# THE (PHANTASMAGORICAL) ASTRARIUM COMPENDIUM

# The (Phantasmagorical) Astrarium Compendium

MARK ROLAND LANGDALE

Copyright © 2015 Mark Roland Langdale

The moral right of the author has been asserted.

Apart from any fair dealing for the purposes of research or private study, or criticism or review, as permitted under the Copyright, Designs and Patents Act 1988, this publication may only be reproduced, stored or transmitted, in any form or by any means, with the prior permission in writing of the publishers, or in the case of reprographic reproduction in accordance with the terms of licences issued by the Copyright Licensing Agency. Enquiries concerning reproduction outside those terms should be sent to the publishers.

Matador
9 Priory Business Park,
Wistow Road, Kibworth Beauchamp,
Leicestershire. LE8 0RX
Tel: (+44) 116 279 2299
Fax: (+44) 116 279 2277
Email: books@troubador.co.uk
Web: www.troubador.co.uk/matador

Cover designed by Naomi Green, Troubador Publishing

ISBN 978 1784622 374

British Library Cataloguing in Publication Data.
A catalogue record for this book is available from the British Library.

Printed and bound by CPI Group (UK) Ltd, Croydon, CR0 4YY
Typeset in 12pt Aldine401 BTRoman by Troubador Publishing Ltd, Leicester, UK

**Matador** is an imprint of Troubador Publishing Ltd

*Thanks to Ben Smith.*

*I dedicate this book to my nephew,
Able Seaman Fraser Valentine-Langdale, good on you, shipmate.*

*In memory of my Great Uncle Len who fought in the Great War.*

## PROLOGUE

## Time & Tide

Now you may find the tale I'm about to tell you hard to swallow (unlike the whale who found Jonah remarkably easier to swallow), in fact you might well find this tale taller than the mast of a tall ship. You might be inclined not to believe a single word that is written down upon the pages before your eyes. There is no doubt you will have to suspend your doubts and disbeliefs and be open to your wildest imaginings for it is true, very little will prepare you for the journey you are about to embark upon. And as long as you do not suffer from either sea or airsickness I'm sure you will survive!

So let us take a sharp intake of breath and drop anchor before we push the boat of our imagination out as far as we may dare. Now is not the time for cold feet or faint hearts… now is the time for every man Jack, and Jill of you to do your duty for queen and country, after all, time waits for no man or woman.

Hoist the mainsail and splice whatever needs splicing and, with the aid of a good compass, some passable charts, a spyglass and a map of both the oceans and the stars let's set sail for the Sea of Imagination… and Godspeed to you all.

# 1
# National Treasures

Gulliver stood in his antiques emporium imagining a national treasure had just walked into his shop looking for some lost antiquity or other which may be hidden there. Hidden in between the large dusty old grandfather clocks, the brass telescopes, antique globes from the seventeenth century, which hadn't put Australia on the map, as back then it was known as New Holland of which the island of Van Diemen's Land was within spitting distance. Gulliver had a smaller antique globe in his shop which when opened revealed a map of the heavens.

Gulliver also possessed a children's vintage Chad Valley globe made of tin the like of which his father owned as a child. There was even a small green and black metallic globe atlas which when opened revealed a lighter, although it didn't work, like a lot of old antiques. I'm afraid I can't shed any further light onto why this was the case other than to say that like Isambard Kingdom Brunel, the owner was a heavy cigar smoker. However, the word 'antique' didn't stretch to the antiquarian timekeeper Old Father Time whose body clock was still ticking over very nicely if you please!

Hidden amongst the layers of dust which, if the particles could have been separated would have told you how long they had been lying there, were the following: sextants, compasses, microscopes, ships logs, astrolabes, weather barometers, oars, an old diving helmet, maps which may lead to national treasures or not (although my guess however uneducated would be not!), naval sailors' uniforms, ships in bottles, both large and small.

Then there were antiquarian books which hadn't been opened since the dawn of time by the looks of them and never mind about the musty smell that they omitted, which most people did! Various almanacs could be found in the antiques emporium if you had the mindset of an explorer or an old gamehunter to hunt them out. These almanacs told you the times of the tides forty years ago and the latitudes and longitudes of the northern hemisphere (very useful I must say if you have a time machine at your disposal!).

Gulliver had several early copies of the famous journal *Mercurius Politicus Gelesen* which kept you informed of what was going on in the revolution of timepieces in the seventeenth century. This was a period in time in which the well-to-do even had their own personal clockmakers, and the owners of these precious timepieces which marked the passing of time were known as guardians. However, once again what good these journals were to anybody but the guardian of time himself, Old Father Time, or the antique presenters of Antiques Roadshow, I'd be hard pressed to tell you. If you did have such an interest then you would probably be hard pressed to listen to my less-than-compendious explanation, needing an old ear trumpet to do so.

Large conch shells were scattered in amongst these priceless antiquities (or should that be antiques?) that as yet had not being labelled with a price tag. The conch shells scattered in what to the untrained eye seemed to be somewhat of a random fashion would have driven anybody suffering from OCD. crazy. Customers would come into the antiques emporium, pick up a large conch shell then put it to their ear and say they could hear the sea. Gulliver said the shells were from Tahiti which meant it wasn't the sea they were hearing but the ocean. Gulliver imagined if a seashell fell from the heavens and you put it up to your ear you would be able to hear the cosmological oceans, he knew this wasn't logical but he just liked the imagery of such a fantastical happening.

In the emporium sat several large, oak ships' wheels which were best steered clear of, as the price tag on them would have told you had you the misfortune to come across them. Barrels which were big enough for a man with a spare tyre or two to fit comfortably into, in fact big enough to climb into and rush headlong over the Niagara Falls if you so desired. Just for the record Gulliver did not desire this as he was not the adventurous type despite his name suggesting the contrary.

Clocks of all shapes and sizes ticked incessantly as if talking to one another. Included in these timepieces was a thirty-hour brass dial lozenge-shaped wall clock, an iron wall clock in black and gold from the Netherlands, maker unknown, and a reproduction of the Gothic-looking astrarium, an astronomical clock made by Giovanni de' Dondi in 1348. A golden lantern clock made by Fromanteel in 1650 hung from one wall; this clock was well known for its preciseness, with its glass dome and ornate fittings. Roman numerals were written upon the face of the clock, and long chain-like pendulums hung down like golden beads of frozen water trapped in time. This particular clock was later to be fitted with an anchor escapement pendulum beating the second, a clock which in its day was seen not only as a timepiece but a status symbol. Gulliver thought some of these clocks were like works of art, or that's the spiel he gave the customer when they wanted to see one in working order!

Gulliver had lost count of the various different carriage clocks he owned, however, a small unique miniature gold clock in the shape of an old diving helmet stood out amongst this sea of chronometers despite its size. Gulliver had so many fob watches on display you would have thought they had been swept up onto the sands of time, and Gulliver had simply gone down to St Mary's Bay in Brixham, Devon, and picked them off the sand like seashells.

One of these many clocks was of the grandfather variety, which Gulliver's grandfather had left to him in his will. An old moon dial and a compendium clock were also hidden somewhere in the shop like hidden treasure and if you looked hard enough I'm sure you would have found them, eventually! The compendium clock had four faces, which was better than some of the two-faced dealers Gulliver came in contact with. Encased within one of its faces was a large fob watch which you could take out of its casing; another face housed a weather barometer and another a calendar. And the final face housed a thermometer which told Gulliver what his blood pressure was rising to as the customer with the annoying laugh and shallow pockets, continued to waste his valuable time haggling over a broken timepiece that most people wouldn't have given the time of day!

Amongst all these ancient timepieces stood a new timepiece, called Midnight Planetarium Poetic Complication made by Van Cleef & Arpels, which in part, to Gulliver's mind, seemed to be based on the

Antikythera Mechanism. The watch featured six planets, each represented a precious stone that orbit in real time around the 'sun' in the centre of the dial. One may well wonder like Alice in Wonderland, how Gulliver could afford this expensive chronometer, well wonder no more because it was as fake as a fake Rolex!

With all these timepieces incessantly ticking away was it any wonder that at times they wound Gulliver up!? It seemed no sooner had he wound the last timepiece up that he had to start all over again, a procedure not unlike that in Victorian London with the gas lamps. But in truth on a slow day this gave him something to do and stopped the shop feeling like a graveyard.

Thanks to all the antique programmes that were now on television everybody thought they were an antique dealer. There was a certain type of customer who he could spot without the use of a brass telescope, one who would walk around the shop with a companion trying to guess the price of the item before their companion told them the real price. These customers rarely, if ever, bought anything and could often be heard to say 'nice little piece but I would never pay that much for it, never in a million years!' to which Gulliver would add under his breath, 'or anything else for that matter!' These customers' wallets and purses had almost as many cobwebs and moths in them as some of the items gathering dust in Gulliver's antiques emporium had living in them!

Somewhere in the shop the Dead Sea Scrolls could be found, but God knows where! Actually that was just a dream that Gulliver once had when one of the three wise men, who was down on his luck, brought them into his shop to see if he could get a good price for them.

Gulliver did have several chests covered in cobwebs

in his antiques emporium, however, there was no treasure hidden within them, unless you counted money spiders to be a treasure, which Gulliver did not! Gulliver even had a rusty iron cannon standing in his shop along with several large cannon balls, which had been retrieved from a sunken ship somewhere in the vicinity of the Bay of Biscay. Gulliver had recently purchased an ivory walking cane which cost him an arm and a leg, or at least a leg, and which when unscrewed revealed an ink fountain pen in one end of the cane and an inkwell in the other. Well, when out walking, one never knew when one wanted to write a note to one's self!

In one corner of this treasure trove sat a large whale tooth, which, had an old sailing ship painted upon it and which rested on a large flat oval orange shell in a glass cabinet full of other seashells. The tooth was so old it probably once belonged to the whale that swallowed Jonah!

A pocket watch had sprung up somewhere in the shop after one of Gulliver's rare spring cleans, which belonged to none other than the great Lawrence of Arabia, with the provenance to prove it. Sometimes Gulliver put this watch in his waistcoat and every time he took it out it instantly transported him back in time, to riding on the back of a camel across the windswept desert, and everybody knew camels were known as the ships of the desert. And there was more besides, so much more besides, Gulliver thought he may need to open another antique shop to fit it all in, either that or make Doctor Who a reasonable offer for his Tardis!

Around the walls of the shop hung paintings of the maritime variety in the most beautiful ornate gold frames, which were draped in fishermen's nets with large green-coloured spheres; paintings from Nelson's *HMS Victory,*

Sir Francis Drake's *Golden Hind* and Charles Darwin's *Beagle* to the Royal Mail Steamer, *Titanic*.

Who was the national treasure now standing before Gulliver in his antiques emporium in the old fishing village of Brixham in Devon? Well none other than the national treasure of all national treasures, that's right, Stephen Fry. Imagine that; well as it happens Gulliver was. Well, Gulliver had been watching *QI* the previous night on television so this was only to be expected, or at least it was as far as Gulliver was concerned.

What if a customer was to come into his shop, which looked like a cross between Aladdin's cave and the Natural History Museum? And what if this imaginary customer asked if they could buy this national treasure, which of course was priceless, as was this imaginary happening? Gulliver was imagining this unlikely event as it happened to be a very slow sales day and those days produced a lot of imaginary customers! Gulliver wondered if he should sell the national treasure that was Stephen Fry, whose expression at the time would no doubt have been priceless! Or would he say he wasn't for sale he was only there for show?

Now there is one more thing I should probably furnish you with about Gulliver's shop-cum-emporium, which was, it wasn't a shop, or at least it was but it wasn't all at the same time. The shop was shipshape but once again, it was and it wasn't!

I know that last statement isn't entirely logical which makes it illogical, a bit like time itself, so I'll explain further. The shop was originally a tall ship which sat in Brixham harbour in four feet of mud; a ship which Gulliver had rather cleverly turned into an antiques emporium. Now most antique shops are anything but shipshape and Bristol fashion 'as they say', being crammed to the rafters with antiques, or in this particular case, being crammed from bow to stern might be a better description of his emporium.

As a child Gulliver had always sat down with his parents and watched *Antiques Roadshow* and was fascinated by the antiques he saw. His father, who had a healthy sense of humour, rather liked to make fun of the show, especially when objects which had cost the owners a small fortune, which they hoped would turn out to be worth a large fortune, turned out to be a fake. After which his father said they probably took the object out the back and either jumped up and down on it or threw it in the dustbin or the recycling bin!

His mother, however, liked the look upon the faces of people who had spent one pound on an object they'd found at a car boot sale only to be told on the programme that it was a priceless antique. Gulliver liked both of these outcomes.

Most people on the programme said their antique was a treasured family item and no matter how much it was worth they wouldn't part with it for love nor money.

The children at Gulliver's school said anyone of Gulliver's age who watched the *Antiques Roadshow* must be old before their time, and further more they wouldn't be in the least bit surprised if he told them he was a member of the Flat Earth Society. Gulliver had been a member of this rather archaic society man and boy, although like a secret treasure stash Gulliver had kept this a secret for fear of being ridiculed.

Like most children Gulliver had always been obsessed with travelling in time. Gulliver imagined himself as an antique dealer who could travel back and forward through time as he pleased, and one who made a large fortune in doing so. And Gulliver would sail on and on through the waves of time in his own shop, which as we now know was a tall ship. Even Gulliver knew this tale was as tall as tales got, but quantum physicists were always saying everything was possible given time, and time is the greatest illusion of them all. Or at least Gulliver knew that Einstein had once said, 'time is the greatest illusion of them all'.

Albert Einstein was the father of quantum mechanics, something Stephen Hawking was later to explore the possibilities of. Eventually Einstein disowned his own theory saying it had more holes in than a Spanish galleon after encountering Sir Francis Drake's *Golden Hind*. Well, actually he didn't say that. However, he did say something along those lines regarding quantum theory, a theory that encompassed the infinitesimally small workings of the universe, which included time. Gulliver had wished he was made of light, because nothing was faster than the speed of light or so Einstein said. Now Gulliver was no Einstein but he figured if he was made of light he could make light work of anything he wanted to make light work of!

One night as he sat watching *QI,* Stephen Fry spoke to him, telling Gulliver quite categorically that he was made of light, before telling him boffins had discovered a particle called a neutrino that could travel faster than the speed of light. This, in theory, made time travel a distinct possibility! At this wondrous revelation Gulliver was blinded by the light, blinded by science and blinded by the glare of Stephen Fry's glasses all at the same time, so much so that he tripped and almost put his head through the screen of his black and white antique television set!

Unfortunately Gulliver's interest in time didn't stretch to his time management skills, which left a lot to be desired as very rarely was he ever on time, either being early or late for an appointment. For Gulliver there were never enough hours in the day, even the eight-day mantle clock which sat on his mantlepiece at home didn't provide enough time for him to do all the jobs he needed to do. That was the thing about running your own business, Gulliver found he rarely had time on his hands, unless he was picking up some antique timepiece from a dealer or antiques fair!

Gulliver had read enough books on the subject of the universe to know that if you wanted to be a quantum physicist you had to sail off into the seas of your imagination to the edge of the unknown universe, and then keep going until you fell over the edge. For the sailors and explorers who sailed the cosmological oceans there was no need for an anchor. This was not unlike the sailors and explorers of Drake and Raleigh's time who had once thought the world was flat so, when they sailed to the very edge of the world naturally they would fall off.

Gulliver's teachers said with a name like his he was destined to travel and he had travelled far and wide. He'd scaled mountains both of the land and the sea, on his way to all four corners of the globe. The trouble was, the only travelling he'd done was in his imagination for in truth, he'd never left the comfort of his home county in Devonshire where he was born. Not only was Gulliver no Einstein, which funnily enough some people were now saying about Einstein himself, but Gulliver was no Francis Drake or Walter Raleigh either, who were both Devon born and bred.

The mountains he found himself climbing more than any others were the ones in the Sea of Tranquility on the moon, and the lands he had sailed to were in the New World, a world which had long since disappeared into the sea mists of time. The seas he had sailed upon were in Drake's *Golden Hind* for he had replicated Drake's voyages around the world in his head, otherwise known as a circumnavigation. Francis Drake, later to become a sir, was the first Englishman and the first captain to achieve such a fantastical fete between 1577-80. Magellan, Elcano and his pals were the first to circumnavigate the globe in 1522, although this was said to be rather by accident than by design. Magellan only made half the voyage, Elcano taking over the captaincy when Magellan was killed in a skirmish with natives in an uncharted island paradise that was so far off the map it wasn't on one! The fights Drake had with the Spanish Armada and their many magnificent galleons were legendary, and often he would have Walter Raleigh standing by his side like the brothers in arms they once were when this happened.

As a boy Gulliver was a legend, a legend in his own lunchtime when he ruled the waves in the geeks' lunchtime computer club. This was the computer club where Gulliver battled it out with other would-be sailors of the low seas in the computer game called the *Golden Hind*. Gulliver found virtual sailing so much easier than real sailing as in virtual sailing you never suffered from sea sickness as Gulliver often did in real life. Sometimes Gulliver got seasick simply just standing on the deck of the replica *Golden Hind*, which sat in the harbour in Brixham going nowhere fast.

Although Gulliver's teachers said he was born to travel, in truth they had never once put on his report card – 'This boy will go far', but then again what do teachers know?!

The truth was that when Gulliver was younger he had no time for school and school had no time for him.

Once he had even been expelled for disappearing in the middle of a class, although I should clarify that further by saying disappearing into a world of his own, in other words not paying attention in class, as the boy was no Merlin and Brixham wasn't the Bermuda Triangle! Rather he'd be daydreaming about single-handedly sailing the seven seas. Now the only seven seas he came in contact with were the vitamin tablets he bought from the local health shop!

It wasn't too surprising that Gulliver replicated Drake's epic voyages to the New World, what with a replica of the *Golden Hind* sitting in Brixham harbour and all. Gulliver loved the story of Don Quixote, which being dyslexic he spelt Donkey Hot-tea and he also loved tales about the sea and Neptune. When his imagination combined the two it came up with Neptune tilting at windmills in the sea, using his pitchfork as a lance, or in this case, tilting at wind turbines. However, Neptune might not have liked his sea space being cluttered up with large ugly wind turbines or wind farms. However, Gulliver found the sight of windmills in the sea, which is what he called wind turbines, a beautiful sight.

Gulliver couldn't understand why man hadn't harnessed the full power and potential of the sea and the waves before now. However, Gulliver had heard of a project called The Time Bell which would harness the power of the waves around the coast line to power a clock that would ring out throughout the lands. The time bell was rung on a ship to signify the passage of time in days gone by.

How Gulliver would have loved to have raised the anchor and sailed off into the sunset on his own boys'-own adventure. He had once again only in his imagination and now he was no longer a boy but a man, and he had responsibilities, even if he was just responsible for himself and his dog, Beagle.

Gulliver's dog wasn't a beagle it was a black Labrador and the reason he had called it Beagle was after another one of his heroes, Sir Charles Darwin. Darwin was the man who wrote *The Origin of Species*, a book that his father had given him on his tenth birthday; a book he had reread so many times he was surprised it hadn't fallen apart in his hands. Charles Darwin had sailed his ship *HMS Beagle* to the Galapagos Islands in search of the answer to his origin of species theory, and had found it there. How Gulliver would have loved to have followed in his hero's footsteps, or at least sailed in them.

But the thing was, it was far safer to sail off into your imagination where there was no chance of being made to walk the plank by some cut-throat pirates. Or falling overboard to be crushed to death by the kraken, the giant octopus in some sea as black as the night. The cosmological oceans were also as black as the night and Gulliver had been lost at sea in those dark forbidding waters many a time, before he was brought back down to earth with a bump. This was a recurring dream he had, although nightmare would have been a better description of it.

The older you got, the more frequent the sailing ship you were sailing off into the sunset of your imagination in became becalmed. Either that or you found yourself all at sea while still being stuck in the harbour with the anchor of your imaginary ship weighing heavy on your mind.

Gulliver loved reading stories about the sea or the ocean and also loved mysteries like Atlantis, the Bermuda Triangle, the *Marie\Mary Celeste* the *Titanic*, and other such stories be they true or otherwise.

Gulliver had read the true story of the island of San Juan de Ulûa in Mexico in 1568 when John Hawkins and his ship *Jesus* had been soundly beaten by the Spanish. The ship was abandoned after losing much of its rigging in the ensuing gunfire. Gulliver had also read the story in the Bible of Noah's Ark. 2012 had seen the worst flooding in Britain since time immemorial, or at least since records began, which was in 1910, two years before the sinking of the *Titanic*.

It had crossed the seas and oceans of Gulliver's mind that one day his antique shop\ship might be washed away in the floods like Noah's Ark, still, as long as he and his beloved dog Beagle were on it at the time then he'd be fine. Mind you if England and Devon did see a flood of Biblical proportions, Gulliver had no intention of dumping his antiques overboard just to make way for an aardvark and a zygote and every living creature in between! Noah could just jolly well come out of retirement and build another ark. The last thing Gulliver wanted was bulls behaving like bulls in china shops\antique shop emporiums. Especially, as he had several priceless Meissen plates, porcelain vases, a seventeenth-century Slipware 'Mermaid' dish and rarer still, a Queen Elizabeth I Verzelini glass goblet, which were made especially for the Crown. Gulliver also had a teapot made of white Devonshire clay shaped as Admiral Vernon's ship. So you can understand why he didn't want any bulls in his antique shop, well not unless they were actually made of china that is! It seemed Gulliver's imagination was really pushing the boat out on this one and what with the old junk stored in both his shop and his imagination, it seemed appropriate that this ship was an old Chinese sailing vessel, in other words, a junk!

That was the trouble with reading books about the

sea, there were so many analogies floating on the written page you were literally all at sea trying to make sense of them all. Words floating on the page were a pretty good analogy for anybody who suffered from dyslexia, which Gulliver did. Gulliver often told his teachers he felt seasick, especially when reading *Moby Dick* or the *Ancient Mariner*. Although, unfortunately for Gulliver this wasn't picked up until after he left school. When Gulliver was a boy stories flowed out of him like a faulty fountain pen, nowadays however, the only writing he did was when doing a stock check or writing out a shopping list!

Gulliver might have had a name for travel but unfortunately he didn't have the courage or the confidence to actually do it. This was borne out by the fact that he had never learned to swim so, if on one of his voyages his boat ran aground against some rocks, which appeared from out of the sea like a giant shark's tooth, he would sink faster than an anchor to the bottom of Davy Jones's Locker. Here in the seas of time he'd lay forgotten along with the sunken treasure of Spanish galleons long since sailed.

Now you may wonder why Gulliver was named Gulliver as it is a name you rarely hear of these days. Well wonder no more, for Gulliver was named after his father's favourite book *Gulliver's Travels*, even though Gulliver was the surname of the character in this book. Some stories aren't really worth telling and the story of Gulliver's name was such a story. Gulliver tried to liven the story up, but who hadn't heard of *Gulliver's Travels*? Once he told people his name they hardly needed a treasure map or otherwise to connect the dots, they certainly didn't need a sextant or compass to point them in the right direction. Having said that, Gulliver was the only boy in his school, and for that matter the only boy he knew, who was called Gulliver so that at least made him feel special. In truth not much else did, for in every other way he was average. He looked average, was of average height and he was an average student who got average marks, which meant university was out of the question. Still, as his father was always telling him, you can learn far more from the University of Life than any seat of learning which is bound within four walls.

Gulliver was thirty-five so as far as he was concerned his ship was never coming in for his ship had well and truly sailed, sailed off into the sunset never to return. He may just as well quit daydreaming and live in the real world like his teachers and his parents had always told him he should, otherwise his antiques emporium would go under and he would end up destitute like many ancient mariners.

Destitute was a word that haunted him like a spectre; he blamed Charles Dickens. But how could he blame Dickens for his wonderful imaginative stories that took him to another time and place? Imagine a world where he got to meet all his heroes like Drake, Darwin, Dickens, Lewis Carroll, Nelson, Einstein, and his heroines too like Queen Elizabeth I and Amy Johnson. That was another thing in his imaginary world, he could fly and swim, whereas in the real world he swam like an overweight walrus. Furthermore, he got dizzy standing on the third step of a stepladder and airsick on a plane, which meant travelling through time was a complete non starter!

## 2

## How Long is a Piece of String in Theory?

Today it was Sunday and as such, being the good Christian boy that he was, Gulliver didn't open his antiques emporium for today was a day of rest. The Bible said Sunday was a day of rest, so who was Gulliver to argue with the word of God who said you had to keep the Sabbath day holy. However, rest is not always forthcoming, or at least it isn't if you own a dog; a dog you could set your antique time piece by, for at precisely eight o'clock Greenwich Mean Time, Beagle wanted to go out and answer the call of nature. Gulliver also knew it was precisely eight o'clock Greenwich Mean Time because his antique grandfather clock told him as much, as did the call of nature, i.e. the dawn chorus. Sometimes Gulliver referred to this time of the day as 'stupid o'clock in the morning' for obvious reasons! Every time the grandfather clock struck it reminded him of his grandfather and what he said to him as a boy. 'Gulliver,' he'd say, peering over his half-moon spectacles studiously,

'Gulliver, you can do anything you put your mind to, anything, nothing is impossible as long as you believe. You've got the whole world to explore and with Old Father Time on your side the only limit is the limit of your imagination, and with an imagination like yours, well, unlike the speed of light there simply is no limit!'

The trouble was, Gulliver was having trouble believing, for his imagination which once took him on unbelievable mind-boggling adventures, was being strangled by reality. How he wished he was a boy again and he could relive some of his childhood, but that wasn't possible. Old Father Time was no longer on his side and one day in the not too distant future they would no longer even be on speaking terms. And when this day came what would he have done with his life, what would he have to show for the time he'd spent on God's flat earth?

Today was a typical Sunday and as such, like every other Sunday he could ever remember, it was dull and overcast and he felt listless. Gulliver wondered why Sunday was called Sunday as the sun never shone on this day, not in actuality or metaphorically. On a Sunday Old Father Time had taken a leaf out of the Bible, putting his feet up reading the *Sunday Times* and taking a well-earned rest. This, according to Gulliver, was why a Sunday dragged interminably. Every second seemed like a minute, every minute seemed like an hour, and every hour seemed like a day. It was as if every time Old Father Time dozed off to sleep, his bored mischievous Time Apprentice would pickpocket his fob watch from out of his waistcoat pocket. Then he would literally rewind the clock so a Sunday appeared to last for ever and a day.

Gulliver often asked himself, how long does a Sunday last? He would have liked to have asked Einstein but he knew he would have told him, time was the greatest illusion of them all, which in all honesty wasn't a great deal of help. Gulliver had heard of string theories regarding the universe so figured the answer must be, how long's a piece of string?! And although Gulliver was good at drawing figures, he couldn't add them up for toffee, or add up the price of toffees in a jar either, (although technically they were out of the jar at the time he had to add them up). Now that last sentence might seem like gobbledegook to you, well, that's because it is!

I was only yanking the chain of your fob watch like Old Father Time's Time Apprentice! It was just that Gulliver used to work in a sweet shop when he was at school, or at least in the school holidays, as working in a sweet shop when you should have been working out Pythagoras theorems was frowned upon by the education board, his headmaster and his parents, although not necessarily in that order. However, if you held that last line up to a mirror it would be in the right order, you do the math… okay I'll do it for you: Pythagoras x Da Vinci = Alice Through the Looking Glass!

As far as Gulliver was concerned the only good thing about a Sunday was it only came round once a week, which was scant consolation for Gulliver at this precise moment in Greenwich Mean Time. *Quantum mechanics was certainly hard to quantify,* Gulliver thought wistfully. As Sunday went on for ever and a day, perhaps this day of all days would be the perfect time to set aside for the reading of Stephen Hawking's timeless classic, *A Brief History of Time.* Yes, I think it is fair to say it wasn't a quantum leap for Gulliver to make this connection. Gulliver had plenty of time for Mr Hawking, however, he found this book to be anything but brief and furthermore, it had far too many words in it that he could not make head nor tail of!

'Okay, okay, Beagle. *You* don't have to scratch the remaining paint off the inside of the front door!' Gulliver said as he wiped the sleep out of his eyes as Beagle completely ignored him.

'That was quite a dream I had last night, old friend,' Gulliver said to Beagle, who looked up at him with his big doleful brown eyes. Eyes which seemed to say, I know, because you kicked me off the bed three times while you were doing your Walter Raleigh impersonation, chivalrously upholding Queen Elizabeth I's good name as you single-handedly fought off the Spanish Armada.

Gulliver opened the door and Beagle flew off down the street towards the harbour as if he had just been let out of a dungeon where dragons weren't the only thing to put the wind up you. Gulliver knew Francis Drake once sailed a ship called *Dragon* and that the Spanish saw him as a magical dragon, who at times seemed omnipresent like God or the Gods. Beagle was no longer in the first flushes of youth, more like the third, although he was still very much young at heart like his owner.

'Don't go too far, Beagle. I want to see you're not getting into any mischief!' Gulliver said as he locked the door behind him and set forth upon his travels. These travels normally meant a walk that took him and Beagle around Brixham, which passed the *Golden Hind* and the fishing boats in the harbour\marina, past the statue of Prince William of Orange, The Berry Head National Nature Reserve quay, around St Mary's Bay, past the cave to Sharkham Point and then back again. This was quite a trek, especially if the wind was in your face, which it always seemed to be, and as you turned around the wind would turn around with you. Probably one of Thor's little jokes, the God of Thunder; well, you know what the gods are like, they do like to play their little games. Mind you, what a Norse god was doing in this neck of the woods was hard to imagine but Gulliver appeared to be able to imagine it!

Gulliver often imagined Sir Francis Drake riding round Brixham harbour on a penny-farthing on a Sunday along with William of Orange, which was a most curious thought and a very strange one to boot!

Suddenly Gulliver felt a chill as if somebody had just walked across his grave and he wouldn't have minded but he wasn't even dead; dead tired, yes, but not dead, certainly not dead in the water as he couldn't swim to save his life.

By the time he'd reached the harbour, Beagle was sniffing around the replica of the *Golden Hind*. Both Sir Francis Drake and Sir Walter Raleigh had lived in Devon at one point in time, that time being the sixteenth century, the golden age of Queen Elizabeth I.

As a boy the *Golden Hind* had seemed big to Gulliver but now it appeared small, it was almost as if it had shrunk. Of course he knew he had grown bigger but not to such an extent that he was now a giant like Lemuel Gulliver in *Gulliver's Travels* appeared to the Lilliputians, after all, Brixham was hardly Lilliput! Gulliver was surprised how small the *Golden Hind* was, he couldn't believe Drake had sailed it so far around the globe; it seemed like a strong wind would literally blow it over. His mother was always telling his father that as a young child he was so frail a strong wind would blow him over, that was before he filled out and became averagely built.

But that was the thing about those old boats like the *Golden Hind*, *Nelson's Victory* and Darwin's ship, *The Beagle*, they were as sturdy as an oak tree, mind you most of them were made out of an oak tree so that wasn't too surprising.

An hour later both man and dog had walked as far as both man and dog had wanted to walk, as the two travelling companions stretched their legs and as Old Father Time appeared to stretch time well beyond its natural limits. So they both turned at Sharkham Point and headed back to the harbour. By now the weather had changed; the clouds were as dark as he could ever remember, it was as if a magician had draped his black cloak over the small fishing port of Brixham and extinguished all light. For a few seconds Gulliver entertained the thought that perhaps he had been swallowed by a giant whale like Jonah and was now ensconced within the walls of its ample belly. Never mind about the whale's ample belly, with middle age just around the corner it was just a matter of time before he had a belly every bit as ample as that of a whale!

The sea, which had previously been as calm as a mill pond, was producing white horses which seemed in somewhat of an agitated state, almost as if they had been spooked by a rattle snake. Thor, the Norse god of thunder was no longer sighing gently but blowing out his cheeks in frustration. Gulliver was happy to have the cobwebs blown away as long as the spiders which had spun them ended up on Mars and he didn't! *The ancient mariner would have loved this weather,* Gulliver thought to himself as he turned the inside of his collar up to protect his face and neck against Mother Nature's sudden mysterious sea change.

Then around about Cod's Rock, which was some way out to sea, something caught Beagle's eye. Something in the dark greenie-grey murky waters seemed to be beckoning him towards it, compelling him like the alluring mermaid-like sirens in Greek mythology had done to many a sailor, only to have their hearts and their ships smashed against the rocks for their troubles. Beagle raced into the sea as if Gulliver had thrown a stick in that direction wanting him to fetch it, it was a game they had played ever since Beagle was a very young puppy. Beagle loved the water and unlike Gulliver, could swim like a fish, like a dogfish in fact. Gulliver wasn't big on jokes, inside his head he was funny but unfortunately, as soon as he opened his mouth he wasn't!

Gulliver's grandfather had a lovely gentle sense of humour which, when you were around him, lapped gently against you like waves lapping at the shoreline. Unlike his father's sense of humour and personality which was like a tidal wave which swept over you and dragged you under. Actually his father's personality was so overpowering it was like a tsunami. Gulliver often thought maybe that's why he was so reserved.

'Come back, Beagle, it's too rough!' Gulliver shouted as the wind blew the words back into his mouth.

But Beagle didn't come back, instead he went out further; it seemed this invisible stick was always just out of Beagle's reach.

And then Beagle vanished under the waves; it was as if Neptune had pulled the waves over his head as much as to say, 'It's time to rest your weary head on the sea bed, old boy.'

Gulliver panicked, Beagle was gone and if he didn't do something quickly he would be gone for good. But Gulliver couldn't swim, no matter, a dog was a man's best friend and he couldn't let his friend down in his hour of need. Gulliver hadn't even got time to strip off to his underpants so he simply removed his shoes, ran into the sea fully clothed and dived in. Within no time at all Gulliver, like his trusty companion Beagle and all those aboard the *Marie Celeste,* was lost to the mists of time.

It was odd, as soon as Gulliver disappeared underneath the unwelcoming waves, the wind died down, the dark clouds passed and the sun came out of hiding.

The water was dark; Gulliver couldn't see in front of his face. It felt like an ice bath although it was the middle of the summer. Gradually, as his eyes adjusted to the darkness, he could just about make out a figure that was falling towards the sea bed. Gulliver was sure it was his beloved Beagle. Gulliver knew he couldn't turn back now so with great fortitude he dived down further, deeper, deeper still; now he was swimming like a fish. Now that wasn't right, swimming like a mermaid, although a merman might have been a better description in the circumstances. Circumstances which didn't really lend themselves to humour, but the mind was a strange thing and even in the darkest of times humour came to the fore. And then another dark-humoured thought followed on closely behind the last one. He had always wanted to be buried at sea, but not yet, the timing wasn't right, he was halfway through a stock check and he hadn't even read the Dead Sea Scrolls. Gulliver was the sort of meticulous person who hated to leave a job half done.

He must concentrate, he told himself, he couldn't afford to black out or all would be lost for him and his loyal companion for he would literally be lost at sea. Gulliver could feel his lungs fit to burst; it hadn't really registered that he was swimming, although, perhaps he wasn't, perhaps this was a dream more like a nightmare in which he was drowning! Don't give up. Remember what grandfather said – 'You can do anything if you put your mind to it'. Gulliver could see his grandfather in his head telling him as much as he stood on the *Golden Hind*, he couldn't have been more than seven at the time, perhaps eight; in truth his early years had rather got lost in the sea mists of time.

And then his thoughts started to drift from one thing to another, drift like the *Marie Celeste* on a becalmed sea as a song from his childhood started to play in his head – *row, row, row the boat gently down the stream, merrily, merrily, merrily, merrily life is but a dream.* Now his head was swimming, unfortunately his body wasn't, then everything went black.

## 3

## What time is it? Why don't you ask Old Father Time?

Gulliver woke up in a cave with Beagle beside him, but Beagle was no longer long in the tooth, as now he was a puppy, and one who was licking Gulliver's face as if he hadn't seen his master for years. Gulliver knew he hadn't washed for a few days but really, *calm down, Beagle,* he thought, *otherwise you'll wash the features from my face, like the sea washes away the face of a cliff.* What a strange thing to enter his head as he remembered he'd had a similar thought when he was twelve when he'd got his first dog, who insisted on sleeping on his bed and waking him up at the crack of dawn by licking his face with great gusto.

'Okay, calm down. It's good to see you too, old friend,' Gulliver said getting to his feet as Beagle jumped up at him in a playful manner. This was obviously just a dream, a vivid one admittedly and one in colour and in 3D HD with surround sound, but a dream all the same.

*Still, no harm will come from going along with it,* Gulliver thought in a manner that could best be described as matter-of-fact. The script writers in his head had come up with a good plot so he may as well see where the story took him, like the spirit walkers in ancient native North American stories and aboriginal tales of dream walkers in the southern hemisphere.

Gulliver noticed his hands were rather prune-like so he must have been in the water a while. He also noticed that his hands had shrunk, he then looked at his feet and they'd shrunk too, as had his body. It was almost as if somehow he had ended up in the Model Village in Babbacombe in Devon. This was like *Alice's Adventures Under Ground* but in reverse. *Alice's Adventures Under Ground* was the original title of *Alice's Adventures in Wonderland*, not everybody knew this fact but Gulliver did, Gulliver was a mine of both useful and useless information. Gulliver often joked his head was like a steam-powered search engine or a steamer which took time to get a full head of steam on!

Gulliver wandered over to the rock pool in the cave and looked into the water that now resembled a looking glass and to his amazement he saw a boy staring back at him in wide-eyed wonderment. Hold on a minute, Old Father Time, he recognised this boy, recognised that messy hair and that lopsided grin, it was him, it was Gulliver!

'Will wonders never cease? I know my name's Gulliver but travelling back in time? Nice touch, the old subconscious is really pushing the boat out in this dream, old fella!' Gulliver said as he knelt down and horsed around a little with the puppy. 'Old fella, I can't call you that, you're a puppy!' Gulliver said laughing out loud as his voice echoed through the cave.

Then Gulliver tripped over his feet and hit his head against a rock.

'Ow, look where you're going, big feet!' Gulliver exclaimed to himself as he rubbed his head. What was that sticky, red substance he felt in his hair? Blood!

'Ow, Beagle, that hurts. I thought you weren't suppose to be able to feel pain in dreams. Mind you if this Dreamland is anything like Wonderland I suppose I shouldn't be surprised by anything!' Gulliver said, taking a handkerchief out of his pocket and holding it against the wound. Suddenly Gulliver was distracted by a light that caught his eye. 'Let's follow the light, Beagle, and see where it leads. I don't know about you but my stomach's rumbling, I wouldn't mind getting a bite to eat.'

Beagle woofed several times in agreement with his master, which in canine speak meant, what are we waiting for? And so they both set off on a journey that would leave most people with a permanent puzzled expression upon their face. But then again most dreams had that affect on you, it was just that being asleep at the time you weren't aware of it.

As Gulliver and Beagle followed the light through one cave after another, its luminosity increased. The caves were like a labyrinth and one Gulliver was starting to wonder if they would ever get out of, he just hoped he didn't bump into the minotaur! What if this was like the maze at Hampton Court? If it wasn't for his grandfather he'd still be lost there, lost in a world of his own, something his teachers were always accusing him of.

Then another strange thought occurred and as it did Gulliver realised these strange thoughts were becoming more and more commonplace. If the dream continued in this vein he'd better start getting used to these strange intrusive thoughts.

This particular strange thought was, *what if this isn't a dream? What if I'm dead and so is Beagle, and this is in fact heaven?!* If this was heaven then he certainly had travelled a long way, perhaps his teachers were right after all and with a name like Gulliver he was destined to travel. But hold on a minute, better make that two, surely you didn't bleed in heaven? And he was sure as he could be in the circumstances (the circumstances being that there was every chance he was going mad like the Mad Hatter!), you didn't feel pain either because you were an angel or a spirit or whatever. If you bled in heaven you'd bleed all over your nice, white angel suit and angels were always white and immaculately dressed. The white suit St Peter wore was pristine and starched to within an inch of its life, so much so you could eat your dinner off it! 'You see, Beagle, funny in my head but as soon as I open my mouth, nothing, nada, zilch! Nothing good will come of this, nothing!' Gulliver said under his breath. *But then again hadn't the universe appeared from nothing as if by magic? So perhaps it would*, his subconscious piped up in a voice that sounded remarkably like Stephen Fry's!

Gulliver could hear his voice echo through the labyrinth of his mind, like his voice had echoed through the caves not a moment ago. Or was it a moment ago? Maybe it was a lifetime ago. Maybe heaven was like a Sunday where time had no meaning! Gulliver was expecting St Peter to pop up at any moment with a clipboard in his hand and say, 'Welcome to heaven, Gulliver. Come right this way. Let me introduce you to your heaven planner'. According to all the stories he'd read about heaven you didn't bleed and you didn't feel pain so logically this couldn't be heaven. Gulliver breathed a huge sigh of relief at the thought that his time wasn't up.

Yes, heaven could wait, after all he was a young boy, this he knew as the mirror he'd recently gazed into had told him as much, or at least the rock pool in the caves had. Now he was sounding like Narcissus the Greek god who was in love with his reflection, the one who thought he was immortal.

Greek gods, heaven, wow, this was like somebody had emptied the entire contents of the set-top box on his television, with its 300 and something channels into his head while he was asleep, probably through the labyrinth in his ears by the looks of it! Well, his teachers had said there wasn't much between his ears so there was plenty of room to fit them all in!

Then Gulliver turned a corner and the light that greeted his eyes nearly blinded him. *The sun in the sky is almost as big as the moon*, he thought. Now that was a strange thought, one even Alice in Wonderland would find strange. Gulliver wanted to utter Alice's famous words 'curiouser and curiouser' but by now he was way past being curious. Gulliver wondered what the word was for 'way past being curious', another curious thought that for the moment would go unanswered.

Gulliver shielded his eyes against the bright light as he stepped out of the caves and further out into daylight, his eyes slowly adjusting like the lens of a telescope. He looked towards the heavens that was... that was, no he wasn't going to say strange or curious, that was peculiar, as there appeared to be a glass screen between him and the heavens. That made no sense and as such it came under the heading of nonsense; Lewis Carroll was alive and well and living inside his head with Alice and the Mad Hatter too by the looks of it. *Now there's a stra– cur– peculiar thought*, thought Gulliver and wondered if that was a double negative or, had he just thought the same thought twice? Could it be that now he had a photographic memory, although all the images he was processing in the dark room in his head appeared to be out of focus!?

Not that strange and not that peculiar as it happens, as *Alice in Wonderland* and *Alice Through the Looking Glass* were two of his most treasured books. He even had a signed first edition of *Alice Through the Looking Glass* under a glass dome in his Antique Antiquarian Emporium. And no, it wasn't for sale, it was just there to be shown off!

The more Gulliver's eyes adjusted to the light the more of this strange world made itself known to him. He was inside a glass dome, it was a bit like one of the glass snow domes you saw in gift shops in Devon or in seaside resorts, well, minus the snow. Mind you, give it time, perhaps it was summer in this strange magical parallel world he'd stumbled into. No hold on, his eyes were playing tricks upon him, *it wasn't a glass dome it was a big, gigantic, large, humongous bottle,* he thought, trying out all the words he could pick out of the thesaurus in his head to describe this bottle. The only difference between him and Alice was he was a boy and he'd fallen through the sea into a cave rather than a rabbit hole. Gulliver's mind was racing, he needed to slow things down, take some time to get his bearings as he was beginning to feel like he was on a helter-skelter ride which had no end. Gulliver felt these analogies needed a little work, so as soon as he found a bookshop he would buy a journal and write everything down, except this journal would be a travelogue. Well, his name was Gulliver and he was travelling so it made perfect sense and this was about the first thing for some time that actually had!

Actually it was like he'd fallen through an egg timer

or an hourglass. Fallen through the sands of time literally, either that or he was dreaming the most vivid dream anybody had ever dreamt in the history of dreamers. There was, however, one other option: he'd eaten a magic mushroom! He'd recently been out picking mushrooms in a field not far from where he lived, *maybe it was one with hallucinogenic qualities!*

Now there was a thought! If Gulliver was going to keep having such thoughts as these he needed to start classifying them into categories of strangeness, that way they wouldn't all blow his mind. The question was, how big was this strangeness scale, was it from one to ten or one to one hundred and ten!? Only time would tell, he must press on with this adventure and he was sure everything would become crystal clear, yes as clear as mud! Gulliver didn't even need a map, a compass, a sextant or a sat nav as the map and his sat nav were all in his head. Possibly like this dream. Nothing was impossible, nothing, his grandfather's voice echoed in his head as Beagle jumped up at his leg several times as if he were upon a trampoline, before scampering off into the distance.

'Slow down, Beagle, slow down. You don't want to get lost!' Gulliver cried as he started to walk towards what looked like a town in the distance.

# 4
# The Pandemonium Emporium

Gulliver took out his pocket watch from his waistcoat and opened it up. Unsurprisingly it had stopped as the water had obviously gotten into the mechanism. *I shall get it fixed at a jeweller's when we get to the town,* naturally enough he thought, and why wouldn't he. He then rolled up his fairly lengthy sleeve which revealed a digital watch. Gulliver surmised the sleeve length of his shirt was due to the fact that he'd shrunk in the water while his clothes had not; surely that should have been the other way round? This happening seemed slightly odd to Gulliver's mind, which meant it hardly registered on his strangeness scale.

The digital watch was going crazy obviously like he was, like a compass in the Bermuda Triangle. *Time to buy a new watch*, Gulliver thought. 'What, that's it!?' Gulliver remarked to Beagle out loud. Didn't his brain want to add anything to this thought, like, when was the last time I found myself in the Bermuda Triangle? And I wonder what time it is in Baffin Land?! No, obviously not, thankfully it was time to move on.

Within what seemed like both an eternity and the blinking of an eye Gulliver and Beagle were standing in a bustling town full of life and vitality. The first shop they came upon was a shop called The Pandemonium Emporium, which seemed nothing more than appropriate in the circumstances, the circumstances on this occasion being that the town was in a state of pandemonium, albeit a happy state of pandemonium, if there is even such a state. Well, it appeared in this world there was!

To Gulliver's mind, which was taking the information it was being given and processing it with remarkable ease, the town looked like a cross between the sixteenth century and the nineteenth century, but it was still Devon, of that Gulliver was 110% sure.

'Let's go into The Pandemonium Emporium, I'm curious as to what they sell there,' Gulliver said to Beagle as girls and boys ran about in the street pushing hoops with sticks, and then a man on a penny-farthing nearly ran him down.

'Sorry, can't see a thing from up here!' the man said with his head in the clouds, as he doffed his top hat to Gulliver before continuing shakily on his way across the cobbled streets. Cobbled together was a very good way of describing this town and this world for that matter.

As Gulliver entered The Pandemonium Emporium a young scruffy urchin ran past him nearly knocking him off his feet for the second time in as many minutes.

'Get out of here and don't come back any time soon, in fact don't come back any time!' said the proprietor of the shop, a strange-looking man in a top hat reminiscent of the Mad Hatter in *Alice in Wonderland*. The only difference being it said 'not for sale' on the top of the hat. Gulliver was half expecting to see a price tag with 10\6 although with this being a parallel world perhaps he should have been expecting the price tag to read 6\10!

Given the strangeness of this world was it surprising that the man standing in front of him looked not unlike the Mad Hatter in *Alice in Wonderland*? No, it wasn't, thought Gulliver sounding more than a little irked, which in truth was better than sounding more than a lot irked!

*The sooner I get my travelogue the sooner I can write that in it, and I'm going to put the first of the many exclamation marks beside it too.* Gulliver had a feeling that this world was going to give him plenty of opportunity to use the exclamation mark!

'Sorry,' said the man gruffly, a man who looked like a cross between the Mad Hatter and Ebenezer Scrooge as he peered from beneath the rim of his hat, which was almost as big as he was.

'Don't give it a second thought,' said Gulliver politely.

'All right I won't!' said the man wearing the oversized hat on his head even grufflier, although for a few seconds Gulliver gave some serious consideration to the thought that in fact the oversized hat might well be wearing him! What was that old expression? 'If you want to get ahead, get a hat' although in this world it was probably the other way round! 'If you want to get a hat, get a head'. Gulliver wondered if this man was a cannibal as he continued to think outside the old hat box. Gulliver was given over to thinking that perhaps he should purchase a mad hatter's hat as it would make him feel right at home in this mad world.

(Gulliver was to later write this line in his travelogue: 'I don't think there is even such a word as grufflier but I like the sound of it so I'm keeping it in!'.)

'Now, what can I do for you? Oh, excuse me where are my manners? Bad morning,' the man said in a matter-of-fact manner.

'Yes, as it happens I have had a bad morning!' Gulliver

said rather taken aback that a complete stranger would ask him if he'd had a bad morning. Of course Gulliver was a little slow on the uptake, after all, this was a parallel world so the man could hardly have been expected to have wished him a good morning now could he. That would have been the height of bad manners. 'Do you have a book without any words in it?' Gulliver enquired politely.

'Take a good look around you, does it look like we've got a book without any words in it in this shop?' said the man with the hat, or was that the hat with the man? Gulliver wondered if the man had been born with the hat on his head and it had grown in size as he grew as the hat was the same size as the man, which was the reason you saw as much of the hat as the man underneath it!

Gulliver did a quick scan of the shop, which to be honest had next to nothing in it, and said as politely as he knew how, while not entirely making sense which fitted into this world admirably, 'Well, actually it does!'

'Well then, we do!' said the slightly mad proprietor matter-of-factly. 'The thing about The Pandemonium Emporium, apart from the fact that it's pandemonium in here, is that whatever you imagine we have then we have it, and,' he paused for dramatic effect before continuing on, 'if you can't imagine it then we don't have it! So in other words we have everything in stock and nothing in stock all at the same time! Everything you see in the shop is cosmetic, although that's one thing we don't stock, cosmetics! Having said that, I suppose we don't actually stock anything!' said the mad hat almost confusing himself.

Now to Gulliver this made perfect sense and in a world where quite clearly nothing appeared to make sense, this he found to be of great comfort.

To Gulliver's way of thinking it was best not to try and figure this world out, rather it was better to just accept everything no matter how bizarre it was because that's what everybody else appeared to be doing. Although, as they say, appearances can be deceiving. When in Rome and all that jazz, not that he was in Rome but the principal was the same. Gulliver thought that as jazz was improvised, it summed up this world rather nicely as the people appeared to be making the whole thing up as they went along, not unlike the great teller of fairytales, Hans Christian Andersen!

Beagle was sniffing around the shop looking into every nook and granny, yes that was granny and not cranny, as there were several old women looking around the shop. The proprietor then walked towards Gulliver's dog with a mad look upon his face.

Now Gulliver was half expecting the man to say in his best gruff voice, 'No dogs. We don't allow dogs in this shop!' However he just bent over and picked Beagle up, put him on the counter and stroked him. *I suppose I should have fully expected that; expected the unexpected,* thought Gulliver dryly. In fact, he was only surprised the man hadn't said, 'Sorry, you can't come into this shop without a dog!'

'Nice dog, how much?' said the proprietor, softly lowering his voice several octaves.

'He's my companion. I've had him ever since he was a puppy nigh on fifteen years now,' Gulliver said proudly and affectionately all at the same time.

'But he still *is* a puppy!' said the man with the big hat and the big head, or vice versa. Now it was his turn to sound puzzled.

Of course Beagle was a puppy, well he was and he wasn't all at the same time. Like Gulliver was a boy, well he was and he wasn't all at the same time. Surely the proprietor understood this, after all he was talking gobbledegook and surely the man understood gobbledegook. Here Gulliver imagined a book called The Gobbledegook Dictionary sitting on one of the dusty empty bookshelves, which then instantly appeared before his eyes like magic, before disappearing back to wherever it came from! Why was he not surprised, but he wasn't, not in the slightest, not for one minute, he didn't bat an eyelid. That was this world all over, everything was all at the same time as time was quite clearly all jumbled up, as were some of Gulliver's thoughts and the sentences in his head. But then again Gulliver was used to this jumbled-up effect, being dyslexic as he was. Gulliver wished some of the junk in his antiques emporium would disappear off the shelves as quickly as The Gobbledegook Dictionary had disappeared off the shelves of The Pandemonium Emporium!

Surely he shouldn't have to explain himself, Gulliver thought! If this was a dream, this part of the dream sequence was like a cross between Lewis Carroll's *Alice in Wonderland* and Charles Dickens' *The Old Curiosity Shop*. As from the moment he stepped into this shop his curiosity had grown like Alice in Wonderland, to the point where it was just a matter of time before he uttered the words curiouser and curiouser.

'Curiouser and curiouser,' Gulliver said under his breath.

'Mmm!' said the proprietor, the gruffness returning to his voice. 'So he's not for sale, pity, he would have made a good guard dog to keep some of the riff raff out!'

'Sorry but no, Beagle's not for sale,' Gulliver said once again as politely as he knew how.

'Isn't that a Labrador?' the owner of the shop said quizzically.

'Yes it is,' said Gulliver. Once again Gulliver was surprised to see a puzzled expression on the man's face, he thought nothing surprised the people of this world.

'So why do you call it a Beagle then? You're a very strange boy you know!' continued the proprietor rudely.

*I'm strange? I'm strange?* thought Gulliver, talk about the pot calling the kettle black, or in this case the man in the oversized hat calling a normal twelve-year-old boy, who in reality was thirty-five, strange.

'I named him after Darwin's ship, *HMS Beagle,*' Gulliver said proudly.

'Who or what on earth is a Darwin?' said the man, perplexed beyond belief.

'The man who wrote *The Origin of Species,* of course,' Gulliver said trying to keep his cool.

'The Origin of what!?' exclaimed the man so loudly that half the shop turned round and stared at this strange otherworldly boy, while the other half of the shop appeared not to notice, but then again the shop was an inanimate object so why should it notice anything!?

'*The Origin of Species,* you know, the book about well, species, the tree of life, where we came from and how and all that jazz,' said Gulliver, words falling out of his mouth at a rate of knots.

'Who's Darwin and what on earth is jazz? Has anybody in the shop heard of a man called Darwin? I presume it's a man, or is it a place?!' said the large hat with the small man inside it.

Everybody in the shop was now looking at one another and shaking their heads in disbelief, 'No, no never heard of a chap called Darwin, have you?' one woman said shaking her head vehemently.

'No, no, the boy's obviously one penny short of a penny-farthing!' said a man who looked like a stepladder in a shrill high-pitched voice, one who'd obviously just sat down on a porcupine.

'Talking of species, the boy's a strange species and no denying!' said a man with what looked like a cardboard box on his head. Unfortunately for the poor man, he didn't have a cardboard box on his head he just looked like he had a cardboard box on his head.

'A tree that's alive? A talking tree? What's the boy talking about? He's clearly talking gobbledegobble. I'll eat my hat if anybody can tell me!' said another who was hard of hearing who had what looked liked a gramophone in his ear with a horn attached to it.

'Never mind eating your hat, I'll eat my words if you can tell me what the boy is babbling on about! In fact, while you're about it, why don't you take a bite out of this book, it's delicious,' said another man chomping his way through a large book made of rice paper. The book had just appeared upon the shelf from out of thin air as if by magic as soon as the box-headed man had asked the proprietor if he had a book made of rice paper in stock.

'I could explain but it's rather a long story,' Gulliver said as Beagle licked the hat several times, although it could just as easily have been the head in the hat Beagle was licking.

'Long story? Long story? No, no, that will never do in these parts, we only like short stories, isn't that right, wife of mine?' said a man who looked like he was dressed in the dusty dust jacket of an old book, to his wife who looked like she'd swallowed a giant Toby jug. In a world this topsy-turvy they were like matching bookends.

'If you want long stories you need to find the Last Book Shop in the World, there you'll get as many long stories as you wish for, so many in fact, one book will last you a lifetime,' said the man wearing the dust jacket, who by the look upon his face thought he was the wisest man in Christendom.

'Of course you'll never find it, nobody ever has. I'm not sure it even exists!' said the proprietor popping his head out of his hat and his eyes out of his head all at the same time.

Gulliver wondered if the book *The Origin of Species* was out of print, or perhaps it had never been in print in the first place to become out of print. That sounded logical enough to Gulliver, however, the thought did occur that if this shop was anything to go by in this world, he shouldn't try to be logical when trying to find an answer for something, but instead be illogical. Being illogical in this parallel world was completely logical, or at least it was in The Pandemonium Emporium. He wouldn't be the least bit surprised if the expression, 'end of story' in this world was, beginning of story!

'Well, you don't mind if I browse do you?' said Gulliver as he picked Beagle off the counter and made his way towards one of the under-filled bookshelves, which looked like it might collapse any minute under the weight of the invisible books that weren't upon the shelves.

'Of course I mind you browsing, I want you buying. Where would I be if I let Old Tom Cobbley and all into my shop simply just to browse? I'd be out of business in ten seconds flat!' the head underneath the hat said abruptly.

Gulliver didn't think it could be said of the large hat with the man underneath it that he was the type of man who at the drop of a hat was prepared to come to your aid if you were in trouble. More likely he was the type to walk by on the other side of the street with his nose in the air as if you didn't exist. In fact, he doubted if the man had ever doffed his hat to anyone in his entire life before. Furthermore, Gulliver thought the hats middle name must be Unhelpful or Disinterested. In fact, the hat's middle name was neither Unhelpful nor Disinterested, although in truth both would have fitted his personality like a hat fitted Isambard Kingdom Brunel or the Mad Hatter!

The fact of the matter was that the hat didn't have a middle name, in fact he barely had a first name, unless you counted Mad as a first name. Although why Gulliver was so hung up on the hat's middle name when he didn't know his Christian name or his surname was a mystery far outweighing either the mystery of the *Marie Celeste* or the lost city of Atlantis!

'Well, I do need a pencil and a pencil sharpener as well as a book with no words in it so I'll browse until I find them, then I'll leave,' said Gulliver making perfect sense in a nonsensical kind of way.

'Mmmm!" said the Mad Hatter lookalike gruffly as if at any moment he would spontaneously combust.

'The boy must be from out of town, doesn't he know you could be in this shop browsing for a lifetime and still you wouldn't have seen half of what's in it, or half of what isn't in it for that matter given the fact there is nothing in it?' said a large caterpillar wearing a smoking jacket which had slipped out of the cover of an antiquarian book called *The Beginner's Guide to Nothing in Particular*. Although in truth Gulliver might have imagined that last bit, the ambience of the shop was inclined to do that to one's imagination.

Gulliver then met a boy in the shop who he struck up a conversation with to pass the time while he waited for the proprietor to fetch his book with the blank pages, pencil and sharpener from out of the stock room. This stock room which in truth was not much bigger than a hat box! Now you may think, hold on a minute, why didn't the book with no words in it, the pencil and the pencil sharpener just appear by magic like the Gobbledegook Dictionary? Good question, I'm glad to see you're paying attention. Well, for a start, do you have to keep asking stupid questions? And for a finish, Gulliver didn't imagine these items, if he had imagined them then of course they would have appeared by magic upon the shelves. What's wrong with you? Why don't you try using your imagination for a change?! Another unwritten law was that if you didn't take the item off the shelf within a few seconds of it appearing, it would disappear.

The boy that Gulliver was talking gobbledegook to said he had an idea for a magic talking box that showed moving images. Gulliver didn't know it at the time but this boy was John Logie Baird who had invented the television, or at least he had in his world. Gulliver shook the boy's hand, which the boy thought a little strange considering he'd only just met him, but how often do you get to shake the hand of one of your heroes? Thanks to John Logie Baird's invention, Gulliver had travelled all around the world without even leaving the comfort of his own front room.

Although Gulliver didn't know it because he wasn't from around these parts, this emporium was a bit like his Antique Antiquarian Emporium and a bit like Doctor Who's tardis, in that it was small on the outside and large on the inside, even though there was nothing in it to speak of. Although saying that, people in The Pandemonium Emporium did seem to speak a lot while saying very little, in some cases nothing at all.

Gulliver thought he'd better not mention Doctor Who otherwise he'd never get out of the shop. 'Dr who?!'

everybody in The Pandemonium Emporium would say in unison. 'Doctor Who, who's Doctor Who?!' and then all hell would break loose or pandemonium if you prefer. However, at this point in the proceedings Gulliver didn't prefer pandemonium to all hell breaking loose, what he preferred was peace and tranquility and above all else, order.

Gulliver quickly browsed around the shop for a pencil and pencil sharpener while he waited for his book with no words to appear, although not for one second did he imagine them in his head. Then when they appeared he could pay the hat for them and leave. After which he'd find a nice peaceful library so he could detail the finer points of his journey so far in the nice white pristine pages of his book with no words in it. Was that really so much to ask? Mind you, if he was in his world, yes, because the word 'hullabaloo' fitted a modern library like it fitted the word 'zoo'!

Now I'd like to say yes, but it wasn't, so that's what happened if you discount the fact that Beagle bit the man who looked like a stepladder because he wouldn't let him climb up him and, if you discount the fact that Gulliver bit his tongue several times as people said, what a strange boy he was.

Gulliver noticed how the shop was lit by candles, which made it rather dark so he asked what he thought was a simple enough question to a man who was looking at nothing in particular.

'Excuse me, sir. Has there being a power cut?'

The countenance on the man's face could best be described as a blank canvas, which is probably why he looked blankly back at Gulliver (now surely you wouldn't expect anything else would you? Good, then you weren't disappointed were you!?). Gulliver pursued the matter further, 'Electricity.'

'What?!' said the man looking puzzled, well at least Gulliver had drawn some expression from this fellow's unexpressive countenance.

'So you've heard of James Watt then?' Gulliver said finally making some headway in this one-sided conversation. Gulliver wondered if he should mention Edison too as the man had obviously heard of James Watt.

'What?!' said the man again as the puzzled expression got more pronounced.

Gulliver could see another Doctor Who moment sailing over the horizon so wisely decided to let it go. Perhaps the proprietor of The Pandemonium Emporium had fallen on hard times and hadn't being able to pay the electricity bill, or perhaps looking like Ebenezer Scrooge as he did, he was too tight-fisted to pay the bill, hence the candles and the poorly lit shop.

Gulliver decided to change tack and asked an altogether simpler question to the hat with the talking head inside it.

'So, my book without words, my pencil and pencil sharpener, you have them?' said Gulliver as he went back to the counter to speak to the proprietor.

'What are you talking about, boy? A book without any words in it? Have you gone mad?' said the head peering from underneath the hat. And then a tall thin man appeared from out back who was a doppelganger for the man who looked like a stepladder, whispered something in the hat's ear and then disappeared as quickly as he had appeared.

'Sorry, I would forget my hat if it wasn't screwed on properly and my head along with it!' said the hat with the head beneath it irritably, who appeared more mad with himself for forgetting the boy's order than anything else.

'Here's your book without any words in it, although I suppose it could be a book written in invisible ink! If it turns out to be a book written in invisible ink, don't bother to come back looking for a refund because we'll be closed for lunch permanently. Enjoy. Oh, and don't forget, too many words spoil a sentence,' the hat and the head said, smiling in unison. What was it that Mark Twain said, something about there being no wrong words just words that needed crossing out.

Considering this was the first time Gulliver had been in The Pandemonium Emporium, the proprietor seemed to know Gulliver better than he had any right to. Mind you, as Gulliver knew full well, you should never judge a book by its cover or a book by its dust jacket either.

'Oh, I nearly forgot, that will be tuppence ha'penny,' said the proprietor taking off his hat and holding it out so Gulliver could put the money in it. The bizarre thing was when the man took off his hat there was another hat underneath it, this one slightly smaller than the one he had just removed. Gulliver wondered how many hats he actually had upon his head, it was a bit like the Russian doll which you unscrewed to reveal another Russian doll, which was slightly smaller than the one before. Well, apart from these were hats and not dolls but apart from that...!

'Tuppence ha'penny, that's more than reasonable,' said Gulliver instinctively reaching inside his pocket and drawing out tuppence ha'penny before dropping it into the large hat, which seemed to swallow it up as if it were a black hole or a large wishing well. Gulliver was half expecting to hear a plopping sound as the coin hit the water in the bottom of the well. However, that didn't happen as Gulliver wished as hard as he could that he was anywhere but where he was right now, which was plainly wishful thinking on his part I'm afraid.

Gulliver's imagination was getting the better of him again, or was that the worst?!

'More than reasonable? I should think it is. Now bad day to you and don't close the door on your way out!' said the proprietor gruffly, placing his hat back on his hat, back on his hat, back on his hat... infinitum. Oh, and there was a head in that description somewhere but where is anybody's guess!

Gulliver wasn't in the least bit surprised that when he had reached into his pocket he found the exact money to pay for his purchases, not a tuppence ha'penny more not a tuppence ha'penny less. Perhaps in this world pickpockets put money into your pocket and not took it out! Well, *it was a parallel world so that must be the case*, Gulliver thought, and then thought no more about it.

A boy then came into the shop blowing a tin penny whistle. At first Gulliver thought his tinnitus was playing up again until he turned round to see the boy with the whistle in his mouth. Unfortunately the boy seemed to only know one tune which he played note for note over and over again. Doubly unfortunately for Gulliver and all in The Pandemonium Emporium was that this tune only had one note in it, which Gulliver's ear perceived to be an F sharp and which was so sharp it was going straight through his head. Unfortunately for Gulliver (times three) it wasn't going straight through his head as it was going round and round his head circumnavigating his brain in the process.

Gulliver feared if he didn't leave this shop immediately, if not sooner, it wouldn't be long before he lost his mind. And as his mother was always saying to him, he would lose his head if it wasn't screwed on properly. The very last thing Gulliver wanted to do was lose his mind, not with his memory, otherwise he would end up like the large hat with the small man underneath it with the even smaller hat underneath that, infinitum. And to Gulliver's mind this man had quite clearly lost his mind some time ago. Whose mind he had borrowed in place of his own, well, God alone knew? But one thing that Gulliver was 110% sure of was that it was none of his business and as such his insides were jumping for joy like Mexican magic beans.

As Gulliver left the shop and heard the bell attached to the shop door ring, he felt like turning back round and shouting to the strangers in the shop, 'Me? Strange? Why don't you take a look in the looking glass!' However, he felt sure that if they did they wouldn't like what they saw looking back at them, that and they would all say 'Keep your hat on, boy!' even if he wasn't wearing a hat. No, they were bound to take umbrage so he wisely decided to continue on with biting his tongue, he just hoped he didn't get a taste for it. Gulliver wondered if he should have tried unintelligible conversation rather than intelligible conversation, perhaps he would have been better understood if he had!

Gulliver had never had any problem with the word 'mad', however, he had no time for the word 'mental' which he felt should be dumped in a graveyard for words and tired old phrases. Buried along with 'It's not rocket science', 'It's in their DNA' and other such unoriginal sayings which had been done to death!

Gulliver walked a little further down the street to find a shop called Mad Hatters which unsurprisingly sold everything but hats! He wondered if the hat owned this particular shop too. Perhaps he owned all the shops in the street.

Then Gulliver came upon a shop called The Compendium which was oblong in shape and looked like a box. Surprisingly this shop actually did what it said on the tin\lid\sign above the shop as it sold games, nothing but games from all around the world. Inside the shop on the ground floor a huge game of Snakes and Ladders was painted upon the floor, although the snakes in this game were from the sea. On the first floor a giant Ludo board was painted upon the floor, and on the top floor chess, drafts and backgammon were painted upon the floors. All of these games had giant dice, chess, drafts and backgammon pieces so anybody could play. That's as long as they didn't mind people walking across the middle of their boards while the game was in progress, as if they were Gulliver in *Gulliver's Travels* and the people playing the games were Lilliputians. In fact, the entire shop resembled a giant compendium hence the name of the shop.

On the walls of the shop were giant paintings of gods playing various games from a giant compendium, and the pieces they were playing their games with were depicted as people. In one of the paintings the gods were playing Sea Snakes and Ladders, rolling huge dice upon a map of the planet. The snakes were like giant sea snakes with grotesque faces wrapped around the rigging of a tall ship. And some of these snakes had sailors in their mouths, not the sort of thing Gulliver had ever seen painted on the walls of Gamely's when he was a child that was for sure. If he had of done he would have had nightmares for evermore.

Another of the wall paintings featured the game Ludo and the gods were trying to get the counters into the pot by pressing one counter down upon the other, except once again the counters were depicted as people! Never mind about giving him nightmares as a child, these paintings would give him nightmares as an adult if he spent much more time inside this shop. Perhaps Gulliver needed to shop around to find a shop more to his taste, like a shop that was made of gingerbread and sweets like the house in Hansel and Gretel; yes, a sweet shop that was edible, that would definitely be more to his taste!

However, the surprising thing was that the children in the shop loved the paintings and stood riveted, gazing up at them in wonder. And what's more they didn't seem in the least bit scared or revolted by them, nor did their parents.

After watching several games being played out in The Compendium and once being nearly knocked to the floor by a giant dice, he continued down the street. Here Gulliver found a huge old ship sandwiched in between a baker's shop called The Baker's Shop and a sweet shop called The Sweet Shop, which just for the record wasn't edible and that's not a fairytale. Gulliver might well have had an imagination as wide as the cosmological oceans but obviously the owners of these two shops did not.

*A ship, a ship in the middle of a street,* Gulliver thought to himself incredulously before he said it out loud!

'A ship, a ship in the middle of the street, really!' Gulliver said as he looked up at the bow of the ship with a woman attached to it. Maybe I should clarify that, for when I say a woman attached to the bow of a ship, of course I mean the carved figurehead of a women. Gulliver had seen several of these figureheads outside pubs in Devon, however, the figureheads normally weren't still attached to the ships!

Gulliver went inside the shop which he found to be shipshape and Bristol fashion, albeit in Devon. The ship had two floors, on the ground floor the shop sold children's clothes and on the second floor it sold men's and women's clothes. Now although the ship only had two floors for some strange reason only known to the owner of this ship, sorry shop, this was how it was presented. Gulliver did enquire as to why the first floor was called the second floor when there was only a ground floor and a first floor, however, the shop assistants were as mystified as he was. All they could say was that the owner had sailed the ship a little too far into the harbour in a massive flood and the ship had ended up wedged between The Baker's Shop and The Sweet Shop. Apparently the ship displaced a cobbler's in the process which had resided there since kingdom come. Gulliver wondered if everybody who worked in this shop was talking cobblers!

Gulliver did find out the shop in its previous incarnation was a ship called *The Neptune*. This shop\ship both surprisingly and unsurprisingly was called The Ship, just to make things even more confusing, as if things needed to be even more confusing. The owner obviously hadn't pushed the boat out naming the shop, however, in the January sales he did hoist two giant sails up the ship's mast advertising these sales. Regarding things being confusing, Gulliver certainly didn't think things needed to be even more confusing, if anything he thought it would greatly benefit all and sundry if things were to be less confusing, however, they weren't so there was no point wishing things were otherwise. Nobody in this world seemed to wish things were otherwise so why should he, wishful thinking was obviously flat-earth thinking to the minds of these people. So Gulliver said to himself from this point on he was just going to accept everything no matter how strange it was. Now whether his subconscious would adhere to this dictum only time would tell.

While in the shop Gulliver bought some new clothes with the money from his magic pocket, fortunately these new clothes weren't like the emperor's new clothes! Before he dumped his old clothes he checked his pockets and found a ten pound note in one of them, a note with Charles Darwin's head upon it. He'd a good mind to go back to The Pandemonium Emporium and show everybody this bank note and then say, 'There, I told you so. I told you Charles Darwin existed!' However, the thought of stepping back into that shop sent a sharp shiver down his spine so Gulliver wisely thought better of it.

Gulliver noticed how the clothes in the shop were either from the sixteenth or the nineteenth century. The dummies in the shop window were dressed in doublets with frilly collars and hose, while other mannequins were dressed in morning suits with waistcoats, wearing silk cravats around their necks and with black satin top hats perched upon their heads. Gulliver didn't want the street urchin look from a Dickensian plot line or the Oliver look either, or even the Little Lord Fauntleroy look for that matter! So he chose a combination of the two. It seemed at least in this world Gulliver was a trendsetter, well, after a fashion, although I'm sure the owner of The Pandemonium Emporium would have just said he was a dummy!

## 5

# The Cost of Repairing an Astrarium Clock is Astronomical!

Gulliver then continued on with his travels bumping into an old man, although at least this time it was figuratively speaking. Gulliver asked the old man for the time, the man looked a Gulliver as if he were mad. When Gulliver asked the man who he was he said he was Old Father Time, however, since the gods had shaken things up around here, as he put it, and he had been given a gold watch, he was now retired. According to Old Father Time there was no longer such a thing as time, or at least not in the traditional sense of the word. Gulliver said that as he was at a loose end would he like to join him and his dog Beagle on his adventures, whatever they turned out to be. Old Father Time said as he had plenty of time on his hands why not, at least it would help to pass the time that no longer existed, and get him out from underneath his wife's feet. Now when I say get him out from underneath his wife's feet, I do mean get him out from underneath his wife's feet. You see Old Father Time had a bad back due to carrying an old grandfather clock around with him upon his back, and his wife often stood upon his back to help him get back on his feet, literally! I hope that's as clear as mud, good!

To say Gulliver was speechless upon meeting the Guardian of Time was undoubtedly the understatement of all time.

And so that was how Gulliver, Beagle and Old Father Time became friends. Gulliver later explained what had happened to him and this time it was Old Father Time's turn to be speechless, in fact you could have said, 'clock the look upon his face,' if you'd had a mind to! This speechlessness lasted about as long as it takes the minute hand of a clock to circumnavigate the clock face. It was fair to say Old Father Time was rather talkative and compendious when words came out of his mouth. Later he apologized for this wordyness but said that being the Guardian of Time you didn't get out much, this comment he was to explain later in minute detail.

This was the shortened version of events of Gulliver's first meeting with Old Father Time. Gulliver wrote everything that happened to him on his travels in this world in shorthand in his book with no words in it. Later he wrote them up in his travelogue in longhand, B. because it took longer and A. because while on his travels he hadn't the time to do so, not with the speed that events were unfolding around him. Gulliver wrote with a pencil which had a rubber attached to the end of it which saved him crossing things out and making his book with no words in it look messy. As I have mentioned before, it was Mark Twain who wrote that there were no wrong words, just words that needed crossing out, or some such nonsense. Gulliver thought Lewis Carroll and Mark Twain would have got on famously had they ever met!

'So, Old Father Time, look I can't really keep calling you Old Father Time, now can I?' said Gulliver looking Old Father Time squarely in the eye.

'Well, Gulliver, I've rather got used to being called Old Father Time, I'm not sure I want to change my name. It's a bit like me saying to you, so, Gulliver, I can't keep calling you Gulliver!' Old Father Time said, making perfect sense.

'Well, as long as you don't mind. It just seems that as a name, Old Father Time is a little long-winded. What if you dropped the Old from your name, then I could call you Father Time?' said Gulliver making just as much sense as Old Father Time had done previously.

'Okay, I can live with that. I must admit being called old does make me feel a little old,' Old Father Time said, continuing to make sense.

So that was how Old Father Time became Father Time. It's true that as a story it wasn't anything to write home about and in truth sending a letter through time isn't exactly what you might call reliable! So instead Gulliver wrote it in his travelogue along with everything else that had happened to him since he jumped into the sea in Brixham in Devon to save his dog Beagle. After which, the book without words and without pictures in it that he'd bought from the Mad Hatter lookalike in The Pandemonium Emporium, now at least had words written within its white pristine pages, if not pictures.

However, it wasn't long before Gulliver lapsed into calling Old Father Time Old Father Time and it was an even shorter period of time before Old Father Time stopped reminding Gulliver that he'd suggested he dropped the Old from his name. It was understandable that Old Father Time, being as old as he was, would forget this but after all, Gulliver was only a boy of thirty-five!

The first thing Old Father Time, sorry, Father Time did, was give Gulliver and Beagle the guided tour of Old Devonshire. This guided tour included the old aquarium, which contained sea monsters and other creatures of the sea like the kraken, a mermaid who couldn't swim but had plenty to say for herself, and a giant killer whale who had lost all its teeth due to all the people it had eaten over the years.

This old aquarium was called an Antiquarium, which Gulliver very much liked the sound of and, as it was positively ancient, this made perfect sense, as did old books and an old book shop being called antiquarian.

Old Father Time showed Gulliver and Beagle around the Antiquarium which gave Gulliver a chance to draw some of the more weird and wonderful exhibits that were housed there. This now meant his book without words not only had words in it but pictures too. Now this was a good thing because it meant if they ever bumped into Alice in Wonderland she wouldn't pull a face and say, 'and what is the use of a book without pictures or conversation?' Well, in this parallel world just about anything was possible, no scratch that, in this world anything was possible, end of story!

How his grandfather would love this place, Gulliver thought and for the first time since he had returned to his childhood, which, as an adult had been one of his fondest wishes, a tiny piece of him yearned for his own time. Mind you this yearning didn't last very long there was just so much going on in this world, that and after a while his old life was very much out of sight and out of mind. That was the strange thing about living in a world without time, with no clocks to remind you that time was slipping through your hands like sand through an hourglass, and as such, now it no longer felt like it was.

This reminded Gulliver of what Einstein once said, 'Time is the biggest illusion of them all.' Old Father Time even showed Gulliver what looked like an old rubbish tip or junk yard, where hundreds of thousands of watches, alarm clocks and old grandfather clocks had been dumped. It was like a graveyard for timepieces. Old Father Time said when he first saw it, it was both freeing and scary all at the same time. He then smiled and said the old jokes were the best and he should know!

After Old Father Time (who of course was now just plain Father Time having dropped the Old from his act, although he was still old), had given Gulliver the guided tour he took him back to his house. Once back at Father Time's house, Gulliver met Mrs Old Father Time, sorry Mrs Father Time, or Old Mother Time if you prefer, which she did if you subtract the old from this title. The Times then introduced Gulliver to their three children, Nicholas, Holly and Ivy. Gulliver thought perhaps Father and Mother Time were a little confused because surely these must be the names of Father Christmas's children, however they weren't, so let that be an end to it!

Mrs Time then prepared a sumptuous meal at rather short notice for Gulliver and there were more than enough scraps left over to keep Beagle happy.

At the meal table Gulliver was keen to glean as much information on this world as possible, which was still called earth, which wasn't unsurprising what with Devon being called Devon in this world.

Father Time explained that this world sat upon a giant antique globe which was exactly the same as

Gulliver's world, he said. But here Gulliver misunderstood Father Time for he meant this world literally stood on an antique globe covered in fish skin which the gods had placed there. This was said to be the beginning of this world and was written as such in a large compendium of rules which was said to be the word of the gods. The gods knew this planet to be called Compendium, translated from the Latin – *Compendious Terra Firma*, however, everybody else knew it as earth which was much less of a mouthful.

Once the gods had decided the general layout of the land and had drawn a rough map and covered the globe with it, they then coated the globe in several coats of varnish to make sure the map was waterproof. Every time a place was discovered the gods wrote the name of the newly discovered land on the globe. From time to time the gods would spin the globe and thus cause tidal waves, tsunamis and adverse weather conditions, which in turn threw some of the people upon the globe off into space. Then the gods commanded Atlas to hold this globe upon his shoulders as a punishment for getting marmalade on his atlas at school, until they could get a green marble statue of Atlas made, which eventually replaced the real Atlas. Old Father Time joked that at the beginning of time, Atlas looked as if he had the weight of the world upon his shoulders as he performed this Herculean task, which in truth he did. According to Old FT the gods had asked Hercules to hold the atlas globe up but at the time Hercules told the gods he was sorry but he couldn't because he was busy washing his hair! The meridian of the antique globe was golden as was the base it was standing upon and along the curve of the meridian was written the degrees 80 at both poles, decreasing '70 60 50 40 30 20 10' until they met in the middle at '0'. Gulliver knew in his world, Atlas was a Titan and was the titan of astronomy and navigation.

Gulliver knew a little bit about the history of the globe in that a man named Crates made the first globe atlas in 150 BC and back then globes were called gores. Gulliver also knew that the original globes were made out of stone, metal, marble, or in some cases, papier mache. Gulliver thought it was lucky this world wasn't made of papier mache otherwise one long hard downpour of rain and it would be goodnight Vienna, providing there was a Vienna in this world!

The gods also had a giant statue of Pegasus, the winged horse, constructed in flight mode out of white marble. The statue was the size of the House of Babel times one hundred, which they placed on the globe in an area which would eventually be named Mesopotamia. The gods were going to place Pegasus in Sparta but to be honest geography wasn't the gods' strong point, Old Father Time said, with a smile on his dial the size of the face of Big Ben.

It was fair to say you really didn't want to upset the gods in this world. Gulliver thought this was funny but not because it was odd, but, because as a child he had felt the world revolved around him, as all children did, like a globe revolved\spun on its axis. However, when he became an adult he realised it didn't and Gulliver had often wanted to shout 'stop the world I want to get off!' and now in this world if he had a mind to, he could, well, in theory at least. However, one would have to say he would have had to be out of his tiny little mind to do such a crazy thing!

On the antique globe, in the precise spot the word 'Greenwich' was written, sat a huge antique compendium clock which had four faces, coincidentally like the one in

Gulliver's antique shop, although not quite. The first of the faces of the compendium clock was an astronomical one, the second a chronometer which could be used in all weather conditions, the third was a small hourglass which sand ran through, and the final face was a calendar. The clock was covered with a glass dome like a lantern clock and was illuminated like a lighthouse. This was where Mr and Mrs Time and their children lived before time ceased to be, this was a bit like the old woman who lived in the shoe, minus the shoe and plus the clock! (A reason for the all-weather chronometer was in case space debris, an asteroid, a comet or a meteor broke the glass dome.)

Mr and Mrs Old Father Time had lived in this clock since time immemorial, which was probably why both Old Father Time and his wife were as deaf as posts, or they were when they weren't using their ear trumpets. This was because the chimes in the clock were ten times louder than if you were living inside Big Ben.

By the side of this clock sat an even bigger astronomical clock known as the Astrarium Chronometer, which although having somewhat of a complex mechanism pretty much took care of itself. Old Father Time only had to check this clock once a century. The Gothic-looking astronomical clock looked almost bare as if its casing had been removed to perform repairs. This revealed the inner workings of the clock with its numerous cogs, wheels, circular foliots, hammers and chimes. The astronomical clock had been going since the year dot and would be the last clock in the universe to stop, along with Old Father Time's body clock, Old FT joked. Old Father Time said if the Astrarium Chronometer ever did go wrong, the cost for repairing it was astronomical, another joke which in Old Mother

Time's case almost always fell upon deaf ears!

Old Father Time also had a large moondial as well as an even larger sundial to check the passing of time on both of these celestial bodies, although once again these dials pretty much took care of themselves.

Gulliver had always been a little puzzled by the expression 'as deaf as a post'. He had never seen an inanimate object such as a post before which had ears!

Old Father Time's full title was The Guardian of Time and his job description was a simple one, to keep things ticking over, nothing more, nothing less. This was one job where clock watching was positively encouraged!

A back-up clock was provided by the gods in case the clock ever stopped. This was an even larger hourglass which the sands of time ran through. Old Father Time's son kept an eye on this hourglass, making sure the mechanism that turned it was well oiled and thus ran like clockwork. There was also a large oriental candle clock as a further back up just in case all the lights in the universe went out! Old Father Time's son was known as Old Father Time the Younger, basically he was Old Father Time's apprentice and thus was known as The Time Apprentice.

Gulliver was surprised that Old Father Time didn't have an atomic clock, which told time to the nearest nanosecond. When Gulliver said this to Old FT, as some of his friends called him, he replied with a world-weary smile upon his face, worn down by time, 'Because the gods are a tight-fisted bunch!'

Gulliver knew that Leonardo Da Vinci had drawn up the plans for a clock that measured infinity. Twelve cogs of exponential size were to be connected in series, with the smallest gear completing one revolution per second. Each successive cog would rotate more slowly than its predecessor, until the final cog appeared to be entirely stationary. But that apparent standstill is deceptive; even the final cog would be turning (like the wheels and cogs of Da Vinci's mind were always turning), albeit unimaginably slowly. It would take a billion years to complete one revolution! *Even Father Time didn't have that much time on his hands to clock watch*, Gulliver thought, *or at least he hadn't until time had ceased to be!*

Gulliver thought that if he invented a time machine he could then pick up all the great minds on his travels through time and create a think tank where these great minds like Newton, Da Vinci, Pythagoras, Einstein, Nostradamus, Archimedes, and Stephen Hawking, could think up fantastical inventions. How's that for thinking outside the old brain box? Gulliver would probably leave Galileo standing at a bus stop thinking to himself, 'Isn't it always the way? You miss one time machine and then two appear at the same time!'

Another way-out thought had occurred to Gulliver, which was what if some boffin took all the theorems of the great minds throughout history and fed them into a super-computer programme. This would then create one giant synthetic brain which could solve all the world's problems… I think, therefore I am. I over think, therefore my name must be Gulliver!

Old Father Time told Gulliver that these giant clocks took quite a bit of winding up as the keys were bigger than he was! Of course Father Time was just winding Gulliver up as he told him later, as the gods took care of turning the key in the clocks so they didn't stop, well that was until they flew to sunnier climes. Old Father Time likened the gods' moonlight flit to a cuckoo in a cuckoo clock that in spring had broken free from the shackles of its tether and sprung forth into the sky to fly where it may. Gulliver thought this quite poetic in its make up. Old Father Time said that on a slow day he often wrote poetry to pass the time. Gulliver wasn't sure if he was yanking his pendulum or not! Gulliver knew a little of Greek philosophy and Greek history, although a lot of it was all Greek to him! Here Gulliver recalls the Greek's philosophy on time which was, that the gods had wound the clock of the universe up, set it down and then just let time take care of itself, doing Old Father Time out of a job. It appeared in this parallel world that the gods weren't so keen on letting time take care of itself, or at least they hadn't been in the beginning when the gods created the heavens and the antique globe atlas that Atlas supported upon his back!

Two giant snow domes sat at each pole, one at the North Pole and one at the South Pole. Scattered across this old globe were hundreds upon hundreds of ships in a bottle where the lands resided like Devonshire. Obviously all these tall ships were laid in the bottle by the gods in the time-honoured fashion with the sails laid flat. The sails and the mast being attached to a fine twine as they lay flat upon the decks of the ships, which were of course laid longitudinally before being slipped into the bottle. After which the gods would pull upon the fine twine and hey presto, the ship was ready to sail, or it would have been had it not been set upon a wooden plinth in a bottle.

Of course! As far as Gulliver was concerned there was no 'of course' about it. 'Of course' was so far off course in this world that it had sailed off the edge of the earth and wasn't coming back any time, let alone anytime soon! However, it seemed to Old Father Time, as it did to the people of this world, such fantastical and phantasmagorical things as their world being a giant antique globe, where giant ships in bottles and snow domes resided, was nothing more than commonplace and the most natural thing in the world.

Perhaps if your name was Darwin or you were a dog named Beagle it was natural but to Gulliver the words 'of course', which Old Father Time and the people in this world used as a matter of course, seemed wholly inappropriate.

Of course, to add to the confusion, from time to time when the gods got bored they would shake things up, literally, and time along with it. Luckily, most of the time the gods left the ships in the bottles and the snow domes alone. Although sometimes when the gods were playing silly beggars, England, otherwise known as Albion, ended up in Italy and Australia (known as New Holland when first discovered) ended up in Greenland.

However, this time it appeared that the gods had disappeared for good and weren't coming back any time, sooner *or* later for that matter. This meant from that moment on, 1.30am Greenwich Mean Time on Sunday 17 March 1743 to be precise, funnily enough, time ceased and Old Father Time was made redundant. Old Father Time joked that before time ended everybody was asking him for the time and as soon as it ended people wouldn't give him the time of day! Although people no longer gave Old Father Time the time of day, Old Father Time being the Guardian of Time was left a golden watch by the gods for services rendered. Of course, this gold watch was nothing more than a fashion accessory, like a fake Rolex was in Gulliver's world, as the gods were as tight as Scrooge in Charles Dickens's Christmas tale and just about as mean to boot!

Although Greenwich Mean Time had ceased to be, the sun and moon dials still kept ticking over, as did the astrarium, the large astronomical clock which was still recoding the space-time of the universe. Although technically Old Father Time was now retired, he still out of a sense of duty occasionally checked this astronomical chronometer, once in a blue moon.

Not only had time ceased but when the gods had shaken up time various time periods had got mixed up with one another. Luckily this didn't affect the snow domes, the south and north poles, as there really wasn't a lot there, although now mammoths could be found at both poles, as could the dodo, which got stuck there while migrating from a different time.

Old Father Time said that in 'The Big Shake Up' some of time had even been mislaid, while some had literally been lost in time. He also said that time was so complicated he couldn't even beginning to explain how time had been misplaced or lost. All he knew was that it had been and Gulliver would just have to take his word for it.

Who was Gulliver to argue with the ex-Guardian of Time, after all, he had barely scraped through O level maths and physics, so he was more than happy to take Old Father Time's word for whatever he told him. Although Old Father Time did say that without clocks, people were now very much reliant on their body clocks, and as such were very adept at guesstimating the right time.

When man was first put on the earth he just used the sun and the moon to tell the time so losing time wasn't quite the disaster it might at first have appeared. After all, Stonehenge is probably just a giant sundial and even the earth has its own internal body clock.

'If you look at things this way, the history books have been ripped up and the pages have been scattered to the four winds and beyond. In fact, it seems the rules for time travel have also received the same treatment. You could well say that history is history!' Old Father Time said drinking down a large flagon of ale to wet his whistle before continuing on. 'At the time of this catastrophic time collapse, something Nostradamus had predicted in one of the quatrains in his book, *Les Phropheties*, it seems from those ripped up history books that the sixteenth century and the nineteenth century got mixed up together and have now settled down comfortably side by side.' Gulliver knew in his world both of these time periods were known as 'the Golden Age'.

'I recently met Queen Elizabeth I out in the street talking to Charles Dickens, and then I saw Sir Walter Raleigh out on a penny-farthing, or should I say I saw him fall off a penny-farthing. He probably didn't have his sea legs with him at the time!' Old Father Time laughed heartily. 'Luckily the people from the nineteenth century are helping the people from the sixteenth century understand some of the latest inventions. Can you imagine when Queen Elizabeth I first saw a hot air balloon in the sky? Well, I can tell you, she nearly fell off her throne. And as you can imagine that's just the tip of the iceberg, well it would be if this was the north or the south snow domes!' Old Father Time said chuckling to himself.

Old Father Time said that according to the legends and myths which were written down in sand-script and hidden in a cave somewhere at the bottom of the ocean. (Well you know what the gods are like, they love a bit of drama and mystery!) The gods had devised several games which they placed inside a wooden box which they called a compendium. Just for the record, the box was made by a guy called Jesus who was a carpenter. Now whenever the gods got bored they would take a game out of the compendium like Snakes & Ladders (although in this world it was called Sea Snakes & Ladders), Ludo, Drafts, etc. etc. and play the game until one of the gods won. 'However, and here's the twist,' Old Father Time said smiling, 'the pieces, or the pawns if you like, they would be using would take human form. The gods would move them across the board which would be the map of the earth. Dice would be thrown and pieces would be moved; most of the time the gods made the rules up as they went along.' One thing was for sure, Old Father Time obviously had never heard of the word 'compendious'! Gulliver, however, had heard of the word 'compendium' and knew that it not only meant a collection of board games in one box, but also a concise and comprehensive summary of information about a subject.

*It was fortunate for the people of this world that the gods hadn't heard of the game Spin the Bottle or Battleships*, thought Gulliver dryly!

Old Father Time said there was a young engineer called Brunel who had constructed a giant hourglass which turned automatically every hour using a design of pulleys, leavers and cogs. Every city had one of these giant hourglasses and some people even had miniature versions on their wrists just so they could keep track of the time that no longer was.

Having thought long and hard about this it still didn't sink in properly, so Gulliver thought about it even longer and even harder and still he couldn't get his head round it. Anymore than he could get his head around this globe, parallel world, whatever it was he found himself stuck up to the neck in! Still, at least he was alive, unless this was heaven, or hell! Gulliver, like Alice from Wonderland, had a mind to wonder if there was a Flat Earth Society on this world, although he presumed it was called The Flat Globe Society! He also had a mind to wonder if some of the Chinese junk boats which had sailed off the edge of the globe atlas and into the cosmological oceans could now be said to be 'space junk'!

Then Gulliver recalled the shop called The Compendium and the paintings upon its walls and now things started to make a little more sense, for in truth they didn't make a lot more sense. *Perhaps that's why the gods had got bored and left,* Gulliver thought wistfully, as they had found another world which had more sophisticated games like Xboxes and computer games! Gulliver then remembered the Einstein quote 'God doesn't play dice with the universe'. God may not play dice with the universe but it appeared at one time or another, the gods in this world had!

Old Father Time then chuckled to himself as he could see Gulliver was finding it hard to take this all in.

But that was the thing, you had to chuckle to yourself in this world otherwise you were likely to go mad, stark raving mad like the Mad Hatter had so obviously done having spent far too much time in the land of wonder, otherwise known as Wonderland, wondering about this, that and the other! Gulliver was later to write something similar in his travelogue and after it he wrote the words, 'Compendious not Mark Twain was right!' Later still, he drew a pencil line through the whole sorry paragraph!

'Don't worry, lad, in time things will become as clear as the Black Sea!' Old Father Time said less than reassuringly. If the truth be told, Gulliver would have preferred if things were as crystal clear as the Mediterranean Sea rather than the Black Sea!

To Gulliver it seemed this world was 'out of this world', which was exactly what he wrote later in his travelogue. This short but concise sentence described this world to a T, minus all the waffle and nonsense, and was one he didn't cross out, in fact, after it he wrote the word 'compendious', Charles Dickens eat your heart out! After he'd dwelt on things further, Gulliver thought, *well, is my world that different from this one?* If before the big shake up somebody from this time had ended up in his time wouldn't they think things had been shaken up? After all, the continents had shifted and now people of all races, creeds and colours were mixed up with one another in all four corners of the globe. The main difference between the two worlds was time, or the lack of it.

This world and his own to some extent reminded Gulliver of a dream he'd had as a child and this is how it went...

Gulliver awoke from a dream as a hell of a racket appeared to be going on downstairs, *perhaps the Mad Hatter was having a late-night tea party,* he thought in his delirious state. However, when he got down into the living room all was quiet, although the books in the bookshelves had been pulled out and some of the books were strewn upon the floor. Gulliver looked around nervously, perhaps they had been burgled by a book thief who was searching for his signed copy of *Alice's Adventures in Wonderland*, that curiously enough he kept in a cabinet of curiosity in his bedroom. He searched all of the downstairs rooms but found no one. Gulliver then put the books back in the bookcase and ascended the stairs back to bed.

A few minutes later the noise started again. *Perhaps it was a ghost,* Gulliver thought, in which case it was best he ignored the noises and went back to sleep, which being a dream he already was. However, Gulliver put on a brave face and went back downstairs to once again find all was quiet but once again the books were strewn about the place. Gulliver happened to pick up *Treasure Island* and read a few pages as he thought it might help send him off to sleep. A few pages in he realised the story had changed, in fact, it had become mixed up with several other stories; characters from *Peter Pan, The Lost World,* and *Hard Times* had somehow ended up in *Treasure Island*. Not only had the words become jumbled up but so had the pictures, as drawings from Roald Dahl's book *James and the Giant Peach* and *Alice Through the Looking Glass* were now in between the pages of the book *Treasure Island*.

Gulliver then picked up several more books and they were also jumbled up, fairytales with mystery stories, fictional books mixed up with non-fiction books, his mother's cookery books were mixed up with his father's fishing books; the whole thing was most curious and perplexing.

Gulliver just shut the books up tightly, leaving Peter Pan clinging to the edge of the spine of *Treasure Island* and the mad March Hare squashed between the pages like a bug. Gulliver feared he had gone stark raving mad like the Mad Hatter and went back up the stairs to bed hoping the nightmare might end. Ten minutes later the noise started again. Gulliver rushed downstairs determined to sort this mystery out only to find characters from all the books on the shelves either fighting with one another, dancing, or slipping in between the pages of the wrong book as if they were slipping in between the bedsheets. It was at this point that Gulliver really woke up (and I don't mean woke up to himself either, although if he had a looking glass on his ceiling then I suppose he could well have done!).

This time Gulliver knew he was awake because he tried the old *Alice in Wonderland* trick and pinched himself several times and it hurt. Gulliver had always had wild and scary dreams ever since he was a very young child and still did up until this very day, and in all the weird, wild and wonderful dreams, Gulliver had never eaten cheese before he went to bed!

The last dream Gulliver had before he ended up in this world was of it raining words and letters, literally raining words and letters! And they weren't little words either, they were big ones like, phantasmagorical, fantastical and presentiment, which according to the dictionary, which he had no reason to doubt, meant – sense of something unpleasant about to happen, which it was! And perhaps he wouldn't have minded so much if the words and letters weren't landing directly on his head knocking him to the ground. And some of these words were heavy like enormity, herculean and weighty. Gulliver felt like he was drowning in a sea of words which soon turned into a wild river which Gulliver was caught up in. Gulliver clung on to a giant letter Z for dear life as he was swept out to sea never to be seen again, end of story!

After this nightmare had ended and Gulliver had awoken he took the dictionary and thesaurus which were in his bedside cabinet and threw them in the harbour! Some dreams had you lost for words and this was such a dream, although not quite, as Gulliver later committed it to his dream journal.

Although Gulliver didn't know it at the time, and not just because there wasn't any time to know about, but his travelogue would be the first travelogue ever written without any times or dates within it. Now one might say this might make it a little\lot difficult to follow, but no matter, one day when Gulliver eventually finished his travels and put his journal to one side it was sure to make an interesting read. Or at least it would make a good paperweight or a bad doorstop!

'This world must seem very confusing to every living person as well as the animals,' Gulliver said when Old Father Time stopped speaking, as he wondered if Noah had ever had an occasion to get his ark out of mothballs and take it for a spin around the globe.

'Well, it's true what you say, Gulliver. At first both the people of our world and the animals didn't know whether they were coming or going. However, eventually we all got used to it and now we don't take a blind bit of notice of the way things are!' said Old Father Time with a wry smile upon his face.

'Is that why everybody is always bumping into one another?!' Gulliver said with a similar wry smile upon his face, and then rather wished he hadn't. 'I told you!' he said to himself under his breath, 'funny in my head but not when I open my mouth!'

'Yes, my boy, I guess it is!' said Old Father Time as a broad smile broke out across his craggy antiquarian features.

'I guess I am funny after all,' Gulliver said still under his breath, but then again, with this being a parallel world it was only to be expected.

Old Father Time did add that, as this world was set on an antique globe, at least when you got close to a county or country the word would be written upon the land in large writing. This was especially useful if you were viewing this world from above, say for instance in a hot air balloon. The problem was of course, since the gods had shaken things up, it meant places weren't where they once were. Devon was still Devon and London was still London but Devon might now be where London used to be and London might be where Devon used to be. It wasn't in this case but some places weren't where you expected them to be or at least weren't where Gulliver expected them to be.

Just imagine for a moment, if you will, waking up on Christmas Day in New Holland (Australia) to find it snowing, which might well be a nice surprise. However, what might not be quite such a nice surprise is to find a polar bear in your back garden! For the reason it's snowing is because New Holland\Australia is now where Greenland used to be and Greenland is, well, God knows where! Old Father Time let out a roar of laughter when he told Gulliver this that nearly shattered Gulliver's eardrums.

Gulliver wondered if Sir Walter Raleigh was still living in Devon and whether any other of his heroes lived there too, like Sir Francis Drake. Perhaps he would get to sail on the real *Golden Hind* and not just stand on the replica which stood in Brixham harbour in his time. Well on this score only time would tell, except of course in this world it wouldn't, or at least Old Father Time wouldn't be the one telling you!

'There is one more thing I should probably tell you,' Old Father Time said as the smile dropped slightly from his face. 'Because time has been shaken up here you may meet my younger self, in fact you may meet my middle-aged self as well. Most of the time this is a rare event as the world is a big place, and there is an awful lot of time to get mixed up, although I should probably amend that to *was* an awful lot of time to get mixed up. Now the rule of thumb (no, not Tom Thumb, this isn't *Gulliver's Travels*, well, it is but it isn't all at the same time, but you know what I mean!), now where were we? Oh yes, measuring Tom's thumb. Now the rule of thumb is if you meet yourself in time it's best if you give yourself a wide berth, you certainly don't want to be getting into fisticuffs with yourself in case you end up doing yourself in. Just like if you travel back in time and meet you parents and run them over on your penny-farthing, otherwise you won't have been born, the old time paradox, you get the picture. However, now time no longer exists this will no longer be a problem as there is no timeline to disturb. So if you come across a book entitled *The Time Traveller's Guide*, feel free to throw it on the fire!' Once again Old Father Time laughed out loud at his own joke before he once again began to be compendious and not so compendious all at the same time!

'I can tell you one thing, I'm certainly glad I've retired. Imagine all the different watches I'd have to have in my pocket to tell the correct time. It is strange that once time filled my every waking moment and now time means nothing to me. Einstein was right all along, time is the greatest illusion of them all. Perhaps I'll become a magician, although I won't be able to perform the old stopping of the fob watch routine!' The smile on Old Father Time's face quickly stretched itself out across his face as if it was about to break into a yawn, which a few seconds later it did, minus the seconds.

Gulliver remembered a conversation he'd had with his father, although as a conversation it left a lot to be desired as mostly it was his father talking at him. In this one-sided conversation his father said he should help himself. Now at the time Gulliver didn't really understand what his father was getting at but now he did. If he met himself (Gulliver) he could help himself (Gulliver). For example if Gulliver got washed up on a desert island and met himself they could both help each other build a boat and then they could both row back to civilization. When they got back to civilization and people called out in jest to Gulliver, 'Gulliver, how were your travels?' both he and himself would turn round at the same time! His father was right, it made perfect sense, he had to help himself. Perhaps he hadn't given his father enough credit, for a split second (which didn't exist) Gulliver felt guilty about not listening to his father and made a mental note that when he got back to his time he would make it up to him while there was still time to do so.

After the conversation with the Times, both Mr and Mrs, Gulliver thanked the couple and retired to bed after what had been a very long day indeed. That day time had passed both quickly and slowly, while not passing at all.

That night Gulliver had some of the weirdest dreams he'd ever had in his life before now but as he was only twelve this wasn't that surprising. However, in reality (whatever that was!) he was thirty-five, although to Gulliver's mind it appeared to him he was neither twelve or thirty-five but a cross between the two. Gulliver was to maths what Archimedes was to the world of fashion (refer the *Emperor's New Clothes* and the Eureka story!), but even he knew that if you added two figures together then divided them you would get another figure, which hopefully would be the sum of the two parts or something like that. This made Gulliver... twenty-three and a half years of age, which meant he would have to wait six months for his next birthday to come around.

In one of those weird dreams he had that night, he was sitting in his bathtub full of baked beans smoking a pipe full of bubbles and singing 'the big ship sails on the alley alley-o, the alley alley-o, the alley alley-o.'

Talking about reality in this world was like a tightrope walker attempting to walk across a strand of gossamer over an active volcano. Actually it was nothing like that but Gulliver wrote the line in his travelogue just because he liked the sound of it. Quantum physicists and philosophers alike were always saying 'what's reality?' and now Gulliver was beginning to say the same thing.

'What's reality?' Gulliver said to a bemused Beagle, who was in fact a Labrador. Beagle just looked up at his master as if he had lost his mind. Perhaps he *had* lost his mind but where had he lost it, in this world or in the world he'd just come from? It was puzzle, all right. No, it wasn't a puzzle, a puzzle was easy to do, even a 3D puzzle of the universe was easy to do compared with making sense of this world.

Gulliver later wrote in his travelogue: 'This world is likely to give you a permanent migraine!' Gulliver was right about one thing this world was tailor made for the exclamation mark.

Gulliver had never been very fashion conscious, however, he had noticed in this world how men dressed like women, in short dresses with high frilly collars or in pantaloons. He had often seen pictures in books and paintings of Sir Francis Drake and Sir Walter Raleigh dressed in such a get-up and in truth, thought they both looked a right Charlie! Either that or the men of this world dressed in smart dark suits with waistcoats and cravats with top hats on their heads, or frock coats like he'd seen Isambard Kingdom Brunel and Oscar Wilde dressed in.

Women's outfits between the sixteenth and nineteenth century didn't seemed to be that different from one another, as women from both centuries wore long wide flowing dresses. Although once again the sixteenth-century dress was frilly and embellished with lace and was lighter while the nineteenth-century fashion went for darker shades. Vintage fashion was very fashionable in 2013 as it was in both the sixteenth and the nineteenth centuries, which was one thing that was most definitely something that wasn't to be expected however, was that later Old Father Time told Gulliver that the antique globe was a part of a Grand orrery. This was a clockwork model of the solar system, Gulliver wasn't sure if the Guardian of Time was winding him up or not?

# 6

# The Antiquarium Revisited

The next day both Gulliver and Beagle woke up late and ate a hearty breakfast which Mrs Old Father Time had laid on for them and which, to Gulliver's mind, was a spread fit for a king and a queen. Gulliver could see why Mr and Mrs Time were both pear shaped.

That night Gulliver had some weird and wonderful dreams which kept him tossing and turning most of the night. One such dream saw him fighting pirates off Penzance in Cornwall, which considering the rivalry between the two counties wasn't that unexpected. Gulliver had a dream in which his face resembled a clock like the one he'd had as a child on his bedside table. And the clock was being thrown onto a giant pile of clocks which were being thrown away and he was suffocating at the bottom of this pile. 'I'll file that dream under nightmare' Gulliver later wrote in his dream journal.

In between these dreams\nightmares he'd also had time to think. Well, he didn't because time had stopped, but he did think, and this thinking led him to wonder how you managed to get out of the bottle with the ship in it. And how come everywhere was green when the clouds, the sun and the moon were all outside the bottle with the ship, Devon, Old Father Time and his wife, the small man with the big head under the even bigger hat who owned The Pandemonium Emporium, his dog Beagle, him and old Tom Cobbley and all in it!? And did birds with very little brain bump into the top of the glass snow dome or sides of the bottle with the ship in it, knocking them senseless in the process?

All these questions needed answering and luckily for Gulliver, as before Old Father Time was happy to provide answers for them, or at least most of them as some questions could only be answered by God or the gods or the God-like geniuses of Einstein, Newton, Archimedes and the like.

After Gulliver rattled all these questions off to Old Father Time this was what he said verbatim, in other words, word for word.

'Dear boy, aren't you the inquisitive one? Well, let me see,' Old Father Time said studiously as he peered over his half-moon spectacles. 'Well, although the sun is outside the glass, as it shines through it, it creates condensation on the inside of the roof of the bottle and thus eventually it produces falling rain,' the old man with time on his hands said as he folded his arms across his chest in somewhat of a contented fashion before adding, 'And as for birds bashing into things, well, birds have got far more sense than most people, they quickly realised that the roof of the world was made of glass, sooner in fact than the pilots of our hot air balloons did!'

'Of course!' said Gulliver as if he was Archimedes and had meant to say eureka instead of, of course!

This reminded Gulliver of a bad joke his father once told him about Archimedes running down the road naked after his eureka moment in the bath tub. After which

Archimedes was stopped by a policeman who said he was arresting him. Archimedes said something to the policeman along the lines of 'have you got a screw loose?' although it could have been the policeman who said that to Archimedes, as this was in Greek it might have been somewhat lost in translation, as the expression goes, 'it's all Greek to me'. Of course Gulliver knew all about Archimedes' invention, the Archimedes screw, otherwise the joke would have sailed right over his head. (To be honest sails did tend to sail right over your head unless they were in the January sales where you often got trampled underfoot!)

'And as for how we get out of the bottle, well we remove the cork, dear boy, we remove the cork,' Old Father Time said in a matter-of-fact manner.

It was round about this time, which didn't exist, that Gulliver thought that actually, this world wasn't quite as complicated and nonsensical as he may have at first led himself to believe it was. Both the answers to his questions were completely logical, which led him onto another question.

'Old Father Time, does this mean that if you need to get to the North or the South Pole, sorry North or the South Snow Dome, you have to take the stoppers out of the bottom of the domes? And furthermore, you have do it very quickly so all the ice and water in them doesn't leak out onto the globe which in turn would lead to the map peeling off!?' Gulliver said hardly drawing breath before sitting back and folding his arms in somewhat of a contented fashion mirroring Old Father Time.

It was almost as if Gulliver was playing a game of chess with Old Father Time. Luckily he wasn't as Gulliver had never been very good at playing chess, while Old Father Time on the other hand often played chess against himself. Well, while ensconced within the giant clock in Greenwich, OFT did have plenty of time on his hands, and there is only so much clock watching you can do without it sending you as cuckoo as a cuckoo clock!

Old Father Time said Gulliver was pretty much correct in his assumptions and, due to time, which no longer existed, the corks in these ships in bottles, which were scattered all over the antique globe had been worn away somewhat so there was a tiny, almost imperceptible gap between the glass and the cork. Through this gap air managed to squeeze its way, as could people at a pinch, the people who climbed through this gap were the ultimate free climbers, Old Father Time joked. If you waited for the tide to rise you could then sail your ship through it, which wasn't a joke because that's what sailors did. The ship in the bottle would face lengthways with the cork and bottle neck pointing towards the sea so when the tide rose people didn't drown in a flood of mythical proportions. The houses, schools, shops churches etc. were set well back from the neck and cork of the bottle. Old Father Time did say that in this procedure it certainly helped to keep a tight ship!

Gulliver wanted to ask Old Father Time whether he'd ever read *Gulliver's Travels* for if he had Gulliver could make a joke of his own. Something along the exact lines of, if he were Gulliver the giant in Lilliput he could stand on a giant stepladder and push the cork out with his own hands. Old Father Time would have probably said one of the gods would be standing there to stop him doing that. The gods were a contrary bunch, they wanted life to flourish, but at the same time they wanted to watch your struggles from a safe vantage point, and have a good old laugh at your expense while very rarely lifting a finger to help you in these struggles. Of course from time to time the gods did condescend to giving you a helping hand or a leg up, well, until the day time had ceased and the gods had swanned off to sunnier climbs, and didn't appear to be coming back any time before, now, soon or later.

'There were also times that Neptune or Poseidon would take the cork out of the bottle just to make sure everything was shipshape and Bristol fashion,' Old FT said, which immediately made Gulliver think of his namesake Gulliver in the book *Gulliver's Travels*. Gulliver, who by now was giving Alice a run for her money in the wondering department, wondered if he might bump into Jonathan Swift the author of *Gulliver's Travels* as he was born in 1667 in Dublin. The thing about *Gulliver's Travels* was that it was a great story for children but at that age a lot of the satire went right over your head. It was only when you read the story as an adult that you could read in between the lines, something which in all honesty sounds like a fairytale as there is nothing in between the lines, literally nothing!

And you won't be in the least bit surprised that there was a Wondering Department in The Compendium, where heads of department would literally get their heads together and wonder about how they were going to improve sales figures and get more customers through the doors.

There was also a Wondering Garden just outside Brixham where people came to wonder about this, that and the other, as they wandered slowly around the gardens taking time to smell the roses as they did so.

'Yes, that's the gods for you, they think they're above us mere mortals. Mind you, I suppose when you think about it, they are!' Old Father Time said laconically.

Old Father Time then went on to describe how the

condensation, falling rain\rainfall could, due to the closeness of the sun, cause flooding. After which everybody including the animals would have to pile onto the gigantic ship, which would now in effect be like one gigantic Noah's Ark. Well, they didn't all want to end up in a whale's belly like Jonah now did they?' Old Father Time said with a smile on his face. He also said water and sunlight, when combined, produced life. In truth Gulliver had been a little\lot perplexed how life inside a ship's bottle could get started and now Gulliver knew this, it was one less thing to keep him awake at night. Talking about Noah's Ark, recently a stone tablet had been discovered from Babylonian times which mentioned a story which was remarkably like the ark story. However, this ark was a giant round coracle. It appeared to Gulliver that the writers of the Bible were obviously no more apposed to plagiarizing than modern writers were!

Old Father Time should probably have dropped the Time from his name, like Gulliver said he should drop the Old from his name. But he'd got so attached to his full given name that he found it nigh on impossible to do so. Being the Guardian of Time made him a somebody, and being a nobody took a bit of getting used to. Gulliver on the other hand had always been a nobody and as he still was he only had to get used to the body of a twelve-year-old boy again. Mind you, if Old Father Time dropped both the Old and the Time from his name he'd just be left with Father, which having two daughters and a son of course he was. In time, Old Father Time would see that being a father was plenty to be going on with and nothing, but nothing, beat being a father to your children.

Old Mrs Time, who rarely spoke unless addressed personally, and that's *addressed* and not *dressed* personally, because she wasn't the White Queen in *Alice in Wonderland* or Queen Elizabeth I and she didn't have her own personal maids. However, Gulliver did address Old Mrs Time personally, although being the perfect gentleman he was, he dropped the Old from her name. Gulliver did wonder if he should be addressing Old Father Time as ex-Old Father Time and his wife as ex-Mrs Time, although as they weren't divorced he saw no reason to do so. Some may have said that this couple may not have been divorced but they were divorced from reality, although in this world in that respect it appeared they were not alone!

This addressing of Old Mrs Time consisted of asking her where she got her dress from, a yellow lace number that flowed outwards from the middle like a river, and had so many ruffles at the bottom of it that to Gulliver's mind it looked like waves breaking on the shoreline. Gulliver certainly found this dress most pleasing to the eye. Old Mrs Time said, 'Oh, this old thing? I've had it for some time.' Gulliver wasn't sure if she was joking or not as she didn't smile at the time she was addressing him. However, after this comment she did go on to say that at the time time ended, Old Father Time's hair was as grey as a grey squirrel and now it was as white as Father Christmas's beard.

This got Gulliver to thinking which led him to wonder how long time had ceased to be? But as there were no calendars and no clocks and no one was recording time since Old Father Time had retired, who could say. Certainly not Old Father Time. Gulliver wondered why nobody had thought of restarting time but with time all mixed up as it was, where were you going to start it at? Perhaps you could restart it at the precise moment it stopped, which was 1.30am Greenwich Mean Time on Sunday the 17 March 1743. But now with time so radically altered, that wouldn't make sense either. I suppose you could calculate a date and time between the sixteenth century and the nineteenth century, which seemed to be the two centuries that had now snuggled up in bed together, metaphorically speaking that was. Perhaps that wasn't a bad idea, however, it was no good him doing the calculations especially, as the only thing they had to hand nowadays to calculate things on was an abacus. Maybe if he ran into Sir Isaac Newton, Pythagoras or Archimedes he could ask them to figure it out and then Old Father Time could come out of retirement. Perhaps Old Father Time could roll a dice or toss a coin but then again, perhaps not!

But what if Old Father Time didn't want to come out of retirement? Perhaps he was happy to be retired with time on his hands. He might not thank Gulliver for interfering, especially as he didn't even live in this world, as his world obviously ran parallel to this one. Or he might thank Gulliver but in a manner that could be said to be tinged with sarcasm, 'Thanks for nothing, Gulliver!' to which Gulliver, being a twelve-year-old boy and not entirely at home with the complexities of sarcasm, would reply, 'Think nothing of it. I was happy to be of assistance.'

Old Father Time said the truth was that they didn't want to restart time as it gave the gods too much power and control over their world. What if the gods were to come back and shake time up again and again and again? This way was better this way they had more control over their own destiny. Gulliver thought of this parallel earth as a twin, albeit not an identical twin.

Although Gulliver didn't think there was anything obvious about anything that had happened to him since he'd woken up in the cave. 'Obvious' or 'obviously' were two words, although they obviously only counted as one word, that he had no business using in this world, along with 'of course'. In fact, if he ever found The Last Bookshop in the World and found a dictionary upon the shelves he had a good mind to go through it and as Mark Twain suggested, cross out all the wrong words like, 'obviously' and 'course' (which of course didn't make sense without the of!). 'Definitely' definitely had to go, after which he'd put it back upon the shelf and walk away with a broad smile upon his face. Of course the editors of the Oxford English Dictionary would have had their collective noses put out of joint but that was a small price to pay for giving the English language a well deserved boot up the gluteus maximus! Of course, being dyslexic Gulliver couldn't spell the words gluteus maximus for toffee, words that to Gulliver's fertile mind sounded like a Roman emperor with piles!

One last thing Gulliver wanted to ask Old Father Time was this... 'What about the church?' Gulliver was hoping he hadn't hit on a sore point! In his world, religion was one of those things you were never supposed to bring up, or at least not unless you were prepared for an argument or a theological debate.

'What do you want to know about a church, other than it's a big, cold, empty building with spires and stained glass windows?' Old Father Time said, yanking someone's dog collar other than Beagle's. Although thanks to the clock at Greenwich, Old FT was more than a little hard of hearing.

'No, I mean what about religion?' Gulliver said, making himself as clear as he knew how, which was by talking slowly and in a loud voice as if Old Father Time was completely gaga. (Gulliver liked Lady Gaga and thought she would have fitted into this world without any problem whatsoever.) Gulliver hoped he would bump into P.T. Barnum the freak show promoter, then he could borrow one of his loud hailers to enable Old Father Time to get the cloth out of his ears!

'Oh religion, well, since the gods deserted this world, the people have deserted God. Most of the churches are now deserted,' Old Father Time said, as if religion wasn't exactly high on his agenda of things to worry or talk about. *There was no doubt about it,* Gulliver thought, *at times this world mirrored both* Gulliver's Travels *and* Alice's Adventures through the Looking Glass.

Gulliver decided not to press the point so changed the subject to the Crown, in other words, Her Majesty's subjects, of which he now both counted and considered himself as one.

'So what about the queen?' said Gulliver as if he and Old Father Time were both playing a game of chess against the gods and he was asking his opinion whether to move the queen or not.

'So what about the queen!?' said Old Father Time, yanking Gulliver's crown. Gulliver wasn't quite sure what to say next to that question other than to say, 'What!'

'You mean who is the queen?' said Old Father Time adding a serious note to the proceedings.

'Yes,' said Gulliver as the conversation at this point seemed to require a yes.

'Queen Elizabeth I and a mighty fine queen she is too. She takes no nonsense from anyone and in this world that's a must,' said Old Father Time earnestly.

It was at this point in the time that no longer existed that Gulliver could see the old man had had enough of being cross-questioned so Gulliver quit jabbering, as to be honest, he was tiring of the sound of his own voice. That and his throat felt like a piece of sandpaper which time had left untouched. Gulliver did wonder that as the time zones of Queen Elizabeth and Queen Victoria appeared to be so inextricably linked, as if their time was hanging upon the same thread, why both queens were not upon the throne at the same time.

After all this think tank-type thinking and Alice-type wondering, Gulliver was only too ready for a good hearty breakfast, which was all Old Mrs Time seemed able to prepare, her being old school in the cooking department. Gulliver didn't think she'd warm to Heston Blumenthal's style of cooking.

Heston Blumenthal, who unlike Stephen Fry, Fiona Bruce and Doctor Who, had in reality actually been into Gulliver's antiques emporium in Brixham at the time he'd been shooting one of his cookery programmes on board the *Golden Hind*. Heston was cooking up a storm by making sweet chips and other weird and wonderful delights. Gulliver thought the people of this world would appreciate Heston Blumenthal's style of cooking. He was only surprised Heston hadn't cooked the books 'as they say' by cooking an edible book, just give it time!

After breakfast Old Father Time took Gulliver back to the old aquarium, otherwise known as the Antiquarium. This was so he could sketch some more of the wondrous creatures on display in the main large tanks, which included some giant seahorses and what Gulliver believed to be the Loch Ness monster. Old Father Time said Gulliver believed correctly because it *was* the Loch Ness monster. The monster had been fished out of Loch Ness some time ago. The Loch Ness monster wasn't the only monster in the Antiquarium as the kraken, the giant octopus-like sea monster, had been captured swimming off Greenland by a whaling ship. Later the kraken was sold to the Antiquarium for both a small and a large fortune in keeping with this crazy mixed-up world. However, Old Father Time couldn't tell Gulliver how long ago these events had happened, and that wasn't because his memory was failing him but because when the gods had shaken things up, in part his memory had been shaken up with it. Old Father Time said his memory was settling down like the flakes in a snow dome but there was still stuff missing. The stuff probably wasn't missing, Mrs Old Father Time said, it was probably just misplaced like her husband always misplaced his socks. Gulliver was glad to see some things in this world ran parallel to his own! Later, after this compendious discussion, Gulliver was to write this in his travelogue: 'To my young mind this world appears not unlike the Land that Time Forgot or the Lost World or the World that Lost Time or something along those lines.' It appeared Gulliver was caught in two minds like this world was caught in no man's land!

Today was the day when Gulliver bumped into a young girl, or should I say she bumped into him? Although in truth it was hard to tell who bumped into whom, it was probably half a dozen of one and half a dozen of the other.

'Sorry!' Gulliver and the girl said in unison and then they both laughed.

'Is this yours?' said the girl, handing Gulliver his sketch pad. To be fair the girl had seen Gulliver sketching and was curious to see if his drawings were any good for she also sketched. This broke the ice between the two of them, having said that, they weren't encased inside a snow dome as this wasn't the North or the South Pole. However, they were encased inside a large ship in a bottle. Later Gulliver was to wonder how these ships in a bottle and the snow domes didn't simply fall off the large antique globe. Perhaps he would bump into Sir Isaac

Newton or Albert Einstein and they would explain things to him, mind you, as they had both found it hard explaining things to him in his world, he didn't think they would have any more luck doing so in this one. Perhaps, once again, I should clarify that last line by saying that the books Sir Isaac Newton and Albert Einstein had written, Gulliver had found difficult to understand. 'What goes up must come down,' Gulliver muttered to himself when this thought made itself known to him. Perhaps everything was stuck onto the globe with super glue, he joked to himself, and perhaps Gulliver being twelve as he now was didn't quite understand the gravity of the situation he now found himself in.

'So do you come here often?' Gulliver asked the girl and then cringed at the corny chat-up line, but then again he always had been tongue-tied around the female of the species.

However, the girl didn't bat an eyelid and replied, 'Yes, I do. I virtually live here, or so the curator of the Antiquarium and my stepmother are always telling me!' said the girl as she looked at her feet as if she needed a new pair of shoes.

By this time Beagle had wandered off as per usual, inquisitive to see what was behind these large walls of glass before returning to his master's side with a puzzled expression upon his face.

'What's your name? My name's Gulliver,' Gulliver said as he stopped looking at his feet as he had just bought a new pair of shoes.

'My name's, my name's Alice,' said Alice a little bashfully.

'That's a nice name,' said Gulliver awkwardly while thinking he had actually wandered into Alice's weird Wonderland.

'So is Gulliver,' said Alice stroking her long golden locks.

Gulliver didn't quite know what to say next, luckily for him Alice did.

'Is that your dog?' Alice said as Beagle wandered in between Gulliver's legs like the Cheshire cat on the make.

'Yes, he is. His name's Beagle and he's a Labrador,' Gulliver said as if he expected Alice to say, 'but he's not a beagle, he's a Labrador', but Alice didn't, but that was children all over, they only asked stupid questions to ones that had obvious answers. There were times when Gulliver wished he hadn't named his dog after a ship, although these times were few and far between.

'Can I have a look at your drawings?' Alice said changing the subject as she reached her hand out for the sketch book she had only just handed back to Gulliver.

'I'm afraid they're not very good,' said a bashful-looking Gulliver as he handed Alice back the book with both pictures and words in it.

Alice took the book and flipped through the pages as a puzzled expression appeared upon her face.

'There aren't many words in this book!' she said as she studied the picture of the giant seahorses more closely, holding the book up in the direction of the seahorses in the aquarium, as if to see how lifelike the drawing was.

Gulliver wanted to ask Alice if she knew that the biggest island in Galapagos was an island called Isabella and to Gulliver and other artists' minds it resembled the shape of a giant seahorse. Well, artists were always drawing comparisons, he could hear his grandfather in his head saying as much and chuckling as he did so. Gulliver wondered if Alice knew that Galapagos meant tortoise in Spanish. Perhaps in this world the Galapagos

Islands were just up the coast where Cornwall used to be, as was Spain, and as such Alice spoke fluent Spanish. She may even be able to speak the mixed-up language of Esperanto.

However, Gulliver didn't say any of these things as he didn't want to seem like a complete geek know-it-all with a head the size of a giant ostrich's egg, so instead he said, 'No, I don't like words, or should I say, they don't like me. I've got dyslexia,' said Gulliver admiring his new shoes again as if they were some priceless antique.

'That sounds painful!' said Alice sympathetically.

'What sounds painful?' said Gulliver sounding like he'd forgotten his own question.

'Dicewhatsia!' said Alice.

'It can be at times,' said Gulliver truthfully.

'Have you seen the crazy mirror maze by the giant tropical fish tank which distorts both the size of the fish in the tank and your face all at the same time?' Alice said gabbling excitedly, grabbing Gulliver's hand and pulling him in the direction of this amazing exhibit.

Gulliver thought the world he was now living in was one big crazy mirror maze but he didn't tell Alice this in case she thought he was as mad as the Mad Hatter. Later he was to ask Alice if she had heard of Lewis Carroll and the Alice stories but she just gave him a curious look as if he was talking nonsense. Perhaps on this parallel earth Lewis Carroll was still a boy like John Logie Baird.

A short while later Gulliver found himself in a long corridor where a large fish tank sat and housed within it were huge brightly coloured fluorescent tropical fish, which all seemed three or four times bigger than in Gulliver's world. In this tank swam the angel, butterfly, and tiger fish and a golden catfish variety which normal resided in Africa and which was as blind as a bat so it had a good excuse for bumping into things. Despite the catfish being blind, it had a knowing grin upon its face like the Cheshire cat in Alice's Wonderland. Gulliver wondered if the golden catfish was daydreaming about another golden catfish. There was no doubt in Gulliver's mind that the golden catfish was quite a catch as it was as pretty as a picture.

There was also a scorpion fish in the tank, which was sure to have a sting in its tail, and several parrot fish which came from the coral reef in New Holland, and some golden jellyfish which came from the South Pacific seas. And that was just to name but a few of the fish in this tank, for if we were to name a lot we would be here until kingdom come.

In fact, there were so many fish in this tank that it seemed fit to burst and they were all lit up like a neon sign. Gulliver wondered if this fish tank was like the Tardis, small on the outside and large on the inside. Not that the fish tank was small but perhaps the fish tank was as big as the ocean, literally as big as the ocean. This was yet another strange thought but how strange was it? He'd have to refer to his strangeness scale later on as this thought weighed heavy upon his mind! I would, however, add that there were several sharks in the tank, and several giant manta rays that appeared to by flying through the water in slow motion rather than swimming, such was the gracefulness of their bird-like motion. There were no flying fish in the tank, one of the staff said they had tried putting them in but they kept flying out; it seemed the flying fish was rather like a fish out of water! Gulliver wasn't sure if the man was throwing him a line or yanking his fishing rod but by the look upon his face I'd say not! Gulliver was later to write this line in his travelogue word for word.

As you walked past the crazy mirror maze you could see your distorted face in the mirror along with the distorted images of the fish, it was quite an amazing sight, which made your eyes go funny.

'Wow!' said Gulliver, his eyes nearly popping out of his head like the eyes of some of the tropical fish appeared to be doing.

'I thought you said you didn't like words,' said Alice, who by now looked twice the size she was before as if she had just opened out like a huge telescope or a giant sea anemone. To Gulliver, Alice looked at least nine feet tall, possibly taller, and her face looked like the giant hat in The Pandemonium Emporium.

Gulliver looked a little puzzled by what Alice had just said. This expression was almost becoming a permanent fixture on his face since he'd stepped into this strange and compelling world.

'Sorry, I'm not with you,' said Gulliver dimly.

'Well, if you're not with me then I don't know who you *are* with!' said Alice as the smile on her face grew so big it resembled a crescent moon. 'Wow, that's a great word. Do you know any more great words like Wow?'

Finally Gulliver realised that he was being a complete dunderheaded nincompoop of the first, second and third order. In fact, he should probably get a brain transplant and be done with it, or swap his brain for one standing on the shelves of the Natural History Museum. Darwin or Sir Isaac Newton's brain would suit his needs, he thought wistfully!

Gulliver wondered what museums must be like in this world, a world without time, a world where history was… was… what was history? History was history, end of story!

'Well, I know the word phantasmagorical but I

couldn't spell it to save my life!' Gulliver said as a large spider fish appeared out of the blue, a fish which appeared to have two heads and which floated past Gulliver's head. 'Two heads are better than one,' he heard a voice in his head say, it was the voice of his grandfather.

'Phantasma-whats-ama-call-it, what does it mean?!' said Alice who had now shrunk to the size of a teapot as a shoal of butterfly fish flew past her ear, or at least they did in the crazy mirror maze attached to the wall.

'It means a shifting quality of dreamlike figures,' Gulliver said sounding like he'd swallowed a dictionary.

'That sounds about right,' said Alice as her head was replaced by the head of a large angel fish. 'I must find a sentence to fit that into. It's sure to impress my friends. In fact, it will probably make my teacher, Mrs Finickity-knickers, have a fainting fit. She normally has a fainting fit or a hissy fit whenever I write left-handed!' Alice said as her head swam away on the body of a giant terrapin. 'There goes my head,' Alice said pointing to the terrapin, who appeared to have taken her head. My father's always saying I'd lose my head if it wasn't screwed on properly! These fish are phantasma… phantasmagori… phantasmagorical,' Alice said triumphantly as she finally managed to spit the word out, which was momentarily stuck to the tip of her tongue.

'I suppose they are,' said Gulliver as his body swayed first one way then the other like weed in a fish tank. 'I think I need to sit down before I fall down,' Gulliver said holding his head tightly as if to make sure it didn't swim off into the distance on the body of some exotic fish.

'Yes, the mirror does make you feel a little light headed after a while,' Alice said taking Gulliver's hand and leading him away to a bench where they both sat down. By now the pupils in Gulliver's and Alice's eyes were as big as saucers, no make that they more resembled blue moons.

A little while later, for it certainly wasn't sooner, Gulliver's pupils had returned to their normal size, as had Alice's and Beagle's, who was still pawing at the glass of the fish tank and barking at the misshapen fish with a puzzled expression on his face. This barking, however, didn't make Beagle mad for the fish was a catfish and everybody knew how much cats and dogs hated one another! This was another line Gulliver was to include in his travelogue, which on first reading appeared to be the sort of nonsense Lewis Carroll was to one day write, for in this world at least it appeared he was still waiting to put pen to paper. However, if you stood on your head or read the line backwards or looked at it in a crazy mirror maze then it made perfect sense!

One has to remember Gulliver was using the right words but not necessarily using them in the right order, a bit like Shakespeare used to do, and in this world that didn't seem to be much of a problem. In fact quite the opposite, it actually seemed to make things clearer!

While Alice and Gulliver were sitting on the hard wooden bench provided for short periods of rest before continuing on with the tour around the Antiquarium, Gulliver started to think. The way things were panning out Gulliver was doing so much thinking perhaps he should consider joining a government think tank. Now it's funny you should mention think tanks as Gulliver was surrounded by fish tanks. Not that fish did much thinking, mostly they did swimming followed by eating, followed by some more swimming, followed by some more eating, not necessarily in that order, although mostly in that order.

Gulliver's thoughts drifted like dead wood upon the sea before stopping at this thought. As Alice went to school, what on earth was on her school timetable? In fact, did they even have a school timetable? They obviously had tables because it was a school and all schools had tables. But now there wasn't any time to speak of, although Gulliver and Old Father Time still spoke of it, surely there wasn't a timetable, or a times table for that matter. Although, you could speak of time if you wanted to as there was no law saying you couldn't, written or otherwise, but as time had stopped this was really just an exercise in futility so most people didn't bother. Gulliver was beginning to wonder if he should bother thinking at all, rather he should just do. After all, his mother was right, procrastination was the thief of time. 'The trouble with an exercise in futility,' Gulliver's grandfather once told him rather un-succinctly, is 'like all exercise it wears you out so it makes perfect sense that nobody wants to exercise their God-given right to this exercise in futility.' 'With such logic philosophers are made!' Gulliver's father once said to him after he'd asked his father to explain another one of his grandfather's pearls of wisdom. Gulliver's grandfather would have fitted very nicely if you please into Alice's Wonderland, as he's written the book on Gobbledegook, Gulliver's father once told him with a wry smile upon his face. Of course it wasn't Alice's Wonderland, she didn't own it as if it was some kind of magical theme park like Harry Potter World or Disneyland, but Gulliver knew what he meant and so it appeared did Alice! It was nice, Gulliver had found a like-minded individual, someone who was on the same page as him, as to his mind nobody in his own world was even on the same planet as him!

So many things bothered Gulliver in this disordered world it was hard to choose just one; this world was a nightmare for anybody suffering from OCD, which unfortunately Gulliver did. Gulliver had said it didn't matter how strange things got in this world, he was going to accept things the way they were like all the people around him appeared to do! But that was easier said than done as Gulliver was rapidly finding out.

The thing that Gulliver's mind had singled out to bother him at this particular moment was how did anybody know when Christmas was or what day their birthday fell on?! Gulliver thought that was another strange expression, 'what day your birthday fell on'. Imagine if all your Christmas and birthday presents fell on you from out of the sky, if that happened you certainly wouldn't say 'all your Christmases and birthdays had come at once' as by then you might well have joined the same club that the dodo now belonged too, the Extinct Club! Luckily there was no television in this world so you didn't have to worry about what time certain programmes appeared, or at least not until John Logie Baird invented television. Having already met a young John Logie Baird in The Pandemonium Emporium it seemed this discovery wasn't that far off. The thought had occurred to Gulliver that the tank of the antiquarium was like a wide-screen HD 3D TV set on the Discovery or the Eden Channel.

When Gulliver was young and he stayed with his grandparents he used to get up in the middle of the night and switch their black and white television set on, even though the programmes had ended. Gulliver would stare in fascination at the screen for hours as fuzzy random dots danced before his eyes. What he was actually looking at was the microwave radiation left over from the beginning of the universe, the big bang. Gulliver's grandparents would find him asleep the next morning snuggled up in a ball in his grandfather's large brown leather armchair. Later, when his grandparents got a coloured set, they gave their antique black and white set to Gulliver. Even to this day when he couldn't sleep, Gulliver still got up in the middle of the night and switched on the black and white set and watched the microwaves until he dropped off to sleep on his settee.

It had occurred to Gulliver that his sponge-like brain was like the sponges in the aquarium tanks and the sponges in his bathroom at home, except they could swim and he couldn't! Mind you, he could think and they couldn't, although right now he was beginning to wish he couldn't as his head was swimming. *Whoever said, 'in reality you spend your whole life living inside your own head' was spot on,* Gulliver thought, although travelling through your own head would put a slightly different spin upon things.

The thing was that unbeknownst to Gulliver, John Logie Baird lived just around the corner from Old Father Time and Lewis Carroll lived a few streets down from him, although he was still being pushed around by his mother in a perambulator. Can you imagine that Old Father Time and John Logie Baird lived on the same street and Lewis Carroll lived just up the road too? Unbelievable, that's what it was, unbelievable! It might even have been phantasmagorical, although Gulliver thought it probably wasn't unless this was a dream and then it probably was! There was nothing worse than using the wrong word for the wrong thing, nothing, or so Gulliver's English teacher Mr Crabapple was always telling him in a crabby manner. 'There's nothing worse than using the wrong word for the wrong thing, Gulliver, nothing. So if you ever have a mind to, it's best you take a leaf out of Mark Twain's book and cross it out before I do!' he would hear that monotonous voice droning on in his head till the end of time. He left school almost twenty years ago and still he could hear Mr Crabapple's monotonous voice droning on like Droning Maud did in the land named Droning Maud Land in Antarctica. This land that time barely remembered wasn't a million miles from the recently named Queen Elizabeth Land. That was the Queen Elizabeth in his world in 2013 and not the Queen Elizabeth in the sixteenth century, unless somebody had invented a time machine in his world while he'd been away. *That would be typical,* Gulliver thought, *he'd only been gone five minutes and while he was away some clever clogs boffin had invented a time machine!*

Although Gulliver had been away from his earth for what to him seemed like a short period of time, it had occurred to him that perhaps he'd been away years. Perhaps in his world people had forgotten he was even missing or perhaps time had virtually stood still. Einstein was right, time was an illusion, and one the gods and the people of this world had become disillusioned with, and one he was rapidly become disillusioned with too.

Gulliver wanted to ask Alice the Christmas question if not the birthday question, but he didn't because he didn't think he'd like the answer, which was a reasonable enough reason for not asking a question if you think about it! So he asked Alice another question that he didn't mind hearing the answer to.

'Alice,' Gulliver said politely.

'Yes,' said Alice equally politely.

'At school what is your least favourite subject?' Gulliver said making small talk which was a lot less wearing than long talk, because long talk made your throat sore.

Alice considered the question for a few moments and said with a grimace on her face, 'Maths!'

'Me too,' said Gulliver in a most agreeable manner. Gulliver knew Lewis Carroll was good at maths but he hadn't held that against him as Alice's adventures had always held him spellbound. Funnily enough dyslexia had also held him spellbound but in a bad way!

'It seems we've got an awful lot in common, Gulliver,' Alice said twiddling her hair into ringlets with her fingers in a dreamy manner, as she continued to look at the exotic fish from a distance without once turning to look directly at Gulliver.

'You're correct, Alice, we do seem to have an awful lot in common,' Gulliver said talking to the side of Alice's face.

'I know, I think you're correct too, Gulliver. In fact I'd go as far as to say I think I've never been more correcter about anything in my entire life before,' said Alice grammatically incorrectly.

It seemed both Alice and Gulliver were revelling in their grammatical incorrectness and they didn't give a tawny owl's hoot about grammar, their teachers old or new, and as far as dyslexia was concerned, it could take a long walk off a short pier. It seemed the only thing that really mattered in this world was being happy, and surely any world in which the only thing that really mattered was being happy couldn't be all bad.

After they'd got bored of sitting, Gulliver and Alice continued to look around the Antiquarium where they saw a huge white whale nicknamed 'Moby', several giant lobsters, and a giant salamander which the Japanese regarded as national treasures. Alice told Gulliver the Japanese were none too happy that one of their national treasures was swimming around inside a fish tank in England. The two countries were going to war over this, however, after Drake caught the legendary Kappa Sea

Monster and brought it home to England all was forgiven, as in Japan it often ate children, presumably because it could fit them in its mouth. The kappa sneaked up behind children as they were playing in a river and gobbled them up, although as it was like a giant version of the giant salamander, in truth it rather sucked them up rather than gobbled them up. Some people or fish survived inside the kappa's stomach for a little while until the digestive juices inside its stomach dissolved them!

'Apparently the man o' war jellyfish was named after the spat between the Japanese people and the British Crown over the capturing of the giant salamander, but that sounds a little fishy to me!' said Alice with a smile as wide as a giant salamander.

'So that's the legendary kappa,' Gulliver said putting his hand up against the glass of the tank as the fish tried to suck him through to his side. Gulliver instantly withdrew his hand and backed away from the tank as he was not entirely sure just how thick the glass of the tank was. Gulliver once had a nightmare of standing in front of a giant tank in an aquarium where the pressure of the water broke the glass and all the fish inside the tank swamped him. This wasn't helped by the fact that this tank contained sharks. Gulliver had hated sharks ever since he'd seen the film *Jaws*, after which he wouldn't even take a bath, in fact, his loathing of sharks got so bad he wouldn't even take a shower!

'I'm glad we're this side of the glass and not the other!' said Alice sensibly.

'Me too!' said Gulliver as he found yet another thing he had in common with Alice.

Elsewhere in the Antiquarium were some ancient deepsea glass sponges which had been fished out of the southern oceans. The sponges seemed perfectly content their side of the glass sponging up what was going on around them. Alice said the sponges were probably wondering how these strange-looking people got inside the tank they were encased in! Three goliath fish from Africa also circled menacingly in the tank and looked uglier than any sea monsters Gulliver had ever seen in films or in books. And an African king fish, which was twice the size of a man. In his world they were only the size of a man so this particular fish had doubled in size between one world and the other. There was a cornucopia of colourful coral which surrounded the deep sea glass sponges, sponges which Gulliver knew had been found off the Great Barrier Reef in Australia, as it was known in Gulliver's world, as it was still known as New Holland in this one. A giant Pacific Ocean octopus, orange in colour and which had 2,000 suckers attached to its tentacles appeared, to be giving Gulliver the evil eye. These suckers were probably the reason the octopus was stuck to the glass of the tank like glue, it also had two hearts and is said to have a high IQ, well, compared with other marine creatures that is. However, despite the octopus's high IQ Gulliver didn't think this one would ever get invited onto the TV quiz show *QI* hosted by the national treasure that was Stephen Fry and say, 'I think, therefore I am'. Gulliver also knew that if a starfish had one of its arms cut off it would regrow. He also wondered if any of these stars had fallen from the cosmological oceans, although he knew this was extremely unlikely and illogical in the extreme.

Gulliver thought in his world when days were at their busiest it would be useful if like the octopus he had eight arms, although technically he knew they were called tentacles. It would also mean he would have to get his mum to knit a jumper with eight sleeves in it!

Inside another tank was a forest of kelp where several giant white lobsters resided. These were caught by Sir Walter Raleigh off the Galapagos Islands and were the only two white albino lobsters ever to be seen in captivity. At first, some of the visitors to the Antiquarium had said that this was a trick. That in fact the lobsters had been boiled alive and then put into the forest of kelp so you couldn't tell that they were actually dead. However, the white lobsters were alive and well and often stretched their legs to prove as much.

Gulliver pointed out to one man who insisted the lobsters had been boiled alive that the more you boiled a lobster the redder it became. The natural colour of a lobster is a drab black-brown colour. If a lobster was naturally bright red he would be rich pickings in the oceans and seas of the world and would probably be extinct by now. So said Gulliver, with great authority and while tipping his hat to Stephen Fry and *QI*, which is where he had heard this strange but true fact. After this the man rebuked several other people who were saying the albino lobsters were fake with his new-found knowledge of marine life.

Gulliver thought the owner of the Antiquarium must be like the famous American showman P.T. Barnum, the man who turned freak shows into an art form.

Another large tank housed a narwhale with a vicious-looking long-horned spike attached to its head, not unlike that of a unicorn. The narwhale was almost as big as a car! Gulliver wouldn't have liked to have been a diver or a shark on the end of that spike. Gulliver wanted to say to Alice that the narwhale was as big as a Rolls Royce but the thought of going through the whole rigmarole of explaining the workings and the history of the automobile was just too much. Imagine telling someone that a motorized carriage had been invented but due to health and safety a man had to walk in front of it with a red flag, and in fact a horse was faster than the motorized carriage. 'Yes, good luck with that one, Gulliver,' he said to himself under his breath as he blew out his cheeks ever so slightly! Mind you, the invention of the motor car might not be that far off, although at this present moment in time the penny-farthing and the horse and carriage were the preferred modes of transport. Gulliver then tried to bring to mind the fact about blue whales and how many buses could be fitted into their ample belly, but he couldn't. Where was Stephen Fry when you needed him? If he had bumped into Neptune in his travels he would have said to him, 'You don't see a blue whale for ages, Neptune, and then two appear at the same time!' In his world Gulliver knew this to be the old bus equation.

Alice then showed Gulliver the shark tank which was full of tiger, hammerhead and great white sharks, which were bigger than Gulliver had ever seen. Gulliver, however, saw little of these sharks as he had his eyes virtually closed at the time, obviously his shark phobia hadn't disappeared as easily as the crew of the *Marie Celeste*.

Gulliver had once seen a basking shark in St Mary's Bay in Brixham in 2002, which he at first thought was a dolphin. One of his friends was a diver who went out to investigate this unusual sighting and swam with the shark for a while before it went back out to sea. It was funny that this sighting happened within a stone's throw from Sharkham Point, Gulliver thought at the time. Synchronicity was a strange science and no denying!

Gulliver would have loved to have some of the species in the Antiquarium in the aquarium in his antiques boat\shop in miniature form. He already had several seahorses in miniature form in his tank, again these thoughts led him to comparisons to the land of Lilliput in *Gulliver's Travels*.

Wouldn't it be cool, Gulliver thought, if he had a snow dome in the bottom of his tropical fish aquarium at home, well you must remember, he was only twelve!

After looking round the Antiquarium in which Gulliver and Alice both lost track of time, like this world had seemingly done, and seeing the fish feeding their faces, it made both Gulliver and Alice slightly peckish. So they found a small bakery which sold hot Devon\Cornish pasties which were savoury at one end and sweet at the other. This suited Alice and Gulliver down to the ground as Gulliver had a sweet tooth and Alice didn't. They found a nice piece of land surrounded by giant oak trees and weeping willows and sat down upon the ground on their knees and ate the pasty, Gulliver eating from the sweet end and Alice the savoury end until they met in the middle.

Gulliver had never kissed a girl before, actually he had, after all he was thirty-five, but he had never kissed a girl named Alice before. This quick and rather embarrassed kiss, although meeting of lips would have been a better description, was both sweet and sour all at the same time, befitting of this world. Well, once again, as they were sharing a Cornish\Devon pasty at the time this was only to be expected. Although in some respects Gulliver had memories of a thirty-five-year-old man and the occasional cynical thought befitting this age, even in his time he was very much an innocent. In this world Gulliver's feeling towards the female of the species was they weren't for kissing but just for friendship. In fact, the thought of kissing a girl was quite revolting and although he liked Alice, his hormones were very much that of an immature twelve-year-old boy.

I must add one thing regarding the pasty and that is, you would never call a pasty in this part of the world Cornish\Devon or vice versa, as famously, the two counties being attached to one another as they were had never seen eye to eye. If you were from Devon then the grockles (outsiders) from Cornwall were the sour part of the pasty and you were the sweet part. And if you were from Cornwall, the pirates from Devonshire were the sour part of the pasty while you were the sweet part! Although as Gulliver was Devon born and bred (and buttered) and the pirates came from Penzance near Lands End (refer to opera by Gilbert and Sullivan), then a part of this analogy left a sour taste in the mouth.

Yes, as analogies go it wasn't crash-hot like the pasty as it happens, however, in this mixed-up crazy world which Gulliver found himself in, it seemed like a pretty good analogy, minus the Devonshire pirates! For this was exactly what he wrote in his travelogue that night before he retired to bed, and before he disappeared into that fantastical and wondrous place known as Dreamland. This world of the imagination, a world with no boundaries and no end, a world where the subconscious breaks free from the conscious mind on a crazy mixed-up voyage that turns the illogical into the logical and back again. Dreams merge into nightmares and nightmares into dreams on the ultimate roller coaster ride of a lifetime. Unless of course you're one of those lucky or unlucky people, depending on your point of view, who never dream. Then of course it's like the universe at the very end of its life, empty! Then Gulliver's steamship of thought sailed off into uncharted waters as he pictured Cornwall and Devon drifting off into the Caribbean due to the continental drifts where pirates boarded the two counties and sailed them up to Queen

Elizabeth Land in Antarctica. Once again this dream was inspired in no small way to the floating mechanical islands in Jonathan Swift's *Gulliver's Travels*.

One thing Gulliver was all too aware of was that any travelogue worth its salt needed some action and some travel in it otherwise it wasn't worth the paper it was written upon. So Gulliver made his mind up that he was determined to find both so as to spice this travelogue up. Having said that, considering Gulliver had never travelled outside of Devon before this adventure, travelling through time to a land where time didn't exist wasn't a bad start to his travelogue. Later still, Gulliver was to write this in his travelogue: 'Only I could travel back in time to a time where time no longer exists!'

Gulliver just hoped by the time he got back to his world he hadn't missed the Brixham pirate festival in May.

# 7

# A Black Mark in Alice's Book!

Some time later, 'No that's not right,' Gulliver was later to write in his travelogue followed by two exclamation marks, which showed just how hard he was finding adjusting to this world. The one good thing Gulliver found was that being different he was used to swimming against the tide (or he would have been if he knew how to swim!), so in a strange way his world had prepared him for this one, as this world gave you plenty of scope for swimming against the tide. It is said that if you are different and you don't fit in, especially at school, later you will go on to have a highly creative life, whereas if you fit in and don't have to struggle, you won't, who can say? Well, Gulliver for a start, and at this point in non-time you would have found it hard to disagree with him!

Later (taking out the word some and the word time), Gulliver and Alice left the Antiquarium to find the library. Now this trip may not have been very far, a short step from the Antiquarium and in truth was not a trip full of spice and excitement, not even between the pages of the books that were housed within the library. However, all travels have to begin with the first step and this was it. What did Neil Armstrong say when first he stepped onto the lunar surface? 'It's one small step for man and one giant leap for mankind.' Gulliver later wrote this in his log of travels, not that he had any intention of walking on the moon either in this world or his. Gulliver knew Neil Armstrong hadn't quite meant to say this rather fluffing his lines as he later put it, although it all turned out well in the end.

Now it was quite clear from talking to Alice that she had never known what time was or had ever had the opportunity to use it, and as such it could be said that she had no time for time. However, Alice had never said such a thing but she could have said it if she had wanted too. Old Father Time on the other hand certainly had said such a thing although in a jocular fashion. This was another thing Gulliver found hard to get his head around. Of course, Alice had no idea that Gulliver was from another time and place and if she had known I'm sure she too would have found it hard to get her head around.

Like I said before, the library was just a little way across town and was the biggest building in Brixham, five times the size of the library in Gulliver's modern-day Brixham. Gulliver couldn't wait to get into the library to see how many wonderful books he could find. However, he didn't find any, not one single book! Although the library looked big on the outside, on the inside it was tiny, never mind about there being enough room to swing a cat in there, there was barely enough room to swing the Cheshire cat's tail minus the Cheshire cat and its smile! The library reminded Gulliver of the glass bookcase he had at home, the one with the sliding glass doors.

The library was the polar opposite of The Pandemonium Emporium, which was small on the outside and large on the inside. The library had those glass sliding doors you often see in modern libraries except these were not electronic but worked upon large rollers, the sort you see ladders moving back and forth upon in large old libraries. The librarian was a woman who could best be described as looking extremely bookish, antiquarian of age and who appeared to be wearing a dust jacket for a dress, end of story! According to her, the library only had four books and they were all out at the moment. And what's more, this bookish woman seemed to take great pleasure in telling Gulliver this fact. However, she did add that she could reserve one of them for him if he so wished but it could take some time before the book came back, especially as time no longer existed. Gulliver didn't wish for this as he thought it somewhat of a wasted wish. So instead he thanked the bookish librarian for nothing apart from wasting his time, even though there was no time to waste. Then both Gulliver and Alice went on their merry way, but only if you redact the merry part from this sentence along with Gulliver's name!

In truth Gulliver was a little irked at Alice for not telling him this was the worst library in the world and probably the universe too! In Gulliver's book this was the first black mark against Alice but he had no intention of throwing the book at her. Alice probably didn't know any different, after all, books in this world seemed few and far between, whereas in his world they weren't. *Mind you, what with the invention of the electronic book, one day they might well be,* Gulliver thought ruefully. Gulliver then recalled to mind the fact that there was an e-library in America where books were nowhere to be seen,

bookcases being replaced by rows and rows of computer screens. First the atoms that records were made of had turned to sand before being sucked into the hole in the middle of their own black disc and then books were disappearing off the shelves in libraries as if invisible elves were thieving them like book thieves, and bookshops were disappearing off the face of the earth just as quickly, and anything but by magic. What on earth was the world coming to? However, one thing Gulliver remarked upon was how silent the library was, what with there not being anybody but them and the librarian in it. Whereas in Gulliver's world libraries were nosier than the local zoo at times! Now it was Alice's turn to look puzzled, 'Weren't libraries supposed to be quiet like a graveyard?' she said quizzically.
Gulliver just said, 'Of course they were!' he was simply just being playful.

'I don't suppose anybody gets in her good books!' Gulliver said out loud as Alice looked at him as if he wasn't all the (library) ticket.

'Sorry, Alice, just thinking out loud,' Gulliver said looking down at his shoes for the umpteenth time. 'Just thinking out loud,' Gulliver repeated under his breath so Alice couldn't hear him.

'You should never think out loud in a library, librarians frown upon thinking out loud in a library!' Alice said admonishing Gulliver, but in a lighthearted manner.

Now Gulliver was beginning to get the hang of this world for this description of the library fitted like the book jacket fitted the man in The Pandemonium Emporium, who looked like several of Dickens's grotesque figures all rolled into one. In truth the book jacket the mad hat was wearing was quite ill fitting, although wearing it didn't make him ill like a not-so-fashionable ill-fitting straightjacket appeared to make you ill in Gulliver's world.

Some of the curious thoughts Gulliver's mind was throwing in his direction were not unlike the thoughts he had as a child, but which as an adult had for the most part disappeared like the Cheshire cat's grin. Gulliver kept forgetting he was a child again and not an adult, his mother was always saying that his father and grandfather were in their second if not third childhoods, or at least in their minds they were. But although Gulliver was a child he was an adult as well and as such, his memories were all mixed up, like this world's history was all mixed up. Having done a pretty good impression of Alice in Wonderland, having shrunk in size, now everything seemed much bigger to Gulliver!

If ever the expression 'man child' fitted a man, it fitted Gulliver like a well-tailored straightjacket fitted a tailor's dummy, or at least it did in Gulliver's time. In this world people were beginning to say Gulliver was old before his time, like they did when he was a boy. Every time Gulliver looked in the mirror he smiled and ran his hands around his chin half expecting to feel stubble. That was one thing he didn't miss about not having an adult's body, shaving!

After Gulliver left the library he couldn't help himself and finally asked Alice why the library was as it was, for what good was a library without any books in it, apart from the fact that you'd never have to pay fines on an overdue book? Alice simply smiled shrugged and said that to her knowledge, which being twelve was limited, it had always been that way, which is what Gulliver expected her to say. *Perhaps it was down to council cuts*, Gulliver thought, and perhaps this world wasn't so different from his after all. Of course there was always the slim possibility that he was or had gone stark raving mad, but he'd explored that theory before and dismissed it out of hand, or relatively out of hand. But still, if the worst came to the worst and he was madder than the owner of The Pandemonium Emporium or a librarian who wasn't all the ticket, was that really the end of the world? What did Alice say in *Alice in Wonderland*? 'All the best people are mad!' Maybe the Alice in this mad world would someday say exactly that.

After this thought made itself aware to him, another one quickly followed on its heels as he recalled a poem he had learnt off by heart at school. The poem was the *Mental Traveller* by William Blake, although he could only bring one verse to mind – 'The guests are scatter'd thro' the land, For the eye alters all; The senses roll themselves in fear, And the flat earth becomes a ball.'

Gulliver knew some people in the sixteenth century were known to be one ship short of a crew as they thought the earth was flat, and that if you sailed too far you would fall off the end of the world. At this point in the story it appears that Gulliver has wisely blanked from his mind the fact that he was\is a member of the Flat Earth Society! When Gulliver thought about the poem the *Mental Traveller*, it fitted his situation as he was a guest in this land, and as for his senses, well, they were definitely rolling themselves in fear as at times were his eyes. And the eye altering all well, he knew the sky wasn't really blue or the trees and fields really green, your eye just perceived them to be that way, at least that was something he did remember from his school days. And this world sat on an old globe which was shaped like a ball, unlike his world which was an oblate spheroid, which in layman's speak meant it wasn't quite as round as a ball. William Blake's poem hadn't made much sense when he had first heard it at school all those years ago, but now, in this world it made perfect sense. Gulliver wondered if it would make sense when he got back to his time, if he ever did, that was.

It appeared to Gulliver that his head mirrored this mixed-up world: half was in one time and half was in another. In his head he had both feet planted in the past, except they were not planted firmly, it was almost as if he was standing on the deck of a ship out on a wild and windy sea. The past was in the Devon of 2013 and the old Devon of both the sixteenth and nineteenth centuries. Gulliver was both young and old all at the same time, although thirty-five could hardly be considered old, however, to a twelve-year-old it could and it often did. In some respects, in his own world Gulliver was old before his time and being surrounded by antiques didn't help, while in other respects he was very much young at heart.

As far as the present was concerned, well, in that respect Gulliver was all at sea. Time no longer existed in his world and for somebody like Gulliver whose life was governed by the clock, this took a great deal of getting used to. It seemed to Gulliver that he was going to have to rely heavily upon his body clock. At times in this world Gulliver felt like Mark Twain, Hans Christian Andersen, Charles Darwin, Alice (in Wonderland), Sir Isaac Newton, Sir Francis Drake and Gulliver (from *Gulliver's Travels*) all rolled into one, no wonder the poor boy was mixed up!

Gulliver thought, if he was going to find books to feed his various appetites for the written word, which he felt compelled to do, he needed to track down The Last Bookshop in the World. Unfortunately, according to everybody he talked to, this bookshop didn't exist, it was just a myth, a good story like Troy or Atlantis, or the

Loch Ness monster, although supposedly Troy had been discovered some time ago and Gulliver knew the Loch Ness monster existed because he had seen it with his own eyes in the Antiquarium. That's, of course, if this was the mythical Loch Ness monster and it certainly looked like the monster, which meant The Last Bookshop in the World also existed, that was only logic wasn't it?

Mind you, in this world a first edition copy of *The Origin* by Charles Darwin didn't exist and nor did the author Charles Darwin, or according to the owner of The Pandemonium Emporium he didn't. Of course, this man was as mad as the Mad Hatter in the Wonderland that Alice didn't own, so Gulliver probably shouldn't put too much store by what he said, or much store of the store that was The Pandemonium Emporium either for that matter. Maybe while in the confines of The Pandemonium Emporium, if Gulliver had imagined Charles Darwin he would have appeared sitting on one of the shelves in the shop, a thought which was even further out there than the thoughts of a quantum physicist!

Maybe Darwin hadn't written *The Origin* yet, perhaps he was the same age as Gulliver or maybe he was in a different time altogether? Gulliver had always thought that if he found an original copy of *The Origin* before it became *The Origin of the Species*, that to an antiquarian book collector really would be like finding the Holy Grail. One thing Gulliver didn't want to do was find the Holy Grail while looking for his Holy Grail The Last Bookshop in the World, as there just wasn't time for all that nonsense!

So Gulliver made finding this mythical bookshop his top priority and he would do it with the help of Alice and Old Father Time, and anybody else he could find along the way to help him. After Gulliver had written this in his book with no words and no pictures, which now had words and pictures in it, he remarked how this quest was beginning to sound not unlike a cross between *The Wizard of Oz*'s, *Alice's Adventures in Wonderland* and *Gulliver's Travels*. Wow, that would be some book, Gulliver wrote in his travelogue, after which he added three exclamation marks!!!

Most if not all travelogues are littered with times and dates, this makes it easier for the armchair traveller to understand where the traveller is at any given point in time in his journey. But how do you do this when there is no time and there is no calendar? Well, by the moon of course, and the stars, like travellers and explorers have done throughout the centuries. Unfortunately, in this world it wasn't quite so straight forward, especially if you take out the word 'quite'! Then you had to take into account the glass between the viewer's eye and the celestial bodies, although of course in your travels, especially when on the sea, you weren't always within the confines of the ship in the bottle. Add the fact that Galileo's telescopes didn't have the scope they had in the year 2013 in his world, and there were no satellite navigation systems, or Google Earth, then as you can see that Gulliver was faced with a dilemma. How was he to make his travelogue easier to understand, not just for him but for anybody who wanted to read it at a later date!?

Of course, reading Gulliver's travelogue at a later time and date in this world was not possible and as such this made it impossible. Now Alice in her land of wonder might be able to think of six impossible things to do before breakfast but Gulliver couldn't and, he was pretty sure Alice had never fallen down a rabbit hole and ended up in this world. If she had done, Gulliver surmised she would probably have spent the whole time (which didn't exist any longer) repeating the word all dyslexics loved with a passion, curiouser!

Apparently the four most asked questions by strangers who confront an explorer or a traveller are the following: Who are you? Where did you come from? How did you get here? When are you going to leave?!

Now up to this point in time nobody had asked Gulliver any of these questions. Perhaps this was because everybody looked out of place in the world and as such he didn't, that and everybody had got fed up to the back teeth with asking one another those four questions! Everybody in this world was an explorer, everybody, so he was just like everybody else. Gulliver had never been like everybody else, he had always been different and everybody had made him feel that way, but not in a good way. There was one more question you could have added to these four questions if you were ever to meet a time traveller and that would be – What time are you from?

To be fair Gulliver, was more than a little nervous of telling people he came from another world; they might think he was an alien or more likely as mad as a hatter. Some people in Gulliver's world thought gods in chariots had come down to earth like Ezekiel in the Bible, and that we were originally from the stars, which we were, but these people of course meant aliens. Some writers had suggested we were from Sirius the Dog Star but then some writers were barking mad, *although in theory, at least Beagle could have come from the Dog Star,* Gulliver thought with a wry smile upon his face.

Children at school had said he was strange, as did most of the people he'd come in contact with in his life, and sometimes he felt like an alien from another planet.

But not in this world in this world, he was normal, whatever that was, well as long as you took out The Pandemonium Emporium from that equation, which he did as did everybody else, as everybody in The Pandemonium Emporium was as mad as a hatter. If when entering and leaving The Pandemonium Emporium the people inside the shop didn't call you strange, then you really must be strange. And although that sounds like gobbledegobbledegook it wasn't because there was no such thing in this world as the word gobbledegook just Gobbledegobble!

Mind you, saying anything in this world was either simple or straight forward was best avoided, perhaps not at all costs because by all accounts Gulliver seemed to have an endless supply of money in his pocket. In fact, Gulliver seemed only to have to reach into his pocket and the money would be there, however much or however little, but always the exact amount he needed, not a penny farthing more and not a penny farthing less, until the next time he needed money. Gulliver felt his pocket was akin to the Bank of England, mind you, if like the song said, 'life was but a dream' and he was simply dreaming, then once again perhaps not. To Gulliver's mind, in his world the Bank of England was now printing Monopoly money to bolster the economy, which was funny because as a child he had buried some coins hoping it would produce a money tree! This was monetary humour of the highest order his grandfather told him when he found his grandson burying the coins, which in all honesty went right over the young Gulliver's head!

The funny this was, or at least it was mildly amusing, was that the people who ran the hat shop, Mad Hatters, weren't in the least bit mad. They were as sane as the next hat shop owner, and most hat shop owners had no intention of eating their own hats, no matter how hard times got. Anyway, who would be mad enough to eat their own hat when the lining of hats contained mercury which was said to drive you mad? Or so he thought he recalled Stephen Fry once telling him on John Logie Baird's magical box of tricks! This was a big relief to Gulliver, or if not a big one, at least a relief. If he thought everybody in this world was as crazy and mixed up as the world itself was simply by judging the first place his journey had taken him, i.e. The Pandemonium Emporium, well then it wasn't. Being illogical might apply when in the confines of The Pandemonium Emporium but it didn't necessarily apply in other parts of this world. Having said that, sometimes it did!

If you discounted The Pandemonium Emporium, which Gulliver wished he could have done, then people in this world were no madder than the people in his world, or for that matter madder than him. Mind you, that wasn't saying much! Maybe this wasn't a dream but a psychotic episode brought on by overwork. His mother had always said he was a workaholic, although his teachers had never said as much on his report cards! His father had said logically, well being a workaholic was certainly better than being an alcoholic, although some people found work drove them to drink! Hopefully not mad enough to drink sea water, Gulliver's grandfather once said, which would send you mad if you drank enough of it.

# 8

# The Quest Begins in Earnest (and about time too!)

So Gulliver, having set his heart on the rather unusual quest of finding The Last Bookshop in the World, sat down and thought about how he would best be able to achieve such a thing. First he thought about this task logically and then he thought about it illogically; Lewis Carroll would have been proud of him, Gulliver had no doubt about that, the scientific community on the other hand not so much so. Gulliver made copious amounts of notes on the subject and talked to both Alice and Old Father Time. According to the proprietor of The Pandemonium Emporium, if you wanted to find this mythical bookshop you first had to face various trials and challenges while finding clues along the way. After trials and tribulations, hopefully The Last Bookshop in the World would appear before you very eyes as if by magic. After which Gulliver looked at the few maps, charts and books he was able to find, drew the logical and illogical together and removed the cobble from his cobbled-together plans until eventually they had an order to them which he found most pleasing. Then after studiously going over the plans with a fine-tooth comb, which he'd picked up in a shop which sold fine-tooth combs, he was ready to embark on the adventure of a lifetime. Oh, and I nearly forgot, after all the studiousness and fine-tooth combing, Gulliver reached into his pocket, withdrew a shiny gold ducat, tossed it in the air and asked Alice to call it!

Well, even the best laid plans have one or two minor imperfections that needed ironing out. So Gulliver did just this by placing his plans on a ironing board and running a warm iron over them as if they were the *Times* newspaper. Gulliver had often seen manservants do this on period dramas on the television as if they were ironing a newly washed shirt, before presenting it on a silver tray to their masters at the breakfast table, the newspaper not the shirt! Then, and only then… did he toss the coin. It seemed in this world that for some strange reason Gulliver felt the need to take everything literally!

Alice called heads which meant they were heading south in their quest to find The Last Bookshop in the World. The coin landed face up revealing the smiling face of Queen Elizabeth I. If one had picked the coin up, and here the expression 'on the other side of the coin' springs to mind, and turned it over to the tails side of the coin, they would have seen a picture of Queen Victoria looking anything but amused at this sleight!

Now you may think tossing a coin to decide which direction you're heading in is not exactly what you might call scientific, and you may well be right. However, in all quests and journeys you must factor luck into the equation, for without Lady Luck on your side you may as well pack up and go home. You see, according to

Gulliver's calculations, to find this mythical bookshop he either had to go east, west, north or south. Now as Gulliver was already in the west in old Devon, then he had two choices, well, that's if you discount the east. Gulliver had discounted the east because he didn't like spicy foods and as such there was little chance of him captaining a cutter and getting involved in the spice trade. So if the Last Bookshop in the World was in the east then the whole quest thing was off, end of story!

In The Great Shake Up of Time and Space, as Old Father Time referred to the time when the gods shook things up in this world, Devon was still where it had always been as, by all accounts, was the west, the east, the north and the south, well, after a fashion. After the shake up, several explorers had explored some of the New World, however, a lot was still to be explored.

The only thing that worried Gulliver slightly was that crosswords and puzzles had never been his forte, especially the ones in the *Times* newspaper. In fact, he hadn't got a clue how to solve them! One of his father's old jokes, so he needed all the help he could get. Some jokes improve with time like a fine wine and some jokes should remain in the wine cellar gathering dust, metaphorically speaking that is.

Gulliver asked Alice and Old Father Time if they wanted to come on his quest to find The Last Bookshop in the World. Alice said she'd love to as it was the school holidays and her wicked stepmother was sick of her getting underfoot, and that wasn't a fairytale. Alice was also looking for a book and when Gulliver asked her what book it was she was looking for, she replied, 'I'll know what it's called when I've found it!' This to Gulliver sounded like his mother's logic, or as his father often called it, female logic. This logic, his father said, really defied logic and was best not put under a microscope and certainly was best not argued against. To be fair, this logic was rarely found wanting, as Gulliver's mother and grandmother often told him. Here Gulliver pictured putting the word 'logic' under a microscope, which after some twiddling of this scientific device, the word becomes clearer. You're right, that wasn't very scientific but then again it was better than being blinded by science! When he was a young child, Gulliver looked at the sun through an old telescope and was nearly blinded for his troubles, this taught him a valuable lesson which was that he should never look directly at the sun, especially through an optical device. Well, we all get blinded by the patently obvious at one time or another in our lives!

Old Father Time said he'd love to come on Gulliver's quest as he had plenty of time on his hands now that he was retired. Old Mrs Time also wanted to do the spring cleaning and she was as equally as sick of Old Father Time getting underfoot as Alice's wicked stepmother was of Alice getting underfoot. Actually, that's another fairytale as Alice's stepmother wasn't at all wicked, although she did have a wicked sense of humour. Still, Alice was of a mind that you should try everything at least once in a lifetime and she'd never run away from home before so why not give it a try? What was the worst that could happen... How long have you got!? In truth, her stepmother and her father said this adventure would do wonders for her self-confidence and would make a woman out of her. So although her parents were a little reluctant to let her go, they agreed to do so, that and they trusted the Guardian of Time to take good care of her.

Old Father Time said he was good at working out clues, as he often did the *Times* crossword while overseeing the clock at Greenwich to make sure it kept perfect time. Old Father Time was also looking for a book, although having already asked Alice what the book was that she was looking for, only to have the book shut on his hand, metaphorically speaking, Gulliver was more than a little reluctant to ask Old Father Time what the title of the book he was looking for was called.

Gulliver, being as curious as the next twelve-year-old boy going on thirty-five, however, did ask Old Father Time what book he was searching for. Old Father Time said the book was called *Time: A User's Guide,* although he said he didn't know the author's name. Gulliver said perhaps he had written it but had forgotten as the passing of time does tend to have that effect on one's mind. Old Father Time said he was sure he would have remembered if he'd written a book. Gulliver said not if he'd forgotten he wouldn't, which was logical. There the conversation ended, which both Gulliver and Old Father Time agreed was probably for the best.

After Gulliver had chosen his companions for his epic journey, which of course included Beagle, who could sniff out a clue a mile away, or at least a bone, he then had to decide what form of transport would best suit him and his travelling companions' needs. Once again science was thrown out the window and the shiny gold ducat emerged from his pocket and was tossed in the air with great gusto. This time Old Father Time called it and the coin came down tails side up, although by the look upon Queen Victoria's face, she was no more amused by this than she had been of landing face down in the dirt. This meant they would take to the air in a hot air balloon. Old Mrs Time said this was appropriate as Old Father Time was full of hot air. Some marriages work perfectly well until the couple retire. Old Father Time said to Gulliver with a resigned shrug of his shoulders. If Old Father

Time had called heads they would have started their journey on a sailing vessel upon the seas and then Lady Luck and Queen Elizabeth I would have been shining down on them. However, as the coin would have been face up Lady Luck and Queen Elizabeth I would in fact have been shining up at them, but why spoil a good or a bad story with such trifling little things like the facts. In truth, facts didn't seem that important in this fairytale-like world! Old Father Time was no ancient mariner and suffered from seasickness so was rather relieved he'd lost the toss of the coin.

Alice said she wished there were such things as magic carpets but Old Father Time said he was rather glad there weren't for with his balance he was sure to have fallen off!

Gulliver wondered what sort of books would be on the shelves of The Last Bookshop in the World; big books, small books, lavishly illustrated books with gold lettering on the spine, paperbacks, hardbacks, ones with no backs at all because the proprietor was wearing them! Gulliver just hoped this bookshop wasn't a let down like the library Alice had taken him to, as the only books upon its shelves were invisible, like elves, now that's what I call a fairy story! The proprietor probably looked like a cross between Stephen Fry and Charles Dickens and the floorspace was so large he would have to cycle around the shop on a penny-farthing holding a lantern on a stick in his hand. Well, as long as he was the polar opposite to the proprietor of The Pandemonium Emporium he didn't care much, or much care for that matter.

Gulliver would love to find a copy of the rare book *The Mariner's Mirrour* published in 1586, the title page of which was filled with globes and ships, with two sailors who looked not unlike Walter Raleigh and Francis Drake. However, although Francis Drake was one figure, the other was Anthony Ashley, another famous sailor of the day. The figures stood in regal pose like giants, not unlike Gulliver standing over the tiny Lilliputians in that book about travels. Drake was standing one side of a statue and Ashley the other with the title of the book written across the top of the statue. Underneath the statue was an inscription in calligraphy-style writing with each word ending in glorious flourishes with the heading – 'Of Navigation', and with the names of both Anthony Ashley and Sir Francis Drake on the title page. The page was scattered with a quadrant, astrolabe, sand-glass and cross-staff compasses and navigator's dividers. It seemed the writer of this book, like Gulliver, was dyslexic as he had spelt mirror, mirrour; the truth was that was how they spelt mirror in the good olden days, or was that the good golden days!?

There was also another book Gulliver would have loved to get his hands upon called *The World Encompassed*, written in 1628 by an unknown author. Books by unknown writers were always fascinating to Gulliver as he wondered who the author actually was. Perhaps they were of royal blood, either that or they were a scoundrel who was blackmailing the publishers into publishing their own personal doctrines and beliefs. Perhaps the publishers had the last laugh when they pushed the unknown author into the printing press so his head was pressed like a grape in a vineyard! Yes, Gulliver did have 'quite the imagination' and would have been happy as a sand\ship's boy living on either the imaginatively titled Imagination Street or the street just off of this street, Wonderland Gardens.

Gulliver wondered how many books on time, both fiction and non-fiction, he would find in this bookshop, especially as now time didn't exist. Would books such as these be much in demand, or as time was no longer, would they be out of print, slipping into virtual obscurity? *Surely books like* The Time Machine *and* Hard Times *would never be out of print*, thought Gulliver wistfully, as they were timeless classics. And if ever a word fitted, then the word 'timeless' fitted this world like a cuckoo fitted a cuckoo clock.

The trouble with having too much time on your hands was your mind has plenty of time to go walk about. The mind is like a bookshop or a library, it needs order otherwise it's complete pandemonium!

Gulliver surmised that The Last Bookshop in the World would probably look nothing special from the outside, while inside it would be so magical books would literally be flying off the shelves like in *Harry Potter*. Gulliver had built it up in his mind so much that it would be like a cross between Buckingham Palace, the Vatican Library and Aladdin's cave. No doubt reality would tear his mind palace down like a pack of cards when he eventually found it, if he ever found it!

That was the trouble with mythical places like Atlantis, El Dorado and The Hanging Gardens of Babylon, they were notoriously difficult to find no matter how good your charts, maps, compasses, sextants, astrolabes and satellite navigational systems were. Most, if not all these places were best kept in the imagination, they weren't meant to be found for as soon as they were the story was dead in the water, or at least Atlantis would have been if it was ever discovered!

Gulliver had heard of a library full of golden books which was apparently hidden in a cave beneath a river in South America in Ecuador, but like the Lost City of Atlantis and El Dorado, the city of gold, it was probably nothing more than a Hans Christian Andersen-like fairytale. And Gulliver did like reading the imaginative Hans Christian Andersen stories, both his fairytales and his travelogues, that man could spin tales like Rumplestiltskin, could spin hay into gold. Hans Christian could make words dance, sing to his pied-piper's tune as they jumped right off the page as if by magic and did a jig of delight right in front of your very eyes, which in truth, being dyslexic could be a little troublesome at times.

A few days later, Gulliver, Beagle, Old Father Time and Alice were clambering into a hot air balloon in a field a few miles outside Brixham, wondering if they were going on an adventure of a lifetime or the exact opposite. The panels of the balloon, which had been stitched together so skilfully (hopefully!), now filled with hot air as the onlookers stood in wonderment at this glorious sight. The balloon was blue and gold in colour and was woven in golden thread reminding Gulliver of the Rumplestiltskin story. The balloon also reminded him of the book *The Golden Hind Airship,* a book his grandfather had given him for his tenth birthday, although he couldn't recall the author's name. Gulliver knew just enough about the history of balloon flight to know that the first balloon flight took place in 1783 in France, although he couldn't recall who had made the flight, however, he did recall that it had been the Montgolfier brothers who had built this marvellous contraption.

Old Father Time, being the ex-Guardian of Time, still had connections in this world so he'd called on one of them literally, banging on the door of the owner of one of the hot air balloons at some ungodly hour. Old Father Time told Gulliver the owner wasn't best pleased, or worse pleased for that matter!

'Now remember, the higher you want to go the more

sandbags you have to throw overboard, but just remember they're heavy, and if they land on somebody's head they are liable to knock them spark out!' the balloon owner laughed like he had just told the funniest joke ever, which went down like a lead balloon with Gulliver.

'And what if we want to come down?' said Gulliver quizzically as he helped Beagle into the basket.

'Want to come down? Want to come down? You haven't even been up yet and already you want to come down? What, don't you have a head for heights, boy!?' said the man bellowing in Gulliver's ear. 'Only pulling your chain, boy, and that's what you'll have to do, pull the chain attached to the gas tanks, this will stop the flow of hot air and you'll come down. Mind you, you might find it harder stopping the flow of hot air that emanates from my good friend's mouth, he's always gassing,' the owner of the hot air balloon said, looking over towards Old Father Time as he was telling Alice about the record-sized turnips he'd recently grown in his vegetable patch. These turnips, according to Old Father Time, had taken no time at all to grow, literally no time at all, he said with a smile on his face.

As the man told Gulliver this, he imagined the balloon falling from the sky like a stone before Old Father Time blew into the balloon, sending it in an upwardly direction. Unfortunately, he could also see the balloon filling Old Father Time with gas until he blew up to the size of a balloon made in the shape of an elephant, like he'd once seen a man do at a friend's birthday party. After which, Old Father Time would float off into the sky before hitting his head on the roof of the ship's bottle. Or worse, he would burst like a balloon which had been pricked with a needle. Neither scenario was a particular comforting one for him or Old Father Time, so he promised himself it would never appear on his radar ever again, or at least not until they were back on terra firma.

Gulliver smiled, trying to put the vision of Old Father Time bursting like a balloon out of his head. He then shook the hand of the man who owned the balloon, who wished him good luck before he walked off into the distance. But just before the man disappeared completely, he turned around and shouted in his best town crier's voice 'Oh, and try not to hit the roof of the world or you might puncture my balloon. If I lose any passengers my insurance premium will go sky high!' and then the man disappeared like a rabbit in a magician's hat.

Gulliver climbed into the balloon using the small stepladder provided, having first placed Beagle in the basket. After which he did his knight in shining armour\Walter Raleigh routine by gallantly helping Alice into the balloon as she too climbed into the basket. Then Old Father Time untethered the balloon from its mooring, climbed the small stepladder, and the Four Musketeers were ready to embark on their adventure of several lifetimes.

# 9

## *Time waits for no man, not even Old Father Time, apparently!*

Ten minutes later the people on the ground had shrunk to the size of toy soldiers and the houses to the size of a doll's house. Twenty minutes later those toy soldiers had metomorphasised into ants and the dolls' houses into small anthills.

'Wow!' said Alice finally finding the right description for such a word, as she looked down at the landscape as it sailed serenely beneath them, which by now resembled one of her grandmother's patchwork quilts.

'So whereabouts did you say we were heading?' Old Father Time said, nervously peering over the edge of the basket as he held on to the side as tightly as his fingers would allow.

'Well, somewhere in the direction of the south coast, which according to the latest maps is not a million miles from where the east coast used to be,' Gulliver said as the wind blew his hair in and out of his eyes.

'Refresh my memory, Gulliver, what did you say we we're going to find there?'

'Portsmouth harbour, which hopefully is full of boats,' Gulliver said confidently while feeling anything but. Gulliver remembered his father once taking him to Portsmouth to see Lord Admiral Nelson's all conquering ship HMS Victory. Gulliver also saw the 600-ton Tudor ship *Mary Rose,* or what was left of her, where she'd sat resting her weary bones on the seabed since 1545.

'Yes, I knew there was a reason my memory was holding something back, I suffer from seasickness!' Old Father Time said, pulling a face as if he had just been forced to swallow a tablespoon full of castor oil, presumably by Old Mother Time.

'And after that?' Alice enquired as Beagle jumped up at her as if to say 'I want to see where we are going'.

'Your guess is as good as mine!' Gulliver said a little too truthfully.

'So you're guessing as to where this mythical bookshop is hidden!?' Old Father Time said as he backed into the centre of the basket where he felt safer.

'Of course I'm guessing, everybody's just guessing. The Last Bookshop in the World is mythical like Atlantis, however, my guesses are educated,' said Gulliver proudly as he pulled out a spyglass from his seemingly infinite pocket and started peering through it.

'Good point, well made,' Old Father Time said forcing a smile onto his lips. It seemed Old Father Time's memory was playing tricks upon him again as he appeared to have forgotten Gulliver was a newcomer to this world.

'Be careful you don't fall overboard, Beagle, as I'm afraid we couldn't afford a parachute!' Gulliver said, as by now Beagle was in Alice's arms peering over the edge of the basket to the land below.

'What's a parachute?' said Alice turning to Gulliver, who turned in her direction without taking the spyglass from his eye, which produced the effect of a very blurred Alice.

Gulliver put down his spyglass and thought for a few seconds before answering, thinking how best to explain what a parachute was and how it worked.

'It's the latest invention by Leonardo Da Vinci,' Gulliver said rather sketchily as he couldn't remember who had actually invented it, mind you, Da Vinci had probably sketched something resembling a parachute at one time or another. A parachute is like a very large tablecloth which you cling to when falling from a great height. This slows down the rate at which you are falling at, and as long as you don't let go of the tablecloth you will be all fine and dandy, land safely, or at least relatively safely, onto the ground.' Gulliver said, pleased with his explanation of a parachute, especially the bit about 'relatively' as it was close to the word 'relativity' which was one of Newton's three laws of motion, what goes up must come down. And it would have made a nice joke but Gulliver thought it too long-winded and that it would only confuse Alice further.

'But we don't have one!' said Alice sounding rather alarmed.

'Well, that's not entirely true,' said Old Father Time, ducking as a seagull flew over his head. 'Old Mrs Time packed a rather nice food hamper which includes a rather large tablecloth so actually we do have a parachute,'

'Good!' said Alice sounding extremely relieved.

'Now as my friend said, we mustn't get too high, we don't want to scrape the roof of the bottle. And we must be careful we don't catch on the mast of the tall ship in this bottle either,' Old Father Time said half jokingly and half not.

The thing was, the ship in the bottle, the one the gods had placed on the land, was big, but it wasn't so big that it overshadowed everything else in the bottle. The bottle itself was big very, very big mind you, if you were standing outside the bottle looking in or inside looking out, everything was big, as glass magnifies, like being a child magnified everything.

To pass the time that didn't exist Old Father Time gave Gulliver a brief history lesson on time. One of the things he told Gulliver was that time changes as we look back on it, an experience that went like nothing balloons in our memory, which seemed appropriate seeing as they were in a hot air balloon. Old Father Time also said the brain is a time machine in that we journey to the past and the future so quickly that we don't notice the leap from the now to the then. Memories become frozen in time, like the house we lived in as a child, which never alters, while in reality the house had probably been demolished some time ago.

Gulliver found this lecture on time most fascinating, telling Old Father Time he could earn a good living on the lecture circuit in his time, if he ever fancied a change of scene. Old Father Time laughed and said he was keeping his options open. However, now he had plenty of time on his hands the world was his oyster, which didn't exclude travelling to other worlds or other times. Of course, travelling to other times could only be achieved if somebody invented a time machine. *Perhaps Da Vinci was already working on one,* Gulliver thought wistfully.

Gulliver knew a good joke about time machines because it was a joke that he had made up and which went exactly like this... 'I want results yesterday, if not sooner,' said the man funding the time machine project to the inventor. 'I need more time!' said the inventor tearing his hair out. 'Time, my boy? You have all the time in the world, or you will have when you've invented that jolly old time machine of yours!' Okay so the joke was a work in progress but it showed promise, it definitely showed promise.

Gulliver had a compendious discussion on antique timepieces with Old Father Time who was most impressed by Gulliver's knowledge on the subject of chronometers and commended him upon this knowledge. 'I can't believe you're so knowledgeable on the subject of chronometers, Gulliver!' said Old Father Time incredulously.

'Well, you must remember, I am old before my time,' joked Gulliver. Gulliver knew that Old Father Time was an horologist, in other words a time keeper, although his official title was The Guardian of Time. Horology was the art and science of measuring time. Horologists studied mechanical timekeeping devices while chronometry more broadly included electronic devices which surpassed the accuracy and precision of the mechanical clock.

Old Father Time, being even older than Methuselah had forgotten that although Gulliver was a twelve-year-old boy he had the knowledge of a thirty-five-year-old man locked up inside his head. Old Father Time joked that his mind used to work like clockwork and at one time you could set your watch by him 'as they used to say in this world', however, now the clock inside his head was running slow, 'as they said' in Gulliver's world.

Several times in this journey of highs and lows, which mirrored a yo-yo in slow motion as the occupants of the balloon's moods mirrored the balloon's motions, Gulliver was given to thinking they may be lost, like words sometimes got lost in his head.

There was one tiny little problem Gulliver hadn't thought of and that was how were they going to get out of the bottle with the ship in it? Here Gulliver took a leaf out of Old Father Time's book when Alice asked him this exact question and replied in a knowing tone, 'Well, Alice, we will simply remove the cork from the bottle, my dear child!' Now as the cork was rather large and weighed a ton, this was never going to happen, and why Gulliver was calling Alice 'my dear child' when he was a child himself Alice couldn't fathom! The truth was they would fly through the gap in between the cork and the neck of the bottle like the ships did. Failing that, a strong gust of air would pull them through the bottleneck whether they liked it or not, which is exactly what happened.

'Wow, that was fun!' Alice said as the balloon got sucked through the bottleneck.

Beagle agreed with Alice in her assessment of this roller coaster ride and barked accordingly to say as much.

'Fun? I'm not sure I would describe it as fun!' Old Father Time exclaimed as he adjusted his attire and brushed the hair out of his eyes.

'Fun? That was the sort of fun you get on a ride at the funfair, which is anything but fun!' Gulliver said looking as white as a sheet as if he had been on a ghost train as he finally opened his eyes.

What had just happened to the balloon and its occupants was not unlike what happens when you jump out of an aeroplane and then deploy your parachute, for as you do this you will be jerked in an upward motion, not knowing whether you're coming or going. Eventually everything will become clear and you will get you bearings. If you have ever made a parachute jump you will know exactly what I am talking about, if not, I am afraid you will have to use your imagination.

Now out of the bottle and with the sea far below them,

Gulliver spotted a seaport which may or may not have been Portsmouth. (Well, you know how time flies! Actually that joke doesn't entirely work as a hot air balloon travels slowly. Having said that, at the time you are flying, time passes, so in some ways it does, although in a world where there is no time it doesn't work on any level!) Gulliver later wrote something similar in his travelogue in a way that was anything but compendious! Gulliver vaguely remembered what Einstein had said about time, that the faster you go the slower the time passed, or some such scientific gobbledegook, and that nothing was faster than the speed of light. This theory, in theory at least, was now being brought into question by the Opera Project in Italy in Gulliver's world. Regarding the speed of light, it appeared the fat lady had finally sung her last aria!

However, there was only one way to find out if Portsmouth was in fact Portsmouth and that was by landing. Actually that's not quite true, as from the air and with the aid of a good optical device, the word 'Portsmouth' would be written upon the ground. In other words, written upon the surface of the antique globe in large capital letters, surrounded by smaller calligraphy writing of places of note. Unfortunately, due to the low cloud cover, Gulliver could hardly see his hand in front of his face.

Now anybody who has ever landed in a hot air balloon knows that the landing can be rather rough, and quite often you can find yourself being dragged across a field with hay, foliage and chickens flying all about you. That's, of course, unless you land in the sea!

'Can you see anything through that optical device of yours, Gulliver?' Old Father Time asked him as he peered through the glass lens, only for the lenses in his own eyes to be met with large white wispy clouds.

'No, I can't see a thing!' said Gulliver leaning out of the basket as far as he dared without doing a good impression of a lemming.

'So you can't see the sea then?' Old Father Time enquired.

Gulliver was just about to say to Old Father Time that he wished the weather gods were on their side when, like a sailor in a strong wind, he was forced to change tack.

'Old Father Time, Old Father Time!' Alice and Gulliver shouted in unison at the top of their lungs. Beagle was going barking mad as the balloon skimmed over the sea like a skimming stone.

Gulliver wanted to close his eyes because this whole experience was beginning to make him feel seasick, which was how words upon the written page sometimes made him feel as their reared up like frightened seahorses. Gulliver thought this probably wasn't the time or the place to say 'hold your seahorses!' as the ship went down, a joke which he would hold back for a more appropriate time and place. As Gulliver was the captain of the balloon he wondered if this meant he was obliged to go down with his balloon.

After contemplating this for a split second, he thought not! In truth, such a question wasn't worth any more than a split second debate and, any more thought on the matter and he wouldn't have needed to answer his own question, for his mind would be made up for him! Frankly, the question really wasn't even worth an answer! However, in that split second, Gulliver, having given this question his full attention and having brought all his life experience to bear in answering it as I said before, he thought not, as a balloon is not a ship. If he had been riding upon the back of a camel in the desert, a camel being said to be a ship of the desert, and was sinking in quicksand, then yes, of course being the captain of said vessel and an Englishman to boot he would have had to go down with his ship! But the balloon wasn't a camel and this wasn't the desert because it was the sea, so as such this question was a no brainer, which meant he wasn't going down with anything!

Here it appeared that Gulliver was rather going overboard, which in the circumstances was probably the best course of action! There were times when you could overthink things and Gulliver thought this was definitely one of them, however, there were other times when you couldn't, like when you worked for a government think-thank!

It's amazing how fast the brain works when it finds itself in times of danger, as Gulliver was finding out. This organ might well look like the sort of sponge found in the ocean, but it really is a marvellous device and an amazing piece of engineering, or at least it is when placed in the right hands, that of a brain surgeon!

Then the balloon stopped its skimming motion, which by all of Newton's laws of motion only meant one thing, that it had to sink like the proverbial stone, as a skimmed stone does when it runs out of steam. The balloon hitting the sea caused a wave of panic amongst the occupants, not helped by a large wave that swept over the balloon. Sometimes synchronicity isn't all it's cracked up to be!

Here Gulliver thinks of a silly little child-like rhyme he made up when he was twelve – *synchronicity isn't all it's cracked up to be when you're out for a swim in the ocean thinking about the kraken then up it pops and gobbles you up for tea!* He then remembered the irregular sonnet by Alfred Lord Tennyson called *The Kraken,* or at least the opening verse: Below the thunders of the upper deep, far, far beneath in the abysmal sea. His ancient, dreamless univaded sleep the kraken sleepeth; sunlight faintest flee. Didn't the myths say the kraken dwelled off the coast of Norway and Greenland? Gulliver hoped the kraken didn't turn up right on cue and prove his synchronicity theory correct. Then he remembered the kraken was tucked up safely for the night in the Antiquarium, sleeping like a baby sea monster. Some demons and sea monsters were real and some were in your own head; Gulliver wasn't sure which was worse, the real demons and sea monsters or the imaginary ones.

Now a balloon is not designed for sailing on the sea, the ocean, or any body of water for that matter, and as such is liable to sink like a ship's anchor at a moment's notice. However, this does depend upon a set of given variables: how fast the balloon lands, the angle of attack to the position of the sea, the size of the balloon, the number of occupants and their combined weight, how many of the occupants have jumped ship before or after the balloon lands etc. etc. Normally, and here I add a proviso with this 'normally' as this is by no means set in stone, normally this process takes a little time but eventually, as the balloon deflates and it becomes heavy with water, it will, and let's make no bones about this, sink like the proverbial anchor! (This is Newton's Fourth Law of Motion Sickness, which he is still working on as we speak, ironing out some of the obvious and not so obvious flaws in it!)

Oh, and one more thing, a balloon not being a ship, it doesn't have lifeboats or lifejackets and at this stage in the proceedings a makeshift parachute/come tablecloth is very little use to man or beast. Here the phrase 'sailing through troubled waters' sprang to Gulliver's troubled mind and he rather wished it hadn't, although 'sinking fast' might have been a more apt description in this worst-case scenario. Luckily Gulliver didn't think of the expression 'worse things happen at sea'!

'Help, help! I can't swim!' said Gulliver as he fought to get out from underneath the canopy of the deflated balloon as the basket continued shipping water. Now Gulliver had heard that if you drank too much sea water, or swallowed it, as drinking it was definitely a last resort, you would go mad. However, if you swallowed too much of the stuff that really wouldn't be a problem, once again, you do the math!

Alice was already free of the balloon, as was Old Father Time and Beagle, who was doing the doggie paddle for all he was worth. In a flash, Alice dived under the balloon like a mermaid and fished Gulliver out. Now all four seafarers were clinging on to the overturned basket and none of them could be said to be fairing well or doing swimmingly. Old Father Time was bobbing up and down in the water like a cork with a large coin stuck in it (as is the custom in some quarters after a special event) and as such was beginning to feel more than a little seasick. Gulliver, who let us not forget couldn't even do the doggie paddle, was only afloat thanks to Alice, who was literally keeping his head above water.

Gulliver looked at his digital waterproof watch, which up until this point in time had stopped working. Gulliver only kept it on for show, that and it was a present from his parents. The watch not only told you the time, day and the date in every part of the world (apart from a parallel world where there was no time, day or date), but when activated acted as a compass too. The watch was going haywire; times, days and dates were flashing up on the screen in random fashion. Perhaps this wasn't

Portsmouth after all but they had fallen into the Bermuda Triangle. Well, what with continents shifting and drifting around like in some crazy aquatic jigsaw puzzle, it could well have been! You're right, you're more likely to see a white elephant in an aquarium, however, a white whale on the other hand, well, let's get Pythagoras to do the maths for a change!

'A ship'! Alice cried, pointing at a boat that had appeared out of the mists of time, or at least from around a large mound of jagged rocks which were not far from the land.

'Hang on a minute, we'll have you out of there in no time at all,' said the captain of the vessel in a fog horn-like voice, as a lifeboat rowed up by the side of the balloon.

Before you knew it, Alice, Gulliver, Beagle and Old Father Time were standing on the deck of a ship in large pools of water, as sailors wrapped large blankets around them to keep them warm. The captain of the vessel was right, it had taken no time at all to rescue them, but then again, that was only to be expected in a world where there was no time.

'It looks like we came along in the nick of time,' the captain said as a broad grin broke out across his craggy features.

The captain was dressed in a high frilly collared tunic with billowing sleeves that could just as easily have been used as material for the sails of a child's sailing boat. The trousers he wore resembled pantaloons, which were in part covered with thigh-length brown boots, boots which were very much the fashion for a sixteenth century sea captain.

Although Gulliver liked the look of the captain's jib, whatever that was, he didn't think he could carry his look off in the Brixham high street of 2013, unless he was appearing in the Christmas pantomime version of *Puss n' Boots!*

'There's enough blue sky to make a sailor's pair of trousers, don't you think, my boy,' the Captain said to Gulliver, who looked puzzled, until he recalled his grandfather once saying exactly the same thing to him as a boy, which apparently meant it was a nice day.

'Yes, more than enough,' Gulliver said stuttering slightly as he addressed the captain, not that he wanted to dress the captain, like lady's in waiting dressed the queen, as he thought the captain quite capable of dressing himself.

Gulliver thought both the captain and his ship looked familiar to him.

'Francis Drake!' Gulliver exclaimed loudly then wished he hadn't exclaimed it quite so loudly as everyone onboard looked round at him as if he were one ducat short of a doubloon!

'How do you know my name?' Francis Drake said stroking his beard with a slightly puzzled expression on his face.

'Everybody knows Sir Francis Drake,' Gulliver said slightly in awe of his hero.

'Well boy, now I'm a sir and my father said I wouldn't amount to anything. It's nice to know someone holds me in high esteem, perhaps one day Queen Elizabeth I will too!' Drake said, laughing loudly. 'I don't know what fantastical feat I've done for everybody to have heard of me. Mind you, I did nearly dock my first ship in the town hall!'

'Perhaps the boy has a crystal ball hidden down his trousers?' said one of the shiphands, who actually had a hook replacing his left hand.

'Maybe we should hang him from the highest

yardarm and if a crystal ball falls out we'll know he has!' said another of the ship's crew as the entire crew fell about with laughter. Although the sailor in the crow's nest didn't, as being as high up as he was he couldn't hear what the commotion was all about. This was probably for the best as if he had fallen about with laughter that would probably, if not certainly, have been his lot!

Gulliver had no wish to be hung from the highest yardarm, or the lowest yardarm for that matter, not that he knew what a yardarm was, it was just he didn't want to be hanging from it. Gulliver couldn't believe his luck, he also couldn't believe how powerful synchronicity was either.

Gulliver started to wonder, what with this being a parallel world and with everything being in reverse, that if he bumped into another one of his boyhood heroes Lord Admiral Horatio Nelson, would his ship be called *HMS Defeat* rather than *HMS Victory*!? Not that he wanted to run into Nelson, or at least not if he was travelling in the *Golden Hind* at the time as he didn't want to sink the *Victory*. In truth it was much more likely to be the other way around, what with the size of the *Victory*, which was big, and the size of the *Golden Hind*, which was small. If this happened then the phrase 'turning victory into defeat' would have fitted this parallel world nicely. Gulliver thought this a little unlikely as Nelson wasn't a defeatist sort of person, and who would go to war in a ship called *HMS Defeat*? With a name like that you were beaten before you started!

'Leave the boy alone, he's obviously just got an overactive imagination. He reminds me of myself at his age,' Drake said walking up to Gulliver and placing his hand upon his shoulder. 'No harm will come to you or your friends, not on my watch. Now let's get you and your friends below deck where you can change into some dry clothes. Then after that we can get you fed and watered. Although perhaps you've already had enough water for the time being,' Drake said as the smile on his face got broader.

By this time the balloon had sunk without trace, like Atlantis or the balloon fish which was now extinct. That's if you discount the last one, which was now swimming happily in one of the tanks in the Antiquarium. Mr Silevious H. Spindlehoffer, the owner of the Antiquarium, was hoping it would mate with another fish and produce a hybrid to at least keep the spirit of the balloon fish alive. The owner of the balloon (the flying one and not the fish, although some fish do fly), had told Gulliver not to scrape the balloon on the roof of the world, in other words the glass of the bottle with the ship in it. However, he hadn't said anything about scraping it on the bottom of the sea bed!

As the four musketeer's went below deck, Francis Drake said he thought he recognized Old Father Time, but Old Father Time said he had that sort of face, people were always saying they'd seen him some place or some time. Old Father Time didn't mind telling a twelve-year-old boy he was Old Father Time but a grown man might take him for being one sextant short of a chart, or one hand short of a pocket watch, or even one hook short of a pirate. However, this wasn't a problem because Gulliver introduced Old Father Time to Drake as Old Father Time!

Later Gulliver said to Francis Drake in a rather respectful tone, 'Captain Drake, where are we heading, sir?' Drake said this voyage would be a short one as they had just travelled halfway round the world, having been to the Caribbean, the West Indies to be more precise, where their was a British Navy outpost. Now the *Golden*

*Hind* was heading into Portsmouth harbour for repairs. When Old Father Time heard this, suffering with seasickness as he did, he was a much relieved man.

That evening over breadfruit and coloured water, the coloured water being port, Gulliver told Drake of his quest to find The Last Bookshop in the World. Drake said this quest sounded right up his Ocean Drive and he wondered if he could sign up for this journey into the unknown. There was another reason Drake wanted to climb on board with Gulliver's idea, as he'd always been a great believer in omens. Now what could be more of an omen than having a hot air balloon land in your path which contained two children a Labrador called Beagle and the ex-Guardian of Time himself? *It had to be a sign, it just had to be,* thought Drake illogically. When Drake told his crew what their next voyage would be, some were given over to thinking that this was a sign, a sign that Drake had obviously lost his ball bearings somewhere in the Baring Straights!

Once again Gulliver couldn't believe his luck, not only had he met his hero but he actually wanted to help him with his quest, even though as a quest it left a lot to be desired. Having Drake on board with his mastery of seamanship and knowledge of navigation, using charts and the stars to guide them through stormy waters, would be invaluable in finding The Last Bookshop in the World. Gulliver had considered that perhaps the reason nobody could find this bookshop was because it had been built near a cliff, and perhaps it had slipped down the cliff into the water, or had floated away and was now an archipelago, possibly part of the Galapagos Islands. Either that or like Atlantis it had sunken so far into the oceans it was now buried deep within the sea bed, like some sunken treasure off a Spanish galleon. Or maybe it had come to rest on the continental bookshelf. No, that was one idea he needed to shelve immediately, if not sooner! Well, as his grandfather was always telling him, you couldn't afford to take yourself too seriously.

So after the *Golden Hind* had pulled into port and had stocked up on supplies and the crew had let off a little steam, Drake said he would be happy to join Gulliver's merry band of misfits, as they attempted to discover this mythical bookshop. Francis Drake said he knew Queen Elizabeth I was looking for a signed first edition of *Romeo and Juliet*. Drake told Gulliver the queen was sick to the back teeth of receiving jewels and gold trinkets, and even more fed up with receiving dirty vegetables from foreign lands that needed to be boiled to death before you ate them! Gulliver hoped Drake wasn't going to add some horribly written history to this story as he knew in the Elizabethan age they didn't shy away from torture. Here Gulliver recalls the torturous history lessons he had to sit through when he was at school, never once thinking he would be a part of living history. This little adventure of his was really bringing history alive, like Dr Lucy Worsley, Stephen Fry and Fiona Bruce did on John Logie Baird's magical box of tricks.

Francis Drake said you couldn't beat a good book, which Gulliver agreed wholeheartedly with. Drake then joked that you couldn't beat a bad one either, as he had once used a copy of a book called *The Captain's Gold* to knock a Spanish conquistador out cold. The book was 850 pages long, which is probably why he was using it as a doorstop. Apparently Drake had even considered stuffing it into a cannon so as to sink a Spanish galleon; Gulliver wondered if that's where the expression 'throwing the book at you' came from! Drake had used the book *The Captain's Gold* to knock the Spanish conquistador over the head after the conquistador had knocked the sword from his hand during a raid on the *Golden Hind*, which was in port in Mexico at the time. The conquistador was knocked spark out in the fight, which left Drake and his men to get away with countless treasures.

Drake said the book now sat proudly in his sparse library on board the *Golden Hind*, he still hadn't read past the third chapter, however, he said the book made a great story even if the story in the book wasn't that great!

Gulliver thought it would have made a great story if Drake had said Walter Raleigh had used some of the bowls he was using in his game against Queen Elizabeth I to fire out of the cannons of his ship when the Spanish Armada attacked England in 1578. However, that would have made a bad story for if he had told such a fairy story, no one in their right mind would have believed him, unless, of course, he was using cannon balls in his game of bowls with the queen. Well, the French used metal balls in their game of boule so why ever not? However, firing bowls out of a cannon would have splintered them into a thousand pieces as soon as the lit fuse came in contact with the gunpowder. I suppose he could have used the bowls to throw at the Spanish in close-quarter fighting on the deck of his ship, or have drilled a hole in the bowls, laced them with gunpowder attached to a fuse and then thrown them onto the Spanish galleons. Now Gulliver's imagination was really pushing the boat out!

Now *that* would have made a great story. Gulliver's grandfather was right, his grandson really did have a wild imagination, so much so he should probably write a book about his travels in this world. Maybe if he ever got back to his own time Gulliver would, and it may even be a bestseller, perhaps he could call it *Gulliver's Travels in*

*Time*. However, if he did, my guess is that nobody would believe a single word, not a tale as tall as the mast of a tall ship, not in a million lightyears!

# 10

# Fairytales? That Ship has Sailed!

Time passed, no sorry, it didn't, but the sun rose and sank a few times and the man in the moon popped his head out of the clouds to see what was going on. By this time Drake, his crew and the four musketeers were ready to continue on with their quest to find The Last Bookshop in the World. Gulliver had heard a rumour that it might be somewhere in the South Pacific. Mind you, the source this rumour had come from had been rumoured to be somewhat of a teller of fairytales. The man's name? Hans Christian Andersen. But still, as this man said he was a travel writer and seemed a good-hearted fellow, perhaps he had an inkling as to where this mythical bookshop was. True, it wasn't much to go on but as Gulliver had nothing else to go on then he thanked Mr Andersen for his help and went on his merry way, or at least Mr Andersen went on his merry way, care of a tavern called The Liar's Inn, wishing Gulliver Godspeed as he did so. At times it appeared to Gulliver that this world was like an archaic fairyland and the people who lived in it nothing more than characters from a fairytale.

From now on till the end of time, when I use the word 'time', I will be using it in the metaphorical sense to aid the flow of the story. And that was exactly what Gulliver wrote in his travelogue as that seemed the only logical way around 'the time dilemma', as he called it. Gulliver was so used to using the word 'time', that it seemed this was the logical thing to do. Logic was another word Gulliver promised himself he would cross out of the dictionary when he found the mythical last bookshop in the world. Imagine if, when he found this bookshop, he found another bookshop called The Last Bookshop in the World and that it was simply part of a chain of bookshops, what a let down that would be. Although as Gulliver lived by the water he did have a soft spot for the bookstores called Waterstones. But by all accounts, according to the myth that wasn't the case, however, the way things were going Gulliver thought that thanks to e-books, by the time he got back to his world there really might only be one bookshop left in the world and Waterstones may have sunk without trace!

The *Golden Hind* weighed anchor and Gulliver's travels were off and running once again, although nobody on the dock cried 'Godspeed'. Gulliver thought it was a funny expression to say 'you weighed anchor'; why would you want to weigh your anchor? You pretty much knew just by looking at the thing that it was heavy as it was made from wrought iron. If you dropped it on your foot you certainly knew it was heavy, as you would if you dropped a cannonball on your foot. Did it really matter how much the anchor weighed? Yes, it probably weighed a little less every time it was dropped in the sea as the salt eroded the metal, but not to the point that you had to weigh it every time you set sail surely?

Gulliver thought it would be a nice touch if Drake made a golden anchor for the *Golden Hind* by melting down the gold the Spanish had been so kind to give to him. But after giving it a little more thought, for in truth it didn't require a lot more thought, Gulliver realised that this imaginary golden anchor would, in a very short space of time, weigh less and less as sailors chipped bits of the gold away with their cutlasses. This would go on until the anchor weighed so little that it would float away into the cosmological oceans, sailing further into the Milkway galaxy, which is still suffering from the tidal effects of the nearby Magellanic Clouds, which have slightly distorted our galaxy's shape. Passing the great ship *Argo*, passing the Jellyfish Nebula on the starboard side then the Hourglass Nebula on the port side (actually all the sides of the ship on this epic voyage would be the starboard side!), as the solar winds carried it further and further on its voyage into the uncharted regions of outer space, where galaxies and stars lay a quintillion lightyears away from earth, as radiowaves were constantly being picked up by radio telescopes all across the planet.

Who knows, maybe this ship might even pass the Voyager space craft, which by then would have run out of steam on the longest voyage a ship has ever been on. I'm sure Sir Francis Drake would have loved to have sailed upon the cosmological oceans on his *Golden Hind*, on a voyage that would circumnavigate the universe using his star charts and sextant. Now Gulliver really was letting his imagination run away with him, pushing the boat out as far as he was able, the only surprising thing was Gulliver hadn't thought of landing on the moon in a hot air balloon… give it time!

Gulliver had once seen a design for a futuristic spaceship in a book which had sails upon it like a mast, which in principal would be powered by the sun in the same way solar panels worked. Gulliver had always been interested in the stars in the night sky and many a night he had watched stars fall out of the heavens with his father and grandfather. He knew many of the constellations by name and the star signs connecting the dots to form the Great and Little Bear and Orion's Belt. Gulliver also knew of the Gems in the Great Ship Argo. Carina, the Keel and Vela, the Sails, were two of the four constellations of Argo Navis which was subdivided by the French astronomer Nicholas Louis de Lacaille in the eighteenth century. The other two are Puppis, the Stern and Pyxis, the Compass.

'Okay, Gulliver, ready for a spot of hands-on sailing?' Drake said as he motioned to Gulliver to take the wheel of the *Golden Hind* and sail it out of Portsmouth harbour, or Ports Mouth harbour as Christopher Columbus was always calling it.

'What me? You want me to sail the *Golden Hind*!' Gulliver said, his mouth open wide like a hungry catfish. Here Gulliver thought it may be wiser if he didn't take the wheel as the wheel should probably stay exactly where it was! Later Gulliver was to wonder what happened to the whipstaff which steered the boat as there was no ship's wheel on the *Golden Hind*. However there was a ship's wheel on the replica of the *Golden Hind* in St Mary's Overie Dock in London, as well as a propeller! Gulliver knew the Elizabethans were top-notch engineers and designers but really, a propeller? *Perhaps this was another of Da Vinci's designs*, Gulliver thought with his metaphorical tongue in his metaphorical cheek!

'Well, I've got to go downstairs and look at my charts and maps. I've got no idea what most of them mean, of course, but it gives the men confidence to think I know where I'm going. To be honest, the Spanish mapmakers are streets ahead us,' said Drake dryly. 'Most of the time I close my eyes and stick a pin in the map, either that or toss a gold ducat!' Drake said as a golden smile sailed slowly across the landscape of his face. 'Anyway, I wouldn't trust my men to sail the *Golden Hind*, they couldn't sail a toy ship in a bath tub let alone navigate their way out of a harbour without sending us to the bottom of Davy Jones's Locker!' Drake continued with his stand-up routine, one day it was sure to come in handy when flirting with Queen Elizabeth I. Women loved a man with a good sense of humour, it said so in all the women's chronicles of the day, and it might just help him to keep his head attached to his shoulder, instead or it rolling around in the gutter!

'Steady as she goes, seaman,' Drake cried out to Gulliver as he disappeared below deck. Gulliver stood upon an old sea chest Drake had put there for him so he could see over the ship's wheel, which was almost as big as he was. It appeared, regarding his size and the fact that Gulliver was now a boy, the wheel had rather come full circle, even if it had done so in an anti-clockwise direction.

'Aye, aye, captain,' Gulliver said holding on to the ship's wheel for grim death. Gulliver had always wanted to say 'aye, aye, captain'. That was another thing he could cross off his wishlist when he got home. Another thing he'd always wanted to say was 'Yo ho, ho and a bottle of rum' but he was only twelve so that didn't quite seem appropriate at this moment in time. Having said that, some boys put to sea as early as twelve and every day a quantity of rum was given out to the sailors, although this was purely for medicinal purposes of course! Scurvy was the scourge of the sailor not getting enough vitamin

C, something Gulliver knew all about; that's why he'd got spots when he was a teenager. Gulliver's mother had told him this was because he didn't eat enough fruit. Whether this was an old wives' tale he wasn't sure, although he was sure his mother was now an old wife so it probably was!

'Wow!' said Alice, as she saw Gulliver sailing the *Golden Hind* out of Portsmouth harbour without touching the sides as a double rainbow appeared magically out of nowhere. If that wasn't a sign, said Drake, then nothing was.

Alice loved using her new favourite word 'Wow!' whenever anything seemed worthy of its use, and sometimes even when it didn't. Her stepmother was always telling her not to overuse things otherwise she'd wear them out, although apparently this didn't apply to soap and Alice didn't think this applied to words either!

Gulliver wanted to say to Alice 'it's a piece of cake' but he didn't, because it wasn't. He had only been at the wheel ten minutes and already his arms felt as heavy as an anchor.

Soon Beagle was on deck jumping up at Gulliver to gain his attention.

'Down, boy!' Gulliver said a little irritably, if he'd told Beagle that once he'd told him a thousand times. Beagle rarely listened mind you, he was a dog and as such Gulliver felt it was only right and proper that he cut his loyal companion some slack. After all it was hard enough for him to get to grips with the English language and he wasn't even a dog.

Beagle was a puppy again and as such he had puppy tendencies, which meant he peed whenever and wherever the fancy took him, and he wanted to play all the time, oh, and he ate like a horse!

'You seem to be getting the hang of things,' Old Father Time said encouragingly as he walked up and down the deck stretching his legs, as if he had been at sea for more than a month rather than ten minutes.

'Just getting to know the ropes,' Gulliver said giving Old Father Time some old rope. What Gulliver should have added to this remark was metaphorically speaking as he wasn't climbing the rigging. However, it seemed to Gulliver that speaking metaphorically wasn't something the people of this world seemed to care much for, although Drake seemed to be an exception to that rule.

'How's your seasickness?' Alice enquired caringly of Old Father Time.

'Fine, I've never felt better, it must be the sea air,' Old Father Time said cheerfully, not altogether making sense.

'So where are we heading, Captain Gulliver?' Old Father Time said as he looked at Gulliver while ruffling his beard to displace the fleas that had bedded down there overnight.

'We're heading in the right direction,' Gulliver said making perfect sense.

'Good,' said Old Father Time as he picked a flea out of his beard and threw it overboard. 'Good, I've always said it helps if you're going in the right direction. It's certainly better than going in the wrong direction, which is what Old Mrs Time is always accusing me of when it comes to doing the washing up after a meal.' Old Father Time then laughed as if it was the last time he ever would.

Drake then asked one of the sailors to trim the sails, an able-bodied seaman known simply as Hamish, or 'the big man'. Hamish was as rough as an uncut diamond and almost as tall as Neptune himself and whose hair resembled the tangled rigging of a ship in a storm.

Hamish roared like a ship's cannon to the ship's boy, who unlike Gulliver, if thrown overboard in a wild sea would float like a buoy. 'Pepper, trim the sails and be quick about it!'

'Yes, Hamish,' said the boy as he sneezed loudly several times, almost filling the sails in the process. The ship's boy then climbed the rigging with the nimbleness and speed of a spider which had spied a fly trapped in its web. Most of the ship's company had nicknames and the ship's boy was no exception, as not only had he a tendency to sneeze loudly but with alarming frequency, which had alarmed all onboard at one time or the other.

Gulliver knew there were more nautical sayings than you could shake a gull's tail feather at, such as – splice the mainsail, steady as she goes, ship ahoy, fire a broadside, come hell or high water, worse things happen at sea, and his personal favourite, trimming the sails. Whenever Gulliver heard this expression he expected a sailor to appear on deck with a pair of scissors in his hand after which he'd climb the rigging and literally trim the sails. That was the thing about being on board a ship, you couldn't take things literally, especially when pirates had a cutlass in your back and were telling you in the nicest possible way that you had to walk the plank or else. It was a bit like the expression 'taking a long walk off a short pier', or plank in this case; it wasn't to be taken literally, after all the pirates were only yanking your anchor!

And to add to the confusion, Drake often said to the ship's surgeon, who was also the ship's barber, 'I think it's time to trim the old sails, a little off the port side and the starboard side should do the trick,' when he was referring to having his sideburns, his beard or his hair trimmed. The ship's surgeon received the nickname of

Dr Sawbones, for obvious reasons; more horrible history I'm afraid!

The morning alarm was sounded by the quartermaster's mate, Gilbert Galsworthy, who frankly, by the end of most voyages wasn't even the quartermaster's mate, more like Billy no mates. Gilbert Galsworthy was as good at blowing his own trumpet as any of the queen's trumpeters, which was probably why he was chosen for the task. Gilbert Galsworthy had his own trumpet that he'd fashioned from an old speaking trumpet and which apparently once belonged to Methuselah himself (a tale as tall as a tall ship's mast if ever there was one!). This early morning call wasn't helped by the quartermaster's mate's cheerful disposition, him being an early morning sort of person and all. Nor was it helped by him singing the song *What Shall We Do with the Drunken Sailor* repeatedly in a voice which can best be described as a strangulated catfish crossed with a fog horn – 'What shall we do with the drunken sailor, what shall we do with the drunken sailor, what shall we do with the drunken sailor early in the morning.' The crew were often heard to say irritably 'Throw him in Davy Jones's Locker and throw away the key!' The only friend Gilbert Galsworthy had was Able Seaman Drinkwater and a chicken he'd named Henrietta, who as yet had not found her way into the cooking pot, but once again, just give it time!

Now sleeping aboard a ship in cramped living quarters is not really a recipe for a good night's kip, especially if some of those sleeping arrangements included hammocks, sleeping on a damp floor in between cannons, snoring sailors and the rocking motion of the ship in a rough sea. Now this rocking motion wasn't the same gentle rocking motion a mother uses to rock her baby off to sleep, and if you thought it was, you must have rocks in your head! Gulliver had always been a light sleeper so wore wax earplugs to block out the noise of seagulls and fog horns. The good thing was there was plenty of wax available in the captain's quarters, which he used for sealing letters as he often corresponded with Queen Elizabeth I.

A few weeks later after some rough seas followed by some calm seas followed by some even rougher seas, Able Seaman Drinkwater, almost driven to drink seawater as the water supplies were running low, thankfully spotted land from the crow's nest. Unfortunately, he also spied a lone magpie, one for sorrow and all that jazz, and sailors back then were nothing if not a superstitious bunch. (Just for the record and the ship's log, this seaman's first name was Abel and that isn't a jape, I am just stating a fact.) Soon every man jack was on deck singing sea shanties, and doing merry jigs up and down the deck, which included Able Seaman Jack Daniel. (Off the record and not to be included in the ship's log, that was a joke, albeit a poor one.) Several of the men climbed the rigging and spliced the mainsails. Even Drake admitted he didn't know what on earth splicing the main sail meant but luckily his men seemed to.

Except they hadn't spotted land, they had spotted the cork in the bottle, which meant they were now on another continent. Now getting from one ship's bottle to another was a tricky business; it was one of the hardest manouevres a ship's captain could negotiate. There was very little margin for error for the gap between the cork and the bottle was no bigger than a hair's breath, whatever that was! The gap was certainly nowhere near the gap which ran along the famous Northwest Passage. First you had to wait for the tide to rise and then you sailed your vessel through the gap into the oceans. Hopefully the tide had risen along with the oceans in the ship's bottle otherwise you were in for a long drop, which was never good, especially if you landed butter side down.

This principle was a little like the procedure a barge goes through when changing locks, because in truth, it wasn't a lot like this principle! Some said this procedure was like falling off the edge of the world. Gulliver remembered reading in *The Book of Aiden* the line, 'When you reach the edge of the world, you can fly'. Unfortunately, these old sailing vessels were not ships of the sky, in other words airships, and despite the amount and the size of their sails, they could not fly! (Having said that, there is a boat called the flyboat and there is a song called *The Skye Boat* song, Skye being an island in Scotland.) This Gulliver included in his travelogue for the nautically minded and the more serious mariner, who may one day at a pinch find himself perusing this log.

Now obviously the ship rested on the land\antique globe so it was imperative that you waited for the tides to come in contact with the bottle, otherwise your meteoric rise would quickly be followed by a fall both metaphorically and literally speaking. Falling from a waterfall as high as Angel Falls in Venezuela into a body of water, was preferable than diving from a high board into an empty swimming pool, if you get my continental drift! Of course the moon had a big part to play in this procedure as the tides were controlled by the pulling power of the moon. Gulliver had seen high tides reach fifty feet high in some parts of Devon and there was an incoming tide which when it came in contact with the river bore looked like chocolate milk to Gulliver's mind. (However, it didn't taste like chocolate milk, as Gulliver once found out to his cost when falling in the river!) When the river reached top speed the waves looked like they should be on Bondi Beach, not in Devon. This river was a big draw for local surfers and this tide was said to be the second highest tide in the world, there was even talk of harnessing this power by building a hydro-electricity station in the local area. Gulliver had often heard seafaring folk talk of the great flood in Devon in the early part of the previous century when houses and people were literally swept out to sea.

As a boy, Gulliver had often put his mother's ironing board onto the living room floor, turned the television on just in time for the title pictures of the TV police show *Hawaii Five-O* to come on the screen, which was of surfers riding on the crest of a wave. Gulliver would then catch this imaginary wave which came into his living room. However, in real life Gulliver couldn't surf to save his life. Of course not being able to swim didn't help his cause in this respect, that and he wasn't really the adventurous type. *If only there had been 3D HD TV at the time*, Gulliver thought wistfully. Mind you, in Devon in 2012 there had been massive flooding and in some cases waves actually did find their way into the living room.

The one thing that puzzled Gulliver was how did the water get onto the antique globe, for he knew gravity kept it there? Although, one might say the only puzzling thing was that it was the only thing that puzzled Gulliver in this rather unbelievable explanation. Well, once again it wasn't the science of navigation or rocket science for the younger reader. A giant comet fell to earth, or rather landed on the antique globe, which of course was waterproof, and as we all know, a comet's tail is made up of ice, and ice when melted becomes water. This is basically the sort of stuff they teach you in first-year science at school, or at least they should, along with white reflects heat and black absorbs heat and what goes up must come down.

Oh, and just one more thing, planet earth didn't look like a green and blue marble from outer space, it looked slightly yellow with brown, orange and dark green patches, as all antique globes look like. If in Gulliver's travels, in this world, he ever got to ride on a horse then he really could say he was globe-trotting! But back to the action…

'Okay, lads, hold on to your rope and tackle, oh, and if you believe in God, a prayer wouldn't go amiss!' Drake said in good humour, although whether you thought Drake's humour was good or not rather depended on your own sense of humour. That's if you had a sense of humour of course. The small man who ran The Pandemonium Emporium with the many hats upon his head infinitum didn't seem to have one, nor did the antiquarian librarian who ran the library without any books in it in Brixham in old Devonshire.

Drake said a little prayer under his breath and hoped his father, who was once a vicar, was in heaven watching over him, as he hoped Andrew, the Patron Saint of Fishermen and St Christopher, the Patron Saint of Travellers were too. Well as Drake was always saying, 'God knows you can never have too many saints on your side.'

The water rose and the *Golden Hind* along with it and soon the ship was in line with the cork. 'Steady as she goes!' Drake cried to an able seaman who had the ship's wheel in his hand, as everybody on board prayed he was as able as his title suggested, otherwise they were all in the dodo's do dos! The ship's company also hoped this able seaman wasn't walking around with this ship's wheel in his hand polishing it, and that it was attached to something, hopefully the steering column!

Within the blinking of an eye the *Golden Hind* was sucked through the gap between the cork and the glass and was falling at great speed as if it had just gone over a high waterfall. For what seemed like a lifetime to Gulliver and the crew, the ship fell in slow motion until with a great splash it hit the water and for the briefest of moments the crew were all at sea. Luckily for all on board, the ship fell butter side up and although everybody was soaked to the skin, nobody fell overboard. However, the ship's cook hit his head on a barrel of rum, that he may or may not have had attached to his lips at the time!

After a while the ship stopped bobbing around in the ocean like a message in a bottle and the ship's company all breathed a huge collective sigh of relief.

Sailing in the olden days was not for the faint-hearted. It was hardly surprising that people felt the world was flat and that you could fall off the edge of it when they heard of such tales.

'So that's how you get out of the ship in the bottle!' Gulliver said to Old Father Time, in a manner which suggested that Gulliver hadn't altogether bought Old Father Time's earlier explanation of simply removing the cork out of the bottle when you wanted to get from A to B, or Z in this case.

And then out of a crystal-clear blue sky a large fish with wings flew out of the ocean and landed upon the deck, and then another, and then another until the sky was literally raining fish. To Gulliver's mind it was like an event ripped right out of the pages of the Bible. The *Golden Hind* was being bombarded by flying fish the size of baby pterodactyls. As one of these fish could quite easily have been said to be a throwback to the prehistoric age of the dinosaur, a song came into Gulliver's mind, 'One, two, three, four, five, once I caught a fish alive, six, seven, eight, nine, ten then, I threw it back again'. And Gulliver would have been happy to have thrown these fish back, back from whence they'd come, namely the ocean, as they were biting anything that they came in contact with, namely a gunner's left ear. However, Gulliver didn't throw any of these fish back into the ocean as he hadn't a mind to lose any of his fingers. Well, he thought sensibly, what if he wanted to take up the violin, the piano or the harp, after all, he didn't want to be all thumbs and no fingers like Tom Thumb now did he!

The gunners, who rarely saw the light of day, mostly being below deck, had brought their cannonballs onto the deck of the ship, so they could both clean them and see some of that light of day. Gunners often suffered from Seasonal Affective Disorder (SAD), due to lack of sunlight. Mind you, Beagle was having a whale of a time playing with the gargantuan fish that were no longer flying but sunbathing upon the deck. Some of the fish Beagle had in his mouth were thrashing about for all they were worth (which to be fair in this part of the world wasn't that much!)

'Duck!' Gulliver shouted to Alice as a flying fish the size of a hammerhead shark sailed across her starboard bow.

'A duck, really, in this part of the world?' Alice couldn't see it or see it coming for that matter as it clipped her right shoulder and she went down like a duck in a shooting gallery. 'Ow, that hurt!' said Alice as she slowly picked herself up off the deck with some help from Gulliver. 'Where did that come from?' Alice complained holding her right shoulder.

Gulliver didn't think this was the right time to tell Alice she should be keeping her upper lip stiff as Nelson so admirably did when being attacked by the enemy. Mind you, in truth Admiral Lord Horatio Nelson had probably never been attacked by baby flying pterodactyls, or ever sailed his ship *HMS Victory* into the seas that time forgot!

Gulliver had always wondered why pterodactyls were called pterodactyls. However, once he'd broken the word down into syllabus he knew exactly why pterodactyls were called pterodactyls, you do the math! (Tero – terror, please do try and keep up as we still have a long voyage ahead of us. And I can't be expected to explain every little minor detail in minute detail now can I?!)

'What's going on?' Drake said logically, not knowing what was going on, having just been awoken from a dream to be greeted by a waking nightmare as soon as he stepped foot upon deck. Gulliver was starting to realise that this saying 'what's going on' followed by a question mark was one of Drake's favourite sayings, and his too for that matter. Later Gulliver was to write this in his travelogue: 'This world is ripe for the saying 'what's going on', followed by a question mark and then an exclamation mark. Several in fact!!!

'Well, Captain, we're being attacked by some large flying fish off both the port and the starboard side and possibly the bow and the stern too!'

'Really, flying fish you say?' said Drake to the second of the ship's mates, who, and I know this is neither here nor there, had recently kissed and made up with another of the ship's mates. In other words, had done a Nelson and Hardy, or at least this was what it was referred to by sailors in this nautical world.

'Yes, flying fish as far as the eye can see,' the second mate said as he ducked several times as incoming fish flew over his head and landed with a loud smack against the deck. After which they were either knocked spark out or squirmed like eels across the deck as they gave their considerable jaws a workout.

For a minute or two Drake just stood there scratching the fleas from his beard as if the situation the second mate had conveyed to him had gone sailing right over his head. Until he said, 'Get the cook up here with all the large cooking pots in the galley and bring a couple of large kegs up here too. I'm sure the cook can make a nice fish stew out of this little lot. We normally have trouble catching fish while these fish seemingly can't wait to be caught. Oh, and be careful how you pick them up, you might want to wear a thick pair of gloves. Oh, and by the time I awake I want to see the *Golden Hind* shipshape and Bristol fashion just in case my calculations are wrong and we're heading in the direction of Bristol!' Drake said as he yawned and went back below to continue his beauty sleep.

'The captain's a cool customer and no denying,' said the first mate to the gunner as he followed Drake below to relay his message to the cook, muttering under his breath 'more fish stew, I couldn't be happier. No really, my heart is doing a jig of delight!' in a manner that could have been interpreted in some quarters as sarcasm, namely the captain's quarters. Drake later said he'd heard this comment and although he didn't exactly know how high the highest yardarm was, or frankly even what a yardarm was, if he wasn't careful he would soon be swinging from it! One thing was for sure, the ship's captain just couldn't afford any mates onboard his ship, having said that, he couldn't afford not to have any either!

By this time the deck was literally swimming in fish, it certainly was a sight to behold. Sailors running round after fish which not only could be said to be all at sea but could be said to be flying off the handle as well, as the ship's company subdued them with the butts of their muskets and cudgels. Some of the fish the cook literally caught in his pots and some jumped straight into the barrels. The gunner returned to the deck with a musket in his hand and started shooting the fish out of the air, which then fell into the barrels. This was obviously where the expression 'Like shooting fish in a barrel' came from, probably!

Luckily Gulliver wasn't a vegetarian otherwise he might have found this sight unpalatable. However, there was no room in the fleet of the Royal Navy for weak stomachs or landlubbers, it was the law of the jungle, although obviously it wasn't as they were at sea!

Moons and suns did what suns and moons generally did before some real land came into sight, you get the general continental drift. This sighting of land occurred when the two sailors in the crow's nests were playing a game of I spy through their spyglasses to pass the time. Sailor A said to Sailor B, although in truth he more shouted it than said it due to the distance between the two crow's nests, 'I spy with my little glass eye, something beginning with L'. After several failed guesses, which included Lapland, which was way off base, but not Lilliput, the lateen sail or the lion's head on the stern of the ship, Sailor A told Sailor B that it might be prudent if he was looking through the right end of his spyglass because, the L their little game of I spy began with, was L for land!

Drake considered this L for land ahoy to be about twenty nautical miles east, or at least east of where he guesstimated they should be at this point in their voyage. This guesstimated point was, of course, as the fish flew or the dolphin swam which, was similar to as the crow flies, and believe you me there are no flies on a crow!

As time no longer existed when involved in the art of navigation, the captain of the vessel could no longer record in his ship's log the following observations – thirty degrees two minutes south, north, east, or west for that matter. Thirty degrees, yes, south, north, east or west, absolutely, but those two minutes being rather closely associated with time, absolutely not! Such an entry into a captain's ship's log made the whole calculation poppycock of the highest order, nonsense, gobbledegook and gobbledegobble. Even the mad proprietor of The Pandemonium Emporium would have howled with derision at such an entry into a ship's log!

Another thing was that a nautical day began and ended at noon, with the noon sighting, not at midnight as in civil time. Just for the record, a nautical mile is 6,076 feet, or one degree of latitude; a statute mile consists of 5,280 feet. Of course in this parallel world, as time had well and truly flown the coup, neither civil nor sea time was given the time of day by sailors or landlubbers. However, sailors did still occasionally use the sandglass, which had enough sand in it for half an hour before it was turned by the ship's boy as regular as clockwork. Unfortunately, as the ship's boy often dozed off during this duty, the sandglass wasn't any more reliable than the ship's boy. Captains often threw the sandglass overboard with the ship's boy still attached to it 'as regular as clockwork', when finding him in neglect of his duty!

Now the land they had spied was also in a large ship's bottle, although the ship wasn't a ship but an extra, extra large canoe made out of bamboo. When Gulliver saw the land he looked at Old Father Time nervously, as he was very afraid of asking him how they got back inside the bottle with the ship, the land and old Tom Cobbley and all in it.

However, it wasn't rocket science, though Old Father Time hadn't told him as much, you just reversed the procedure. Old Father Time had never even heard of the expression, 'it's not rocket science'! And even if he had, he was far too polite to use it. Although Stephenson's Rocket had recently been invented by a chap named Stephenson, although in this world one can never be too sure of anything. However, a rocket hadn't as yet been invented that could voyage forth into the cosmological oceans, certainly not one powered by steam, but give it time and it will come to pass, as all quantum scientists were so fond of saying. Gulliver had already imagined a spaceship in the style of an old steamer making its way across the cosmological oceans and a Chinese junk, well everybody's heard of space junk so why ever not!

Yes, you could set your watch by quantum mechanics saying as regular as clockwork 'it's just a matter of time before the big end goes, the rocket booster's packed up, or the sprocket has a meltdown! No sorry, we haven't got the time to fix it right now, unless you've got deep pockets that is'. (And for anybody who owns an automobile I shouldn't have to quantify that last statement.) One must remember that although Gulliver looked twelve, in part he had the mind of a thirty-five-year-old man and as such he wasn't born yesterday!

In this world Gulliver appeared to have deep pockets, pockets as endless as the universe and as endless as his imagination. It was just a pity he didn't have endless pockets in his world, he thought with a wry smile on his face that the man in the moon would have been proud of.

In his travelogue Gulliver wrote that quantum physicists wouldn't last five minutes in a time where there was no time for they wouldn't be able to say 'everything will come to pass, given time'. Actually, quantum physicists with their out-of-this-world theories would have fitted into this world very nicely if you please.

So to spare you all the boring details, Francis Drake waited for the tide to rise in line with the canoe in a bottle before sailing the *Golden Hind* through the gap and into the South Pacific seas. All I will say was that after falling through the gap as if falling over a waterfall, the *Golden Hind* landed Queen Elizabeth I head side up! Or if you prefer the toast analogy, the *Golden Hind* fell butter side up. However, I will add a couple of things to this procedure. If the ship in the bottle was sitting on a land mass that was slightly tilted one way or the other, then either of the following happened; A: If the bottle was slightly raised the water would move further down the bottle and the living accommodation would be tree houses or houses built upon bamboo stilts. Also, the houses would be built closer to the shoreline, this sometimes occurred in the South Pacific islands. Or B: If the bottle was on a slight downward slope, houses would be built upon the hills and away from the shoreline. Also the water would collect closer to the bottleneck, thus making it easier to get in and out of the ship's bottle. If there were a lot of ships in a queue waiting to get through the neck of the bottle, this, like in Gulliver's world, was known as a 'bottleneck'! However, having said all that, most of the ships in the bottle lay relatively flat upon the land, or in this case the antique globe.

So to fast forward a little, some more metaphorical sand fell through the hourglass as well as some actual sand before an island came into view.

'Well, boy, how's your first experience at sea been?' Drake said as he peered through his spyglass at the land mass that was rapidly coming into view.

'It's been an experience,' Gulliver said making perfect sense again.

'Good, I'm glad you said that because I remember my first sea voyage and that's exactly what I told my captain when he asked me the exact same question. Great minds think alike, that was what my father was always telling me. Being at sea is a bit like being on land, well, if you take the water out of the equation, and as long as you keep things shipshape and Bristol fashion you'll be fine,' said Drake not entirely making sense. 'Some of the experiences are good and some are not so good and some are bad and some are not worth talking about!' Drake said as he continued to survey the land mass which appeared to be an island. 'Soon we can weigh the anchor, perhaps the natives of this island have heard of your mythical bookshop?' said Drake sounding doubtful as he knew that most natives couldn't read and most hadn't even seen a book, let alone read one.

'The last thing in the world natives have time for was reading books, most of the time they are too busy eating one another!' Drake said as he put down his spyglass and turned to Gulliver as ever so slowly a smile yawned its way onto his lips revealing his less than perfectly even teeth. Tobacco was the cause of his yellowing teeth, chewing it rather than smoking it. Walter Raleigh had already discovered potatoes and tobacco, but thanks to the gods shaking up time, he'd now have to discover them all over again, perhaps this time Drake would discover them and Raleigh would circumnavigate the world. Maybe this time round Francis Drake might beat Magellan, Elcano and his pals to the world's first circumnavigation, in effect airbrushing them from the history books. Or maybe there would be an around-the-world race in which Columbus, Magellan, Drake, Raleigh and Marco Polo would take part!

How Sir Walter Raleigh would have loved to have

found a magic lamp with a genie attached to it, then he could have wished for a magic telescope. He could then peer into this magic telescope and as the mists of time lifted, he could see himself discovering tobacco and potatoes, then at least he would know where to look for them when it came time for him to rediscover them! Mind you, Walter Raleigh might have preferred a crystal ball to peer into, then he would have known where to look for the head he was later to lose along with his marbles!

About a day and a half later, the *Golden Hind* dropped anchor just outside an island Drake was later to name Gulliver's Island. (Thankfully the ship dropped rather than weighed anchor, which at least saved a bit of time.) The island did have a name but it couldn't be seen on the antique globe as a high tide had covered it up. However, a lot of the islands in this part of the world hadn't been named as some weren't inhabited by man or beast.

Gulliver wondered if these natives were restless or if they'd gotten out of the wrong side of the hammock, never a good thing to do if the sea's on that wrong side and that sea contains sharks. Well, you know how quickly the tide rises, perhaps these natives were revolting, there was nothing worse than revolting natives, another one of Gulliver's grandfather's bad jokes!

Gulliver, giving Alice a run for her money, then wondered if he might meet a boy named Friday on this island, like Robinson Crusoe had done in the book of the same name written by Daniel Defoe. This book was one of Gulliver's favourite books, along with his father and his grandfather, a book he had read so many times his eyes had nearly rubbed the words from the page, his mother once teasingly said to him. Mind you, if this was simply just a vivid dream he was having and he was in his bed asleep and it was Sunday, then perhaps the boy would be called Sunday and not Friday!

## 11

## Never get on the Moon's Dark Side

No sooner had Drake's men rowed a long boat onto the island did they discover the leader of the tribe of natives was very well read. As a small aside, as Gulliver was in the long boat, he found himself whistling the tune *Row, row your boat gentle down the stream* before he even realized he was doing so. The leader of the natives had read Shakespeare, Plato, Newton and the Bible. He did tell Drake, however, that one year when the rains stayed mainly on the plains of Spain giving their tiny islands a wide berth, his people were so hungry they ate the pages of the books in their library, as the pages in the books were made of rice paper. The library was made out of bamboo with the roof being covered in the leaves and branches from several large palm trees, *surely this library must have more books in it than the one in Brixham in old Devon,* Gulliver thought dryly.

Apparently a Portuguese ship had sunk when it came in contact with a blue whale, whose internal sat nav had gone haywire in the shake-up of time by the gods. A great deal of the ship's library was washed up upon the shores of their island. However, the books that were illuminated in gold and were of more than 400 pages long sank like the proverbial anchor.

The chief said his people dried out the pages of the books they recovered from the wreck in the sun, like they often laid tobacco leaves in the sun to dry. Gulliver, being as inquisitive as any twelve-year-old boy, asked the chief what books he and his people had eaten. 'The boring ones first and the ones they had already read,' was the chief's logical reply. He did add, however, that nothing could bring him to eat the books of Shakespeare's plays and sonnets, he'd rather starve, he said, than eat the words of the great William Shakespeare, either that or he would be forced to eat one of his fellow natives! The chief then bellowed with laughter so loudly, it was as if they were standing next to Big Ben!

For Gulliver this conversation bought to mind the expression 'I'll make them eat their words', most writers would have said this at one time or another regarding the critics. However, not many of these critics lived on a small island in the middle of nowhere, where people got so hungry they had to eat other people's words.

Drake was a little disappointed there were no cannibals on this island as it would have made a great story for his journal and the ship's log. However, Gulliver was more than happy that he actually got the chance to write in his travelogue that there *weren't* any cannibals on this island! Gulliver found the natives of this island to be as friendly as any people he had ever come across, so friendly were they that Gulliver wondered if this island was called the Friendly Islands, however, it wasn't, so let that be an end to it!

This tiny South Pacific island in the middle of nowhere ticked all the right boxes as far as idyllic South Pacific islands went. The sea was crystal clear and as blue as the ocean, the sand underfoot was as white as the fur on the back of a polar bear, the palm trees, which were in great abundance, swayed gently in the warm Pacific breeze, and all the girls wore grass skirts and had colourful flowers draped around their necks. However, if cannibals had lived upon this island then one of those boxes would have had to have had an X placed within it, like an X marks the spot on one of Long John Silver's or Black Beard's treasure maps.

Gulliver wondered if this island had any national treasures like his world had Stephen Fry and Fiona Bruce.

As Gulliver and Drake sat around an open fire chewing the fat\tobacco with the chief and some of the island's people, they told the chief of the tribe of their quest to find The Last Bookshop in the World. The chief said there was a wise man named Solomon who lived on the dark side of the island who might be able to tell them where The Last Bookshop in the World resided. This man was a very wise man indeed and was filled with much knowledge the chief said, smiling warmly. Drake asked the chief how they would recognize this man when they saw him. The chief said when they saw him they'd recognize him. The chief wondered if Drake was one of these right Charlies he'd heard so much about and said as much; the chief, of course, was only yanking Drake's anchor. 'No,' the chief said picking a piece of boar meat out of his teeth, 'you can't miss this wise man because he has such a big head, which is how everybody on the island knows this man's head is full of knowledge.'

While Gulliver was on the island he had time to study the charts and the maps, some of which had been mapped by the Spanish. Gulliver wondered if the Spanish had been yanking Drake's anchor as one of the maps didn't look right, in fact, it looked as if it were a fake. Perhaps knowing the English revered their mapmakers, the Spanish had slipped Drake a forgery so he'd get lost at sea.

Gulliver had wondered why Drake had sailed around the Cape of Good Hope to get to the South Pacific, passing literally thousands of islands both large and small in the process. Some of these islands were so tiny that whichever part of the island you were on the sound of the waves was ever present. Gulliver thought Drake could just as easily have taken the short cut, sailing through the Mediterranean Sea, through the Suez Canal and into the Red Sea where they might possibly see a ship called *Jesus* that had run aground, and some sail fish. If they had taken this route they would have sailed past the Maldives and Sri Lanka, reaching the Equator and the Indian Ocean, passing Indonesia as they did so, where Gulliver might have seen the giant Komodo dragons, which to Gulliver's mind resembled miniature dinosaurs.

Whenever Gulliver had seen a Komodo dragon on the television, he heard the song *Puff the Magic Dragon* in his head. Now how did it go? 'Puff the magic dragon lives by the sea something, something, something, something in a land called Galilee'. Gulliver never could remember the words of the song. Words often disappeared from his head like the lost world where Komodo dragons lived. Or at lest they did according to old black and white films, that was before they invented CGI! And then finally on this imaginary voyage of discovery they would make for the Pacific Ocean where they would drop anchor onto the head of some poor unsuspecting sea monster who would probably have wished them further. If the anchor had landed upon the head of Puff the Magic Dragon, God knows where they would have ended up.

Gulliver knew old sailors threw sounding weights into the sea to see how deep the waters they were sailing in actual were. *If any of these weights landed upon Neptune's head they were bound to hear about it*, thought Gulliver dryly. One thing he wouldn't be if Neptune ended up with a sore head, dry that is! Later, as Gulliver and the *Golden Hind* sailed into oriental waters, he would pass what looked like lighthouses, which were in fact giant candle clocks. But here, once again like inpatient elves and hungry cannibals, we are rather getting ahead of ourselves!

So in other words, regarding Drake's navigational abilities, although the same words would probably have done just as well, they would be taking a short cut rather than going the long way round, like Magellan thought he was doing in his voyage of discovery. Later, Magellan's pals, including Elcano, would discover this wasn't a short cut but a long cut which led them to be the first to circumnavigate the world. If Drake had taken this imaginary route they might have had time to take a quick scout around the general area of Troy where they might have found the Lost City of Atlantis. However, to cut a long story short, or at least shorter, none of this happened!

The thing was, Gulliver may have been looking at the map through his twenty-first century eyes as he was seeing places that had yet to be discovered, and of course there were the shifting continents to take into consideration, which quite clearly he had not. (Gulliver never had been very good at mapping things in his head!)

To Gulliver the map might have looked ancient but to Drake it was the most up-to-date map that was available. However, saying all that, the map Drake was using was clearly a forgery so Gulliver accidentally on purpose dropped it in the sea until it turned to papier mâché. Or should I say, he made an origami boat of the map and sailed it out to sea, the origami boat which had slowly filled with water before becoming junk mail! Sorry, that was another nautical jest not worth the paper it was written upon!

Talking about continents shifting or drifting or whatever they did, Gulliver often saw continents in the sky drifting around, or should I say clouds that looked like continents or countries floating around in the vast blue yonder. Gulliver once saw a cloud in the sky that to him resembled the British Isles, which was to his left while another cloud to his right looked remarkably like Italy with the Island of Capri floating just below it. And slap bang in the middle of these two cloud islands he saw the continent of Africa before all three clouds drifted off some place else, or with a little bit of help from Mother Nature, magically transformed themselves into something entirely different. There were definitely times when Gulliver's judgment was clouded and this was probably one of them!

This still left an authentic Spanish map, although being in Spanish as it was it wasn't always easy to understand. Gulliver had done O level Spanish at night school so knew a smattering of the language, he also knew Latin, which was useful being an antique dealer, especially when it came to deciphering old maps. He also knew the lost language of Esperanto, which nowadays was no good to man or beast!

After some rest, which was fairly lengthy as everybody

aboard the *Golden Hind* was tuckered out, they then trekked to the dark side of the island.

'So why do you think they call it the dark side of the island?' Old Father Time asked Gulliver as they climbed the mountainous path, which in truth was a little hot underfoot.

'Because that side of the island is thick with undergrowth and trees which are huddled together to keep warm!' said Alice making some more sense while throwing in a little humour for good measure. How Alice would have loved to read the Alice chronicles, Gulliver thought, although *Gulliver's Travels* might sail right over her head what with it being somewhat less than compendious in most of the places Gulliver travels on the map.

'Do you need me to draw you a map?' Gulliver could hear Jonathan Swift say slightly irritably.

'Yes, if you wouldn't mind,' Gulliver said politely as this imaginary conversation ended rather swiftly!

'Maybe the dark side of the island is full of devil worshippers!' Drake said with a straight face.

'Or because they haven't paid their electricity bill!' said Gulliver with a face that was the polar opposite to Francis Drake's.

Everybody was just about to say, 'Electricity? What's electricity when it's at home!?' when they were distracted by something more pressing.

'Are your feet hot?' Old Father Time asked Alice as she wiped the sweat off her brow.

'Yes, they are a bit, but then again I put that down to the fact that I've been using them to walk upon,' Alice said making a lot of sense.

'Rambling!' Drake muttered as he stopped to gather his breath.

'Pardon me!' Alice said abruptly.

'You're pardoned,' Drake said sounding like Queen Elizabeth I as he rubbed his beard with great gusto. No doubt one of Old Father Time's fleas had jumped overboard and had landed on Drake's ample chin.

'I'm not rambling, I'm talking perfect sense,' Alice said scowling, hands on hip as she stared daggers in Drake's direction as she threw her toys out of the perambulator.

'No, you misunderstand me, child I didn't mean *you're* rambling I meant *we're* rambling, as in we're walking, and walking makes the feet hot, especially in a warm climate.

'Oh!' said Alice as she looked at her shoes to see if they needed a good shoe-shine boy to give them a good polish, which they did.

Gulliver then stopped dead in his tracks as several wild animals who were wild about something or other, came rushing past him in somewhat of a hurry. Then large flocks of birds flew overhead making what can best be described as a hullabaloo, the sort of yahoo the Mugwumps in the Houses of Parliament make at feeding time!

'Duck!' Gulliver said as a big bird nearly took his head off and Alice's along with it.

*Here we go again,* Alice thought irritably as she heard the word duck and looked up.

'It wasn't, you know!' Alice said as she stood up and brushed the hair out of her eyes.

'What wasn't?' Gulliver enquired in Alice's general direction.

'It wasn't a duck, it was an albatross. Did you know the albatross is said to be an unlucky bird?' Alice went on in Alice-like fashion.

'Are you sure it wasn't a dodo?' Drake said as the bird continued to fly off the handle.

'Never mind the albatross being unlucky, we were lucky it didn't take our heads clean off, did you see the size of it!?' Gulliver said looking around him to see if any other birds were heading in his direction.

It was round about this time in the land that time forgot, or forgot time, whichever you prefer, that Gulliver had a bad feeling in the pit of his stomach, although it could just have easily have been a bad case of indigestion!

'This mountain we're climbing, did the chief tell you anything particular about it?' Gulliver said looking towards Drake as a frown appeared upon his brow.

'What in particular did you want to know about it?' Drake said raising his eyebrows.

'Well, you know, something like, the mountain in question is an extinct volcano, that's if you take out the word 'extinct', and leave the word 'volcano' in!' Gulliver said sarcastically, reverting to the age when men get a bad case of the grumps. Here Gulliver wished he had an iPad surgically attached to his arm like some of the people of his world appeared to have and then he could have Googled this information. Gulliver didn't own an iPad or a computer so had to use the steam-powered search engine in his head, or the umpteen volumes of the *Encyclopedia Britannica* he had sitting at home upon his bookshelf and which just for the record was made on the continent. Gulliver didn't hold with the World Wide Web as there were too many trolls lurking there who could definitely not be said to be wizards with words!

'Volcano!' Old Father Time said as a look of panic appeared on his face. It's amazing how powerful one word can be when it's used at the right time with the right tone attached to it.

Gulliver just hoped Alice didn't think this was the right time to wheel out the word Wow!

'It's not is it, a volcano that is?!' Alice said deciding this wasn't the right time to use her favourite word.

'Well, you see that fast-moving carpet of red and gold that's heading towards us at an alarming rate of knots? Well, I think that's what they call molten lava and I'm as sure as dodo eggs are dodo eggs that molten lava comes out of a live volcano! Molten lava by and large doesn't come flowing out of an extinct volcano. Mind you, this is a parallel world so perhaps it does!' Gulliver said, rambling.

'What's a parallel world?' Drake said with a puzzled expression on his face.

'I wouldn't worry about it,' Old Father Time said as he turned around to start running for his life, 'on the other hand this volcano, which has now become quite active considering its considerable age, *is* something to worry about!'

Gulliver thought that this wasn't the time or the place to be sharing his knowledge of volcanoes in that they were hot enough to melt gold and, he didn't think it was worth interrupting Old Father Time when he was in mid flow, although he would quite happily have interrupted the erupting volcano in mid flow, given half a chance. However, that quite clearly was wishful thinking so instead Gulliver chose a word from the Oxford English Dictionary that was short and to the point.

'RUN!' Gulliver said without expanding upon it further.

'RUN?' Alice, Old Father Time and Drake said in perfect unison as they looked at Gulliver in horror. Beagle also barked something out which sounded remarkably like 'RUN?' It seemed in this case that Gulliver's friends were all on the same page of the dictionary as he was.

'Yes, RUN!' Gulliver repeated the word as a wild river of red hot lava headed towards them. The reason Gulliver had to repeat the word 'run' was probably because for a split second they had all become frozen to the spot in fear, even though that split second no longer existed in the real sense of the word. As a child Gulliver had always wondered how many times you could split a second before it no longer existed, as he had often done regarding the splitting of the atom. Time was a river and as such the past, the present and the future never actually existed in real time, which was a hard concept to grasp, as was time, as like water and like sand it just slipped through your hands. So although Einstein may or may not have been right about the speed of light, he was right about time being the biggest illusion of them all, or at least Gulliver thought so. That was, of course, until the boffins invented a time machine and then everybody would say, 'Einstein was no Einstein!'

For the time being, that's enough about the vagaries of time so let's get back to the present…

Now the good thing about mountains, apart from the fact that most of them aren't active volcanoes, is that it is easier to run down them than run up them. And it's just an added bonus that you can do this running faster when going down them as you're being chased by a river of hot molten larva. When the old adrenalin kicks in you can usually manage to get up a fair head of steam, well, as long as the river of hot molten lava doesn't outrun you!

Now the general rule of Tom Thumb when trying to avoid being mummified in molten ash is, not only to run in the opposite direction of the river of molten lava, standard procedure in situations such as these, but also to run towards water, the ocean in this case. Lava doesn't like water and once it comes in contact with it, it tends to run out of steam, well, it does and it doesn't (think about it, but not for too long as we haven't got time, because in this world there isn't any!)

So Gulliver, being the seasoned traveller he was and fortuitously having recently read *The Idiot's Guide to Outrunning a Volcano*, did just that, as everybody followed his lead. Twenty minutes later Gulliver, Drake, Alice, Old Father Time, Beagle, the chief and over a hundred of the population of the island were now standing knee deep in the ocean twiddling their thumbs. The lava had attempted to follow them into the water but after dipping its toes into the water decided better of it. Now Gulliver had always wanted to be a trailblazer and not a follower, however, this wasn't quite what he had in mind when that particular thought first made itself known to him!

'So now what?' Gulliver said to the chief as they both stood in the ocean and as ash fell from the sky like snow. Gulliver felt he was in a situation that could definitely be said to be between a coral and a hard place. The molten lava was still letting off steam in front of them as the chief, who had previously been bent double stood to his full height, which was about the size of a Shetland pony.

'Well, we just have to wait until the lava cools down,' the chief said coolly as if this was an everyday event, which it wasn't.

'And how long will that take?' said Gulliver as he watched several large colourful fish nip at his toes.

'How long's a piece of fishing line? To be honest, your guess is as good as mine. The last time the volcano erupted was a hundred years ago?' said the chief shrugging his shoulders.

To be honest, Gulliver and his friends were just lucky this island wasn't full of cannibals otherwise they might well have seen this as a sign from the gods for a good fry up! The good thing was that since the gods had deserted this world for sunnier climes, the natives no longer felt they had to please them with human sacrifices to make sure the harvests were plentiful and the weather was benign. Gulliver was extremely grateful to the gods for their sudden disappearing act for it meant he wouldn't end up on a plate next to a half-cooked potato! Mind you, if it had of happened, his subconscious told him it would serve him right for going off on a half-baked quest in a land he knew little about. And what sort of quest was it anyway, looking for a mythical bookshop? Why not go on a quest for hidden treasure, or thinking outside the old box, what about a quest to find Pandora's Box? Now that would be a quest worth risking life and limb for. Life and limb, who on earth did he imagine he was? Long John Silver the pirate with one leg!

Although Gulliver wasn't altogether happy to be chased by a river of molten lava, he knew enough about the history of earth to know that if it wasn't for the magma and lava inside the planet's core, man might not have even swum out of the primordial soup. For at one stage in the earth's development it was nothing but a large snowball and it took the magma and lava to thaw it out. Gulliver also knew that by using neon scanners and computers, it made predicting volcanic eruptions possible, as could observing increased $CO_2$ levels in volcanoes.

Mind you, he didn't want to bore the chief to tears and perhaps the chief already knew how the earth worked, after all he wasn't a right Charlie, that and he didn't want to blow the chief's mind with talk of computer technology, that and computers were like a different world to him, that and... no, that was it! Since Gulliver had discovered the Discovery Channel he was a mine of both useful and useless information. Gulliver wondered if this antique globe atlas was hollow like the supposed Hollow Earth Theory which stated that the earth was… HOLLOW!! He also wondered if this earth globe had a meridian arm like on the toy atlas globe he had sitting on his Victorian cabinet of curiosity at home, or was it like the antique globes which were encased inside what appeared to be a box or a table? And were the poles magnetic like on his earth? Well, a globe was made out of metal so probably, although the words 'probably not' could just as easily have fitted into this line, a line which at a later time and date Gulliver was to write in his travelogue. One had to wonder why Gulliver hadn't wondered how it was even possible that a volcano had sprung up on a giant antique globe! Well, for anybody curious as to how, then wonder no more, for like an American B-movie title 'it came from outer space', like the giant meteor that wiped out the dinosaurs and flattened the forest in Russia known as the 'Tungsted Event', or something along those rough lines!

Drake suggested that instead of everybody standing in the ocean like lemons freezing their whatsits off, how would they like to join him on the *Golden Hind* for a right royal knees up at Queen Elizabeth I's expense? As she, along with Sir Christopher Hatton was funding this voyage. All who were freezing their whatsits off unanimously decided this was a good idea and it beat having their toes nipped by large colourful fish, that obviously hadn't eaten for a week or more. Still, at least the fish weren't piranha, Drake joked. Later still, Drake told Gulliver that he was used to dealing with mountainous waves and winds that tore the sails asunder and snapped the masts of his ships in two like dry twigs, but dealing with erupting mountains was a whole new experience for him. But Drake liked new experiences, which is probably why he was always sailing off to here, there and everywhere at a drop of a navy admiral's hat. Gulliver wondered if there was a place called Here or There or Everywhere for that matter, or if they were just metaphorical lands like the Middle of Nowhere. In this world, Gulliver mused, there probably was a place called the Middle of Nowhere, which he found amusing even if everybody else thought he was one ship short of an anchor!

Drake did say that he had experienced an earthquake in South America which had a most peculiar effect upon the tide, which rose up the beach quickly to a high-water mark, but not in great waves as one might have expected, almost as if someone had speeded up time. And then just as quickly, the tides returned to their normal level where they had been before the earthquake had happened. Drake thought it might be the gods stirring things up again, although it could just as easily have been Mother Nature, Old Father Time said on overhearing the conversation.

Later, Gulliver introduced everybody to the game of charades which brought much frivolity and laughter and sometimes puzzled expressions to the natives, and the ship's crew for that matter. Never more so than when Gulliver tried to do a mime of the film *Jaws* by acting out the whole thing, which he did by opening and closing his arms in a jaw-like motion. It wasn't that the ship's crew and the natives couldn't guess that he was portraying a shark, although it could just as easily have been a crocodile, no, it was that the film hadn't been made yet, or the cinema to show it in either! Most of the charades performed were taken from books like *Moby Dick* or were stories out of the Bible, or in the chief's case

Shakespeare's plays or Greek tragedies, which in truth weren't a barrel of laughs.

Gulliver sometimes forgot he wasn't in his own world and sometimes he forgot there was no time to remember or forget, or to forget to remember, or remember to forget. After that night, Gulliver wrote this in his travelogue: 'Perhaps soon I will become so immersed in this world and its culture that I will completely forget my own world, although somehow I doubt that.' He also wrote the following: 'It has always annoyed me that in my own world the clocks go forward and back twice a year disturbing everybody's body clocks in the process, as most people neither wish to gain nor lose an hour, apart from the odd farmer in the far reaches of Scotland. At least in this world the clocks stay constant, although it is true, not having any time to move forward or back does tend to help in this respect. Surely it is just a matter of time before the clocks in my time are left as they are. After which time people will shout out from the very rooftop of the Greenwich Royal Observatory, 'About time too!' It did occur to Gulliver after he read this passage back that he must be the most irritable and cynical twelve-year-old boy that has ever lived in any world, be it parallel or otherwise! Perhaps he needed to take a leaf out of Old Father Time's and Neptune's book and just let things wash over him.

Many a time in this world people had been taken aback by things that had come out of his mouth, which didn't seem as if they should have come out of the mouth of a boy his age. However, the more time people spent around Gulliver, the more time they were given to thinking he was just old before his time, like the children at his school had done when they found out that he watched antique programmes on television and was a member of the Flat Earth Society.

Gulliver had read several books on travel in his thirty-five years on this planet and most of them he found ideal late-night reading matter as they often sent him off to sleep. Gulliver was forever jumping large passages of the book or speed reading it. Although funnily enough, whenever he came to a bit about the Northwest Passage he would take his time as this passage had always held a strange fascination for him. To his mind, most of these travelogues contained far, far too much detail. Why spoil a good story, or even a bad one for that matter, with details? Who cared about how wide and high the tree was? Surely it was enough that the tree was there without giving minute descriptions on the bark, the colour of the leaves, the insects which lived on it, the fact that when it was cut down it would be made into a book, etc. etc. etc. blah, blah, blah. Nobody wanted to read about the etc. or the blahs. Journeys should be exciting, full of danger, drama and romance. The etc. and the blahs were all fine and dandy if you were an insomniac trying to lull yourself off to sleep but if you weren't, they were no good to man, beast, beauty and the beast, or beauty and the geek for that matter! Gulliver loved Charles Darwin and his *Origin* book but the descriptive prose of his travels in minute prosaic detail left a lot to be desired at times.

Gulliver was determined to keep the descriptive prose in his travelogue to a bare minimum, the story was all that mattered. The only exception he would make would be for humour, for a travelogue must have humour and with that Gulliver logged off!

That night everybody slept like a log, some of the more hard-headed of the islanders even used a log as a pillow, although those logs were made of soft wood. Most of the natives were more than happy to sleep on the deck of the *Golden Hind* underneath the stars.

Three days later when the island had cooled sufficiently, which was a lot quicker than the earth in Gulliver's world had done millions of years earlier, everybody traipsed back to the island through the waves with heads as sore as rutting stags on a hen night. Three days solid partying will do that to one's head. Gulliver soon found out he did not have hollow legs, although he most certainly did have a sore head. Gulliver never had been able to hold his liquor, although most ship's boys could and often had to hold liquor being seen as glorified waiters to the senior sailors onboard the ships.

Some of the islanders had gone back early as one of the island traditions was walking across hot coals and, as such the soles of most of the islanders' feet resembled galvanized rubber due to this practice. Drake was to make the comment, 'No sense no feeling,' although in a parallel world that was probably, no feeling no sense!

The chief said he was as sure as albatross eggs were albatross eggs that the volcano had let off enough steam, and probably wouldn't let off any more for another hundred years. Gulliver was a little wary of the word 'probably' because it wasn't the word 'definitely', still, it would just have to do. Gulliver was as determined as ever to climb the volcano and get to the dark side of the island where he could meet the wise man with the head full of knowledge.

Later, minus the time, Gulliver and his fellow adventurers had scaled the volcano and had reached the dark side of the island. By now the lava and ash was cool enough to walk upon, although it did make the climb more treacherous, especially for Old Father Time, who wasn't exactly in the first flush of youth, the old in his name rather gave the game away on that score.

'How are you feeling?' Gulliver asked Old Father

Time, who looked for all the world like he was about to meet his maker. 'Old!' Old Father Time said managing a semblance of a smile as he blew out his cheeks, which looked redder than Father Christmas's outfit.

'We should probably rest here,' Gulliver said looking around him at his fellow travellers, who by now were all weary. Old Father Time would have been happier to have heard the word 'definitely', we will 'definitely' rest here. But he'd just have to make do with the word 'probably' for the time being.

This side of the island was dark and why this surprised Gulliver even he wasn't sure, especially as the chief had told everybody that this side of the island was called the dark side of the island. It was probably because he thought the chief was being metaphorical and not literal, although it appeared he was being literal for the island was as dark as the bottom of the ocean. Now if it had been night time, then that was only to be expected, but it wasn't night time and so it wasn't to be expected, which meant it was unexpected (even bearing in mind the chief had called this part of the island the dark side). To Gulliver's mind this part of the island was like the dark side of the moon.

'How are we going to see where we are going?' Alice said squinting to see Gulliver's face in the darkness.

'Why don't we find some thick tree branches and then find some lava that's still warm, which should be hot enough to light the branches and we can use them as torches?' Old Father Time said sensibly. Gulliver couldn't see OFT'S face, he could only hear his voice but he agreed with the voice wholeheartedly.

'Capital notion,' Gulliver said, sounding like a nineteenth century gentleman in a swanky London club, probably the Reform Club where Phileas Fogg and his manservant Passepartout arrived after completing their epic round-the-world voyage in eighty days.

So that's what they did and soon the dark side of the mountain was flooded with light and now no longer resembled the dark side of the moon but resembled a moon that was of the gibbous variety. The word 'flooded' reminded Gulliver of a passage from the Bible and one thing Gulliver didn't want was to be caught in a flash flood, not after yesterday's events, although it was hardly an event, more like a nightmare. An event was something exciting, something you looked forward to. Yesterday was something he wanted to forget about and as quickly as possible, although not before he wrote it in his travelogue for once again it made a capital story. However, in truth this yesterday wasn't yesterday but the day before the day before yesterday, as when this Biblical-like event happened, when fire rained down from the heavens above, it wasn't a Sunday! No, this yesterday, when all Gulliver's troubles were far away, was a metaphorical yesterday, as to Gulliver's mind 'yesterday' was any day that had come and gone and any day that wasn't either 'today' or 'tomorrow'. After that descriptive passage, the expression as clear as mud springs to mind!

Once again this was all fine and dandy unless some boffin egghead like Archimedes, Leonardo Da Vinci, Sir Isaac Newton, Galileo or Pythagoras invented a time machine. You do the math and good luck to you because I have a feeling you're going to need it!

A travelogue was only a good read if the journey was filled with excitement and wonder and being chased by a river of molten lava into the ocean was just such a story. At the time he might not have thought so, but looking back it's just what his travelogue needed to liven it up. The balloon crashing into the sea was also a good story, as was ending up in a cave with his dog and then finding the fountain of youth. And then there was The Pandemonium Emporium, meeting Old Father Time and visiting the Antiquarium where the Loch Ness monster and the kraken were now sleeping like babies, or at least he hoped they were and nobody had released them into the seas to join the other sea monsters that were drawn upon Drake's sea charts and maps. Yes, his little travelogue wasn't a bad read, it still needed more stories, more close shaves, but it wasn't half bad; the grammar left a lot to be desired, as did some of the writing, but after all, he was a dyslexic twelve-year-old boy. Now whether logically it being not half bad meant it wasn't half good, or it was only half good while the other half was bad, Gulliver wasn't too sure, and to be honest he was too tired to care.

After a camp fire was built and food was passed round, mainly coconuts and bread fruit, everybody, now close to exhaustion, fell asleep. The evening passed followed by the night, which was full of disquieting noises, but nobody heard them as they were all dead to the world, which is what they might have been yesterday if the gods had still been around playing silly beggars!

The morning came, although you would have been hard pressed to tell the difference from the night, although if you were press-ganged into it, like some of the crew of the *Golden Hind* had been at one time or another, you would probably have said the morning was a little lighter than the night had been. Everybody had a good hearty breakfast, albeit a little boring, breadfruit washed down with coconut juice, and certainly not a patch on the continental breakfasts Hans Christian Andersen had enjoyed in his travels to such far-flung places as Constantinople and Mesopotamia. The coconuts were kindly cracked open for them by the gargantuan robber crabs, which Gulliver thought resembled giant nutcrackers. Some of these creatures grew up to four meters in length, with legs up to a meter long. In a nutshell, the robber crabs had been given a taste of their own medicine, for as they broke the coconuts up with their giant grabbing arms, some of the braver sailors aboard the *Golden Hind* robbed their prized possessions from right under their very noses. Gulliver wasn't even sure if robber crabs had noses, but once again you get the continental drift, which was exactly what Gulliver wrote in his travelogue!

After breakfast, everybody set off on their journey of several lifetimes, minus the time, in good spirits to find the man with the knowledge buried in his head like treasure. Gulliver, Drake and several sailors each held a lit branch of a tree to light their way.

After walking through a forest of palm trees, which thankfully had large lit pumpkins sitting in between the branches (which meant they could see the wood for the trees), they found the wise man named Solomon with the big head full of knowledge. The chief had been right, Solomon did have an awfully big head, which looked remarkably like a pumpkin. In fact, if you believed him you would have taken him for a genius. Solomon listened intently to Gulliver's tale up to this point in the time that no longer existed, Solomon said time never had existed on this part of the island as it was like a black hole in space, which sucked up everything that came within spitting distance of it, including time.

Solomon, having pondered on Gulliver's quest, said, 'It's written in the stars.' Gulliver's whole body literally shrank in disappointment like a tortoise's head shrank into its shell in times of danger. This man wasn't as wise as he had been led to believe by the big chief, who was tiny, as this was quite obviously mumbo jumbo of the highest order.

That was until Alice said, 'Look, look at the stars!' and sure enough it *was* written in the stars. The stars in the heavens had rearranged themselves into words and the words said, 'The place you seek is to be found somewhere bleak,' then the stars disassembled themselves.

'Can you believe your own eyes?' Old Father Time said with a look of wonderment upon his face. 'I'm not sure a man of my advancing years can, but I'm sure you young pups can!'

'It's written in the stars and that's good enough for me, after all, the stars have never let me down on my journeys before,' Drake said as he put his hand on Old Father Time's shoulder as if to say, 'Your eyes weren't playing tricks upon you, old man.'

Alice was inclined to think this was all black magic and Solomon was some kind of witch doctor. Gulliver was inclined not to believe in black magic, rather to believe that someone had spiked their coconut juice with hallucinogenic, mind-altering drugs, albeit of the natural variety, like magic mushrooms.

Gulliver thought some of the doctors in his world were nothing more than better-dressed witch doctors, however, both kept their council.

'Well, bleak suggests somewhere cold and desolate,' Gulliver said as the wheels and cogs of his mind turned and whirled into action, like the internal workings of a clock.

'What about the North or the South Pole, they're both pretty bleak?!' Old Father Time said looking at Gulliver.

'That's it, the snow domes!' Gulliver said, sounding like Archimedes again.

'You mean The Last Bookshop in the World is in the North or the South Pole? I don't suppose they do much business there!' Alice said disbelievingly.

'I'm not sure the stars were saying the bookshop resides there but it might well be where we will find our next clue,' Gulliver said thoughtfully.

'I think you might be right, my boy,' Old Father Time said, agreeing with Gulliver.

'I hope we're not reading too much into these stars, like astrologers do in my world,' Gulliver said thinking out loud, which produced a few puzzled expressions.

'Well, we'd better not waste any more time hypothesizing. We'd better get back to the *Golden Hind* and sail for the Arctic Circle, otherwise the old girl will think we've forgotten about her,' Drake said good humouredly, referring to his ship once again as a lady, as was the custom for seafarers to do, probably to get Lady Luck on their side Gulliver surmised.

'Or Antarctica?' said Gulliver, adding a note of caution.

'Good point, Gulliver,' Drake said nodding his head. 'We'll consult the charts, the maps and the stars, and I'll get the compendium out of mothballs, the one the clockmaker, Humphrey Cole, was kind enough to make for me, and then we'll toss a coin!' Drake said laughing his pantaloons off. Although he didn't say as much, Drake quite clearly had a mind to think that Solomon had just sold them the snow job to end all snow jobs!

Gulliver was amazed to see Cole's astronomical compendium dial with its five gilt-brass leaves, which incorporated a compass, a calendar and a geometric square, which when aligned with the lunar and the solar dials, enabled Drake to calculate the phases of the moon. This fantastical compendium, a marvel of ancient engineering, enabled Francis Drake to become a master of both time and tide. Okay, so this wasn't quite on a par with Archimedes' Antykythera Mechanism but it wasn't far off. Humphrey Cole had made this device on the bequest of Queen Elizabeth I, and it was now sitting in the Greenwich Maritime Museum in Gulliver's time, although nobody wanted to pin their colours to the mast, so to speak, regarding the ownership of this compendium. However, Gulliver certainly thought this came under the heading of a good story if nothing else.

'How could one object be in two places at one time?' Gulliver said under his breath when Drake showed him the compendium before adding, 'Where's a quantum scientist when you need one!?'

It was the old Schrodinger's cat in the box theory, which stated that a cat in a box could be both alive and dead at the same time. Gulliver wondered if this cat in the box belonged to Pandora and if it did, he was rather grateful that he wasn't going on a quest to find Pandora's Box! Gulliver then recalled Schwarzschild's 'Magic Sphere' theory, and a magic sphere was something this world could well be described as, in fact, that was exactly what he wrote in his travelogue. Then Gulliver stopped wondering as he realized he was blinding himself with science again and it was giving him a blinding headache!

Now, going down the mountainous volcano should have been relatively easy but due to the large amount of ash that now littered the mountain, it was anything but. In fact, it was harder going down than coming up, of course this time they weren't being chased by a river of molten lava. Old Father Time said it was all in the mind, although

Alice, Gulliver and Beagle weren't convinced, as far as they were concerned it was all in the legs. It appeared to Gulliver as if they still had their sea legs on and that the land they were walking upon was like the shifting sands of the desert, or the shifting sands of time. With every step they took, they sunk down to their knees until they sank down to their ankles until they brushed the ash aside as if it were nothing more than a slight smattering of snow. Eventually they reached the beach and collapsed in a heap.

The beach looked like every beach should on a tropical island paradise, however the beach wasn't covered in sand but white ash. After the search party had recovered, Drake, Gulliver, Alice and Old Father Time bid a fond farewell to the native people promising one day they would return with books aplenty. The chief said he would be most appreciative if when they did return they could bring him any of Shakespeare's new works. Drake said he promised he would and he would make sure they were written upon rice paper, just in case food supplies ran low. Gulliver wasn't sure if he'd ever be in this part of the world again so he gave the chief a long hug, almost as if he were his long lost son. However, Gulliver wasn't the chief's long lost son, that really would have been some story to write home about, but Gulliver hadn't the time to write home about it, that and he didn't think his letter would ever reach home, especially if it was a message in a bottle.

The chief and his people had fashioned a canoe out of bamboo and a palm tree and gave it to Drake as a gift and as a mark of the high esteem they held both him and the Queen of Eng Land, as the chief so charmingly called England. However, some people who were still a little old fashioned in their ways, mostly the Elizabethans, still called England by its old name of Albion.

The chief did leave Gulliver with one piece of homespun philosophy, saying that the real treasures were to be found close to home and not in some treasure chest in some far-flung distant land. Gulliver took this advice on board, although he was standing on the shore at the time. Although later he did take this advice on board, onboard the *Golden Hind* where he shared it with Alice and the coxswain, who simply just rolled their eyes to the heavens!

The chief also told Gulliver that not all that glittered was gold; this Gulliver already knew because the snow dome that sat on his dressing room table at home in Brixham in 2013 was full of silver glitter, but he thanked him for the advice all the same.

As the *Golden Hind* sailed off into the sunset, its keel carving its way through the pristine waters of the South Pacific, the native people waved until the ship was the size of a dot on the letter i upon the horizon. Gulliver and his companions waved back until the island was just the size of a starfish and then little more than a grain of sand. Gulliver was sad to leave the islands which Drake had told him he'd named after him. Solomon was none too happy about the name change as in his mind the islands were called the Solomon Islands. But the chief liked the sound of Gulliver's Island and liked it even more when Drake said the islands were now a part of the British Empire and, as part of this package, they were ruled over by Queen Elizabeth I. To the chief's mind, this gave his island great kudos so he told Solomon he could like it or lump it because the name change stood. When the chief told Solomon this, the expression 'his face was a picture' was an apt one indeed. The picture Solomon's face most resembled at the time was of an angry sea, possibly the painting Turner did after being strapped to the mast of a ship in a storm.

Solomon was dark on the chief for quite some time to come but as he lived on the dark side of the island it didn't seem to matter, or at least it didn't to anybody but Solomon, who put a death curse on the chief. This curse was for the chief to be swallowed by a giant Solomon fish, which according to legend could grow to the size of a python and had a mouth as wide as a cave. However, these fish normally resided in the Zambezi River so unless their internal sat nav was all at sea there wasn't much chance of this happening. Having said that, what with the shifting sands in this world, nobody could be 100% sure of this fact. The chief died, but only after the passing of a thousand full moons, which meant he died a very, very old man. Ironically, Solomon died when the next full moon passed, this unfortunate incident happened when a female albatross mistook his head for one of her eggs and sat on it while he was asleep, suffocating him. Well, it was dark and he was as bald as a bald eagle! This meant all the wisdom in his head was lost, like Atlantis, but as they say, that's life. It appears that the albatross suffers from Jonah and the whale syndrome in that they are unlucky, it seems at least one myth was true!

As the *Golden Hind* left Gulliver's Island behind them in their wake, a rainbow appeared over the ship, although of course it wasn't over the ship, it being an optical illusion. Gulliver then noticed that Drake was dressed as Isambard Kingdom Brunel, stove-pipe hat and all, and Brunel, the ship's master, was dressed in Drake's attire, frilly shirt, leather thigh-length boots and pantaloons worn on the outside that were starched within an inch of their life. Was this just an optical illusion or had both men got up on the wrong side of the hammock!? In this world it appeared one could never be quite sure what was and what wasn't an optical illusion! However, one could be quite sure, the rainbow was smiling down upon the *Golden Hind* because its arc was upturned. In this upside down world and being in the southern hemisphere, this was once again only to be expected. Perhaps if Gulliver saw a straight rainbow he might have been more surprised, give it time!

Sir Isaac Newton knew all about colour, light and prisms. This discovery, along with his three laws of motion, was for him the gold at the end of the rainbow. However, Newton, being a keen alchemist, was still determined to find a way of turning base metals into gold. Gulliver wondered if in this world he had succeeded? Did the rainbow appear inside or outside the ship in the bottle? I hear the enquiring scientific mind ask. In truth I couldn't possibly say, other than to say that regarding this question, refer the prism!

Later that night, Gulliver had a nightmare where he was being chased by a tall man who had a pumpkin for a head and whose eyes were ablaze with anger, although this man was carrying his own head! And if that wasn't bad enough, he was joined by another man who was made of red hot molten lava and who appeared to want to give the bogeyman a run for his money!

## 12

# A Snow Job of the Wizarding Variety

The *Golden Hind* now journeyed south towards the Artic, passing what Gulliver knew as Japan and Drake knew as the Land of the Rising Sun, here they must be careful not to run into the mythical sea dragon or they would be sunk. Drake showed Gulliver the old map, or at least it looked old to Gulliver's eyes, though according to Drake it was the most up-to-date chart available to him. Drawn upon this map Gulliver could quite clearly sea a large, coiled sea dragon breathing fire, swimming just off the coast of Japan. If they ran into the giant sea monster they really were sunk! It was here that the *Golden Hind* passed a giant oriental candle clock encased inside what looked like the glass of a lantern clock which had been converted into a lighthouse. It was also here that the ship got caught in a freak lightning storm and having left the safety of the ship\canoe in the bottle, and not yet being under the protection of the glass snow dome in the North Pole, it seemed to the crew that all hell was breaking loose. Drake wrote in his ship's log: More fun and games – maybe the gods have deserted us for a desert island in the cosmological oceans, but the devil has obviously stayed and is having fun at our expense! Having said that, the devil normally works down below stoking the furnace, although as they were not a million miles from New Holland (Australia), which Drake knew as the Land of the Giant Kangaroo, perhaps this was the work of the Tasmanian devil. In this upside down, topsy-turvy world, that was more than likely!

The main mast was damaged, as were several sails, Old Father Time's beard was partly singed and Hamish, otherwise known as 'the big man', caught a lightning bolt in his hand and threw it back in the direction from whence it came. Drake may have been talking metaphorically on that last one, although if you had ever stood in Hamish's shadow you would probably think not.

Gulliver and Alice had somehow managed to sleep through the whole thing, although they both had similar nightmares of the gods taking lightning bolts from their quivers, placing them in their bows and firing them in the direction of the *Golden Hind*. Gulliver saw several bolts of lightning shooting through the air ablaze, which struck the water all about the ship, causing huge plumes of steam to rise like geezers. In Alice's nightmare a lightning bolt hit a small island setting the whole thing into a blazing inferno in seconds.

After this little incident, the *Golden Hind* found a deserted desert island and stayed in the relative safety of the sheltered harbour. Here they repaired the damage to the masts and sails, gathering some more bread fruit and coconuts before continuing on with their voyage into the unknown. At some unknown time later, they were to run into a steamer, literally, although this steamer was broken down. Here they picked up a chap named Brunel, who had steam coming out of his ears as his crew appeared to have deserted him for the same deserted desert island that Drake had found. Now you may well have heard of Brunel, Gulliver certainly had, but that's another story we will save for a little later.

Leaving the Tropic of Cancer behind them and with a new shipmate aboard, they sailed into the Bering Sea, passing through what Gulliver knew to be the International Date Line. This line was drawn on the maps in Gulliver's world, however, this line was something Drake had not the foggiest notion about. In this world Gulliver was slightly surprised not to see this line written in the sand, for if it had of been then he would have known where the expression 'drawing a line in the sand' had come from.

Gulliver was aware that there was an imaginary line between the North and South Poles called the equator, and by all accounts, according to Old Father Time, this was then written upon the antique globe upon which they were now sailing. Of course, it had been written on the globe by the gods before the comets hit the earth bringing water with them, which eventually became the oceans and the seas. So this line was only visible to divers and creatures that inhabited the oceans as it was written upon the ocean floor.

Funnily enough, due to some fog, which literally came out of nowhere, it was in the Bering Sea that Drake temporarily lost his bearings. This meant the charts, compasses and sextants went out of the window, although thankfully for the crew of the *Hind* not literally. This unexpected turn of events meant Drake went back to the tried and trusted method of all good seafarers and trusted to Lady Luck.

Drake tossed his golden ducat and it landed head side up, that head thankfully being Queen Elizabeth I and not Queen Victoria, as she was often amused, unlike Queen Victoria who wasn't! This Drake was sure was an omen, a sign that they were in Lady Luck's goods books. It also meant they would find The Last Bookshop in the World and that Queen Elizabeth I would let him keep his head, unlike his friend Walter Raleigh, using her sword to knight him rather than to remove his head with it, hopefully!

Gulliver hoped this omen was indeed of the good variety and the *Golden Hind* didn't get hit by an iceberg like *RMS Titanic* and sink, or get trapped in the ice and crushed like a walnut in a nutcracker. Mind you, he wasn't sure whether *Royal Mail Steamer Titanic* had even been built yet or as time had stopped, if it would ever be built. Perhaps if things were preordained, not even time would stop this happening.

Gulliver wrote in his travelogue that it was a pity they hadn't invented a sat nav for the sea in Drake's time, although technically they weren't in Drakes time as there was no time to be in. The closest thing they had to a satellite navigation system in this world was Coles' compendium.

An iceberg was spotted from the crow's nest so Drake knew they were now in the Artic Ocean, although the extreme cold told most of the crew aboard that this was indeed the case. Drake said that at this point he guesstimated they were roughly 75 degrees east and 165 degrees north of the equator, as the dodo flew!

'Talk about one extreme to another!' Old Father Time said as they sailed towards the coldest place on the God's earth. Being the oldest on board the *Golden Hind*, he felt the cold more than most, felt it to his very bones, he told Gulliver.

Gulliver told Alice that Old Father Time's skin reminded him of sugared almonds and Old Mother Hubbard's shoe.

Gulliver thought about how they would get into the snow dome. Old Father Time had told him you only had to remove the plug at the bottom of the dome, like you did on the snow domes you found in novelty shops on the seafront. But was he joking, or was that exactly what you had to do? But how did you get underneath the snow dome, and how did you get into the dome without A, drowning in the onrushing water and B, flood the rest of the planet in a catastrophic event of Biblical proportions? Or C, would the water be frozen solid so you couldn't possibly get inside it? And D, well, he couldn't think of a D but he thought there probably was a D followed by every letter in the alphabet! Of course there was a D, D for dodo, which he obviously was!

Surely Old Father Time would know the procedure to gain entry into this winter wonderland, that's if he could remember! He wasn't being disrespectful but old people forgot things, he knew this because he had two grandfathers and two grandmothers and Old Father Time was older than all of them put together.

However, he couldn't worry about that now, he'd worry about it later. He had always been good at putting things off till later, unfortunately most of the things he put off hadn't turned out well. Procrastination was the thief of time, or was that the gods! Homework, chores, paying the rent the harbour required for leaving your boat\antique shop in the harbour permanently, turning the tap in the bath off before it flooded his parents' house when he was nine before he sat down to watch *Doctor Who*, rather than *after* watching *Doctor Who!* Yes, but that was in his world, the world he was living in at the present moment was a parallel world, which meant everything was in reverse. Which meant in this world if he put it off till later, everything would turn out just peachy, probably! It was just lucky that Gulliver hadn't left his bath tap running before he went gallivanting off through time and space, otherwise when he returned his world would be flooded!

The moons passed and the sun came up and then went down again which happened more times than Gulliver had had hot dinners, or at least had done lately, and the *Golden Hind* seemed no nearer to reaching the North Pole. Drake was standing on deck trying to navigate by using a gizmo called an astrolabe, which was a heavy circle of brass with a rotating arm at its centre bearing two plates with a hole in each. The instrument was hung vertically, the arm was moved until a beam of the sun shone through both holes and a pointer on the arm indicated a reading on the circle. However, using this device on a swaying deck in a rough sea was far from easy. Drake often used the pole star to help guide him to his destination when, he could find it. 'Have you looked up towards the heavens recently, boy? The place is cluttered up with stars, it's hard to tell one from the other!' or so Drake often said in jest!

The sailors were scuttling around the deck like crabs busying themselves with one thing or another, although Gulliver had no clue as to what tasks they were involved in regarding the sea as he was still something of a greenhorn in such matters. Four men were climbing the rigging, unfurling one of the larger sails. These men appeared like monkeys on a vine or spiders in a web. Gulliver wrote as much in his travelogue and on the opposite page drew a picture of these men who were risking life and limb and whose only safety net was the sea. Having said that, if the sailors were lucky and Neptune had arisen from his seabed, there was always his net to save them. Gulliver wondered if this is where the expression 'casting your net wide' came from, probably, he thought, then changed his mind and thought not!

'Are we getting close to the North Pole?' Gulliver asked as he tried to keep his balance as the ship rolled one way then the other, as he felt like a ball bearing on one of those puzzle games he'd played as a child.

'Well, according to my calculations... I haven't the foggiest notion!' said Drake shaking his head several times. This remark rather left Gulliver thinking that Drake was obviously no Phileas Fogg!

'I mean, we must be getting closer as it's getting colder and colder but if the North Pole got displaced when the gods shook time up, well, we could be hundreds of miles off course. The pole star is still in its rightful place, thank God, or at least thanks to the gods who don't appear to have moved any of the stars in the map of the heavens or we really would be up a creek without a paddle!' Drake said managing a half smile. A little later the captain was heard to utter the well-worn nautical term, 'full sail ahead'.

Then a boat appeared upon the horizon and gradually came into sight until it passed within a league of the *Golden Hind*. Drake held up his spyglass and then smiled as according to the nameplate on the side of the boat, it was called *Godspeed*. Drake waved as it passed by, although he couldn't see anybody onboard and Gulliver wondered if it was the famed *Marie Celeste*. Later Drake wrote in his ship's log that to him it appeared this was like a ghost ship and being called *Godspeed*, its crew, like the gods of this world, had all disappeared. Either that or all the crew had been partying late into the night and were all asleep, which was the more likely. 'Godspeed to you,' Drake cried as they passed like ships in the night, although it was still late in the afternoon.

Once again Drake took the safest course of action, steering well clear of it for it could well be a trap set by pirates, a Trojan Horse of the sea if you like. This Trojan Ship was one of the favourite tricks of the infamous pirate Black Beard, who now captained the *Queen Anne's Revenge*, a ship he had captured and renamed. The last thing Gulliver wanted to do was run into an angry band of cut-throat pirates with cutlasses to grind on his neck, that and he, like a lot of other people, was (sea) sick to the back teeth with pirates, especially ones who inhabited the Caribbean Islands! Sometimes it was expedient to let sleeping sea dogs lie, that and finding the mythical Last Bookshop in the World was a far greater treasure than some ship, which by the looks of her was not much more than a floating tree trunk. Gulliver knew that some old ships were said to be nothing more than floating coffins and he hoped this would never be said about the *Golden Hind*!

The ship was probably a private sea vessel transporting its cargo to the mainland, or at least Gulliver hoped it was!

The day wore on and night fell, although thankfully not on them otherwise they really would be sunk without trace! To Gulliver's mind the stars at night seemed like glitter which had been sprinkled upon a black piece of card, something he had done as a child as part of a school project on the night sky.

Then it happened, Gulliver spied land with the help of Drake's brass retractable telescope, which Drake had been kind enough to lend him. At first the word land wouldn't come out of his mouth, it was as if in all the excitement he had been struck dumb, unless a pirate had cut his tongue out! More nautical horrible history I'm afraid and that was exactly what Gulliver was afraid of, nautical history!

'Land!' Gulliver croaked, 'Land!'

'What?' said the ship's first mate. 'I can't hear you!'

'Land!' Gulliver repeated the word as he pointed wildly at the horizon.

'I think the boy's eaten a frog,' the boatswain's mate joked, although funnily enough the boatswain and the boatswain's mate couldn't stand the sight of one another.

'That's the cook's fault!' the ship's master said, joining in with the fun.

'Well, the boy doesn't want to get scurvy now does he?' the cook's assistant said in a cheery manner.

It seemed everybody was in high spirits and not a drop of rum had passed their lips that day, despite the cold. In fact, Gulliver was surprised nobody had said 'Shiver me timbers!' Mind you, the cook did say that it was a rum do that no rum had passed his lips that day, so for the time being he would just have to make do with the cooking sherry!

Then Gulliver passed the telescope to the ship's first mate as he continued to gesticulate wildly in the direction of the horizon. The first mate put the brass telescope up to his eye, which by now was so cold that all you could see at the end of it were crystal patterns resembling a large snowflake under a microscope. That and the metal eyepiece of the telescope was ice cold so he immediately withdrew it and instead scanned the horizon from east to west with the naked eye before he exclaimed, 'Land! Land!'

It was at this exact moment that Gulliver rediscovered the power of speech, 'Land! Land!'

'It seems we've got a parrot in our midst!' one of the sailors joked as he patted Gulliver so hard on the back he almost fell overboard.

'Pieces of eight, pieces of eight,' said the midshipman in jest, or at least Gulliver presumed he was a midshipman as he was standing in the middle of the ship at the time.

'What's all the noise about? I was trying to get fifty winks,' Drake said, as he staggered out of his cabin onto the deck. In truth, sailors were lucky if they got ten winks a night let alone the full fifty.

'Land, Captain. The boy's spotted land!' the ship's second mate said beating the first mate to it by a whisker. You could see by the expression on his face that the first mate wasn't best pleased at the second mate stealing his thunder. At this rate these men were never likely to be mates other than Billy no mates, something that was often said about Barnacle Bill!

'Thank the gods for that. Well done, my boy, well done. If it wasn't for you we may well have sailed right past the North Pole!' Drake said half in jest and half not.

Soon everybody was on deck shouting 'land' including Alice and Old Father Time who belied his age by doing a jig of delight a man half his age would have been proud of, and what's more, he had Alice upon his shoulders at the time.

Soon the great glass dome was in sight and it was time for Old Father Time to spill the beans on how they would get inside it. All the snow domes Gulliver had seen in the gift shops in Brixham were full of water and snow, or something which resembled snow, normally glitter, which often being silver didn't really resemble snow. However, Old Father Time had said that the snow dome was full of ice, although at certain times of the year that ice was broken up. But how do you lift a large snow dome up that is sitting on an even larger antique globe?

Soon these questions were answered for it was apparent to Gulliver and all aboard the *Golden Hind* that there was only one way into the snow dome and that was through the hole in the top.

'Well, Gulliver, there you have it, that is our way into the North Pole!' Old Father Time said pointing to the hole in the glass dome.

'So how… what… why… when?' Gulliver said as the words flowed from his mouth like sand through an hourglass.

'Well, the how, and the what, are one and the same, for the hole was made by a gigantic meteorite. The why, well, you'd have to ask the gods that question, but as you know, they're no longer around. The when was 5001 BC at 3.31am precisely Greenwich Mean Time. I remember it well for the noise woke me up. How Mrs Time slept through it God alone knows! I can tell you, it gave the polar bears and the woolly mammoths quite a scare when it hit, still, at least it didn't wipe all life from the area like the comet that wiped out the dinosaurs!

Gulliver was still a little puzzled as to how they were going to get through this hole, which reminded him of the hole in the ozone layer.

'And your next question is how do we get into the dome through such a hole, well, that's easy enough, or should I say answering the question is easy enough. We, or should I say Drake's able seamen, are going to shoot several lines with grappling hooks attached to them from out of a cannon until one of them finds its target. After which they will climb the ropes, attach some new ropes to the existing ones and abseil down them onto the ice, for as you can see, most of the water in the dome is frozen over. I hope that's all crystal clear.'

To be honest, to Gulliver it wasn't crystal clear as he was having trouble seeing clearly as ice crystals had formed pretty patterns upon the glass of the snow dome, like they'd done on the lens of the brass telescope.

Old Father Time, as he was often accustomed to doing after making the illogical appear completely logical, then folded his arms across his chest to signify he was more than satisfied with the explanation he had given.

'Oh!' said Gulliver, sounding like the wind had been taken out of his sails as he folded his arms across his chest to signify that he was far from happy with this explanation.

'I hope you found that answer to your satisfaction, young Master Gulliver,' Old Father Time said as he did his best to contain a smile that was desperate to break free from his lips and do a jig of delight.

It seemed to Gulliver that Old Father Time had been yanking his anchor all the while, and Gulliver had swallowed it hook, line and sinker! How Gulliver could have swallowed such a tall story as the one Old Father Time had spun him he couldn't possibly imagine, and this from the boy whose grandfather had said he had 'quite the imagination'. I'm mean, did he really think Drake's men, even being as able as they were, were going to lift a giant snow dome up, crawl underneath it and pull the stopper out so they could enter the North Pole? To even contemplate such a thing was simply madness. Gulliver wasn't sure if it was he that was mad or this world, or perhaps it was a combination of the two. This adventure made him feel like part of the crew of *HMS Investigator*, which had been lost in the Artic in 1850 and had been found in 2010 in Mercy Bay near Banks Island.

But luckily, Gulliver didn't have to contemplate his own sanity for too long for the excitement of seeing Drake ordering his men into action. Cannons were brought on deck and positioned at the bow of the ship, which was no mean feat in itself as a cannon was a rather heavy object. And you could see just how heavy the cannons were by the strain on the faces of the sailors that were carrying them. It took six burly men to carry a cannon and two to carry a cannonball and woe betide any of them who dropped the cannonballs on their feet. Once the cannons were brought on deck they were reunited with the wooden blocks with wheels which they sat upon.

After this tricky and arduous task was done, the men then laid four wooden planks side by side at the starboard side of the *Golden Hind*, which enabled them to tilt the cannons to such an angle where the grappling irons might stand a chance of A, reaching the hole in the snow dome and B, the hook actually staying in place when it did so.

Unfortunately, the weather wasn't exactly helping make this task any easier as the wind was beginning to get up, which made the *Hind* roll from side to side. If things continued in this vain the weather might well wreck their chances, in which case they may have to put the task off till a day when the weather was more favourable. The sails had already been severely tested by both the galeforce winds and lashing rain. The sail maker, Wilberforce Worthy, who, in some cases had found them wanting, joked that if the sails got any more rips and tears in them, the only use they would be would be to make shirts with. He then went on to say he didn't want to give the sailors onboard the ship the needle, but they might have to donate their shirts to the sail fund, after which he would stitch them all together like a patchwork quilt and make a sail out of them!

According to Gulliver's body clock and the sandglass the ship's boy was turning (or should I say supposed to be turning, as at the time he was fighting pirates, mind you, luckily for him and the ship's company, this fighting was taking place in his sleep!). For nigh on two hours the sailors discharged the grappling hooks from the cannons in the direction of the snow dome without success. Most attempts just hit the glass of the dome, which made a sound like two champagne glasses clinking together followed by a scraping sound of the grappling hook scraping down the side of the dome. However, when I say 'for what seemed like hours' in actuality, without time it was difficult to know how long it took, although you could just as easily have said that about everything in this world.

It was at this point in the proceedings that Gulliver wished the snow dome was the same size as the one resting on his dressing room table in his bedroom at home. Or he was the size of one of the people from Brobdingnag in *Gulliver's Travels*. However, neither was the case and all the wishful thinking in the world wasn't going to make it so. And, of course, logically if he were a giant he would have been too big to fit inside the snow dome and his weight alone would have sunk the *Golden Hind* and... and nothing, as his grandmother was always so fond of saying! Unless, of course, there was a potion on hand like Alice drank in her wonderland to shrink her down to the size of a teaspoon. However, there wasn't, so let that be an end to it!

Then eureka! The gunner Able Seaman William 'Barnacle' Wigglesworth, finally got his eye in and the grappling hook sailed through the hole without touching the sides. Able Seaman Wigglesworth, nicknamed Barnacle because of his first name, William, or Bill, Barnacle Bill, rather than his disposition being scratchy or bumptious in any way. No, to cut a long story shorter, Able Seaman William Wigglesworth had always been an able archer in his youth and was beside himself with joy when he hit his intended target, as was the whole ship's company, which before that moment had been anything but good company. This ship's company, included Beagle, who seemed to have gone barking mad and was chasing his own tail in a frenzy of excitement. Beagle had now become the ship's mascot and was spoiled rotten by all onboard with titbits, and if not careful was in danger of looking like the bow of an old ship as it sagged in dry dock. The ship's cook teased Gulliver, saying that the crew were fatting Beagle up in case supplies ran low, or at least Gulliver hoped he was teasing him!

'Well done, lad, you've done it!' Drake said, as he smiled in a contented fashion as he looked at William Wigglesworth, who at that moment in time was certainly no Billy no mates. Of course, that wasn't the end of it, not by a long chalk, for now the line with the grappling hook had to be pulled back through the hole securing itself on the rim, otherwise it would all have been for nothing.

Drake gave the signal to weigh anchor so the ship could be closer to the snow dome but not so close as to put the *Golden Hind* in danger of smashing against the glass side of the dome. After the anchor was weighed, which all took time that they really didn't have, it was dropped into the icy waters below, breaking the ice as it did so. Then the gunner set about the task of securing the grappling hook. Drake knew he was between a dome and a hard place, for if he spent too long in these perilously icy waters the game might well be up. As the ice closed around the *Golden Hind*, eventually the hull would be crushed like a walnut in between a pair of nutcrackers and if that happened the crew would be sure to call Drake a complete numb nut!

'Steady as she goes, Will,' Drake said in a firm but calm manner as the able seaman's hands trembled a little as he pulled on the line. Everybody held their breath as foot by painstaking foot the line was pulled up, and by now several other crewmen were pulling on the line with the young able seaman.

Finally the sailors gave one last tug and the line was secure.

'Thank God,' Drake muttered under his breath before crying out, 'Well done, lads, you all deserve a keg of rum for your troubles!' Drake said euphorically, although the ship's supply of rum was dwindling faster than the ice in the North Pole in Gulliver's world.

'Yes, well done, Barnacle,' all the sailors cried as they surrounded the young seaman.

Then two brave sailors who were adept at climbing the rigging in rough seas, shinned up the rope with additional ropes wrapped around their necks and waists. Watching the men climb held everybody on the *Golden Hind* spellbound for one slip and they would fall to their deaths.

Every once in a while the men would stop and draw breath before continuing on; twice they slipped and dangled from the rope with one hand before regaining their grip on the rope. Both men wore leather gloves for the weather was so cold icicles were forming upon the faces of the whole ship's company. Then finally, after much struggling, the two men were sitting on the top of the world waving in the direction of the *Golden Hind*. From a distance, it appeared as if they were nothing more than children who had just climbed a tree in their back garden, and were now waving at their concerned parents who were telling them to get down.

The men then abseiled down the line and when they got to the end of the rope they tied another one around it, securing it with a fisherman's knot, the strongest, most secure knot in the world. They then continued with their abseil until eventually they jumped the last twenty meters onto a glacier covered with thick snow.

Drake said that this would be far too dangerous for any of the children to attempt and perhaps it would be expeditious for Old Father Time to sit this one out too.

Gulliver said that as he was fairly light, couldn't he be strapped to one of the sailors? But Drake said this would still be too dangerous for a child. Old Father Time, being the wisest man onboard the *Golden Hind*, said what if they designed a pulley system like he had seen in coal mines, where buckets were attached to a line? Drake thought this a good idea so Old Father Time and the master of the *Golden Hind* got to work on such a system.

A few days later the system was finished and put in place and it worked like a dream, in fact, you could say it worked liked clockwork, although nobody did. This system was far quicker and safer and meant Gulliver and Alice could ascend to the top of the dome by wrapping themselves around the men and be transported safety onto the Arctic surface. The system involved taking some double-sheave pulley blocks from the rigging mechanism and attaching them to the ropes and securing them by using a wooden horn cleat to the *Golden Hind*.

Just for the record, the name of the ship's master was Isambard Kingdom Brunel, who was born in Portsmouth in the earliest part of the nineteenth century. Brunel dressed as a master should in a tall black stove-pipe hat, a long black frock coat with a black waistcoat and a fob watch in his pocket for show, obviously, and underneath a stiff white-collared shirt with a blue silk necktie around his neck. He sometimes carried a walking cane too when the fancy took him, although he was definitely no dandy. You rarely saw Brunel without a cigar in his mouth, whether it was lit of not, some said he even slept with one in his mouth. The crew hoped this wasn't true as they had no wish for a Viking burial at sea!

Again one has to remember that the sixteenth and nineteenth centuries had been mixed up in the great shake-up of time and space.

Brunel had already designed revolutionary dock systems which were invaluable to Drake when the *Golden Hind* had to get from one ship's bottle to the next. Brunel's great dream was to build a ship that was powered by steam of all things, and to build a great railway which would connect one end of the country to the other. Of course, the Elizabethans thought he was one viaduct short of a railway line, but no matter, they liked the cut of his jib and that was all that mattered. Another thing they liked about their ship's master was that he liked a joke, and was more than happy for the ship's company to send his middle name up, which was Kingdom. Regular cries rang out upon the *Golden Hind* of, 'My Kingdom for a horse!' Well, a seahorse or a wave carrying white horses upon their backs perhaps!

'Unbelievable!' Gulliver said as he sat on top of the world, otherwise known as the snow dome, otherwise known as the North Pole.

'Wow!' Alice said as she surveyed this winter wonderland. And if this didn't qualify as a 'Wow!' moment then nothing did.

Gulliver then lifted his shirt and for a moment Alice thought he had gone quite mad, especially as the temperature outside was minus twenty-five. However, Gulliver hadn't gone quite mad, and that wasn't because he was already as mad as the Mad Hatter, as he took out a sketch pad from his trousers and started sketching the snow dome with the *Golden Hind* far below him.

The good thing was that Gulliver and his fellow travellers had arrived at the Arctic at the right time as it was the end of the summer, which meant there was no night, however, the ice was still fairly thick. Drake was still finding it hard to imagine, The Last Bookshop in the World would have set up shop here, although funnily enough, Gulliver could imagine selling snow domes to the Eskimos in this desolate place. But then again, Drake was an adult and his childhood had sailed off into the sunset some time ago. However, the stars had never let him down before so he must assume what was written in the stars must be correct.

## 13

## Darwin in New Holland, Whatever Next?!

While all this was going on, a young stowaway had crept onto the deck of the *Golden Hind* to see what all the ballyhoo was about. You may or may not be interested in knowing the boy's name but, I will furnish you with it all the same. The boy's name was Charles Darwin. Not much of a name it has to be said and being saddled with such an unimaginative name he was hardly likely to amount to anything, which is exactly what his father once told him.

Now unbeknownst to the ship's crew, Charles had stowed away when the ship was docked in Portsmouth harbour. Most of the voyage he had slept through, occasionally being awoken from his slumber in the ship's stores by the rolling of the *Golden Hind* as it sailed through choppy seas.

'So who do we have here?' said a big burly sailor in a loud booming voice, a sailor with a barrel chest and whiskers like a walrus, as he picked Charles Darwin up by the scruff of the neck and dangled him from port to starboard as if he were nothing more than a fish hanging upon a line.

'Put me down! Put me down!' Darwin exclaimed as he swiped at fresh air.

'Look here, lads, I've caught myself a fish, although it's not really big enough to eat. Perhaps I should throw it back into the sea where it came from!' the sailor laughed heartily.

'Put the boy down, Wilf, we've got bigger fish to fry!' the coxswain said joining in the fun.

The sailor who resembled a walrus did as the coxswain asked and Charles Darwin found himself sprawled upon the deck, squirming like an eel in a net.

'I wonder where the original origin of this species came from,' said a sailor who went by the name of Henry Higginbottom, or by the nickname of curly as he was as bald as a coot. This ironic nickname was what passed for humour in maritime circles, and as far as Gulliver was concerned, it was right up there with his father's lack of humour, which by and large hardly jarred his funny bone.

'So, boy, if you want to earn your keep and not be thrown to the fishes I suggest you make yourself useful. Now what skills do you possess?' the coxswain asked Darwin in a straightforward manner becoming of a man in his position, which at this present moment in time was due east of the starboard bow.

As Darwin picked himself and his dignity off the deck of the ship and straightened his attire so he was shipshape and Bristol fashion, he spoke in the measured manner of a boy who had been well educated.

'My name's not boy, it's Charles Darwin and all my teachers are impressed with my knowledge of biology and my grandfather says I show a keen interested in horticulture too,' Darwin said as he put his foot down while he held the lapels of his jacket like he'd seen his father often do when talking down to him.

'Darwin, isn't that a place somewhere in New Holland?' Curly said, giving young Darwin some clog as he polished his bald head with the unbuttoned sleeve of his shirt. Darwin ignored this comment giving the sailor the cold shoulder.

'Interested in horticulture are we? Well in that case, Charles my boy, I think you might make a half-descent gardener's assistant. And let's hope the biology we come in contact with is as impressed with you as your teachers are, otherwise you might end up in the stomach of a whale like Jonah!' said the coxswain sounding impressed with Darwin's manner while adding a note of caution.

'Did you know that there is a jellyfish in the Arctic called a Marrus orthocanna, which can reach two meters high in length and which floats through the icy waters of the Arctic Ocean on a gas-filled raft? And whenever it gets hungry it just casts out a line and waits for its meal?' Darwin said, showing he wasn't all mouth and trousers. The cold definitely made it harder to think straight but at the moment it didn't appear to be having an adverse effect on young Charles Darwin's brain. The way things were going, one day Charles Darwin's brain would sit pickled in a jar on a shelf in either the Museum of Mankind or the Science Museum in London, well, as long as they didn't encounter any cannibals en route!

'In that case, young Darwin, I shall endeavour not to fall into these waters!' said the coxswain navigating his way through uncharted waters as befitting of a man in his position.

'Hello, boy, how are you doing?' Darwin said as Beagle

introduced himself to the boy with a big wet sloppy lick of his tongue on the side of his face. Nobody onboard the *Golden Hind* would be aware of the significance of this meeting other than Gulliver, and that because of this extraordinary meeting, one day Darwin would name a ship after this excitable puppy named Beagle, probably, possibly, highly unlikely if the truth be told!

And so that was how Charles Darwin became a fully fledged, paid-up member of the crew of the *Golden Hind*, end of story, well not quite...

By this time, metaphorically speaking, Alice and Gulliver were holding on to two sailors' waists for grim death, although both were strapped to the men with belts as a safety precaution. It seemed that even in this world there was health and safety, albeit a scaled down version, and at least this health and safety wasn't health and safety gone mad like in Gulliver's world.

'How are you doing?' Gulliver shouted across to Alice, who was hanging off the rope running parallel to the one Gulliver was sliding down.

'Fine, it's plain sailing,' said Alice with her eyes firmly glued together. 'Although I've got to be honest, I'll be finer once my feet touch the ground!'

'Yes, I can quite see where you're coming from,' said Gulliver, although he couldn't as he too had his eyes shut tight.

Later than sooner, Gulliver and Alice were finer as their feet were now planted upon terra firma like an old oak tree, of which the *Golden Hind* was in part made up of, albeit that terra firma being under quite a few feet of ice and snow. And yes, both Alice and Gulliver were being grammatically incorrect again, unless you counted the song in Gulliver's world which rhymed the words 'finer' and 'Carolina' in the same breath. Both Alice and

Gulliver wondered if as the earth was called terra firma, they had a good reason, or a bad reason for that matter, to be worried, as terra sounded an awfully lot like terror to their young ears.

Gulliver and Alice wouldn't have to wonder for too long to find out that they had quite a lot to be worried about and at least half of that worrying would include the word 'terror'.

Although the captain said it would be unwise for Old Father Time to join them in the north snow dome, Old Father Time wisely reminded Drake that they may require his wisdom, and so the ex-Guardian of Time joined them in their great adventure.

After all the sailors and their equipment were gathered together, Drake gave the crew a little pep talk. Drake was good at giving pep talks, in fact, he prided himself on his pep talks and only Walter Raleigh and Queen Elizabeth I were better at giving pep talks to their men than he.

'To the ship's company of the *Golden Hind*, I say I'm proud of every man jack of you.' Drake then looked at Alice before adding, 'And Jill. Now according to the stars, here we will find what we are looking for so let us hope those stars know what they are talking about!'

'What are we looking for, Captain?' one young sailor cried eagerly, who in a manner of speaking appeared to be all at sea as a jet of steam shot from his open mouth.

'Pray, my good man, didn't anyone tell you of our quest?' Drake said as he tried to make out where the voice had come from amongst the ship's crew, who by now were all huddled close together as the wind and the cold started to bite.

'You know me, Captain, I'll follow you to the ends of the earth without question,' said the loyal sailor.

'Well, that's good because we *are* at the end of the earth so let's not have any more of those silly questions!' Drake said sounding a little put out that his captaincy was being bought into question.

'The Captain's here to name this land after Queen Elizabeth,' said the cook.

'Now don't put words in my mouth, Cookie,' Drake said in jest.

'So why are we here then, Captain?' piped up another voice.

'We're here to name this land after the queen,' Drake said putting the cook's words back into his own mouth before spitting them right back out again. If Drake had thought this through he would have bought a vintage bottle of champagne with him and then smashed it against the glass of the snow dome as if he was christening a ship, but he hadn't so, 'Stick that in your pipe and smoke it!' as Walter Raleigh was fond of saying.

Drake hadn't thought of naming a part of the North Pole for Queen Elizabeth I but now the sailor had mentioned it he thought it was a capital notion. To be fair, even Drake thought it sounded a little daft looking for a bookshop in the Arctic Circle, an ice hotel yes, but a bookshop, have you lost your marbles?

'I hereby name this Queen Elizabeth Land,' Drake said triumphantly and he stamped his right boot down upon terra firma and raised his right fist to the heavens.

'What did he say?' the coxswain said to the boatswain as the wind sailed through the labyrinth in his ears before coming out the other side.

'He said he wouldn't book a holiday in this Godforsaken place if it was the last place on God's earth and why would any queen want a land this barren named after her!' the boatswain said with a straight face, making it up as he went along like in a game of Chinese whispers.

'I've always said our captain's a barrel of laughs,' said Horatio the boatswain in similar jocular fashion.

'Well, we must find a sheltered place out of the wind to set up camp and then we can have some food and bed down for the night,' Drake said authoritatively.

'But there isn't any night at this time of the year!' said one of the midshipmen.

'You see, I told you the captain was a barrel of laughs,' Horatio said grinning from ear to ear.

'Right now I'd rather he was a barrel of rum than a barrel of laughs, my whatsits are being frozen off here!' the coxswain said as he bashed his gloves together and stamped his feet to keep the blood from freezing in his veins.

Now you might wonder as to where all this wind was coming from and no, it wasn't all coming from the captain's mouth or out of the backsides of the sailors either, who had eaten too many sprouts to keep the scurvy at bay, or at least in the Bay of Biscay. In the past, the gods spun the antique globe, which produced the effect of wind on the globe, but since they had sailed off to gods knows where, the solar winds were now doing that job and doing it admirably I might add.

Gulliver had read somewhere that Sir Walter Scott had said that the Antarctica, which in this parallel world was the south snow dome, was a Godless place and although he was now in the north pole or the north snow dome, Gulliver was inclined to agree with this famous explorer. The gods, having flown off to sunnier climes, certainly weren't likely to set up home in this Godforsaken place, no, the gods liked their creature comforts too much to rough it!

So after much walking, a campsite was found inside

an ice glacier, which after further exploration turned out to be a cave. This cave was ideal as not only was it sheltered against the wind and cold, but also the further the caves went into the ice glacier, the darker they became. This meant they could sleep there for it was hard to sleep properly when the night was as light as the day.

'How are you two doing?' Drake aimed his question at Alice and Gulliver, who in truth were looking blue and I don't mean as in fed up but as in cold, although not as cold as poor Old Father Time looked, who right now could have done a good impersonation of Father Christmas or an ice sculpture of Rudolph the red-nosed reindeer!

'Cold!' Alice and Gulliver said in unison as if they were twins separated at birth.

'I'm sure as soon as we get some hot vegetable soup inside us we will all thaw out,' Drake said cheerfully. Then Drake turned to the cook and said, 'How's the soup going, Cookie?'

'Won't be long, Captain. I've managed to catch a few fish to go with the vegetables,' the cook said proudly

'Good man, I can always rely on you, Cookie, not to drop us in the old proverbial soup,' Drake said patting the cook on the back forcefully as a smile as wide as the Artic Circle appeared on his face.

'Thank you, Captain, it's nice to know someone likes the taste of my cooking,' the cook quipped back as he continued to stir the broth that was boiling wildly.

Gulliver wanted to quip that the cook had probably got the fish out of one of the deep freezers at Iceland, but thought the joke would probably go sailing right over Drake's and the cook's heads, like a sail fish or a fish of the flying variety, so he kept it to himself.

That night everybody slept like a baby seal and woke up the next morning refreshed and raring to go.

'Good nights sleep, Gulliver?' Drake enquired as Gulliver appeared, slightly bleary eyed, from the nightmare of having polar bears chasing him all night, or at least in his dreams.

'Dawn breaks yonder?' Drake said cheerfully as the day dawned without actually dawning, as it dawned on the captain that at this time of the year there was no dawn, or sunset either.

'I'll have to pass on that question, Captain, until I get my sea legs back,' Gulliver said stifling a yawn, as to Gulliver's body clock it still felt like it was set to stupid o'clock Greenwich Mean Time!

'I had a dream about Big Foot last night. As a child my mother said I had the biggest feet she'd ever seen. She said with feet like mine I was destined to achieve great feats!' Drake laughed as his hot breath hit the cold, resembling a boat under full steam.

'As we appear to be somewhat in the dark, I think we should probably explore these caves don't you, Gulliver?' Drake said peering into the darkness.

'Yes, it would seem like a logical place to start. I just hope the gods weren't yanking our chain with their message written in the stars,' Gulliver said cautiously.

'I thought the gods had left this world for ever!' Alice said with a puzzled expression on her face.

'For ever's a long time, my dear, an awfully long time, and you know what the gods are like, this might just be another one of their little games,' Drake said equally cautiously.

'Note to self, when we have more time, and if we ever get back to the *Golden Hind* in one piece, ask Old Father Time how long for ever actually is.' Gulliver said under his breath before thinking of the line 'how long's a piece of string?' In theory, as long as the spool it's wound around. Gulliver then thought of when he was a child when he tied string to two baked bean cans to make a telephone. Perhaps he could use this telephone to talk to the gods, making sure to reverse the charges!

So after a not-so-hearty breakfast of leftover fish soup from the night before, washed down with some fresh snow, the ship's company, or the ship's company that for the moment had parted company with the ship, went on another voyage of discovery.

# 14

# Time to put the Wizards on Ice

Some time later, how long is a mystery what with there not being any time and all, but for the purpose of this story we shall say… about the time it takes for a man to find his socks in the morning! Okay, not that long, but about the length of time it takes for a tram\ bus to appear while you're waiting at a bus\tram stop! Okay, not that long, but the lifespan of a mayfly should probably cover it.

'These ice caves seem to go on for ever,' Drake said as he held a lantern to light the way.

'It's like a labyrinth, I've never seen anything remotely like this before in this part of the world, or in any world for that matter!' said Gulliver in wide-eyed wonderment as he looked at the large ice stalagmites sticking up from the floor and stalactites hanging from the ceiling of the ice labyrinth. At the time Gulliver saw this remarkable sight, it reminded him of the jaws of the great white shark he had seen in the Antiquarium. This was a sight he rather wished he hadn't seen as he'd had nightmares of being swallowed by a giant white shark ever since.

'You've been here before?' Drake said in amazement.

'No, I mean I've never seen anything on the television like this before,' Gulliver said covering his tracks badly.

'What on earth is a... What did you call it, a television!?' Drake said as his amazement turned to disbelief.

'I mean in the picture books I've read,' Gulliver said hurriedly.

'But you said a television, unless my ears need waxing,' Drake said as he edged forward into the darkness.

'No, what I said was, perhaps we'll soon tell if Solomon's vision was correct,' Gulliver said thinking on his feet.

'In that case, once when get back to Albion I'm going to ask the queen's physician to wash my ears out! To be fair there's probably enough wax in between them to seal a thousand letters,' Drake said in jest, hopefully!

'It's like Hampton Court Maze in here,' said Alice before continuing on, 'without the hedges!'

Gulliver thought this description a little strange but considering all the strange things that had happened since he had ended up in this world then in comparative terms it wasn't that strange. Gulliver was looking forward to visiting Hampton Court Maze in this parallel world, as the original maze was a lot bigger than it appeared to be in his world. In fact, there were four compared to the one that now stood in his world, which in truth wasn't much bigger than a postage stamp. He was bound to get lost, of course, but half the fun was getting lost in a maze, Gulliver wondered what the other half of the fun about getting lost in a maze was. He'd have to wonder about that question a little more before letting himself know the answer!

'Is this place the end of the world?' one of the midshipmen said, sounding lost without the deck of the ship underneath his feet.

'Technically it's one end,' said Alice using her common sense to great effect.

'Did you hear that?' said Drake as he stopped and stood as still as an ice statue in the North Pole's version of Madame Tussauds, although in this case perhaps Ripley's Believe It Or Not London might be a more apt description.

'Yes, I think I did?' said Gulliver, turning his head so his left ear could hear exactly where the sound was coming from.

'There it goes again!' said Drake as he held his lantern a little higher.

'You don't think it might be Big Foot?' Gulliver said nervously, which brought to mind a tale his grandfather had once told him of a tribe in the lost continent, later to be named New Holland and later still Australia. The tribe members were supposed to all have one massive foot, under which they could shelter from the sun. Now given the fact that Australia was like a dust bowl and hotter than an oven, and the North Pole was as cold as a freezer in Iceland, then bringing this story to mind did seem a might strange. However, in the context of this tale perhaps this does not seem in the slightest bit strange at all, in fact, in this parallel world it seems to fit in quite nicely, like in a puzzle entitled Parallel Worlds.

'It's more likely to be a family of polar bears,' the coxswain said matter-of-factly as Gulliver came walking out of his daydream.

'Or extinct mammoths that due to the summer have thawed out,' the cook said in jest.

'Yes, we can probably rule that one out,' said Drake as he continued to peer into the gloom. 'Well, there's only one thing for it, we must continue on with our journey and see where it takes us,' Drake said stating the patently obvious but doing it with great conviction. Drake was good at stating the patently obvious but doing it with great conviction. In fact, nobody was better than he at stating the patently obvious but doing it with great conviction.

Gulliver thought that surely this must be the land that time forgot, but as this whole world was the land that time forgot then that wasn't any great earth-shattering discovery, although discovering this parallel earth most certainly was!

Suddenly Gulliver heard a voice in his head with an American accent say, 'Picture this if you will, somewhere far, far away in another time and dimension, in a world where nothing is quite as it seems.' *'The Twilight Zone,'* Gulliver said out loud, as his voice echoed through the caves and caused a noise which rumbled like thunder towards them then disappeared before returning once more.

'It's big Hamish's stomach that's rumbling,' the cook said with bravado.

'Get down!' shouted Drake as the ceiling started to cave in.

'It's an earthquake!' said one crewman.

'More like an icequake!' said another.

'It's a landslide!' said another.

'It's an avalanche!' another sailor cried, although he wasn't crying when he said it, as it was so cold the tears would have turned to icicles halfway down his cheeks.

It was none of these things, what it actually was, was the ice, which was moving as it tended to do in this part of the world.

For a moment all went quiet as most of the lanterns were extinguished by the falling snow and the stalagmites and stalactites which rained down upon the ship's company from above like a hail storm, although in this case an ice storm would be a better description.

And then a voice was heard. 'Is everybody all right?' it was Drake who looked as white as an ice sheet as by now he was covered in snow and ice from head to toe.

Various moans from various directions were heard until the sound of bodies moving and feet scrapping upon the ground joined them.

Then a light could be seen waving back and forth; once again it was Drake with lantern in hand making sure everybody was still in the land of the living.

'Are you okay, Gulliver? How about you, Alice,' Drake said showing fatherly concern as he appeared out of the darkness like a spectre.

'I'm fine apart from my head hurts a little where the ice hit me,' Alice said rubbing the side of her head.

'No, no, I can't move. Some thing's pinning me down!' said a panic-stricken Gulliver.

'Hold still, lad, there are four large icicles pinning you to the floor,' Old Father Time said with a horror-stricken look upon his face.

'Don't move a muscle, boy, I'll free you,' Hamish barked in Gulliver's direction as he bounded over towards him like a huge mountainous dog. Hamish bent down and tugged at the icicles with all his might until they loosened enough for him to pull them out. Two of these icicles were in fact stalactites, while the other two were stalagmites. For a minute Gulliver thought he was asleep and was having another nightmare of being eaten by a great white shark. Or worse, this was a waking nightmare where he and a great white shark had been trapped in the ice like a mammoth and had now thawed out. The ancients said you could predict the future through dreams and for a few seconds Gulliver thought they were right!

'How's everybody else?' Drake said looking around at what at first appeared to be living snowmen but were just his men covered from head to foot in snow and ice, as he was not a moment ago. Having brushed himself down Drake was once again shipshape and Bristol fashion, however, shipshape and Arctic fashion might be a better description of how Drake looked in the circumstances.

'I'm fine thanks for asking,' said the cook before adding 'I guess it's true what they say no sense no feeling!

'I'm fine too,' said Able Seaman Ivor Gracegirdle cheerfully, whose hair looked as white as Father Christmas's beard, so he shook the snow out of his hair in a violent manner as if he were a dog shaking the water out of his fur having just been for a swim in the sea. The cook shouted, 'It's snowing,' before he realized it was just the able seaman shaking himself down.

'Wow, that was close!' said Gulliver looking at the holes in his jacket where the large ice stalagmites and stalactites with points like arrowheads had pieced the material in his coat.

After a while everybody had shaken themselves down and were ready to continue on. It seemed no bones were broken, although some of the crew's spirits were severely shaken. Still, better that than any of the crew ending up as spirits of the ghostly variety!

'If anybody wants to go back, just say the word,' Drake said looking stern while trying not to shout just in case the glacier gods got angry again and caused another icequake, for Drake could see some of his men were all at sea in this strange alien environment.

For a few seconds, which no longer existed, you could hear an icicle drop.

'Okay, then on we go,' Drake said relighting his

lantern and then pointing it in the direction of where the noise had at first emanated from.

And so the crew of the *Golden Hind* continued deeper into the ice labyrinth, not knowing if they would ever see the light of day again.

'What's *The Twilight Zone*?' Alice asked Gulliver in a hushed voice when all the hullabaloo had died down.

'It's a zone which twilight falls into. It's a scientific term stargazers use,' said Gulliver making the whole thing up as he went along like storytellers were so fond of doing.

Gulliver really didn't like keeping secrets from Alice but wasn't sure how she would react to him telling her that he was from another time and dimension, one in which time still existed. He decided he would tell her but he had to wait until the time was right, although in this world there never would be a right time.

Gulliver, Alice, Old Father Time, Drake and his men, pressed on further and with a growing sense of trepidation at what they might find within this labyrinth of ice. And then Drake saw a light at the end of the tunnel, no, he really did see a light at the end of the tunnel, as at the end of one of the tunnels a bright light appeared as if to light the travellers' way. As far as Drake was concerned, when lost in the dark, metaphorical lights were no good to man or snow beast.

'Look!' said Drake pointing at the light at the end of the tunnel. Further light shone on the proceedings when the travellers reached then end of this tunnel, to be greeted by a brighter light and an oval room which seemed almost as big as the Arctic Circle itself. The ship's company were now all gathered together in the room staring in disbelief at hundreds of old men with white beards and in white cassocks. Although they may have been young men whose beards had frozen over due to the cold, it was hard to tell as most had hoods upon their heads. That was all apart from one wizard, who must have been the head wizard as he was wearing the conical golden 'wizard's cap' which was intricately embellished with astronomical symbols. Gulliver had seen such a wizard's hat on a documentary on television, which was associated with the druids and Bronze Age discoveries. These symbols suggested the ability to predict the movements of the heavens, including the lunar cycles. Gulliver knew the cap dated from around 1200 BC and none had been found outside Western Europe.

Well, Gulliver had now discovered such a hat outside Western Europe and it was attached to a wizard's head. Gulliver brought the saying 'if the cap fits' to mind but couldn't find anything suitably wizardly as yet to hang his hat on regarding this saying. Gulliver, with his encyclopedic knowledge, was also aware that in 1991, 140 paintings and engravings were discovered in a cave in Marseilles, France, called the Cosquer Cave. The archaeologist said this discovery meant that other treasures may remain undiscovered in caves submerged at the end of the Ice Age. 'Well, it appears the archaeologists were right,' Gulliver said under his breath when he saw the wizards in the ice caves. Gulliver thought archaeologists in this world would permanently have puzzled expressions on their faces trying to fit together the pieces of this parallel world's past after the gods, in their wisdom, had shaken time up. In fact, the expression 'you're history' definitely applied to the history of this world.

It appeared to Gulliver that he was now standing in the Magic Ice Circle.

'Don't be shy, gentlemen, we don't bite. If your

looking for cannibals, may I suggest you look no further than the far-flung reaches of the Amazonian jungle, or the South Pacific?' The old man laughed out loud, as did the men at the round white table, which had the effect of filling the room with steam, or as one might say if one had a mind to, hot air!

'Welcome to the magic circle,' said another man, who lifted his hood to reveal half a jagged beard which appeared as if it had been starched and then snapped off. It appeared Gulliver was right!

'I knew it! Wizards, they're everywhere. You just can't escape them. Just give it time and I'm sure Bilbo Baggins will appear. Who would have thought it, wizards in this neck of the woods?' Gulliver said sounding as cynical as if he had suddenly metamorphosed into a middle-aged man as he went on a one-man witch hunt, although wizard hunt would have been a more apt expression in the circumstances, of which you are all aware. Gulliver was half expecting the man to be called Gandalf, or Harry Potter who had aged prematurely. The only surprise was that he wasn't carrying a staff. Gulliver wondered if any of these hooded wizards had been on board *HMS Hood*, he also wondered if they might eventually find themselves in a magical forest full of Christmas trees as white as Father Christmas's beard!

As far as Gulliver was concerned, the real wizards were Newton, Einstein, Archimedes, Da Vinci, Hawking, Nostradamus and the like. Mind you, like wizards, they were poorly dressed and had long beards and white hair, so perhaps there wasn't much difference between them.

Gulliver thought he had better not upset these cold-hearted ice wizards, otherwise they might turn him into an ice sculpture and leave him in the sun, especially as these wizards weren't exactly snowed under regarding having anything to put a spell upon. To be honest, the last thing you want when you're enclosed within an ice cave is fireworks of any kind. Let's face it, you had to have ice in your veins to tangle with an ice wizard.

Gulliver recalled from his history lessons at school that the Spanish believed Drake had used wizardry on the Spanish galleons when relieving them of their gold. Gulliver thought Drake should therefore have no trouble communicating with the wizards sitting before them.

'The stars said you were coming,' said the second man sitting around the ice table who was wearing a tall pointy wizard's hat, but this one was white, unless it was the shape of his head. Gulliver had seen pointy wizard's hats in the gardens of Hampton Court, but they were green topiary.

Gulliver thought this story was beginning to sound somewhat familiar, as if the Bible had got mixed up with *Lord of the Rings* and *Harry Potter*. But then again, why not? As time had gotten mixed up in the big shake-up, why wouldn't books be mixed up like the dream Gulliver had as a child? To be honest, in this world it was only to be expected, but Gulliver hadn't expected it and nor had Drake or Alice by the look upon their faces.

Then the second wizened wizardy type with the ice frosting stuck to his beard added to the stars that spoke routine, 'Oh and word gets round. You know, rumours, gossip, Chinese whispers, table talk, hearsay, tittle-tattle, newspaper speculation, idea afloat, i.e. message in a bottle and the like.'

Drake said under his breath, 'Pecksniff, saltimbanque, knave trickster, magician, charlatan,' which was old-speak for a liar. Luckily the old ice wizard was hard of hearing so he didn't hear these derogatory terms.

'So we hear that you are looking for The Last

Bookshop in the World,' said the third wizened old man around the table without lifting his hood.

'Yes,' said Gulliver excitedly. 'Is it here?' He then heard a voice in his head say, 'Wizard!' however he did not voice this as he wasn't an excitable 1950's schoolboy who read the comic *Boys Wonder*!

'No!' said the hood. Now *that* Gulliver *was* expecting!

'However, we can tell you where you might find it.'

Suddenly the white table, which resembled as smooth slab of ice, started to melt in the middle, which revealed a pool of water in which a vision appeared.

'Come closer, young man, come closer and you will see for yourself the journey you must embark upon to find this mythical shop of books,' said the first ice wizard who'd spoken, who by the look upon the face of the fourth ice wizard around the table, had spoken out of turn.

Gulliver was invited to sit at the table with the hoods, as were Alice, Drake and Old Father Time, who looked as if he could easily have been a member of the wizarding fraternity, in looks at least. Suddenly a ship appeared over the horizon in the vision, fighting against a rough sea and passing what looked like a giant seahorse. Then the pool started to freeze over until the ice broke up and once again the water returned. The *Golden Hind* then appeared out of the mists of time at the foot of a large land mass, which appeared to be Africa, although in all honesty, like in a fairytale, it was hard to tell. Then Drake was looking at a compass which was reading due east. After which the ship and Drake disappeared over the horizon as a comet blazed its way across the heavens above, leaving its icy tail like an aeroplane's smoke trail hanging in the sky.

Gulliver hoped this wasn't one of those bad omens. Perhaps they had hit some rocks and sunk. Then the mists of time once again froze over until a little while later the pool of water returned and this time Gulliver was in a busy marketplace and by the look of the sweat upon his face, it was hot. Then, as if by magic, Gulliver and Drake were sat around another table talking in earnest to four men and then Gulliver appeared to be suffering from snow blindness for everything in front of his eyes went white. A few minutes later his sight returned and the vision was over.

'Well ladies and gentlemen, I hope that helps,' said the fourth of the hooded wizards, who had finally got to say his piece. It was fair to say that these wizards weren't exactly wizard with words, more the brooding silent types with ice in their veins. Perhaps these wizards couldn't spell any better than Gulliver!

'Now, you have to excuse us as we were in the middle of building a giant snowman,' said the unhooded wizened gentleman with ice in his veins, who now appeared to speak for all the ice wizards.

And then the meeting, if indeed it could even have been called a meeting, was adjourned and Gulliver, Drake and Old Father Time were left to decipher what the vision actually meant; Alice just thought it was a nice fairy story. To be honest, Drake thought they had been going round in circles and getting nowhere fast. *It was a puzzle all right, actually it wasn't,* thought Gulliver with a puzzled-looking expression on his face. Jigsaws might well be a puzzle but a puzzle would have been easier to complete than the puzzle they were now faced with. Gulliver had never liked puzzles of any kind and this puzzle was hardly endearing him to the joys of the puzzle and their solutions thereof, if there even were solutions thereof to this curious puzzle!

Well, not wishing to bore the reader further, in *Gulliver's Travels* in *The Land that Time Forgot*, Drake thanked the wizened wizard hoody types and they went on their merry way, if you take out the word 'merry'.

One by one the wizards disappeared as Gulliver stopped to ask one of them how they ended up in such a Godforsaken place. One ice wizard said, without batting an eyelid, which was because both of his eyelids were frozen to the top of his eyebrows, 'The Snow Queen banished us here after we refused to do her bidding. That woman has got a heart of ice. Still, I'm sure one day some prince will come along and thaw her heart and some time in the not too distant future, we'll be brought back in from the cold.'

And with that the wizened ice wizard disappeared too. Gulliver wasn't sure if the wizard was joking or he was suffering from temporary brain freeze!

As Drake made his way back across the ice to where the ropes were still dangling down from the top of the snow dome, he asked Gulliver if he had the faintest notion what the vision had meant.

'So, Gulliver, have you the faintest notion what the vision meant?'

'Well, the seahorse reminded me of something and then it came to me, a giant seahorse resembles one of the islands of Galapagos, which isn't a million miles from Africa, possibly North Africa. The market looked a little like the ones I've seen in the book *The Arabian Nights*, perhaps it could be Marrakesh. I saw some men in the background smoking those long bubbling pipes they call hookahs.'

'So you think we should sail in the general direction of South America and then turn right at the jagged pointy bit of land at the bottom to get to North Africa?' Drake said as he stroked his beard, which meant he was unsure of what to do next.

Gulliver wanted to say to Drake 'Hold your seahorse!' if nothing more than to lighten the mood, but decided the joke could wait until they got to the Galapagos Islands, which by that time, hopefully he would have forgotten it!

'Perhaps we might find some more clues in the Galapagos Islands,' Gulliver said as the sea mists from his mind cleared further.

'Mind you, at least there was a comet in the vision. A vision without a comet in it isn't worth the ice sheet it's written upon!' Drake said stroking his frosty-looking whiskers.

'One thing does puzzle me though,' said Gulliver, once again looking puzzled.

'Only one thing?' Drake said laconically, as he knew this was just the tip of the iceberg regarding puzzles in this world, as the smile returned to his face. A smile that had been missing for some time, almost as if it had been circumnavigating the world and had finally returned home.

'I thought time no longer existed, yet these old men talked of time as if it were still around. I mean, if we were seeing a future event in this vision that just doesn't make sense, unless they're referring to space-time. I suppose we should ask Old Father Time, he's bound to know the answer to that question, what with all the time he'd spent in this world!'

But before Drake could ask Gulliver what space-time was suddenly from behind them they heard a growl followed by another and then another. Drake and Gulliver looked round and saw a marauding pack of polar bears heading in their direction.

'I think we may have a problem!' Drake said in an agitated manner that Gulliver didn't associate with Drake's normal calm and cheery one.

'Don't they say you should never try and outrun a polar bear? Shouldn't we all just make like an ice statue and hope they go away?' the cook said as his eyes widened in fear.

'That's an option, or we could attempt to out stare them,' Drake said trying to keep as still as he could. 'Or being as close to the ropes as we are, we could make a run for it,' said Drake, turning first from the ropes that were ahead of him and then back at the pack of polar bears, who seemed to be getting up a full head of steam.

'I choose the third option!' said the cook as he turned round and started running, which in the snow and ice was like running in black treacle, like in a nightmare.

'Come back, man! You'll never outrun a polar bear, not with the blubber you're carrying!' Drake said as steam came pouring out of his mouth.

The cook wanted to tell Drake he was skating on very thin ice with the jokes, but decided better of it as he didn't want to be left out in the cold, either literally or metaphorically.

Gulliver then bent down and started to make a snowball, after which he threw it with all his might in the direction of the polar bears. This hardly made the polar bears flinch but Drake thought this third option, which he hadn't previously entertained, was a good one so he bent down, rolled a snowball and fired it in the direction of the polar bears. After which, the entire ship's crew, including the cook, Alice and Old Father Time, were making snowballs and lobbing them at the polar bears, which by now had slowed to a walking pace. Ten minutes later the polar bears had been vanquished, or at least had turned tail and were heading in the opposite direction.

'Good thinking, Gulliver. Sometimes I forget you're so young, you seem to have an old head on young shoulders,' Drake said patting Gulliver on the back.

'If only you knew, if only you knew,' Gulliver said under his breath.

After this brief moment of excitement, Drake and Gulliver went back to pontificating on the ice wizard's vision.

'Yes, it's a puzzle all right. I suggest we consult Old Father Time, he has plenty of wisdom,' said Drake using some wisdom of his own. Gulliver didn't want to seem a complete know-it-all so instead of saying 'all ready ahead of you on that score' he said, 'What a good idea I wish I had thought of that.'

Then everybody heard a creaking sound reminiscent of the creaking floorboards on a ship, which continued to get louder as the ice started to move underfoot. It appeared it wasn't just Drake that was skating on thin ice as all the ship's company started waddling around like inebriated penguins before falling on the ice like pins in a bowling alley.

'AHHHH!' exclaimed the cook as the ice opened and swallowed him like he was being swallowed by a narwhale, otherwise known as the unicorn of the oceans.

Drake managed to get to his feet and helped Alice and Gulliver to their feet too although in truth they all knew where their feet were on the end of their legs!

'Where's cookie?' Drake said as he looked around him.

'I think his goose has been cooked, Captain!' said the boatswain, tottering on his feet as he tried to regain his balance.

'Now who's going to do the cooking?' one of the able seamen said who was able to stay upright as large chunks of the ice broke up around him.

The ice was breaking up so fast it now resembled stones laid across a stream and the only way across to where the ropes were hanging was to jump from one piece of the broken ice to the next.

'Okay,' said Drake with much authority, 'follow me.'

Drake jumped from one block of ice to the other with great speed until he was on the other side of the rift.

'The only way across is if you take a run at the ice and keep going, otherwise you'll lose your balance and end up in the water. Drake knew if you fell into the ice water you wouldn't last long and the way the ice was shaking and breaking up, soon there would be nothing to stand upon.

Gulliver took Alice by the hand and told her to stay with him as they both skipped across the ice hand in hand in unison, like skimming stones. Halfway across Alice stumbled and looked for all the world to be falling into the water, until Gulliver pulled her across to the block of ice he was standing upon and they continued on until they reached the other side.

'Captain, Captain! Over here, over here!' cried the cook, whose hands appeared on the top of the ice as his rosy cheeks followed along quickly behind.

'The cook! Rescue the cook otherwise we'll all starve,' shouted Drake with bravado more than anything else as now even he was scared.

The coxswain and Drake reached the cook and somehow hauled him from the jaws of death.

As the ground shook everybody made it to the ropes and started to climb as the ice disappeared from beneath their feet like ice cream in a heatwave, to be replaced by freezing cold water.

'Jump! Jump!' cried Gulliver to Alice as the ice beneath her feet was just about to break into a hundred separate pieces.

'I can't! It's too far, I can't reach it!' Alice said as the panic rose in her like a tsunami.

'Yes, you can!' Gulliver cried, who by now was attached to one of the seamen's waist as he reached down and offered his hands to her.

Alice looked at her feet as the ice she was on became smaller and smaller and she knew she didn't have long as she bent her knees and with all her might jumped up and grasped both of Gulliver's outstretched hands. For a split second Alice's hands started to slip through Gulliver's until she only had the grasp of his left hand as she dangled over the breaking ice. Then Gulliver grabbed Alice's loose hand and with all his might pulled her up to his waist and she gratefully wrapped herself around him, like he had seen koala bears do in wildlife documentaries on television as they hung on to their mothers.

'Gulliver, get Alice to climb up your body and then she can hold on to mine and then I'm afraid you'll have to climb on your own. Can you do that, Gulliver?' the able seaman said, straining to hold on to the freezing cold rope.

'Did you hear that, Alice?' Gulliver said as he looked down at a petrified Alice.

'Yes, yes, I think so,' Alice said as she gulped in a breath of cold air and started to climb Gulliver. A few minutes later, Alice had her arms and body wrapped around the seaman, who was slowly climbing up the rope, leaving Gulliver to climb the rope on his own.

'Are you all right Gulliver?' Drake shouted in Gulliver's, direction as he clung on to the rope for grim death as if he slipped it really would be a grim death as he would freeze to death in no time at all.

'Yes, I think so,' Gulliver said as he looked down at the water below him and the floating ice. He hoped the ice wizards were safe within the cave in the labyrinth, which still seemed to be standing. He also hoped the polar bears had found a safe haven; perhaps it hadn't been the snowball volley that had scared them but the fact that they had sensed the vibrations of the moving ice, animals always had a keen sense of impending danger.

For what seemed like a lifetime, the crew of the *Golden Hind* struggled to climb up the dangling ropes as their lives literally hung in the balance, until everybody was safely sitting on the roof of the world breathing heavily.

'Wow, that was quite a roller coaster ride!' Gulliver said as he tried to ignore the ice burns on the palms of his hands!

'What's a roller coaster ride?' Alice said as a puzzled expression appeared on her face without the least bit of help from magic.

'It's an expression my father likes to use, it means going up and down quickly,' said Gulliver, knowing if he explained what it really was he'd have to tell Alice he wasn't from this world and now didn't seem the right time for such an explanation and all the questions and answers that would inevitably follow such a revelation.

As a child, Gulliver had a dream of riding on the biggest roller coaster in the world, which literally went all around the world. It started it England and wound its way across the whole globe, which meant several changes of clothes. When it arrived in Africa and Australia it was stiflingly hot so Gulliver had to strip down to his boxer shorts and when it reached Russia and the North and the South Pole he had to put on several thick layers of clothing to combat the freezing conditions. The entire roller coaster ride took three months to complete and went through so many different timezones, quite frankly you didn't know whether you were coming or going, and sleep, well, quite frankly you could forget about it!

And the price for a ticket on this roller coaster ride of a lifetime, £100,000, cheap at half the price. Anybody who bought a ticket for this ride was told that if they suffered from travel sickness then this experience probably wouldn't be their cup of tea. Saying all that, Gulliver suspected that Gulliver from *Gulliver's Travels* would have loved it, as would the Mad Hatter!

Gulliver's mother once said that Gulliver could dream for Great Britain; in 2012 he had a dream in which he won ten gold medals in the pool and he couldn't even swim!

Some time later, still metaphorically speaking, all the crew, Alice and Gulliver were back on dry land, or should I say dry wood as they were now back on board the *Golden Hind*. The sailors were rubbing butter into their palms as most had rope burns for their troubles. Gulliver wrote in his travelogue that things happened so fast there was no time to think about things and as such, long-winded explanations and descriptions of events were best avoided, as were long words he couldn't spell. Gulliver had no desire for his travelogue to read like *Lord of the Rings*, which to Gulliver's mind was perfect reading matter at bedtime as it was guaranteed to send you off to sleep! Gulliver just hoped he didn't run into Tolkien in this parallel world for if he did, he was sure to throw the book at him, and if it was his book *Lord of the Rings*, it being as heavy as it was, well, he'd be sunk without trace, end of story!

'Captain, I'd like to introduce you to the latest member of our motley crew,' the ship's master said as a boy appeared from behind his back as if by magic. 'This is Darwin, Charles Darwin, our new gardening assistant,' said Isambard Brunel with a smile upon his face not far shy of the hole in the ozone layer in Gulliver's kingdom.

'Another stowaway? We attract them like flies,' said

Drake in jest, knowing full well the ship's master was cutting a short story even shorter! 'Well, boy, I can't be too critical as I once stowed away on a ship called the *Pandora* and got my ears boxed for my troubles, so welcome aboard. And as fortune has it, we are heading for Islands where we may well need your skills,' Drake said as he reached out and offered Darwin his hand, who shook it willingly, if not a little nervously.

The ship's master then introduced Darwin to the crew and Alice, Gulliver and Old Father Time. Beagle had already been introduced earlier and was now following Darwin around like a lost puppy. The job of the ship's master was often to bridge the gap between the officers and the seamen, whether they be able or not, and Isambard Brunel was a man perfectly suited to this task.

Gulliver was having a hard time digesting everything, not only the visions he had seen in the ice labyrinths but now young Charles Darwin had turned up on the scene just at the right time. This, to Gulliver's mind, which at this moment was reeling somewhat, seemed like synchronicity gone mad but there seemed no other choice than to go with the flow.

Drake took a reading from the stars which had appeared in the night sky for the first time in what seemed like ages, as he set a heading due west and the journey and quest was once again resumed in earnest, even though as per usual Ernest was nowhere to be seen!

'So what do you make of the vision in ice?' Gulliver asked Old Father Time with both of his eyebrows raised in a quizzical manner, without going overboard like Fiona Bruce's eyebrows appeared to do at times on the *Antique's Roadshow*.

'Well, it appears that some people are running on a different time to us!' said Old Father Time as he mused upon the vision. 'You see, Gulliver, time is an illusion and it slips through your fingers like sand through an hourglass. And not only is time an illusion, but let's face it, some people are delusional and that, I am afraid, is all I've got for you at this point in time! I know I'm supposed to be as old and as wise as Methuselah himself, but that's not quite the case. I mean, when you're stuck in a large chronometer, quite frankly time drags and you end up clock watching for there is really very little time for anything else,' Old Father Time said, making as much sense as the next timekeeper.

But to be fair to Old Father Time, this explanation wasn't far off the beam as Gulliver knew Einstein had said, 'time is the biggest illusion of them all', and he knew some people were delusional, he just hoped he wasn't one of them.

Another thing that had puzzled Gulliver was where had the gods disappeared to? So he put this question to Old Father Time and this was his reply, 'Well, Gulliver, from my limited knowledge on such theological matters, I'd say they climbed into their orbiting cathedrals and flew off to find another planet they could make a complete mess of!' Gulliver wasn't sure if Old Father Time was joking or not when he said this, however, judging from the tone of his voice and the countenance upon his face, it was a mixed bag like this world, some truth, some fairytale.

Gulliver wrote this in his travelogue: 'Although there is no time in this world, by and large the people who inhabit it seemed to have plenty of time for one another. Whereas the people in my world, who have time to spare, have very little time for anybody else but themselves. Which wasn't as nonsensical as it sounded.'

## 15

# The Land of the Giant Seahorse

The *Golden Hind* sailed east around Greenland and up to Baffin Bay, unbelievably passing Devon Island, past the Arctic Circle in the Arctic Ocean. Past Alaska, where they saw an aurora borealis, which appeared to Gulliver and the crew as a ghostly glow in the sky; undulating gossamer curtains of green and reds and blues. This truly was a magical sight and prompted Drake to say that perhaps the gods hadn't deserted this world after all. Drake told Gulliver that you could use auroras to forecast the weather and that the lights were known as 'wind lights' and 'weather lights'.

Old Father Time said that if you whistled gently the lights would respond by drawing closer, almost as if they were a living breathing entity. Alice and Gulliver tried but all to no avail, Drake joked they should probably wet their whistle and then try again.

When Gulliver saw the aurora, to him it looked like the waves of the ocean, especially when the lights were blue. He could imagine a ghost ship sailing into this magical aurora and coming out in another world, the New World. Gulliver's mind was hot-wired differently to other people, he knew that much. He could see colours in words and see patterns when he heard music, this apparently made him a 'synaesthete'. However, Gulliver's brain went one step further, turning these patterns into holographic images which he saw in his mind's eye gathered from his subconscious and transferred to his conscious mind. At times, being dyslexic and a synaesthete made words appear to rise and fall on the written page like a wave upon the blue Pacific Ocean or the Red Sea.

Gulliver kept this gift to himself as he thought if he told anybody they would think he was round the twist, resembling a DNA strand. That and he couldn't see any practical use for this so-called gift, other than keeping him entertained when there was no access to television. As of yet, John Logie Baird hadn't invented his magical Pandora's box of tricks, but give it time, just give it time.

Still, there was no point complaining, everybody had their Southern Cross to bear. Gulliver was lucky enough to have seen the Southern Cross when he was in the South Pacific seas. There he saw the Jewel Box, Musca, Triangulum Australe and the Crux jewels shining in the heavens above, which is how he described this sight in his travelogue, although the spelling of some of these jewels in the jewel box of the universe did leave a little\lot to be desired! Drake said he had once seen paintings on the bark of a tree in New Holland depicting the stars in the Southern Cross, one a shark and the other a stingray. Gulliver presumed these were painted by the indigenous population of the outback, which he now knew as the Aboriginal tribes. New Holland, Drake said, was a land of many riches where gold ran like a river. However the outback was the most inhospitable place on God's earth, full of snakes, spiders, scorpions and other delightful creepy crawlies, giving the North and South Poles a run for their money, minus the creepy crawlies!

In his world, Gulliver perceived time as a river which flowed with great speed. While in this world the river of time had become becalmed to that of a mill pond. But was that the case? Only time would tell. If Gulliver remained forever young like Dorian Gray in Oscar Wilde's book *The Picture of Dorian Gray* having found the elixir of youth, he would know that time and its affects had ceased. This, in Gulliver's mind, would be like a mammoth trapped in the ice, or like an insect caught in amber, except unlike the mammoth and the insect, he would still be alive.

The *Golden Hind* continued its voyage, sails billowing in the trade winds, through the Bering Seas past America, or at least what Gulliver knew to be America as of yet Columbus still hadn't gotten his finger out and discovered it. Into the North Pacific Ocean and the Tropic of Cancer, past Hawaii, again, yet undiscovered as the *Hind* veered towards the coast of Mexico. Here Drake would have loved to have landed and filled the *Golden Hind* with gold but decided this would not only weigh the ship down but also slow their progress. Eventually the *Golden Hind* reached the Galapagos Islands, where the giant seahorse was laying down in the water as if asleep. Now Gulliver could see for himself why these islands were known as the Land of the Giant Seahorse.

On this epic voyage Gulliver had more time to think, and fishing in the sea of his imagination he caught several ideas in his net and this was one. What if while sailing on the seas of time, they ran into *RMS Titanic*? Answer, they would sink! This was because the *Titanic* was made of iron and the *Golden Hind* was made of wood and not gold as some of the Spanish people believed. But should they draw alongside the *Titanic* and shout to the captain 'beware of icebergs off the starboard bow'? In this theoretical and moral discussion that Gulliver was having with himself, he seemed to have forgotten there were no waves in time to sail upon, not even gravitational waves, not in this world, and as such 1912 no longer existed. So this meant they wouldn't be racing against the *Comet*, the first paddle steamer, in 1812 along the river Clyde either, or in 1712, 1612 etc. But no matter, with the time being as mixed up as it was, this still didn't preclude the *Titanic* hitting an iceberg and sinking, it was just that the incident wouldn't be recorded with a time or date. Once again this was Gulliver pushing the boat of his imagination out into unchartered waters so far that it was just a matter of time before they reached the cosmological oceans.

Gulliver, being the mine of useless information he was, knew that the first steam engine had been invented by a man called Newcombe in Dartmouth in Devon, and the line of the Great Western Railway, which the first steam locomotive ran along, reached Devon.

Drake thought that perhaps it would be better if this time they left the *Golden Hind* parked outside the ship in a bottle and used the long boats to transfer from the sea to the bottle. This would be more dangerous and could only be performed when the tide was at its highest point as falling any great distance in a long boat was never going to end well. At least in the confines of the ship, if you fell butter side up you may well be shaken and stirred but at least you were still alive!

When the *Golden Hind* finally reached the Land of the Giant Seahorse, they dropped anchor just off a cove in the largest island known as Isabella. A few members of the crew then rowed onto the island to replenish its bread fruit and coconut supplies. As the long boat rowed into the island it was flanked by several bottle-nosed dolphins which were in a playful mood, jumping over the boat in turn as if they were performing tricks in an aquarium or at Sea World. As one of the dolphins jumped over the long boat in an arc motion, Gulliver reached up his hand and stroked the belly of the dolphin, which produced a contented gurgling sound, as if the dolphin was talking to Gulliver, saying, 'More please, I like having my belly stroked.' Beagle also loved having his belly stroked but you couldn't teach an old dog new tricks, or a new dog old tricks, so Beagle was never going to be able to compete with the dolphins in the showboating department!

Then both dolphins arced over the long boat together, one coming from the port side and one from the starboard side as if somehow this was their party piece, which produced a long round of applause from all in the long boat. Both dolphins thrashed their flippers in the water in appreciation of their own efforts. Dolphins really were the Brains Trust of the oceans, they certainly were the think tank of the Antiquarium back in old Devon, of that there was no doubt.

The moon had done its stuff moving the tides to the exact positions where the changing of locks was possible and the long boat was able to slip into the bottle with relative ease (and no, the bottle-nosed dolphins didn't follow the long boat into the bottle, that would plainly have been ridiculous!) That was the good thing about a long boat, it might well be long but it was a lot slimmer than a ship, and without God's speed but with a lot of help from Newton's laws of physics (what goes up etc. etc.), and as everybody onboard either prayed or shut their eyes, or shut their eyes and prayed, the long boat thankfully landed butter side up. In truth, the gap between the cork and neck of the bottle was so wide even the *Titanic* could have fitted comfortably through it, but why spoil a tall story with trifling-like things like the truth, for if one had done so it would no longer be a tall story!

Alice seemed to enjoy the whole experience, but then she was a child and children by and large enjoyed theme parks, roller coaster rides, etc. etc. rather more than adults did, even though Alice had never been on a roller coaster before. Gulliver rather less so, probably because he couldn't swim, something he was determined to overcome sooner rather than later. Alice said when they had the time she would teach him to swim as she swam like a mermaid. Gulliver thought until time was restarted this would never happen, and he may well have been right, or he may well have been wrong, only time would tell!

Meanwhile, on board the *Golden Hind* Darwin had a question to put to Drake.

'Do you mind if I go ashore, Captain; I could do with stretching my legs?' the young Darwin said looking up at Drake as if he were some sort of Greek god.

'By all means, lad, I'm sure the gardener could do with a hand. See what you make of the islands and then report back to me. Perhaps when we've got more time we can come back here, you never know, we might find untold treasures buried here. I quite fancy a bit of treasure hunting,' Drake said with his spyglass firmly glued to his right eye before he had to remind himself there was no more time as the sands of time had run out some time ago.

'Thank you, Captain, I won't let you down,' Darwin said enthusiastically and he didn't, turning down all opportunities to play with Alice and Gulliver in favour of recording everything he saw in minute detail. Gulliver wrote in his travelogue that he liked Darwin even though he was a very serious boy, which reminded him of himself when he was a boy. Gulliver then had to further remind himself that he still was a boy, even if he was a boy of twelve going on thirty-five!

After the first long boat signalled that the island was free from cannibals, the second long boat, with the gardener and the new gardener's assistant, namely Charles Darwin, in it made for the bottle which the island of the Land of the Giant Seahorse was encased in. After which Drake sailed out to the island in a third long boat, having no fear that he would end up surrounded by hungry cannibals with a spear to grind, or worse, end up in a large cooking pot full of garlic. The one thing Drake hated above all other was garlic, although he wasn't that fond of French cooks or their cooking, especially if he was on their menu! All the long boats successfully navigated the procedure of changing from sea to bottle without too much fuss.

The only hiccup was Old Father Time, who got a bad case of the hiccups just as the long boat got to the neck of the bottle, like one sometimes does at the top of a roller coaster ride and which was probably down to nerves. This case of the hiccups lasted two days until Hamish crept up behind Old Father Time and scared the living daylights out of him by pretending to be a head hunter. Still, it worked a treat even if for some considerable time after, Old Father Time looked as white as a sheet!

Now perhaps I should explain that all the ships in the bottles which the gods had placed upon the antique globe with their fair hands, represented (if not resembled) large mountain ranges to the peoples of these lands. And that these mountain ranges were often scaled by mountaineers who placed flags on the top of the masts to signal that they had climbed these treacherous mountain peaks. Another thing I should probably explain is that as these islands were so close to one another, the ships in the bottles were considerably smaller than the ones in say Africa and America. This was only to be expected, Gulliver later wrote in his travelogue, or at least he was pretty sure it was only to be expected.

By the time they had left the Galapagos Islands, which to everybody but Gulliver was known as the Land of the Giant Seahorse, Darwin had begun to come out of his shell, or at least he did after Gulliver sketched a picture of him posing inside a giant tortoise shell! Gulliver wondered if the famous old giant turtle, Lonesome George, was alive and well on this island; he could well be a baby when in his world unfortunately he was as dead as a dodo! Gulliver then thought of Schrodinger's cat in a box theory being both alive and dead at the same time, so perhaps Lonesome George the giant turtle could be both alive and dead at the same time, although as there was no longer any time in this world, that made the implausible theory even more implausible, didn't it? Gulliver wasn't sure, although he was sure this thought should be put into the box in his head marked Pandora which was never to be opened under any circumstances!

'So what do you think?' Gulliver said showing the sketch to Darwin.

'Very good, Gulliver, you've got a good eye,'

'Hopefully I've got two,' Gulliver said breaking the ice, although they'd left the ice far behind them in the Arctic.

'These shells would make a good shelter if you were backpacking around the world and you wanted to do it on the cheap,' said Gulliver, which rather went over

Darwin's head like the dolphins had done a few days earlier.

'Do you ever feel like things are preordained, that they're meant to be?' Darwin said with a slight frown on his face.

'Undoubtedly,' Gulliver said with a slight smile on his face.

This rather took Darwin aback as he wasn't expecting Gulliver to agree with him on this point. In fact, he thought the point might go right over his head like the arrow did when it split the apple on the head of William Tell's son.

'Did you know that Leonardo Da Vinci thought that whatever nature could do, people could copy and the last word he ever wrote was "etcetera"? And did you know the Latin genus for seahorse is Hippocampus, which means sea monster?' Gulliver said giving his cerebral muscle a work out.

'The first thing I didn't know, the second thing I did,' Darwin said matter-of-factly in true Darwinian style. 'Did you know that the male seahorse gives birth to its babies?' said Darwin impressed by Gulliver's knowledge for a boy, while showing he was no slouch in the geek department either. Darwin thought Gulliver was almost as bright as he was. Of course Darwin didn't know that Gulliver was literally an overgrown schoolboy and had a photographic memory and had read and committed to memory the complete volumes of the *Encyclopedia Britannica*.

'Yes, as it happens I did know that the male seahorse gives birth to its young. I also know that seahorses communicate with one another by using clicking sounds, and that the biggest seahorse is the big-belly seahorse, which can grow to over thirty centimetres long, and that there are over fifty species of seahorse, and that when seahorses want to go to sleep they attach themselves to weed or coral so they don't sleepwalk!' Gulliver said doing his geeky best to outdo Darwin. 'You know the biodiversity on the Galapagos Islands is quite amazing. To think Darwin spent five years here with the *Beagle*, it's like stepping back in time,' Gulliver said in wide-eyed wonderment forgetting for a moment that Darwin was standing right in front of him.

A puzzled expression appeared on Darwin's face as he looked at Gulliver as if he'd lost his senses somewhere in the Bermuda Triangle.

'Bio-di what? And what did you say about me and your dog?'

'Sorry, my mother told me I shouldn't mumble! I said perhaps if you've got time you could keep an eye on Beagle for me while I do some more sketching, Darwin,' Gulliver said covering his tracks.

'But I'm sure I heard you say a word I've never heard before, "biodiversity"!' Darwin said as the puzzled expression got deeper. That was the thing about this world, sooner or later a puzzled expression was likely to get etched upon all the members of the crew's faces like carvings upon stone.

'I might have mentioned biology,' Gulliver said as he spun another fairytale. 'You need to get out more, Charles, get some fresh air into those lungs of yours,' Gulliver said as a smile the size of an upturned rainbow appeared on his face.

'That and I need to get my ears washed out like Drake and Old Father Time,' said Darwin as he scratched his head.

*Another musket bullet dodged*, Gulliver thought to himself. It was wearing at times trying to keep everything he knew about the outcome of people's lives under his mad hat, especially when he wasn't wearing one!

'One day you're going to be a great man, Charles Darwin,' Gulliver said trying not to let the cat too far out of the bag as for the briefest of brief moments he pictured Darwin as a marble statue in the Natural History Museum in London.

'Do you really think so, Gulliver?' Darwin said innocently.

'Aye, that I do, lad, that I do,' Gulliver said mimicking the big man on board the *Golden Hind* otherwise known as Hamish.

'In that case, so will you. You'll become a great explorer and circumnavigate the world,' said Darwin with an earnest look upon his face.

'Aye, happen I might,' Gulliver said mirroring Darwin's expression.

'Aye, happen I might too,' Darwin said in parrot fashion.

Then both the boys fell about with laughter, so much so that Gulliver fell down a large rabbit hole nearly disappearing for good, until with the help of Darwin and Alice he managed to scramble out. Luckily this was one of those friendly islands that were often mentioned on documentaries on the Discovery Channel in his world. Later Gulliver joked to Alice that he swore he saw a rabbit in the hole that was carrying a fob watch in his waistcoat pocket! However, Gulliver did find something in his pocket when he crawled out of the rabbit hole, a ten pound banknote with a picture of Charles Darwin upon it and in the headshot he was old and as bald as a bald eagle with a long grey beard, which made him look not unlike a wizard.

Gulliver wondered if he should show young Darwin

a picture of how he would look when he got old. This was one of those no brainers they talked a lot about in his world as he saw a picture of himself in his head raising both of his eyebrows towards the event horizon. This Gulliver took as a sign, a sign which read 'No, under no circumstances should you show young Darwin a picture of old Darwin, not unless you want to see Darwin spontaneously combust in front of your eyes!'

One thing Gulliver didn't have to wonder about was how he looked when he got old because he already had some idea. Not that thirty-five was old, although to a twelve-year-old boy I suppose it was.

Perhaps the whole incident had been another one of Gulliver's vivid dreams. Like the one he had two nights ago of being encased inside a great big bubble which floated into the sky and into outer space, past the Hubble telescope where the dream rather turned into a nightmare when the bubble burst! Gulliver was thirty-five so he was used to people and life bursting his bubble; no doubt if he bumped into Sigmund Freud he would tell him his dream signified as much. Gulliver had already had a dream where he was lost in a forest of clocks of all shapes and sizes, although predominately the forest was full of large grandfather clocks, clocks which chimed so loudly they made his ears bleed. As time passed, Gulliver got more and more panic stricken as he couldn't find his way out of this forest of clocks. He distinctly remembered thinking that if a tree falls in a forest and there is nobody around to see it fall, does it make a sound? Gulliver thought about this question, although he didn't want to lose any sleep over it, before he heard a voice echo through the labyrinth in between his ears 'Yes, if you are in a forest of grandfather clocks it does!'

When Gulliver awoke from this dream-cum-nightmare he was given to think that if there was such a forest of clocks in this world then all you would be able to hear was an eerie silence. Gulliver then thought of the phrase 'the silence is deafening', which to him made no more sense than either his world or this one!

There was a plentiful supply or bread fruit and coconuts on the island as were there wild boars. Gulliver was amazed to find giant turtles which carried semi-detached houses around with them on their backs, or so it appeared to him. And the birds were every colour of the rainbow. This gave Gulliver plenty of opportunity to get his sketch book out and record all he saw. Something he'd rather not have seen were the volcanoes on this island; most of them were dormant but most was not all. Later the people of these lands and waters were to name these volcanoes 'sleeping giants' and to be honest, after the run-in with the volcano on Solomon's Island, now known as Gulliver's Island, Gulliver had pretty much had his fill of volcanoes, dormant or otherwise. Gulliver had recently watched a documentary on television about a recently discovered volcano in a little place in the Middle of Nowhere called God Knows Where, which had been called The New Galapagos. Actually in truth it was in Papa New Guinea but Gulliver liked the sound of the Middle of Nowhere and God Knows Where. Here, so many new species had been discovered it was untrue, even though it was true, the scientists had been flown into the volcano by helicopter and had set up camp in the volcano and was studying these new lifeforms. While Gulliver was on the Land of the Giant Seahorse he was picturing all this on the television set in his head, known to most people as their mind's eye.

Gulliver had always wanted to go to the Galapagos Islands and here he was, he could barely believe it.

Nowadays it would have cost him an arm and a leg to visit the Galapagos Islands, that's if he'd even be allowed on the islands as the amount of people being allowed onto them was being restricted as it was such an important ecological site.

Gulliver saw several colourful chameleons on the islands, one as large as a cat and a dwarf chameleon no bigger than the head of a match. When he was at school he wished he could change colour like the chameleon to escape the school bullies. He also wished he'd had the chameleon's eyes, which worked like 3D cameras in that the left eye worked completely separately to the right, which gave the chameleon 3D images. Its brain could send separate signals to each eye giving it a panoramic view of its surroundings. Mother Nature really was a marvel at genetic engineering. Gulliver later wrote this in his travelogue, along with another incident. This incident occurred one night when the night sky was lit with tiny moving pinpricks of light that weren't shooting stars but fireflies dancing above their heads.

Gulliver had often seen people let off Chinese lanterns into the sky in his world. This magical sight reminded him of golden jellyfish swimming to the surface as the sunlight streamed through the water, images caught on film in wildlife documentaries he'd seen on John Logie Baird's magic box of tricks.

These images had always made Gulliver want to travel but until now the only travelling he'd done was in his imagination. Now he was actually seeing these things for himself and at times he found it hard to believe this wasn't simply just another one of his vivid Technicolour dreams in HD 3D.

The crew of the *Golden Hind* spent a week on the island

of Isabella and when the time came, most were reluctant to leave. For a minute or two Gulliver wondered if Drake may have a mutiny on his hands like on the infamous mutiny on the *Bounty*. 'Mutiny, Mister Christian. Hang him from the highest yardarm!' Gulliver could recall Lieutenant William Bligh's voice giving the master's mate, Fletcher Christian, the instructions to do just that to one of the mutineers. This was of course from the film *Mutiny on the Bounty* as Gulliver hadn't been in this world long enough to witness such an event. However, the thought had occurred that surely it was just a matter of time before he witnessed such an historical event. Gulliver wondered that if he did and he got involved and changed the outcome of the event, would that somehow have an effect on the timeline that no longer existed. Not only was Gulliver intent on giving Alice a run for her money in the wondering department but it also appeared he wanted to surpass her in that department too!

On the island, Gulliver and Alice enjoyed stretching their legs chasing wild boar or moreover being chased by wild boar. Darwin and Gulliver were amazed at the many different species of hummingbird, all the colours of the rainbow and some not much bigger than his thumb. One appeared to be wearing Joseph's amazing Technicolour dreamcoat and another hummingbird was indigo violet, another's emerald green coat looked rather oily in the sunlight, while another hummer had a shimmering fluorescent hue to it. Gulliver knew the hummers had poetic names like the Coronet and the Jacobean, which made Gulliver wonder how Shakespeare would have described them. Gulliver had little doubt he would have described them in the most glowing and poet of terms. The island of Isabella was like the enchanted garden he'd seen on a nature programme on the television filmed in Colombia, except bigger much, much bigger. On the programme on television Gulliver had seen hundreds of hummers drink from sugared waterfeeders, sucking the water through their large curved beaks as they hung in the air as if frozen in time; hummingbirds that could beat their wings at over fifty times a second and could fly backwards, as if it were the most natural thing in the world.

For Gulliver, seeing the hummingbirds close up was even better than having a HD 3D television. The Galapagos Islands were like a giant enchanted garden, Gulliver was later to write in his travelogue. Darwin wasn't so given to such poetic musings, rather being more prosaic and technical in his observations and writings about what he had seen and collected in specimen jars on the islands. However, he marvelled at the extremes he saw on the islands from the giant turtles with shells big enough to climb into, to the Tom Thumb-sized hummingbirds, this island truly was a paradise on earth. Gulliver had also seen a documentary on the Indian Ocean where certain countries were planning national parks in the seas to protect the environment and the life that lived in these environments, this was so fish could be protected from overfishing. Gulliver then thought of the game he played as a child with cardboard fish with magnets stuck upon them which you had to catch with a fishing line with a magnet attached to it, and as the globe in this world was metallic, then you could see why this thought came to mind, that and large fish often swallowed metal objects that were lying on the ocean bed.

'Hold that thought,' Gulliver said to himself under his breath as he remembered seeing a modern globe in a toy shop in Brixham in Devon which was made in an antique style with metal meridians and had physical cartography upon it, raised mountainous areas and ocean troughs. This reminded Gulliver of the globe he was standing upon as if he was a Lilliputian and if he wasn't careful the globe would start spinning and he would have to run on the spot so as not to fall off as if he was running on a treadmill, a treadmill that was slippery! As this globe was antique, in theory this meant he should find the Seven Ancient Wonders of the World somewhere upon it, but only if he had a good map at his disposal. Did Gulliver want the gods or a master cartographer to draw him a map? You bet he did!

Gulliver let go of this curious thought as while sitting under the palm tree he recalled to mind the cave in Ecuador where there was supposed to be a mythical library full of golden books. However, that was in his world and the vision and the compass they had seen in the table made of ice hadn't seemed to point in that direction. Gulliver didn't want to send Drake and his crew on a wild goose chase, or an even wilder one than they were already on, anymore than he wanted to be chased by a pack of wild geese! So Gulliver, having given it much thought, decided to trust his instinct and the ice wizards and put it to the back of his mind. While sitting under this palm tree, a small coconut fell on his head, which reminded him of Newton's laws of motion: what goes up etc. etc. must come down etc. etc. However in this particular case, he rather wished what goes up stays up, like space junk!

Just before they left the island, Darwin discovered what he thought was a new species which he named a flat fish because it was as flat as a skimming stone. When he first saw it lying in the shallow water by the shore, he went to pick it up only to get the fright of his life as it squirmed away. Darwin then found a school of flat fish, one the size of a large dinner plate, which Drake said would make a good addition to the Antiquarium. So several seamen that were able, including Able Seaman Able Drinkwater, went out in a long boat with a net and after much hilarity from the rest of the crew caught this rather large flat fish. As several seamen who appeared not to be so able fell overboard into the sea attempting to haul the flat fish into the long boat, a song broke out upon the shore. A chorus of a song Gulliver knew well: 'One, two, three, four, five, once I caught a fish alive, six, seven, eight, nine, ten, then I threw it back again.' This song could be heard all along the beach as the slightly inebriated rum-soaked crewmembers fell about with laughter!

When several of the fish were brought aboard they were stored in an old powder keg filled with seawater. Drake joked that if supplies ran out this new species may well end up in their bellies rather than in a tank in the Antiquarium in Devon.

Darwin was surprised to say the least that sea lions and penguins found a home in the Land of the Giant Seahorse, but that was the thing about these islands, they were full of hidden treasures, full of surprises.

So the Golden Hind's crew rejuvenated and in high spirits after their week's holiday on the Land of the Giant Seahorse set sail again this time for the continent of Africa.

By this time Gulliver was convinced that it was Africa that held the answer to the question of where his mythical bookshop was hidden away. Gulliver knew Africa was the cradle of mankind and where his ancestors had sprung from. He had read many books on Africa and on explorers such as Stanley and Livingstone. How he would love to meet them. Mind you, with this being a parallel world, perhaps they weren't explorers, perhaps they were carpet makers and lived over a tiny shop in Cricklewood and had never travelled further than the end of their street. Of perhaps as this was a parallel world, it had been Livingstone who had said to Stanley, 'Stanley, I presume,' instead of in his world where Stanley had said to Livingstone, 'Livingstone, I presume.'

As Drake was a sailor in this world and Darwin was well on his way to discovering and writing *the Origin of Species*, so it followed that there was every chance he'd get to meet his heroes. After all, why not? He'd gotten to met Francis Drake who, God willing (but no thanks to the gods), would one day get his knighthood, becoming Sir Francis Drake. Unless like Raleigh he fell foul of Queen Elizabeth I! Gulliver wasn't sure he wanted to meet Queen Elizabeth I, by all accounts she could be a little fiery and unpredictable and he had grown rather attached to his head.

Gulliver had always wanted to meet Queen Elizabeth II in his world, but right now that seemed as unlikely as him ever getting back to his own time.

On their journey towards Africa they saw several Spanish galleons but wisely the Spanish gave the *Golden Hind* a wide berth. Drake had no time to get embroiled in a skirmish with the Spanish, that could wait for another time and place. Drake couldn't afford to take his eye off the prize, which was The Last Bookshop in the world, which supposedly housed all the rarest books ever written, some were even said to be written in gold. On this part of the voyage Gulliver asked Old Father Time what he perceived to be a rather tricky question which was, 'What was there before time?' Old Father Time gave this question much thought, stroking his beard more times than Gulliver had ever seen him do before. After several sandglasses had been turned on their heads, he gave this studious reply, 'Well, Gulliver, I'm afraid that was before my time!' In truth, Gulliver probably should have seen that one coming.

Some time later, having sailed across the equator, through the Tropic of Capricorn in the South Pacific Ocean, passing New Zealand, or at least Gulliver knew it as New Zealand, past several small unnamed islands, around the foot of South America seventy degrees west of the Greenwich Meridian, passing Cape Horn and into the South Atlantic Ocean until finally the continent of Africa came into sight, which was a sight for sore eyes for all on board the *Hind* and after all that sailing and lack of sleep, believe you me these sailors had very sore eyes!

Now Gulliver didn't want to tell Drake his business, after all the only boats he'd sailed were in his imagination or in his bathtub, but he had wondered why they hadn't taken a short cut through the Panama Canal but instead had gone the long way round Cape Horn. *Perhaps it hadn't been built yet, or perhaps Panama hadn't even been mapped,* thought Gulliver. Gulliver had no wish to fall out with his hero or be thrown overboard for being a bigheaded know-it-all egghead geek who for once wasn't Greek. And he didn't want to incur the wrath of Queen Elizabeth I when they got back home to England for sailing too close to the wind either, so sensibly he kept his council on the matter. The truth was that Gulliver's knowledge of Panama and its canal left a lot to be desired as the Panama Canal wasn't opened until 1914. Still, one has to make allowances, after all Gulliver was only a boy of thirty-five! Drake later made a joke saying he hoped they didn't sail too far off course and run into pirates in the Caribbean. It appeared that Drake had perfectly good reasons for not sailing through the Panama Canal besides it not being there! Gulliver wondered what Drake would make of the film *Pirates of the Caribbean*, he'd probably say it was a fairytale and nothing more!

So once again the *Golden Hind* had to go through the rigmarole of waiting for the tide to rise so it could sail out through the gap between the cork and the glass, and splash down in the South Atlantic Ocean as if it were an Apollo space capsule. This time the manoeuver wasn't exactly plain sailing as one of the masts was damaged when the *Golden Hind* got wedged in between the cork and the glass. The sailors had to pull several of the planks from the *Hind's* decking and slowly and carefully lever the ship until it was free.

Unfortunately, due to the unpredictable currents in this part of the world, the *Golden Hind* then had to freefall like a skydiver until it hit the water, where it rolled several times before righting itself. Eventually all the crew managed to get onboard and miraculously only one sailor was lost at sea, however, this may have been the sailor's own stupid fault! And the reason for this being the sailor's own stupid fault was that while his colleagues were in the business of freeing the *Golden Hind* from its unfortunate predicament, he was drowning his sorrows in rum!

'Help, help! I can't swim!' Gulliver cried. However, luckily Beagle could and was coming to his master's aid at quite a rate of knots. Beagle was of course doing the doggie paddle, which was only to be expected. Soon Beagle was at his master's side and helped keep Gulliver's head above water before a keg of gunpowder sailed their way, which they clung to for dear life until a long boat picked them up.

Alice, who could swim like a fish to such an extent that

the crew nicknamed her 'the Mermaid Girl', rescued several sailors who couldn't swim like a fish but could sink like a stone. One of the sailors said while he was in the water he swore he'd seen Alice with a large fish tail attached to her body. Drake said perhaps he needed to get his eyes tested!

But all's well that ends well, and apart from some very wet sailors who looked like drowned rats, plus a few objects upon the *Hind* that were not properly tied down and which parted company with the ship's company, luckily only one hand of the ship's company was lost, although he probably didn't think it was lucky! Gulliver wrote these exact words in his journal while adding that at least the sailor in question who was lost at sea was probably too drunk to know much about it!

Drake stayed onboard, as was the practice of captains; the last thing you wanted was your captain to end up being roasted on a spit over an open fire like a wild boar. However, it was fine if any other member of the ship's company ended up as toast!

'Land in sight, Captain!' shouted the midshipman in the crow's nest.

'We'll we've made it, Gulliver, but where on earth are we?' Drake said scratching his chin vigorously and sounding like Magellan halfway around his circumnavigation of the globe.

'Africa's a big place, Captain. All I can say for sure is that Africa is on our starboard bow and we're coming alongside it and once we've found the bottleneck it won't be long before we're in the heart of Africa,' Gulliver said bluffing his way through his cobbled-together, less-than-compendious explanation of the patently obvious.

'Yes, that sounds logical,' said Drake as the sun started to dry the ship and its company out.

'I think it's best we sail along the coast until we reach

North Africa, that's where the vision appeared to be pointing us towards. Wouldn't you agree, Gulliver?' Drake said, looking at Gulliver to confirm his summation of the situation.

Gulliver was finding this all a little hard to believe; here he was standing upon the deck of the *Golden Hind*, one of the most famous ships of all time, and not the replica that stood in Brixham harbour, or the one docked in London either. And believe it or not Sir Francis Drake, no less, was asking his advice, even if he wasn't a sir yet. It was bonkers there was no other word for it; he'd looked through his pocket dictionary and the only word that fitted this situation was the word bonkers, bonkers with a capital B; Bonkers, Bonkers, Bonkers, although mad with a capital M wasn't far behind it!

The *Golden Hind* sailed along the coastline for what seemed like quite some time until it reached North Africa. Once at the tip of North Africa they sailed into shallow waters and the crew disembarked via the long boat, this time with Drake on board. Drake said to Gulliver as he climbed aboard the long boat, 'Now is not the time for faint hearts.' Later still, when the tide rose and was of equal height both inside and outside the bottle, they slipped from the sea into the bottle with the ship in it. Drake had said that perhaps it might be a might safer if they pushed the long boat off the top of the ship's bottleneck and either dived into the water below or abseiled down the ropes, like they had in the snow dome. However this all took time, which they didn't have, so in the end they took the waterfall approach and crossed all their fingers and toes. The fall wasn't as great as it had been before and, although a few of the crew fell off the long boat into the water, they all managed to get back onboard relatively easily.

Gulliver noted that whichever country he came to

the ship in the bottle took the shape of that nation's national boat. In other words, a canoe in the Pacific Islands, a Viking long boat in Norway, a Spanish galleon in Spain, a junk in China, a giant lavish golden barge with oars to match in Egypt, a gondolier in Italy, and an ark in Israel, actually Gulliver was only yanking the reader's anchor on that last one. However, if things ever got so bad and a flood occurred you could always scale the mountainous ship and hole up there until the floods passed!

# 16

# The Think Tank to end all Think Tanks

The crew of the *Golden Hind* were not met with any opposition of any note, in fact they found the African people only too obliging, especially when they found they had not come to round them up and put them in the cargo hold of their ship and then take them halfway around the world before selling them into slavery.

It wasn't long before Gulliver, with his O level geography grade B and his knowledge of old sea maps, realized they were in Morocco. A little while later, with the help of several of the local people, they found themselves in Marrakesh. It appeared to Gulliver from his travels in his head with the aid of picture books and HD television, which included the History, Eden, Discovery and National Geographic channels, that in this part of the world after the great shake-up, time had become even more mixed up than in England.

Then fate smiled kindly upon Gulliver when he bumped into a man, who knew a man, who knew a man, who thought he knew a man who could help them. After some argy-bargy, bartering, begging and pleading, the man who knew a man who thought he knew a man actually did know a man who could help them.

Now you may or may not be interested in who this man was, well, whether you are or not I'm going to tell you anyway, for their meeting was either an amazing coincidence or synchronicity gone mad. For this man was none other than Hans Christian Andersen, the storyteller that Gulliver had bumped into in Portsmouth within spitting distance of The Liar's Inn.

Anyway to cut a long story shorter, Hans Christian Andersen pointed them in the direction of a small shop that sold carpets that weren't magic. And how did they know these carpets weren't magic? Well, because they weren't flying off the shelves and out the door!

Gulliver told Hans Christen Andersen about the quest and as Hans loved books he asked if he could join them. Gulliver said that as it was he who had directly and indirectly got their quest started, then it would be a pleasure to add his company to the ship's company, if you get my continental drift. And that was how Mr Hans Christian Andersen joined the ship's company of the *Golden Hind* and, after hearing about Alice 'the mermaid girl' this was how Hans Christian Andersen came to write the fairytale *The Little Mermaid* and that's not a fairytale, even though in truth it is!

Gulliver, Alice, Drake, Old Father Time and Hans Christian Andersen were shown through a beaded curtain into a back room of the carpet shop where four men sat around a table playing backgammon and one puffing on a hookah pipe. The room was filled with the scent of musk, myrrh and frankincense, which at first was more than a little overpowering. The men stopped their backgammon doubles match and introduced themselves.

'My name is Isaac Newton,' Newton said, standing up and welcoming them, 'and my colleagues from left to right at the table are, Nicolaus Copernicus, Archimedes, Pythagoras, Timaeus and the fellow at the end gazing into the distance likes to be known only as Nostradamus. Gentleman and ladies will you please be seated?' Isaac Newton finished speaking then moved the table with the help of Pythagoras and sat cross-legged in the middle of the room, as one by one his colleagues joined him,'

'Now we've heard it on the grapevine that you are looking for The Last Bookshop in the World and you've come halfway around the world to find it. My first question to you has got to be, are you stark raving mad? Have you lost the senses God gave you or just your sense of direction?' Newton said with a straight face before he and the five most original minds on the planet broke into laughter.

'You'll have to excuse my ebullient friend, he has quite the sense of humour you know, or at least he thinks he does!' Nicolaus Copernicus said smiling warmly, 'In this part of the world we are known as the Think Tank, or at least I think we are. Unfortunately two of our members aren't present at this juncture in time, Leonardo Da Vinci, who's painting somebody's last supper, which to be honest is his bread and butter, although from time to time he moonlights on this little think tank of ours. Well, I suppose it keeps the big bad wolf from the door!'

Gulliver knew Leonardo Da Vinci lived in the fifteenth century but then again he always was a man ahead of his time so this fact shouldn't have surprised Gulliver unduly.

'The brains of the operation has also gone walkabout, that's Albert Einstein, sometimes that man thinks he's

God Almighty. At the moment he thinks he's discovered the theory of everything and won't be disturbed until he's checked his calculations several times over. Frankly, I think he's one brain cell short of a brain stem! The other day he thought he'd discovered the theory or relativity. I mean no one denies the guy's a genius but sometimes he can be a loose cannon, if you know what I mean!' Copernicus said raising both his eyebrows to their zenith.

Drake knew exactly what he meant, several loose cannons had run over his foot the last time they were in a rough sea. Although Queen Elizabeth I admired Drake's buccaneering qualities, at times she thought he too was a loose cannon as he didn't always adhere to the principles of her fleet. Drake was always having run-ins with Sir Thomas Baskerville, who was admiral of the navy, but then again, Drake was a privateer and was never a great lover of authority to boot! Gulliver wondered why Galileo wasn't in this think tank; could it be that the Vatican, who thought he was a loose cannon, still had him under house arrest for his unorthodox belief!?

'So tell me why you want to find this mythical bookshop, which by the way isn't that mythical,' Nostradamus said quizzically.

'Because we like books,' said Alice making more sense than all the greatest thinkers in the world put together, well, minus Einstein and Da Vinci!

'The kid's a smart cookie there's no denying that,' said Isaac Newton, who at this point in time hadn't had a knighthood bestowed upon him.

'Yes, she's certainly a lot smarter than Cookie the ship's cook that's for sure!' Drake said lightening the mood.

'Well, I don't know about you boys, but I say we put our eggheads together and solve this little mystery right here and now!' Archimedes said enthusiastically. 'Oh no, I think I left my thinking cap at home!' he said with a worried look upon his face.

'Don't worry, Archie, you can borrow my fez,' said Newton thoughtfully

'Piece of cake,' said Nostradamus tucking into a piece of dried cake.

'Piece of cake, that's funny because the last time you tried to divide a piece of cake up you clearly showed how little you knew about mathematics!' said Pythagoras rather abruptly.

'Don't worry, kid, we'll figure it out in no time,' said Pythagoras as he looked at the miniature sundial on his wrist before looking at both Alice and Gulliver at the same time, which made him appear boss eyed. Then Pythagoras started counting on his fingers, which to Gulliver did seem a little archaic but still, as he had only just scraped through O level maths, who was he to argue with such a computer-like brain as the one that was ensconced within Pythagoras's skull?

'I was thinking,' said Archimedes before he was interrupted by Pythagoras.

'You know where thinking got you, Archie,' said Pythagoras raising an eyebrow or two.

'Sorry, not with you, old chap,' said Archimedes, mirroring Pythagoras's expression.

'Well, the last time you tried thinking you shouted 'Eureka!' jumped out of a bath full of water, ran down the street as naked as the day you were born and were nearly arrested for indecent exposure!'

'I was thinking,' Archimedes said before continuing. 'I was thinking and thanks to your untimely interruption now I can't remember *what* I was thinking!' said Archimedes with a puzzled expression on his face.

'No, I can't think what you were thinking either, running down a street naked in the middle of the day!' said Pythagoras, moving the beads of an abacus first one way then the other. 'That's the trouble with Archie, he's always thinking outside the old bathtub when he should be thinking outside the old box!'

Then Timaeus, an astronomer of the old school who in truth Gulliver had heard little of, mostly because he rarely spoke, stepped outside to consult the stars. However, having been blinded by the patently obvious, the sun in this case, and realizing it was still daylight, came back into the room and shook his head. It seemed the stargazer couldn't give them the time of day and he went back to smoking his hookah.

'Timaeus!' Gulliver said sounding like Archimedes when he exclaimed eureka before adding 'Plato!' Drake hoped Gulliver wasn't going to go through the whole of Greek history picking out historical figures of note as Greek history was all Greek to him, that and if he did they would all be here till kingdom come!

Timaeus stopped smoking his pipe and said, 'Plato, who's he when he's at home?' He then smiled and went back to smoking his hookah as if to say 'my work here is done.'

'Tell us all you know and we'll see what we can do,' said Newton, in a polite but austere manner hoping to restore some sort of order to the proceedings. To be honest Gulliver was rather starstruck at seeing one of his heroes in the flesh and shook Newton's hand rather too vigorously.

'I'd like to congratulate you on the Newtonian reflector,' Gulliver said trying not to gush too much.

'Well, thank you, young man, that's most kind of you to say so. Now when did I invent that?' Newton said stroking his long beard as a frown creased his already creased forehead.

'1668, sir,' Gulliver said as his brain ticked over and then produced the correct year at something approaching the speed of light.

'Really, was it that long ago? It seemed in those days I had all the time in the world. Little did I know the end of time was just around the corner!' Newton said reflecting on the passing of time and his invention all at the same time.

'I'm thinking of building a place and filling it with telescopes, then we can put names to all those bodies and faces out there and stop calling everything the planet X!' Newton said, with a wry smile on his face.

The search for the planet X, now that was a quest Gulliver wouldn't mind going on; a voyage to the distant far-flung reaches of the galaxies, sailing upon the cosmological oceans in a ship that travelled across time and space. Gulliver was daydreaming again and was only brought back down to earth by the sound of Newton's voice.

'What do you think of me calling it a planetarium, a bit like an aquarium minus the fish and plus the telescopes, stars and the planets?' Newton said, looking at Gulliver studiously over his half-moon spectacles.

As soon as Newton finished his sentence Gulliver was imagining astronomers in wetsuits immersed in water in tanks looking up at the stars through waterproof telescopes. Mind you, water did magnify things so was this so far-fetched? Don't answer that!

'I, I couldn't think of a better name for it,' said Gulliver knowing at this exact moment that he was a part of history, albeit an alternative history as Gulliver knew that the planetarium was original called an orrery and that in fact it had been Galileo who had invented the first planetarium in the third century BC, which was a rotating globe which could illustrate the movements of the 'seven wonders' which were the sun, the moon, Mercury, Venus, Mars, Jupiter and Saturn. He also knew that Galileo had called the telescope a perspicillum in his 1610 paper 'Starry Messenger'. Perspicillum, a word which didn't exactly roll off the tongue but which Gulliver liked the sound of, even if it was a bit of a mouthful and he couldn't spell it for toffee. Gulliver wondered, like his hero Professor Brian Cox, if he should tell Newton it wasn't his destiny to discover the planetarium but Galileo, but perhaps in this crazy mixed-up parallel world it was Newton who was to make this giant leap for mankind.

Gulliver had recently read in the *New Scientist* that quantum boffins thought it was the big silence which kicked off the universe and not the big bang. *More boffin eggheads blinding us with science again,* Gulliver thought when he'd read this article.

Newton looked extremely pleased with himself, like the astronomer who found the planet X one might say. Gulliver knew it was a man named Clyde Tombaugh who had found the planet X, or as they later called it Pluto, which a few years ago had been downgraded to a dwarf planet, and Gulliver thought this world was crazy!

Anyway, to cut a long story even shorter still, Drake, Alice, Gulliver and Old Father Time left the think tank to end all think tanks to think about their little problem.

Gulliver wondered if this place should have been called Boffin Island as it was full of Boffins, well, why not? After all, there was a place called Baffin Island. Why not indeed? It's hard to argue with logic like that, although I'm sure the boffins at the new Crick Institute in London would give it a pretty good go!

Archimedes was putting figures into the abacus in his head to see if the numbers stacked up to the abacus that he was holding in his hand. Newton was scribbling equations and figures out on a blackboard in seemingly random fashion. Pythagoras was still counting on his fingers, while Nostradamus was doing a very passable impression of Rodin's statue, The Thinker, adding two and two together and making five!

In less than one turn of the sandglass later Archimedes said, 'Eureka!' Well I ask you, what else was he going to say? After all, this is Archimedes were talking about, the guy who ran naked down the road after flooding his house!

Then Archimedes handed Gulliver a folded bit of paper which he unfurled to reveal nothing, as there was nothing on the paper. At first Gulliver thought that it must have been written in invisible ink.

'Sorry, boy, we haven't a clue where the Last Bookshop in the World is, it's a complete and utter mystery and it's probably best left that way. I mean, since they found the Loch Ness monster nobody's been within a mile of Loch Ness! If they found Atlantis or Big Foot what would we all talk about?'

Gulliver, Alice, Drake and Old Father Time just stood there open-mouthed, this never happened in a Dan Brown novel, one clue would lead neatly to the next, or if not neatly at least it led to the next clue. All this time Hans Christen Andersen had kept his council and just scribbled upon a pad. Later it transpired that he was writing a story which may well have been a fairytale, on that score I could not say one way or the other.

Surely the greatest minds on the planet could solve this puzzle. All right, admittedly the think tank was down a few hundred thousand brains cells as neither Leonardo

Da Vinci nor Albert Einstein were around. Still, you would think the think tank to end all think tanks could solve this humdrum conundrum. It seemed this think tank couldn't think straight, in fact, it seemed they hadn't the brains they were born with, which in truth and to be fair to them, as brain cells start dying as soon as you're born, they hadn't!

Then Newton walked forward and handed Drake a screwed up bit of paper with writing only an inebriated spider could have written, with equations, compass directions and various doodles which looked not unlike hieroglyphics but weren't.

Drake looked at the piece of paper, frowned and handed it to Gulliver, who frowned and passed it to Alice, who frowned and then passed it to Old Father Time, who smiled and said, 'Thank you, gentlemen, for your help. We're most obliged to you.'

'Sorry, just yanking your anchor!' said Archimedes with a smile almost as wide as the Milky Way.

'I apologize for my mischievous friend but if we don't let him get his own way he throws his calculus equipment out of the perambulator,' Isaac Newton said as a slight smile lightened the dark side of his face.

And then before you could say, *'Ali Baba and the Forty Thieves'* or, *'One Thousand and One Tales of the Arabian Nights'*, they were on their way, leaving the think tank to end all think tanks arguing over whose turn it was to put the rubbish out.

'So what does it all mean? It was all gobbledegobble to me!' said Drake quizzically as they walked back through the dusty marketplace.

Gulliver's head was in such a spin he could have given a whirlpool galaxy a run for its money as left, right and centre in the bizarre marketplace throngs of people bartered for goods in a hubbub to end all hubbubs that would eventually turn into a hullabaloo!

'Luckily, Francis, I've always been good at languages, especially gobbledegobble. Basically it means we have to turn right at the seas of the Mediterranean, take a long walk across Constantinople, across the sea which is blacker than a sailor's foot, hop, skip and jump our way across Persia and then somewhere in that general area, if my calculations are correct, or should I say, the Brain Trust's calculations are correct, we should find The Last Bookshop in the World, or not!' Old Father Time said sounding rather pleased with his less-than-compendious explanation, which to the others was as clear as mud!

'I've been to Constantinople,' said Hans Christian looking up from his writing pad. 'Its like living in a fairytale with its minarets, palaces and towers. Admittedly it's poorly lit and would benefit from some fairylights but the whole place oozes mysticism. It's a fantastical place, like Paris combined with Venice and the fantasy,' Hans said as his eyes widened to that of a child waking up on Christmas Day. Later, Hans told Gulliver he was among the first wave of modern tourists to arrive in this exotic land. Hans Christian might not have said much but when he spoke you hung on his every word. Gulliver wrote this in his travelogue, which reminded him of his nightmare with words raining down from the sky upon his head and hanging on to the letter Z as he was swept out to sea.

Gulliver asked Hans Christian Andersen if he had any more ideas on the whereabouts of The Last Bookshop in the World, unfortunately he said he did not. Despite having been to this part of the world before he had never come across the bookshop, and to be honest, he had thought the whole thing was nothing more than a fairytale.

'This mythical bookshop is probably like Plato's Troy, nothing more than a golden tale extracted from the imagination of a writer,' Hans said smiling warmly. Gulliver didn't want to tell Hans that a German archaeologist in his time had discovered the lost city of Troy in Turkey. Well, why spoil a good fairytale with little details like the truth.

Unlike Gulliver, who at times was a mine of useless information, Plato's mind was full of gold which he'd extracted from his head and put upon the written page, as did Hans Christian Andersen. They were both storytellers from the old school and could make words dance to their tune like the Pied Piper. Gulliver was hoping to mine some of that gold from Hans Christian's mind, or at least pick his brains as he knew he was a seasoned travel writer.

'Well, time waits for no man, not even a knowledgeable one like Old Father Time, so we'd better get back to the *Golden Hind* and splice whatever needs splicing!' Drake said as he turned to Gulliver and rested his hand upon his shoulder in a less-than-reassuring manner.

On their way back to the *Hind*, Old Father Time told Gulliver that Leonardo Da Vinci had invented a clock that could measure infinity, although he never actually got round to building it. According to Old Father Time, the greatest expert on clocks to ever live, this was how Da Vinci's infinity clock worked: twelve cogs of exponential size were to be connected in series, with the smaller gear completing one revolution per second. Each successive cog would rotate more slowly than its predecessor, until the final cog appeared to be entirely stationary. However, that apparent standstill would be deceptive; even the final cog would be turning, albeit unimaginably slowly. It would take a billion years to complete a single revolution! Old Father Time joked that this would be the ultimate clockwatcher's nightmare. Such a valuable timepiece as this one would have to be guarded around the clock to make sure it wasn't stolen by a time thief! Gulliver didn't want to burst Old FT's bubble by telling him he had actually told him this story when they were in the hot air balloon.

After Old Father Time had retold Gulliver the tale of Da Vinci's Infinity Clock virtually word for word, it started the cogs of Gulliver's mind turning and the result was that he could imagine a thief stealing time. This the thief would do by travelling through time and stealing time from people, i.e. if they were catnapping or gazing into space, he would literally take this time away from them and add it to his own timeline. And if the thief was caught and tried for this crime, he would enter a plea of not guilty, his lawyers claiming he was only stealing people's free time, so how can you steal something that is free? Lawyers are a crafty bunch and they will always find a loophole! Nostradamus was well known for his fire and water gazing technique to predict the future, so Gulliver was sure the time thief would make a beeline for Nostradamus's timeline. *If anybody was going to build a time machine, surely it was Leonardo Da Vinci, with a little bit of help from Timaeus of course,* Gulliver thought and then smiled to himself!

In no time at all, literally no time at all, almost as if a time machine had transported them through time and space, they were back aboard the *Golden Hind*. It was funny but nobody aboard was musing about anything or gazing into space wondering about the universe or time as there wasn't time for such flights of fancy. Onboard there wasn't time or space to be bored as things on the ship needed splicing so things could be shipshape and Bristol fashion, this was just in case they ever got back to England where Bristol lay. To be honest, Gulliver wasn't sure if Bristol was still in Bristol, it may well have left the safety of its harbour and floated off God knows where, coming into port somewhere off the coast of New Holland! Or perhaps Bristol was now where Baffin Island was and Baffin Island was now where Bristol used to be. If this was the case then Gulliver thought Bristol wouldn't be all shipshape and Bristol fashion, Bristol would probably be complete pandemonium!

The trouble with Gulliver, apart from the fact that he was obviously a greatly troubled individual, was that he had a tendency to overthink things, as the Think Tank was to tell him before he left them. Talk about the pot calling the kettle black, or the greatest thinkers and minds on the globe telling Gulliver he was overthinking things!

'Do you think we're going in the right direction?' Alice enquired in a low voice into the labyrinth in Gulliver's right ear.

'Honestly, I think we're making the whole thing up as we go along, like Hans Christian!' said Gulliver with both his eyebrows raised to the crow's nest.

'I thought so!' said Alice sounding like she was on a wild moose chase, well, they had recently past North America.

Gulliver thought it was just a matter of time before they were forced to admit they were lost at sea. After which they would have to go through the whole rigmarole of tossing a gold ducat, until it landed the queen's head side up, to decide whether they went left or right at the next bit of land that jutted out. At times it appeared to Gulliver that Drake had lost the plot... of land he was looking for!

So the *Golden Hind* navigated its way through the Mediterranean in between Italy and Malta, on past Greece where historians and writers would have loved to have lived in the past, on their way to Constantinople, where Niccolo Polo, the father of Marco, and Niccolo's brother Maffeo had sailed to in the year of our lord 1250, collecting a cargo of riches from Constantinople when they arrived there. Or at least they did according to the history books in Gulliver's world, but then again, as his grandfather once told him, 'Half of history is a fairytale and the other half is made up!' Here in the Aegean Sea on the very cusp between Greece and Constantinople\Turkey, they parked the *Golden Hind* and left the meter running, leaving most of the crew on board.

Then Alice, Gulliver, Hans Christian, Old Father Time, Francis Drake, the coxswain Horace Hortop and Able Seaman Gracegirdle went on their merry way as the men carried the canoe upon the top of their heads. This was the canoe the chief of Gulliver's Island had so kindly given to them before they canoed their way across the Black Sea, making good time as they did so. That was the good thing about the land compared to the sea, the land was reasonably well marked out, what with the gods having been good enough to have clearly written place names upon the globe in the beginning when they created it.

On this journey, Gulliver had plenty of time to overthink things, even if the sailors didn't, and while doing some of this overthinking, his thoughts turned to the story of King Midas who was the king of Phrygia in modern-day Turkey. Now if this story was true and not another one of these myths\fairytales, then if they found his tomb they may find large quantities of gold. However, as his mother was always telling him when he was a boy (although technically he still was), you must concentrate on one thing at a time, for if you didn't you would end up like *Jack and the Beanstalk*, in other words you wouldn't amount to anything more than a pile of beans!

This, however, didn't stop Gulliver wondering how the history books of the future would read in a time where there was no time. *Rather confusing*, Gulliver thought, *not unlike this world as times*. But as philosophers were always saying, everything is judged in comparison to something else, or at least the philosophers Gulliver came in contact with were telling him that, or at least Archie Medes had! If you are used to a way of doing something, however alien it might appear to someone else, your way is the right way, and often the only way you know how to comprehend whatever it is you are supposed to be comprehending. After all, Gulliver didn't comprehend the English language half the time, or most of the people on his own planet, who either spoke a foreign language or spoke gobbledegook. Therefore comprehending the incomprehensible becomes fairly comprehendible, if you get my continental drift!

As they canoed down the Black Sea in a southerly direction, that's if you're holding the map in front of your face, which Gulliver was at this exact moment in non-time, which meant he couldn't see exactly where he was going! Gulliver suddenly dropped the map in the canoe as he heard a loud gurgling noise which appeared to be coming from the water far below them. This set Beagle off and he went barking mad, almost falling over the side of the canoe as his curiosity nearly got the better of him. This, Gulliver thought was one of Sir Isaac's Laws of Motion, every action having an equal and opposite reaction. To Gulliver's mind the Black Sea wasn't anywhere near as black as its name suggested it to be, or had been painted by some artists, as something in the water then caught his eye.

'Captain, I think I saw something moving in the water!' Gulliver said as a look of concern appeared upon his boyish face, prematurely ageing him somewhat.

'It was probably the sea, lad. Seas do have a tendency to do that, you know, move!' Drake said as a smile flickered across his face.

'No seriously, I thought I saw something large moving below us!' Gulliver continued.

'It might be a sea monster, Captain!' Able Seaman Gracegirdle said with a look of horror upon his face.

All aboard the canoe were jumpy and in that respect they were all in the same boat together, both metaphorically and literally speaking.

'There's a light down there!' Old Father Time said looking over the starboard side as he peered into the gloom.

'A light, it could be a USO!' Gulliver said instinctively.

'A what?' everybody bar Gulliver exclaimed with a puzzled expression on each and every one of their faces.

'An Unidentified Submersible Object,' Gulliver said matter-of-factly.

Hans Christian said nothing, as usual, but you could see by the look in his eyes what he was thinking, *this would make a great story.*

It was round about this time, or perhaps a smidgeon earlier, that Gulliver realized he actually was in the *Twilight Zone.*

Now to be fair, explaining what a USO was, which frankly could have been anything from a diver, to a sea monster, to a large piece of floating debris, wasn't the hardest thing he'd had to do since he fell down Alice's rabbit hole. And at least it wasn't a UFO, which would have taken a lot more explaining. Although if that happened he would probably have explained it away as the gods returning in their chariots, or some such nonsense.

Perhaps this was just another vivid Technicolour HD 3D dream like the one he'd had the previous night of ships sailing in the depths of the oceans like submarines; an underwater world where trees blossomed and delivered fruit and flowers grew. And where a large dome sat which wasn't filled with water but which housed a whole city and the city was called Atlantis.

Gulliver's flashback was cut short as the able seaman shouted, 'Bubbles! I can see bubbles!'

Bubbles started rising to the surface and became larger and larger and more and more frequent as time passed.

'What on God's flat earth is that!' Drake exclaimed loudly, as something resembling an overturned tin bathtub rose to the surface about a fifty feet from the canoe, nearly tipping it over.

Soon the top of the submersible contraption peeled back like a sardine tin being opened to reveal a man with dark curly hair and a beard, for to describe the man as anything but hair and a beard would have been a falsehood or a fairytale. A contraption was how Gulliver was later to describe this Underwater Submersible Object in his travelogue before adding that it reminded him of Nautilus in Jules Verne's story *Twenty Thousand Leagues Under the Sea*, or should I say the bathtub in the Nautilus!

'Does anyone know the way–'

Gulliver was half expecting the man to say 'to Amarillo'!

Then two songs vied for attention in his head, one was an old song his grandfather used to sing in the bath,

'Show me the way to go home, I'm tired and I want to go to bed.' Perhaps Gulliver was already in bed and this was just a dream, or more likely than not he'd got out of the wrong side of the bed this morning and this was turning into a waking nightmare. The other song was a childhood favourite of his and one he still sang in the bath today, 'Row, row, row the boat gently down the stream, merrily, merrily, merrily, merrily, life is but a dream.'

'Does anyone know the way to the nearest dry dock? I think I've sprung a leak!' the captain of the vessel said in an Italian accent and in a surprisingly cheerful manner considering his perilous predicament. 'You know, you can't see a thing down there, it's as black as an octopus's inkwell. Mind you, it didn't help that I dropped my torch,' the man continued with a smile on his face.

'I think you need to head that way,' Drake said pointing to where they had just come from.

'That way, you say?' the captain, said pointing in the same direction as Drake.

'Yes, just turn left of the jutty-out bit, then right of the other jutty-out bit and you'll find the land where the water ends. You can't miss it, it's well signposted,' Drake said in what some might say were less-than-nautical terms.

'*Magnifico!* I'm most obliged to you all, *arrivederci*,' and then the man and his submersible contraption disappeared in a mass of bubbles.

'Who on earth was that, and moreover, *what* on earth was that?!' said Coxswain Horace Hortop disbelievingly, which to be honest, was better than hearing Drake say, 'Where on earth are we?' and Gulliver replying, 'Don't ask me, I couldn't circumnavigate a ship around a bathtub!'

'I think it was Leonardo Da Vinci, or at least if it

wasn't it was his doppelganger. He was probably roadtesting one of his latest inventions,' Gulliver said thinking on his feet while seated in the canoe.

'Doppel what?' said Horace Hortop the coxswain, almost as disbelievingly.

'Doppelganger, somebody who looks like somebody else,' Gulliver said matter-of-factly and making perfect sense while at the same time sounding as if he wasn't.

This incident reminded him of a bathtub race he'd once been witness to as a child, but thought the telling of such a story would only muddy the waters further. And let's face it, when you're in the Black Sea, submerged deep within a parallel world, you really don't need to be muddying the waters any further than they were already being muddied. So once again Gulliver held his tongue, which was better than biting his tongue and a darn sight less painful if the truth be told. 'The truth? You must be joking!' as Hans Christian Andersen was always saying in jest.

'Well, whoever he was, I like the cut of his jib. With an attitude like that he'd make a good Englishman,' Drake said in admiration.

So the crew of *HMS Canoe* rowed on until they came to the end of the Black Sea.

Drake said they should leave the canoe in a safe place so nobody would steal it, so this is exactly what they did, finding a nice large rock to hide the canoe behind, after which they covered it over with tree branches. Hopefully they would recognize this rock on the journey back if, in fact, there was to *be* a journey back. They were now a stone's throw from Persia.

Two suns plus two moons later they found themselves in Persia where they trekked on foot until on a mountain pass they came to a sign which read: 'This way to The Last Bookshop in the World. Please don't drop litter'.

Gulliver was a little disappointed they hadn't been attacked from the skies by a pterodactyl with jaws and teeth the size of a great white shark, like in the book *The Lost World* by Sir Arthur Conan Doyle, as this would have made his travelogue a little more interesting. Having said that, if that had happened then the last entry in his travelogue may well have been, end of story! Hans Christian Andersen, having written several travelogues of his own, the most well known one being *A Poet's Bazaar*, had told Gulliver that you couldn't go around making things up just to make the story more exciting, or at least not in a book about travel, unless of course this book about travel was a fairytale with the highly imaginative title of *Gulliver's Travels*, then you could! One thing Gulliver was determined to fit in his travelogue at the end of the book was: 'This world is literally out of this world, end of story!'

'The Last Bookshop in the World straight a head, Captain!' shouted the sailor standing next to Drake looking through his spyglass, the sailor, who it has to be said, was normally in the crow's nest.

'There's no need to shout. I'm not deaf you know!' Drake said as the sailor bellowed in his ear.

'Sorry Captain. Old habits die hard!' the sailor said a little red faced.

Drake gave him that steely eyed glare he often saved for the Spanish or Sir Thomas Baskerville, almost as if to say, 'You will die hard if you ever do that again!'

'Can you believe it, Alice!?' Gulliver shouted in Alice's general direction, avoiding Drake's ears and eyes as Beagle jumped up into his master's arms like the excited puppy he now was.

'No, can you?' Alice shouted back as she saw the sign come into view.

'No, perhaps we're both dreaming!' said Gulliver disbelievingly.

'Which means we're both in one another's dreams, cool,' Alice said picking up on another one of Gulliver's expressions.

Gulliver was half expecting The Last Bookshop in the World to be underwater so you had to climb into one of those old-fashioned diving suits with the lead boots, the ones with the big metal helmets with the long oxygen pipes attached to it, if you wanted to enter the shop. Either that or the mythical bookshop would be on the moon! Gulliver's grandfather was right, Gulliver did have a vivid imagination, but nothing could prepare him for what happened next.

# 17

# At Last... The Last Book Shop in the World!

What happened next... Well, I'll tell you what happened next, after a long hike they reached The Last Bookshop in the World, unfortunately the sign on the door said, 'Closed'.

Only yanking your anchor, what it actually said was – 'Closed for Lunch (be back sometime, not sure when as time no longer exists)'. And everybody lived unhappily ever after, end of story!

No, but seriously, the shop was open for business and looked not unlike The Old Curiosity Shop in Charles Dickens's story of the same name.

'Well, it appears I was wrong, The Last Bookshop in the World isn't just a fairy story it really exists, when I write this in my next travelogue everybody will say 'Oh Hans not another one of your fairytales!' Hans Christian Andersen said in wide-eyed wonderment.

No sooner had they come through the door did a bell sound and they were greeted most courteously be an old gentleman who looked even older than Old Father Time. This certainly gave Old Father Time a second wind, making him feel young and as spritely as a newborn unicorn, or so he was later to admit to Gulliver.

'Welcome to The Last Bookshop in the World. May I take your hats and coats and dogs? You can retrieve them later from the rest room, unless you desire to keep them on your person,' the wizened-looking old man said as he smiled serenely. 'Now before we go any further, you must sign a contract to say you will not breathe a word of the exact location of our fine establishment, after all, we have a reputation for exclusivity and a client list that includes kings, queens, princes and princesses, prime ministers and heads of state from all around the globe. If you feel you cannot hold your tongue, then please close the door on your way out!' the wizened old man said without a trace of malice in his voice or on his face, although what he said he meant most earnestly.

All seven members representing Queen Elizabeth I of England and the *Golden Hind* were more than happy to sign this agreement. Beagle even signed it with his paw print, although he hoped the wizened old man was joking about putting him in the rest room along with the hats and coats, as he was as excited as anybody to see what this vast emporium contained. Gulliver knew full well he could hold his tongue as he put his fingers to his mouth and did just that, 'Yes, I can hold my tongue, see?' Gulliver said acting like a child.

'What if we were to break this agreement?' enquired the coxswain inquisitively, which was exactly what the other members of the *Golden Hind* were wondering.

'Well, if you tell anyone where this shop resides then you'll find out!' said the old man and by the look in his eyes, for the first time you could see he meant business.

In fact, he had the look of a captain of a pirate ship who was about to tell one of his captives he would soon be keel hauled around the bottom of the ship's barnacles and all, before taking a long walk off a short plank in shark-infested waters! Gulliver thought that this man would probably throw the book at them if they reneged on this contract, literally!

'Now, although from the outside this little shop of ours looks, well, looks little, tiny, minute even, however, inside it is almost as endless as the universe itself and we have a copy of every book ever written,' the old man continued without hardly drawing breath. 'Now if you want a guide we will provide you with one and all our assistants can levitate, which I'm sure you will find a great help as the bookshelves almost touch the sky. And you will most certainly need a map and a compass and a portable telescope as the bookshop is so vast. Transport is also provided; we have everything from a penny-farthing and a magic carpet, to a boat that literally flies through the air, one of Leonardo Da Vinci's latest inventions. Mr Da Vinci is one of our best customers, do you know him?' the old man enquired but didn't wait for a reply before continuing on as if he was in a hurry. 'We also have hot air balloons and airship, although they are both comparatively small compared to the ones you see in the skies above us.

'Now some of the books upon our shelves are very lifelike, in fact, you can get so lost in the story you might never leave, not being able to put it down and being so mesmerized by what you find within its pages, reading it over and over and over again. Some books will drag you in from the very first sentence and before you know it you will literally find yourself trekking through the lost world of the Amazon jungle, or fighting off sea monsters around the Cape of Good Hope, or flying side by side with Icarus on his way towards the sun, that one I wouldn't recommend!

'The Bible is a good case in point, some readers have picked up the book, sailed off into a world of imagination in their head and have never left. A boy can come into our bookshop and leave an old man like myself, although I'm not that old, I'm only 708 years old, hardly as old as Methuselah!' said the wizened old man as he took the contracts from each crewmember of the *Golden Hind* and put them under the counter, chuckling under his breath as he did so, muttering, 'The old jests are the best.'

The old man added that as long as they did not open the pages of the book they would not be drawn into the story and as such would not be sucked into the story.

It seemed that The Last Bookshop in the World operated under the same rules as the universe, ordered chaos!

This was a lot of information for everybody to take in in such a short space of time but everybody seem to take it in their stride. Gulliver thought the old saying was true, 'never judge a book by its cover, or a bookshop by its outward appearance.

'Well, off you go. As they say, time waits for no man,' the old man said as he winked at Gulliver and disappeared under the counter, literally!

Gulliver took out his brass spyglass from his pocket and held it to his left eye, criss-crossing the bookshop to see what he could see. Gulliver spied an old man resting his back against one of the tall bookshelves which appeared to tower over him like a mountain. The man was staring dreamily into space holding a book called *Dreams and their Meanings*. Gulliver asked the proprietor who this man was and the proprietor, having disappeared out of sight, now reappeared as if by magic, actually *exactly* by magic would be a better description of this happening. The wizened old wizardly man, peering over his half-moon spectacles, couldn't see who the man was as he was too far away so Gulliver handed him his spyglass. A few seconds later the Guardian of Books, as Gulliver liked to think of him, as if he was in fact an anthropologist protecting an endangered species rather than inanimate objects, having picked the man out with the spyglass who was staring dreamily into space, said with a smile on his face, 'Oh, that's another of our loyal and respected customer. He's always in here, in fact sometimes I think he lives here. He goes by the name of Mr Dreams. Oh, and Mr Fairytale is over there, he wrote the book on the magical and the unbelievable.'

Gulliver thought he must engage in conversation with these two men at some point, what with him being a dreamer and like most children, a teller of fairytales and as such they were obviously both on the same page as him. However, now was not the appropriate time for such a conversation as Gulliver could see by the look upon Mr Dreams' face that he was utterly engrossed in the book entitled *Dreams and their Meanings*. Mr Fairytale, well, he was away with the fairies, which was only to be expected!

Gulliver then asked the wizened old man another question. 'As Mr Dreams is so engrossed by the story, why hasn't he been sucked into the book yet?'

'Well, I'm not sure Mr Dreams is engrossed in the story, he suffers from narcolepsy and he's prone to walking in his sleep, so right now he might well be asleep dreaming,' continued the proprietor without batting an eyelid, as if this sort of behaviour was the most normal thing in the world, which in The Last Bookshop in the

World it quite clearly was. Gulliver then spied another book which was taller than he so inquisitively he asked the proprietor what was in the book. The wizened old man smiled and said, 'It's full of tall stories,' Gulliver smiled back because he was pretty sure the old man was yanking upon the tassel of his bookmark. Perhaps he should take a leaf out of his book and disappear into a book, he thought wistfully.

Gulliver found a suitable bookshelf, shut his eyes and picked a book from one of the shelves at random. He sometimes took books off the shelf of his library in this random manner, taking them home without reading the blurb on the back cover either, to find he had found a treasure chest full of rare jewels, or a treasure chest that was as empty a vessel as the writer who wrote it. Gulliver picked a book up called *The Search for the Lost Plot* by Grimstone Cadwell. Gulliver looked at the back of the book so he had some idea of the plotline as in this magical bookshop he knew he couldn't be so cavilier in his approach to new reading material. The plotline was that the author had lost the plot, or to be more precise, his manuscript, and spends the entire book looking for it, and when he eventually finds it, the story ends. It seemed to Gulliver that the author certainly had lost the plot. Gulliver opened the first page and read the opening line, half expecting to be sucked into the book at any minute and half not. Nothing happened so Gulliver flicked through the book and read random pages and still nothing, so he closed the book.

Now you would have thought Gulliver would have replaced the book on the shelf in its proper place as all librarians hoped the reader would do. This was only good library etiquette, however, Gulliver didn't, instead he placed the book upon the floor, which being a fairly weighty book of 700 plus pages long, he was happy to do so.

Gulliver was then momentarily distracted as out of the corner of his left eye he spied what he thought were giant butterflies, the sort you see in the rainforest, or the sort he had only ever seen on the Eden and the Discovery Channels on television. However, as he drew closer he could see they were books that were opening up like a butterfly wings as if to tempt you to dive straight into the story. Despite everything, Gulliver was still a little cautious, he wanted a little more to go on before he jumped in feet first, like the title of the book or a brief synopsis of the story on the back cover, at least that would give him some idea of what awaited him inside the book. Despite everything, Gulliver wasn't feeling adventurous enough to take this sort of devil-may-care attitude, despite being named Gulliver and despite his unbelievable adventures up until this point in non-time.

Gulliver then went back to Grimstone Cadwell's less-than-riveting book which he had placed upon the floor not a moment earlier and stared at it for the briefest of moments, he then stood upon the book, which meant he was able to rest his left foot on the second rung of the bookshelf, from where he proceeded to climb, as if he was a seasoned mountain climber.

Within a very short space of time Gulliver and Alice were both scaling large dusty bookcases and pulling out musty-smelling books, with pages with gold edging that rustled like leaves in the breeze when you turned the snowy white pages. Gulliver picked up a book called *Scaling the Mountains of the Andes*, and within seconds of getting into the book he got into the book literally as he soon found himself trekking across the vast mountainous lands of the Andes.

This antiquarian bookshop really did house a cornucopia of weird and wonderful delights as Hans

Christian Andersen was finding out as he picked up a book with a dark cover written by the Brothers Grim and was sucked into the book never to be seen again.

Alice had picked up a little book called *The Arabian Nights*; not many people had heard of it and, having read the first paragraph and while not even halfway into the second, she was transported into the land of the Arabias. Here Alice found herself riding on the back of a white stallion with the wind sailing through her hair as the sands of time flowed all around her like a river.

Drake picked up a book called *General and Rare Memorials* written by Dr John Dee and he was instantly sucked into the book, literally like a star being sucked into a black hole. The book's cover was made of brown leather with several ships sailing across with a smiling sun in the sky and an angel in the heavens playing a lyre. The spine looked as if it were made of gold, probably because it was.

For Drake, this book was like looking into his own future for it mentioned Queen Elizabeth I, him and Walter Raleigh. On the title page the title was followed by the words: 'Pertaining to the Perfect Arte of NAVIGATION' and underneath that was written: 'Annexe to the PARADOXAL Cumpus, in Playne: now firft published: 24. yeres, after the firft Inuention thereof'.

Now one must remember that in the sixteenth century the language and writing was different from today, which didn't make it any easier for someone suffering with dyslexia to understand. Gulliver gave these books a wide berth as he couldn't make sense of a word the author had written. Gulliver certainly found it easier to understand the Victorians in this world than he did the Elizabethans.

The coxswain Horace Hortop and Able Seaman Gracegirdle had reached for the same book at the exact same time, a book called *The Great Whale*. Now, as the coxswain could read and the able seaman couldn't, the coxswain was kind enough to read it to him. Unfortunately, or fortunately depending on your point of view, both men were soon sucked into the pages of the book. The wind blowing their hair to the four winds as they shrank and disappeared in between the pages of the book ending up floundering in the Southern Oceans just off New Holland as a great whale came into sight on the horizon.

Old Father Time, not wishing to be wise after the event, although being as old as he was he always would be no matter what and, having seen his friends and colleagues disappear into the pages of the books they were reading, decided to simply browse. This Old Father Time did by hiring a penny-farthing and a lantern upon a stick so he could ride around the bookshop at his leisure imagining the stories which were hidden behind the musty covers rather than actually picking up the books and turning the pages. Quite frankly, he was just too old to be gadding about on such adventures at his time of life, he surmised wisely. Or as he was to later put it in his memoirs – 'Going on one adventure of a lifetime is more than enough for a man who has previously spent most of his life housed within an old clock in Greenwich marking time.'

## 18

# A story inside a story, a curious chapter of events

And so it went on, members of the *Golden Hind* would find themselves being shrunk like Alice in Wonderland and then being sucked into a book and then sucked back out again to regain their full size. Now you would think that once was enough but not a bit of it, this jumping from one book to another in somewhat of a butterfly fashion was so addictive, making it hard to stop. This brought a whole new meaning to the phrase, 'I'm really getting into the story\book.'

'Open sesame,' Alice and Gulliver cried instinctively in unison as the cover of the book opened and they were sucked into the story.

'Alice! Alice where are you?' Gulliver cried looking all about him in somewhat of a panic, seeing nothing but sand.

'Behind you, I'm behind you!' Alice cried hanging on for dear life to the reigns of a camel. To Alice's mind, riding on the back of a camel was all a bit of a pantomime and it was not far from giving her the hump.

Gradually Gulliver managed to find the brakes on his camel and Alice caught him up.

'And I thought a ship was hard to steer!' Gulliver said managing a smile.

'I can see why they call camels the ships of the desert now!' said Alice squinting in the glare of the sun. In truth, Gulliver couldn't see why they were called ships of the desert as they looked nothing like ships and the desert was full of sand with hardly a drop of water in sight!

Then something made Gulliver turn round and he saw a posse of white horses being ridden by what to him looked like Arabian knights, who were all brandishing knives that you were never likely to find in your cutlery drawer at home. It seemed that Gulliver and Alice had found themselves in the eye of the storm 'as they say'.

'Where's a genie when you need one?' said Alice trying to lighten the mood a little.

'I wonder what's ticked them off?' said Gulliver as the wind blew up and he swallowed a mouthful of sand.

'I think we have!' said Alice as hanging down from her saddle was a brown leather bag and in it a golden hourglass.

'What's that?' said Gulliver as Alice held the hourglass up to see sand pouring from the top to the bottom.

Upon seeing the hourglass, a thought flashed across Gulliver's mind, if you rested a sandglass on its side, would that stop time? And if so and they did, would that stop the Arabian knights catching up with them and giving them a piece of their minds!

'I think it's the sands of time!' said Alice innocently.

'That thing's an antiquity, it's priceless!' Gulliver said as a bead of sweat trickled down his forehead and past his left eye, which made him look as if he was crying. 'Time we were on our way don't you think, Alice?' Gulliver said as the Arabian knights were almost upon them.

'We could just give them the sands of time back, after all it belongs to them,' said Alice sensibly.

'Look, Alice, there's no time to argue, the sands of time have nearly run out and by the black look upon their faces, I don't think they're in any mood to listen to reason, and as my mother is always telling me, procrastination is the thief of time.'

'Never mind about procrastination being the thief of time, I think it's us who are the thieves of time!' said Alice jump-starting her camel into life.

'Perhaps we can take the sands of time back to your world and time can begin again.' Gulliver said as he too jump-started his camel, which didn't look best pleased at this rather archaic way of getting his ship of the desert into gear.

'I don't think it works like that Gulliver, remember what the old man in the bookshop said, nothing is as it seems and some people have got so lost in a book they never return to their world.'

'It's so hot, I wish there was a cloud in the sky which we could shelter under,' Alice said looking into a cloudless sky.

Then Gulliver spied something in the distance so naturally he got out his spyglass and to his amazement saw a large old boat becalmed in the sand. The ship was stuck in a sand dune and by the looks of her she'd been stuck there some time. However, this was one ship that wasn't encased inside a bottle. Gulliver's eye strained to see what the name written upon the side of its hull was. He wasn't finding steering his ship of the desert any easier than he'd found steering the Golden Hind. For his ship appeared to be like a ghost ship, steering itself, changing tack of its own accord, first veering to the starboard side and then to the port side as if a drunken sailor was at the helm.

Gulliver slapped the side of his camel, making it clear to the beast that he wanted to go full steam ahead and in doing so almost fell overboard. Luckily he just managed to cling on, eventually managing to sit into an upright position. Gulliver knew he wouldn't be able to sit down for a week after this bumpy ride, he couldn't say he was saddle sore because there was no saddle, no, Gulliver was just saddled with a stubborn mule of a camel! Then he nearly fell overboard for the second time in as many minutes when the name of the boat becalmed in the sand dune made itself known to him, it was Noah's Ark, or at least it was an ark!

'Alice!' Gulliver cried, beside himself. 'Alice, I think we've discovered Noah's Ark!'

However, Gulliver had discovered from his life experiences up to this point in time that not everything is as it at first appears, or disappears for that matter. Perhaps his eyes were playing tricks upon him and this was nothing more than a mirage conjured up by a heat haze which would soon vanish into thin air.

And then in a flash of light with the Arabian knights in spitting distance, a sand storm blew up from out of nowhere and engulfed them all, now they really were both in the eye of a storm. Before they knew it, both Gulliver and Alice were sucked into a spiralling whirlpool of pages and words, which blurred together as one until they found themselves back in The Last Bookshop in the World.

'Wow!' said Alice with eyes as big as the big bad wolf in the fairy story *Little Red Riding Hood*.

'Wow!' Gulliver said, his eyes mirroring Alice's the

last time she looked into a looking glass. 'Where are the sands of time?' Gulliver said looking at Alice while spitting sand out of his mouth.

'I must have dropped them,' Alice replied. 'Perhaps it was for the best otherwise the Arabian knights might well be chasing us round this bookshop right now!' said Alice finally finding that cloud with a silver lining.

'I wondered where you kids had got to,' Old Father Time said, relieved to see Alice and Gulliver were safely back in the real world. Gulliver was wondering if he had been in touching distance of making the greatest archaeological discovery of all time just to have it disappear right before his very eyes like a conjuring trick.

Luckily Old Father Time was on hand, otherwise the crew of the *Golden Hind* would never see their shipmates or their ship ever again, engrossed in a book that they couldn't get out of, never mind put down. This was a strange world indeed; Gulliver never imagined in his wildest imaginings, which let's face it, had always been pretty wild, when it could be said that reading a book was more of an adventure than a real-life adventure, or at least no less of an adventure. The amount of times his father had said, 'Get your head out of that book and get some fresh air into those lungs of yours,' and 'Gulliver you need to live a little,' and 'Gulliver, you do know that time waits for no man, don't you?' If his father could only see him now he wouldn't believe his own eyes. In truth, Gulliver was having trouble believing *his* own eyes at times.

'Gulliver that's enough, it's time to return to the real world!' Old Father Time said grabbing Gulliver's shirt sleeve as he appeared from out of a book called *Tales of the Arabian Nights*.

'But, Old Father Time, I'm having the time of my

life, or at least I was until you grabbed my shirt!' Gulliver said rather indignantly. 'I've just seen a copy of *The Time Machine–*' Gulliver said but before he could continue Old Father Time interjected.

'Yes, that's all well and good, young master Gulliver, but we haven't the time to be playing silly beggars, and anyway, what's the good in a quest if you do not return to tell others about it,' Old Father Time said playing the old vanity card.

'But that's the point, we can't tell anybody about this bookshop, we've signed a contract,' Gulliver said brushing his unkempt hair back out of his eyes and straightening his attire.

'Contract! it's not worth the paper it's written upon!' Old Father Time said gruffly. 'Anyway, you don't have to tell anybody exactly where The Last Bookshop in the World is, you only have to say you found it but you're sworn to secrecy on pain of death, as Queen Elizabeth I had told the crew of the *Golden Hind* in his world after Drake's circumnavigation of the world in 1580. However, that doesn't stop you telling of your adventures in finding it, now does it?' Old Father Time said, sounding very convincing in his argument.

'I suppose not,' said Gulliver thoughtfully.

'There's no supposing about it, my boy, no supposing whatsoever,' Old Father Time continued on in a similar tack.

'Where's Alice?' Old Father Time enquired.

'Somewhere in Wonderland,' Gulliver said as he had seen Alice pick *Alice through the Looking Glass* off the shelf and be sucked into the book immediately, if not sooner.

'Well, young Gulliver, as soon as Alice appears from her wonderland, grab her and I'll grab Drake and the others and we can be on are merry way otherwise Old

Mrs Time will have my guts for garters for being late or early. Mind you, whatever time I turn up I'll just give her the usual excuse any Guardian of Time gives their spouse and simply say I just lost track of time!' Old Father Time said as a large smile found its way onto his dial.

To Old Father Time the bookshop resembled a maze or a labyrinth of neverending bookshelves which was as vast as the imagination itself, which was as good a description as any.

Then Gulliver spotted Alice popping up out of *Alice through the Looking Glass*, along with Wonderland, like in a child's pop-up book and just at that exact moment one of the bookshop assistants was riding on a magic carpet past the bookshelf so Alice jumped onboard. 'Alice, Alice, we need to be on our way!'

Alice heard Gulliver and shouted and with the wind in her sails and her hair blowing all about her she cried in an excited manner, 'Wonderland was so magical, I want to go back, or should I say forward?' as Alice asked the bookshop assistant to steer her towards a red leather-bound limited edition copy of *Alice's Adventures in Wonderland* by Lewis Carroll. 'Don't worry, I'll be no time at all,' Alice said with a grin on her face as wide as the Cheshire cat's. No sooner had the words fallen from her mouth like a waterfall and Alice had opened the book to the first page did she disappear into it taking her grin and the rest of her atoms with her. Now Alice didn't appear to be making much sense when she said, 'I want to go back or should I say forward?' but actually, unlike the real Alice in Wonderland, she was making perfect sense, although it might have made a might more sense if she had read *Alice's Adventures in Wonderland* first and *Alice Through the Looking Glass* second, rather than the other way round, but then again, where would the fun be in that?

'Nooooo!' cried Gulliver to no avail.

'Sorry!' the guide said apologetically to Gulliver, 'but you can't hold back an imagination like that!' he continued, shrugging his shoulders as the magic carpet whizzed off across the tops of the bookshelves before it too disappeared in between the pages of the now open book.

'Now what?' Gulliver said looking at Old Father Time quizzically.

'You'll just have to follow her,' Old Father Time said matter-of-factly.

'I won't be long,' Gulliver said climbing up the bookshelf as if he was Hillary or Tensing climbing Mount Everest.

The trouble was, Gulliver couldn't find a copy of *Alice in Wonderland*, the book had obviously disappeared along with Alice and her Cheshire cat-like smile.

'What now?!' Gulliver muttered under his breath and then it came to him, 'Eureka!' Gulliver then climbed a little higher and then moved along the bookcase a little to the left where he found a copy of *Alice Through the Looking Glass* 'Of course!' said Gulliver. 'Of course!'

Gulliver turned the pages of the book but where to enter the story, the beginning, the middle, or the end, and would he be able to find Alice? The logical thing to do would be to find the rabbit hole and from there he would be able to go from one book to the other. This was both logical and illogical thinking all rolled into one. Gulliver was thinking outside the book and the compendium box all at the same time, which considering there was no time was quite some feat.

'Here goes nothing,' Gulliver said taking a sharp intake of breath before turning to page ten where he started to read the poem that was printed there: 'Child of pure unclouded brow and dreaming eyes of wonder! Though time be fleet, and I and thou are half a life asunder, Thy loving smile will surely hail the loving gift of a fairytale.' And just as Gulliver finished the word 'fairytale' he was sucked into the book and was gone.

Suddenly, as the blinding light evaporated and Gulliver's eyes adjusted, he was standing in a room and looking up at a large gold Victorian gilt-edged mirror.

'Will wonders never cease? Of course, forget the rabbit hole, it's the looking glass I need to climb through the looking glass like Alice!' Gulliver said realizing his illogical logic was a little flawed.

Gulliver following both the Alices footsteps, climbed onto a chair and stepped into the mirror. At once he found himself on the other side of the mirror and standing on the floor staring up at the back of the clock on the mantlepiece as a little old man grinned back at him. 'This really is a great book,' Gulliver said smiling and looking all about him to see if he could see either of the Alices, but at first glance he could not, however, he could see Tweedle-dee and Tweedle-dum sharing a book. Gulliver, like Alice, was curious to see what the book they were reading was as they both had puzzled expressions upon their faces. Gulliver, not wishing to interrupt them, crept around their blind side until he was in a good position to see the title of the book. The title of the book was *Rudimentary Chess for Beginners*, no wonder they had puzzled expressions upon their faces, perhaps it would have been better if they had chosen the book entitled *The Dummies Guide to Chess* as the thoughts of Gulliver's older self popped out unexpectedly and made him cringe. Gulliver left the Tweedle twins stuck on the same page as when he first saw them huddled together on the grass with the book resting in between the two of them.

After some time, he managed to track down Alice who was conversing with a couple of chess pieces, the Red Queen and the Red King. However, it wasn't Gulliver's Alice but the real Alice from the book, if that made any sense, and curiously enough, to Gulliver it did. Gulliver wondered if he should track down a copy of the book *Gulliver's Travels* and meet the real Captain Lemuel Gulliver. But then again, perhaps he would be disappointed after meeting him 'as they say' you should never meet your heroes, even if they are fictional.

With all this talk of looking glasses, this made Gulliver recall the end of *Gulliver's Travels* when Capt Gulliver returned home and pondering on his journey he says, 'To behold my figure often in a glass, and thus, if possible, habituate my self, by time to tolerate the sight of a human creature.'

In his world Gulliver had often shunned mirrors, even as boy he had always loathed his own appearance and time had not helped to alleviate this distrust of mirrors and looking glasses. People of Gulliver's world had often told him that perhaps if he looked into mirrors his outward appearance might be much improved, however, he hadn't heeded this advice. In truth, Gulliver no more liked looking into those metaphorical mirrors than he did the real thing. Having said that, hadn't he climbed into the looking glass in *Alice Through the Looking Glass* and done it without even thinking? But that was Gulliver all over and like Alice in *Alice in Wonderland\Through the Looking Glass* he spent far too much time overthinking things and wondering, when he should just concentrate on doing. More of his father's and his grandfather's words of wisdom ringing in his ears, he thought, making his tinnitus worse!

'Excuse me?' said Gulliver not wishing to appear rude

as he tried to break into the conversation between Alice and the Red King and Queen as the White King and Queen sat upon a shovel and two castles walked by as if they had not a care in the world.

'Excuse who?' said the Red Queen indignantly.

'Yes, excuse who?' said the Red King even more indignantly, if that were possible, which it seemed it was.

'Could I have a quiet word, Alice?' said Gulliver nervously.

'Yes, of course you can have a quiet word, which quiet word would you like to have a quiet word with, silence? Or perhaps you would like to have a quiet word with the word quiet,' said Alice mischievously with the cat-that-got-the-cream look upon her face.

'Oh, I see you're yanking the chain of my fob watch like the rabbit in *Alice in Wonderland*,' said Gulliver mirroring Alice's smile.

'Alice in who?' Alice said as a puzzled expression came across her face, an expression she couldn't keep there for long before bursting into laughter.

'My name's Gulliver and I am looking for Alice,' Gulliver blurted out without properly thinking it through.

'Then you've found her, haven't you?' said Alice acting up.

'No, another Alice,' said Gulliver a little red faced.

'Another Alice in Wonderland. That's going to be ever so confusing isn't it?' said Alice as the puzzled expression returned to her face in earnest.

'Well let's see,' said Alice thinking.

'Yes let's see,' said the Red King and Queen ear wigging into the conversation.

'Well, Gulliver, if you travel in that general direction as the rabbit jumps and turn left when you see a mad fellow with a big hat on his head, but don't stop to ask him for directions for I fear you won't get any sense out of him. Then turn right at the rabbit hole, or is that left? No, no, right at the rabbit hole, and according to the map in my head you've got as good a chance as any of finding you friend Alice,' Alice said sounding extremely pleased with herself.

As the Red King and Queen said in unison, 'Yes, you've got as good a chance as any of finding your friend Alice,' before they turned away and the Red Queen said, 'The boy will fall down the nearest rabbit hole and will never be seen again!'

'Almost certainly, you can see he hasn't the brains he was born with,' said the Red King before adding, 'the boy wonder has got two chances of finding his friend Alice, little and none!'

'Madder than the hatter if you ask me. Asking for an Alice when an Alice is standing right there in front of him, surely one Alice is every bit as good as another!' said the Red Queen indignantly.

'Yes, especially as Alices are ten a penny farthing in this neck of the woods. I don't know, some people are never satisfied,' said the Red King dismissively.

Gulliver ignored the Red King and Queen, treating them with the contempt they quite clearly deserved, before thanking Alice for telling him where Alice at a pinch might be holed up.

Gulliver followed Alice's instructions to the letter and fell down a rabbit hole, which resembled a helter-skelter, pulling the wool over his own eyes. Perhaps I should put some flesh onto the bones of that last comment. Gulliver was wearing a woolly hat at the time and didn't want to see what he might come across in this rabbit hole so he pulled the hat over his eyes! So you see, not everything in Gulliver's travels is as complicated as it may at first appear. In fact, even the most illogical of things can be explained fairly easily when logic is properly applied to them. Just ask the wizards of the scientific think tank and I'm sure Newton, Einstein, Archimedes, Da Vinci, Copernicus, Pythagoras and the like would only too readily agree with that last statement, as would the logician Lewis Carroll himself I wouldn't wonder!

Some indeterminate period later, Gulliver found himself somewhere else other than where he was before, if that makes any sense. No? Good, then we can continue!

'Gulliver!' Alice cried out on seeing him as he shot out of a rabbit hole as if being shot out of a cannon and landing on the side of a hill.

'Alice!' Gulliver said mirroring Alice. 'Is this *Alice in Wonderland*? I mean the book *Alice in Wonderland*?' Gulliver said picking himself up and dusting himself down.

'Of course, where else would it be?' Alice said instinctively.

'Where indeed,' Gulliver said blowing his cheeks out. 'Old Father Time said it's time we got back to the real world,' Gulliver said breathlessly and as he did so he thought, *the real world*, really!' It seemed at last Alice and Gulliver were on the same page!

'Okay, I'm ready when you are. To be honest, I have been here for several weeks and I'm getting a little tired of talking to flowers, and to be even honester, I've never understood the game of chess,' Alice said as she pointed to another rabbit hole about twenty yards from the one Gulliver had just appeared from.

'That rabbit hole's got our name written on it,' said Alice as she took a copy of *Alice in Wonderland* out of her coat pocket and opened the book.

Five minutes later Alice and Gulliver were spiralling

down another helter-skelter as Alice was attempting to finish the story. 'Ever drifting down the stream – Lingering in the golden gleam – Life, what is it but a dream? The end' and no sooner had Alice said the words, 'The end,' did Gulliver and Alice find themselves sprawled upon the floor in The Last Bookshop in the World.

'That was a short story,' said Old Father Time smiling as he helped both Alice and Gulliver to their feet.

By this time Drake had been drawn into a mystery novel about an art theft so this line seemed somewhat appropriate.

Gulliver had seen Livingstone and Stanley in the geography section of the bookshop, picking up and reading a book called *The Lost Continent of Africa* and then they disappeared and were never seen again. Gulliver surmised they were probably still searching for the source of the Nile or at least Stanley was in his boat the *Lady Alice*. Gulliver wished he could have talked to the two men then he could have said, 'Stanley and Livingstone, I presume!' After which they would look at the boy and say, 'Gulliver, I presume, I see you're still on your travels,' Gulliver had often had imaginary conversation with his heroes as a boy. Well, if you're going to have imaginary friends then you may just as well make them famous figures from history who can keep you entertained with their imaginative tales. The truth was that Livingstone had challenged Stanley to a hippopotamus race and, at this precise moment in time they were both riding upon the backs of two reluctant hippos somewhere in the region of the Congo Basin. After which they would probably go giraffe or elephant racing, or perhaps their imagination would allow them to straddle a giant pink flamingo where they would soar above the plains of

Africa looking down at the greatest national wildlife park upon the planet. Well, that's if Stanley and Livingstone had a head for heights that is!

Gulliver knew from his school days that when translated from Arabic, a giraffe meant 'the charming one', which seemed fitting for such a graceful and peaceful creature. Mind you Gulliver had once seen giraffes fighting, although this was on the wonder that was the television. The giraffes were using their necks to knock one another over, so they weren't always utterly charming by any stretch of the imagination. But compared to some Homo sapiens, who could have definitely done with a spell at charm school, they were, Gulliver thought, reverting to his natural state of being, which was a thirty-five-year old man who occasionally suffered from the grumps!

Just before Gulliver left the bookshop he spied a book by Arthur Conan Doyle upon one of the shelves, *this was obviously before he got his knighthood*, thought Gulliver, that's if he did get one in this parallel world. Perhaps in this world Arthur Conan Doyle was a struggling writer barely making a crust, his real job being a baker in a bakery, which is where he probably got his idea for where his great detective Sherlock Holmes would live, Baker Street, now Gulliver really was stretching reality to unimaginable lengths! The book was entitled *The Lost World* and he recalled that he had read the book as a boy, he further recalled how Sir Arthur had written a short verse at the beginning of the book which went exactly like this: 'I have wrought my simple plan. If I give one hour of joy, to the boy who's half a man, or the man who's half a boy. Gulliver realized this line suited his situation like a book fitted a book's dust jacket, as at this moment he was both a boy and a man. He then realized he had known his dog Beagle both man and boy 'as they say'.

Gulliver thought what a great adventure it would be to get lost inside the pages of this particular book as he would have to canoe down both the Orinoco and the mighty Amazon rivers, climb mountains that touched the stars, and cross rickety bridges that in truth at times were simply tree trunks which had fallen across a deep crevice. One might say crossing such a bridge was a bridge too far, it certainly was if you fell! In this land that time forgot he would fight off pterodactyls with nothing more than his bare hands, his imagination and his courage, tools which would serve him well in his rites of passage in the art of making a man out of a boy. But then he came to the little senses he possessed and thought, perhaps not! It was bad enough being lost in this lost world without being lost inside a lost world within a lost world, that really would be like climbing a mountain and crossing a bridge too far! Having said all that, Gulliver surmised that if he got lost in any of the books in this bookshop, especially the historical ones, this would be the closest he was ever likely to get to travelling back in time. Well, apart from his little excursion into this world of course!

Gulliver wasn't exactly well read but he wasn't poorly read either, if that even makes the slightest semblance of sense, and knew Sir Thomas Baskerville was the head of Queen Elizabeth I's Royal Navy. He also knew Baskerville Hall was the basis for Sir Arthur Conan Doyle's book *The Hound of the Baskervilles*, but that's another story we don't really have time for. However, if you have a mind to read it, may I suggest you head for the mighty Amazon and order a copy!

*Just imagine*, Gulliver thought wistfully, *getting lost in one of Shakespeare's imaginative tales.* Oh, he certainly could do that all right, without any problem whatsoever. Imagine himself in the audience at the Globe Theatre with the great unwashed enjoying the dynamic performance of the thespians of the Royal Shakespeare Company. However, the only clue he would have as to what on earth they were wittering on about would be by their body language and by the colourful scenery upon stage. Still, at least back then time still existed and being old before his time he probably would fit in rather nicely if you please. And what's more, even though he was dyslexic, as hardly anybody could read or write back in Ye Bad Old Days, he would be seen as some sort of literary genius giving William Shakespeare a run for his money! *Perhaps, perhaps, perhaps not,* Gulliver thought, as his imagination continued to run away with him!

Some unrecorded time later all the ship's crew were back together and all disappointed they couldn't continue on with their reading matter, however reluctantly, all agreed that Old Father Time's course of action was the correct one and that it was time to be on their merry way. So they all gathered together books that they liked, or they thought the ship's company would like, or they thought they could make a tidy profit from, or they thought would make a good doorstop or boot scraper and then went on their merry way.

Gulliver got several books and almanacs on horticulture and biology for Darwin, although not *The Origin of Species,* even though several copies of the book were sitting upon the bookshelves. Gulliver didn't want to freak Darwin out and as he wasn't sure how time now worked, or didn't, he wasn't sure if Darwin would rewrite *The Origin,* or perhaps he wouldn't write it at all and would get fed up with nature and become a sail maker instead! Every time a book was taken off the shelf in The Last Bookshop in the World an exact copy replaced it as if by magic, exactly by magic as it happens, or so said the proprietor smiling warmly.

Gulliver also found several books by the wizard Leonardo Da Vinci, one which was entitled *Codex Atlanticus*, which was a treasure trove of information, drawings, diagrams of helicopter-like vehicles, submersible, even things which looked like flying machines. According to his writings it was just a matter of time before there were self-propped vehicles and as usual he wasn't wrong.

Later Gulliver was to find out, when talking to the proprietor of the shop, that he had bought an ordinary old oak chest with metal clasps that was said to have belonged to Da Vinci. At first the proprietor of The Last Bookshop in the World thought this was just a fake but, after much reading and research and testing of the 10,000 pieces of papyrus drawings and manuscripts for age, and the handwriting, he found this lost treasure trove was in fact genuine. The old man told Gulliver it was hard to believe the writings and drawing in this chest were one man's work, for at first glance they appeared to be a compendium of writings of hundreds of writers.

However, the wizened old man said, with a look in his eye as if he had just caught lightning in a jar, as this object was priceless, it was another object that couldn't be removed from the shop. You were quite welcome to delve into this treasure trove but you couldn't take any of the contents away with you. Gulliver wished Leonardo had invented a photocopying machine! Gulliver asked the proprietor how this could be, with a curious look upon his face. The proprietor said, it just was, so he should just accept it. After all, time was all mixed up and let that be an end to it. Gulliver took this to mean the equivalent of 'end of story'. However, regarding Leonardo Da Vinci it was far from end of story!

It had occurred to Gulliver that as Galileo had written a paper on the making of spheres it was he and Leonardo Da Vinci who had designed this antique globe and the workings thereof. However, even in this world, surely that wasn't possible. Some things had to be impossible, didn't they? There must be a limit to what was possible for if there wasn't they may as well take the word 'impossible' out of the dictionary. If you took 'impossible' out of the equation, what was there left to strive for as it had always been the impossible that made things possible? If you get my continental drift!

Gulliver saw a bookish-looking lad of no age at all take a book off one shelf, strip the book of its dust jacket before putting it on as if it were a coat, as he muttered under his breath, 'It fits perfectly. Almost as if it were tailormade for me,' the lad said admiring himself in an antique gold gilt-framed mirror that was standing in the shop.

And if you're wondering as to what book the lad took the dust jacket off before he put it on, well wonder no more, for the book was called *The Emperor's New Clothes*. So the next time you're given over to wondering, I suggest you take a leaf out of Alice's book and give it a wide berth!

Gulliver was finding all this hard to take in. The contents of this shop, which from the outside seemed unassuming enough, but when one stepped through the door and looked upon its contents it was literally mind-blowing. Gulliver could almost feel the neocortex and pathways in his head sizzling as he tried to assimilate the information that was now being fed into his brain. At this point in non-time there was a real chance of his head exploding like a champagne supernova. This Gulliver did not want for he had his heart set on his brain being pickled in a jar to end up sitting on a shelf in the Natural History Museum, although for the moment that could wait!

Gulliver also spotted a book called *The Antikythera Mechanism* by an unknown author. This tatty-looking book, which was almost falling apart, some of the pages even crumbled in the hand, claimed that both Leonardo Da Vinci and Archimedes, the great sphere maker himself, had built this mechanism together. Highly implausible it must be said, but never the less a darned good old-fashioned yarn to read on a long cold dark night in the midst of winter. This instrument is on display at the National Archaeological Museum in Athens and is said to be an instrument or device that could predict the motions of the sun, the stars and the planets.

The proprietor of The Last Bookshop in the World said the Greeks and the Italians were great ones for writing in code or disguising their works under the text of prayer books, both Da Vinci and Galileo had done this to protect their secrets. The Greeks, who invented the art of stenography, often hid messages under the wax of writing tablets. Later Gulliver wrote in his travelogue that Drake had made a bad joke, saying that it was all Greek to him, before adding, especially Greek!

Gulliver remembered as a child one of his teachers saying that both the British Museum in London and the New Acropolis Museum in Athens were squabbling over the Elgin Marbles. Gulliver wondered why anyone would squabble over a few coloured marbles and, was given over to thinking that perhaps it was the curators of these two-world famous museums that had lost their marbles!

Gulliver also found Freud's book *The Interpretation of Dreams*, which was guaranteed to send him off to sleep at night. Perhaps he could buy it and give it to Mr Dreams as a present, that's if he ever woke from his slumbers. And a book called *The Golden Book of Spells*, written by an unknown alchemist simply known as Dr Magic, which was either very badly spelt or Gulliver's dyslexia was playing up again. According to the proprietor, when this book first came out it was so popular it literally flew off the shelves! Gulliver wasn't sure if the wizened old owner of the shop was yanking on the chain of his fob watch or not.

Gulliver also found a copy of Homer's *Odyssey* which features a voyage home that Gulliver hoped the *Golden Hind* would not be duplicating. As well as the Iliad, which featured the wooden horse, Helen of Troy Paris and the lost city of Troy, which an antiquarian book collector in his world would pay a large fortune for.

As soon as Gulliver heard Troy had been found his heart sank for he knew once any mystery had been solved it completely destroyed the image you had in your head of the place. It was not knowing and wondering that made Troy, Atlantis and the Loch Ness monster special. Gulliver secretly hoped they would never find Atlantis and he was glad in his world that Nessie had found a safe hiding place that nobody could find.

It seemed that in his world there weren't many more mysteries left to solve and soon, when they solved the mysteries of the deepest oceans and the cosmological oceans of the universe, the big bang and everything, then what!? Nothing, that's what. Nothing. A big fat zero! Imagine a world with no mystery; how dull such a world would be. How dull? Well, Gulliver had imagined it and he found it to be unimaginably dull, that's how dull!

*Unless the scientists were going to invent a time machine, perhaps it was best they all retired before they spoiled things for everyone*, thought Gulliver irritably. No doubt soon they would find a magical elixir of life and we would all live for ever. Gulliver couldn't think of anything worse than living for ever, apart from having to relive his school days, and until he turned twelve for the second time he thought school really was out for ever! To be honest, Gulliver thought that if scientists with their big eggheads couldn't get their collective heads around a tiny little problem like time travel then they were certainly no Einsteins!

Gulliver also came across a little known work by an author called Plato, a book with the rather unimaginative title of Plato's *Timaeus*, but as the condition wasn't bad he bought it. You never knew, it might turn out to be one of those surprise reads, a real page-turner, a book you couldn't put down if you tried because you'd spilled some honey on the cover while reading it at the breakfast table, or not! However, Gulliver couldn't find the book's twin Critias anywhere in the bookshop and there was supposed to be a third of the trilogy *Hermocrates* however Plato never put quill to papyrus to write it.

*Oh, how authors loved to see their own names in print,* Gulliver thought to himself. He also got his hands upon a respectable enough copy of a book called *A Dissertation on the Topography of the Plain of Troy* written by Charles MacLaren and first published in 1822, or at least it was in his world, although the copy was a second edition. Both books featured the story of the mythical lost city of Atlantis, a story which in Gulliver's world of 2013 people were divided upon. Some said the story of Atlantis rested entirely upon Plato's imagination. While others had discovered sunken islands in Greece which they said could well have been the islands which Plato had based his story upon. Some even said that one of these islands was Atlantis and had mapped the streets and towns by the outline of the town on the ocean floor and by the archaeological finds they had dug up there. From reading these books on the journey home to England, Gulliver made a discovery of his own, that Atlantis is an adjective derived from the word 'Atlas' which describes a father\daughter relationship. Literally translated, Atlantis means 'Atlas's daughter'.

The wizened old proprietor of the bookshop said that Gulliver may be interested in Jacob Bryant's six-volume encyclopedia entitled *Analysis of Ancient Mythology*, being the subtitle of: Wherein an Attempt is made to divest Tradition of Fable; and to reduce the truth to its Original Purity. With a title like that, Gulliver joked, no wonder the author needed six books just to fit it all in! Gulliver thanked the wizened old man but said they had to carry the books several miles back to a canoe which, was only made out of bamboo and as he couldn't swim, he didn't want the canoe to be so loaded down by weighty books that it sank beneath the weight of them all! The proprietor said that for a small price he could send them by sea mail if he liked, although they might take a while to arrive, if they arrived at all, as the waters in this part of the world were full of pirates.

Gulliver said he would love to have acquired this historic set of encyclopedias as he could use them to stand upon to reach the books on the top shelf of Drake's library on the *Golden Hind*! Gulliver also wondered how small this price was so in the end decided against this purchase; it seemed the e-book did have its uses after all! Gulliver kept this thought to himself, as he knew any self-respecting bookshop owner would throw the book at him if they could read his mind!

Gulliver then came across a book which must have had over a thousand pages in it and was so heavy he could hardly lift it up. The book was called *The Book of Imagination*. With the help of a guide, Gulliver managed to get the book off the bottom shelf and open the heavy cover, which weighed almost as much as a ship's anchor. Much to Gulliver's surprise, his eyes were met with nothing, nothing but pristine white pages which appeared to turn themselves as if by magic. Gulliver was lost for words, obviously like the writer, unless of course it was a book by Da Vinci and he had written it in invisible ink.

Gulliver asked the guide why this was the case and he said, and I quote, 'Well, you know some writers, they've got no imagination!' Of course the guide was just yanking on the chain of his fob watch and said as much before adding. 'The secret to this book is to concentrate very hard upon the unwritten page and let your imagination do the rest. Before you know it you'll be making up your own stories, which as soon as they finish will disappear like invisible ink.' Gulliver had to agree it was a real page-turner!

Gulliver instantly slammed the cover of this weighty book shut, making dust fly all about him, for he remembered what the wizened old owner of the bookshop had told him about getting lost in the story and knew that with his imagination, if he got sucked into this book he would never get out!

Francis Drake purchased several of Shakespeare's most recently published works in book form for the chief of Gulliver's Island, one being a signed copy of *The Tempest* with the great storm and shipwreck that opens the story. And the other being *Twelfth Night* when the captain tells Viola how her brother tied himself to a floating mast after the vessel went to pieces. Drake also purchased a book called *Frankenstein* by an unknown writer called Mary Shelley and several romantic novels for Queen Elizabeth I. He also purchased a book for himself entitled *Shipwrecked*; being shipwrecked was something Drake hadn't experienced before and hoped that by reading this book he would avoid the pitfalls of doing so in the future.

Several bespoke royal manuscripts illuminated in gold with pictures in them which could definitely be said to be works of art, sat in specially designed glass cases. These priceless books could only be viewed if you donned a pair of white gloves and were prepared to handle them with the utmost care. Some of the manuscripts were predictions of royal futures and one was even said to have been written by Merlin himself, astrology mixed with science. How Queen Elizabeth I would have loved to have got her hands upon this book which was wrapped in a red velvet cover with gold clasps to keep it tightly shut. However, once again these were not to be removed otherwise Drake would have bought the *Bedford Hours*, one of the rarest medieval books ever written. This priceless book included pictures of the Tower of Babel, Genesis with Adam and Eve in the Garden of Eden and a stunning picture of Noah's Ark with all the animals going into the ark two by two.

There was also a book upon the shelves called *Guide to the Holy Land* which Gulliver wanted to look through. Some of these royal manuscripts were bound in what looked like gold covers and were illuminated with so much gold it was hard to lift the covers and turn the pages. All these books and manuscripts literally reeked of history and some, Gulliver mused, reeked of too much history, making you slam the cover back down no sooner had you opened it! The work and detail which had gone into both the drawings and the calligraphy of such manuscripts was quite staggering. Gulliver was later to write this in his travelogue after Drake had showed him these majestic-looking manuscripts.

Gulliver knew enough about antiquarian books to know that in his world this royal manuscript collection was safely housed within the walls of the British Library. It seemed to Gulliver that because these books and manuscripts were bespoke and were to be read by only a chosen few, it made them more valuable. This Gulliver mused must give all authors who only sell a few hundred of their books great comfort, in that their books were rare and one day they would be highly collectable to antiquarian booksellers and as such worth a small fortune, or not! Gulliver found this muse of his quite amusing, although he didn't think the nine muses would, other than Thalia, the muse of comedy and choral song!

As Gulliver looked through these books, he could imagine kings and queens turning the pages and reading about their own lives. When he turned the pages of these books it felt to Gulliver like he was standing over Elizabeth I, Queen Victoria and Henry VIII, reading over their shoulders, after which they would turn round and say in a voice which wasn't in the slightest bit amused, 'Gulliver, how do you feel like reading some horrible history in which you take the starring role? You wouldn't? Well then, pull your head in before you lose it!'

Gulliver told Drake he thought this bookshop was like stepping back in time, which was strange what with there not being any time in this world to step back into.

Alice got a first edition of *Alice in Wonderland* and *Alice through the Looking Glass*, both signed by Lewis Carroll. Gulliver couldn't believe these books were originals and not fakes. The proprietor of The Last Bookshop in the World had to tell Gulliver three times that this was indeed the case by repeating the line, 'What I tell you three times is true!' The wizened old man was obviously a fan of Lewis Carroll too by the sounds of things.

The coxswain and the seaman, who it had turned out was more than able to deal with any situation that came his way, got different versions of the Bible, authors unknown, and several picturebooks on sea creatures and dinosaurs. Old Father Time also got a copy of the Bible, the Old Testament version of course, and several ancient lexicons in Aramaic, as well as a copy of the Dead Sea Scrolls as that was something else you couldn't remove from the bookshop. Old Father Time also got to read the Eleven Commandments, not ten, as one had recently been found in the belly of an extinct fish by a fisherman in the Red Sea. All the commandments were literally written in stone so you couldn't remove them from the shop for obvious reasons. Old Father Time was a little concerned he may have broken the commandment which stated you shouldn't worship any god other than God, which included the gods. Old Father Time had told Gulliver that it was the gods that had interviewed him for the position of Guardian of Time and had eventually given him the job, well, after the obligatory 500-year probation period of course! Here Gulliver wasn't sure if the ex-Guardian of Time was yanking his timeline or not!

I wish I could tell you what that Eleventh Commandment was, however, if you want to know you'll have to visit The Last Bookshop in the World, as this is one tablet that you will not be able to get your hands upon as it literally is out of this world! All I would say regarding this subject is use your imagination, it may well help. That's if the modern world with its technological wonders haven't dulled it to such an extent that it no longer works properly!

The Eleven Commandments were kept in the mythical golden Ark of the Covenant, otherwise known as the mercy seat, which was apparently found in Jeremiah's grotto. The first time the Ark was opened it nearly blew The Last Bookshop in the World off the face of the earth. According to the proprietor, this was all written in stone in the original ledger of The Last Book Shop in the World, unfortunately it had mysteriously disappeared into thin air after the last stocktake sometime before time ended, he said, or so it was written 'as they say'. After some extensive restoration work The Last Bookshop in the World was restored to its former glory.

These religious antiquarian antiquities were said by some to be just a good story and nothing more and the real gods were the ones who had written the rules of Compendium. These were the same gods who had deserted this world for another so how much store you wanted to place in them was really up to you. Old Father Time hoped this was nothing more than a good story as he had no wish to be struck down by a lightning bolt with his name upon it, as in his mind he still had a lot of living to do.

As the proprietor of the shop went to lift the lid of the Ark of the Covenant, some people in the shop dived for cover expecting all hell to break loose. One woman exclaimed, 'God help us all!' Another old man said, 'Have mercy upon our souls!' After this firework display turned out to be somewhat of a damp squib, metaphorically speaking that is, the old man looked towards the heavens and said, 'Thank God!'

Old Father Time also picked up a book called *The Chronicles of Time (Time is Your Oyster)* by Reginald

Clocksmith, almost certainly a pen name, and a book called *Clocks throughout Time* by Wilton H. Timepiece.

When Old Father Time first picked this book up and opened it, it fell open at a page about the first pendulum clock, which was originally made by a man named Christian Huygens, a clockmaker of some repute, who finished the clock at 12.32 on Christmas of 1656. Well, clockmakers had always been known for their preciseness. And a book so rare that only one other copy had ever been seen outside The Last Bookshop in the World a book entitled, *A Compendious History of Board Games throughout the Ages* by Algernon Merryweather. Although only two copies of this book were printed as the printing press at the time it went to press went up in smoke, that and all the workers on the printing press were press-ganged into sailing in Queen Elizabeth I's fleet.

As there were far too many books to carry or fit in the canoe, all the books were put on Drake's tab on trust of a later payment, and as Queen Elizabeth appeared to trust Drake, this was good enough for the proprietor of The Last Bookshop in the World. The proprietor informed the purchasers of the books that they would make their way to the buyers in six working weeks, no more, no less, carried by the ever-reliable postal service known as the carrier pigeon, which in actuality was a giant albatross! It seemed to Drake's mind that having to do such a Herculean task as this meant the poor bird permanently had an albatross around its neck!

Before Gulliver left the shop he ran into a man who introduced himself as Jonathan Swift. To say Gulliver was taken aback would be the understatement of all time, although in this world that would just be an understatement. Mr Swift asked Gulliver if he could get a book high up on the shelf for him as he suffered from vertigo and didn't want to use the stepladder provided. Gulliver was happy to oblige. You may be interested to know the book Gulliver procured for Mr Jonathan Swift, well, to satisfy your curiosity, the book was a travel book called *A Poet's Bazaar* written by Mr Hans Christian Andersen. Gulliver told Mr Swift he loved his book *Gulliver's Travels* and that his name was Gulliver and at this exact moment in time he was on his travels around the globe. He also told Mr Swift that he'd been christened after the character in his book. Swift by name and swift by nature, Mr Swift apologized to Gulliver as he hurriedly bid farewell to him. The reason for this hurried departure might well have had something to do with the fact that he hadn't even written the book yet.

Later Gulliver was to ponder on this unexpected meeting when he told Mr Swift what he'd told him, which was that he loved his book and that his name was the same as the surname of the character in this book. And at the time he told Mr Swift this fact, his face was both one of puzzlement and a picture. Gulliver was then given to wonder if it wasn't this chance meeting that had given Jonathan Swift the idea for the book *Gulliver's Travels* in the first place. And his hurried departure was not because he thought Gulliver was one library short of some books, or not all the (library) ticket, but that he was hurrying home to begin the story! Was this so unlikely? Certainly not, as hadn't Daniel Defoe, the author of *Robinson Crusoe* been told a story in an inn about some sailor being washed up upon a desert island, and then went home and wrote a similar story? What's more, after a chance encounter with a Persian fisherman, hadn't one of the writers of the Bible gone home and written the Noah's Ark story? Yes, I agree the whole thing's extremely fishy!

On this historic meeting, Gulliver surmised that Mr

Swift was around about fifty-five years of age so he could and could not have already written the book. And like Raleigh having to rediscover tobacco and the humble potato, Jonathan Swift may well have had to rewrite *Gulliver's Travels* too! It was hard to get your head around all this and it certainly was all going round and round Gulliver's head like a neverending circumnavigation of the globe.

'Where's Hans?' Gulliver said looking all about him.

'He got sucked into that Brothers Grim book about fairytales and to my knowledge he's still in there!' said Old Father Time raising a bushy eyebrow or two.

'We can't just abandon him!' Gulliver said compassionately.

'Look, we haven't the time to stay here any longer. Anyway, didn't you say Hans has been to Constantinople before and he's a travel writer? He'll find his way home, I'm sure of it,' said Old Father Time sounding very assure of himself.

'Do you think so?' said Gulliver nervously.

'Yes, I'm 100% sure of it,' Old Father Time said reassuringly.

'Well, if you think he'll be all right,' continued Gulliver, rather wishing Old Father Time had been 110% sure of this fact rather than only 100% sure of it!

'Look, if a travel writer can't find his way home, what hope have any of us got?' Old Father Time said logically.

And so they left Hans Christian Andersen in the same state they found him, in a world of his own. Except he wasn't on his own, he was in the world of imagination and in that world you can never truly be said to be alone.

Gulliver thanked the proprietor of The Last Bookshop in the World and said the time they'd spent there was literally and literary out of this world. It was just a pity he'd never got to chat with Mr Dreams, who by now was resting his head against the bookshelf snoring extremely loudly. The entire crew said they would honour their contracts and the wizened old man said he would expect nothing less as he knew an Englishman's word was his bond.

Later Gulliver was to make an entry into his travelogue that he almost needed a separate travelogue for his travels inside The Last Bookshop in the World. And he wrote that he most certainly would have done had they spent any more time there, although if you wanted to be pedantic, as there was no time to speak of, they didn't spend any time there at all. Gulliver added that the time they had spent in The Last Bookshop in the World had passed so quickly it felt like they had been in there no time at all. So although this narrative in his travelogue sounded very much like gobbledegobble it actually made perfect sense, in a manner of speaking!

All I can say is that as an outside observer it was just fortunate that Gulliver had not picked up the Bible in The Last Bookshop in the World and been sucked into its pages, otherwise we would all be here till kingdom come!

# 19

# A Golden Moment for the Hind

And so without wishing to bore the reader further, all Gulliver wrote in his finished travelogue word for word was: 'The *Golden Hind* and its crew did the journey in reverse, that's if you took out them journeying to the North Pole, visiting the Land of the Giant Seahorse, otherwise known as the Galapagos Islands, and when in Marrakesh having a heart-to-heart with six of the greatest minds on the planet. Then added a fight with some Spanish galleons, Titan, Neptune and catching a sea monster, before ending with, "end of story".'

Drake had caught this sea monster in one of his nets, which he regularly trawled over the side so as to catch fish for the crew's fish supper. This strange-looking specimen looked like a cross between a Portuguese man o' war, a squid, a sea snake, and a catfish and must have been hiding in the very depths of the deepest oceans since the beginning of time itself. The creature had more spikes on it than a medieval weapon and when Gulliver first spied it he thought it was the mythical kraken until he remembered it was now living in the Antiquarium in Devon. At one stage the creature slipped across the deck of the *Golden Hind* leaving enough slime in its wake to fill several Olympic-sized swimming pools. Some of the sailors on deck at the time nearly drowned in this slime. It was at this point that Gulliver said to himself ruefully, 'I wish I had a camera phone on me, then I could have taken a picture.' Luckily everybody was too engrossed with the sea monster to ask what a phone or a camera was. There were times Gulliver wished he was viewing these fantastical HD 3D moments from a rather safer viewing platform, like his couch, the one with his HD 3D television in front of it. Viewing it on his antique black and white set wouldn't have been quite so compelling viewing, although I have no doubt it would have kept his imagination on its toes!

Gulliver was glad he got to shake John Logie Baird's hand in The Pandemonium Emporium, even if young Master Logie Baird thought he was slightly strange for doing so, considering he had only just met him!

And then the sea serpent swallowed the *Golden Hind*. I bet you didn't see that one coming, no, nor did Francis Drake or anybody aboard the *Golden Hind*, including Gulliver who in his travelogue wrote this exact account, word for word: 'This really was a fantastical voyage and a dark one as the *Golden Hind* slipped down the creature's throat like it was going down a water slide before sailing around upon a sea of blood in the sea serpent's body, navigating through its veins and capillaries and reaching its heart with many lanterns placed around the deck of the ship to light its way. (It also helped that the sea monster had swallowed a lighthouse and several large flourescent fish earlier that day.) Here the *Golden Hind* fired so many cannons into the chambers of the monstrous creature's heart that it was forced to spit the *Hind* out. Drake said it obviously thought it had indigestion and it was true, this encounter had left a bad taste in the creature's mouth. Luckily, the *Golden Hind* landed in the sea butter side up. It seemed the gods and the lucky lady of the sea hadn't completely deserted them.

Can you imagine such a thing? Oh, Gulliver could imagine it all right, because he had seen it with his own eyes, and he was sure his eyes weren't playing tricks upon him, or at least they weren't when they were open for at some points in this fantastical voyage his eyes were tightly shut. Anyway, you know Gulliver, as far as his imagination was concerned, he never had any trouble in pushing the boat out. Drake said the Antiquarium in Devon would pay him a pretty penny for such a unique specimen, but perhaps now wasn't the time or the place to be taking on this sea monster. However, Drake charted the place they had come in contact with the sea monster on his map so he could come back at a later date and catch the creature for the Antiquarium. Where did they see this serpent on the sea map brought to life? Well, it was the Scilly Isles, which seemed appropriate in the circumstances, whatever they were! Where are the Scilly Isles you ask? Do you want me to draw you a map? Well, I may well have had to as on the antique globe the Scilly Isles were not far from Nova Gvinea, which in plain English is New Guinea, the gods were playing silly beggars, again Gulliver thought with a wry smile upon his face. Gulliver noticed how this old map had huge ships and sea monsters and waves as high as skyscrapers drawn upon it, which were almost as big as some of the countries upon the map.

Being the artist that he was, Gulliver drew a comparison seeing the parallel between the antique sea maps in his antiques emporium and the ones he'd seen

Drake use. He'd always thought they were drawn for effect rather than drawn to scale, obviously not! Gulliver thought some of the huge waves drawn upon the antique maps were obviously modern-day tsunamis. Gulliver knew James Cook had drawn some of the most reliable and accurate maps of the oceans during his epic sea voyages, and it had been he who had discovered New Holland in the *Endeavour* in 1770. On Cook's last epic voyage to find the Northwest Passage, which at the time was said to be in the region of Nova Albion, Nova meaning new, he stumbled upon the Artic and later still on this voyage of discovery he met his death as so many other adventurers would. This was often the ultimate price to pay for the adventure and one Gulliver hoped hadn't already been written for him by the gods. However, as the gods of this world were no longer writing the script, the script rather having being torn up, he had nothing to worry about. The trouble with Gulliver was in truth he kind of liked having things to worry about, it was when he had nothing to worry about that things really worried him!

After this amazing journey into unchartered regions, Gulliver wrote in his travelogue: 'This happening was a bit like Jonah and the whale, minus the whale and minus Jonah and plus a sea monster and the *Golden Hind*! Or a David and Goliath battle minus David and Goliath and– Yes, we get the picture!

Gulliver was once again surprised how easily Alice seemed to take this experience in her stride. However, Old Father Time said that this part of the journey was his least favourite as he had always had an aversion to sea monsters, and this voyage hardly did his seasickness any favours. Old Father Time did get an idea from the lighthouse inside the sea monster's stomach, which was, having spent an inordinate amount of time inside a giant clock, he would feel quite at home working as a lighthouse keeper. This position could be on a part-time basis and would keep him out of Old Mrs Time's hair and out from under her feet.

One of these days Gulliver was going to push his boat out so far into the endless seas of his imagination that he wouldn't be able to make the return journey. It seemed that Gulliver's, imagination like the universe, was expanding and the more it expanded the faster it did so. One day you were more likely as not to find him in a home for the mentally incapacitated, sitting in a rocking chair and staring into space in what seemed like a catatonic state. Although being the idiot savant he now was, he wouldn't speak, although from time to time he would grimace or just simply smile as if he'd found Nirvana or heaven. Either that or he had found the crew of the *Marie Celeste* standing onboard Noah's Ark in the harbour of the lost city of Atlantis as he was just in time to witness Noah and Plato opening the Ark of the Covenant!

After which, Gulliver would probably be imagining a genie inside a bottle that was inside a ship's bottle encased inside another ship's bottle. Not unlike one of those Russian dolls that keeps getting smaller and smaller until it disappears completely, like the crew of *Marie Celeste* did in 1872 while carrying alcohol between New York and Italy. Some had said the *Marie Celeste* had disappeared inside the Bermuda Triangle, having presumably been sucked into some sort of time warp. One of these nameless somebodys was a nobody named Gulliver, who after this circumnavigation was to become something of a somebody of note in this world and not just a footnote in the history books either, but quite a big cheese!

However, just for a brief moment we need to turn the clock back to the battle between the *Golden Hind* the three British ships which came to its rescue, four unnamed Spanish galleons and the sea gods Titan and Neptune, who refused to desert this world like the other gods. This was exactly what Gulliver wrote in his travelogue in quill and ink. The ink Gulliver used to dip his quill pen in was that of an octopus caught by Able Seaman Benjamin Smith and his twin brother Alexander, which was then hauled aboard the *Golden Hind* off Gulliver's Island by six of the ship's company several moons since passed. I hasten to add the octopus in question was not harmed in any way but was put in a glass tank designed by the ship's master, Isambard Kingdom Brunel. The octopus was given the nickname of Curly by the ship's company as they said its head resembled the sailor aboard the *Golden Hind*. Later, Curly found its way into the Antiquarium in old Brixham in the county known as Devonshire.

Date unknown – 'On the end of our journey of several lifetimes, Able Seaman "Barnacle Bill", aka William Wigglesworth, spied two giants in the sea from the crow's nest, one to the south and one to the north, converging on one another with great speed. This produced a wave on the ocean reminiscent of a tsunami which almost capsized the *Golden Hind*. And then from the west came two Spanish galleons within half a league of one another and by the look of the cannons sticking out their port sides, they too were spoiling for a fight.

As usual the captain (Francis Drake) was as calm as a mill pond and told the gunners to make ready to defend the *Golden Hind* and queen and country, which included the honour of Queen Elizabeth and the whole of the lands that were known as Albion. For myself, I felt anything but cool, calm and collected, in fact, the butterflies in my stomach had a fit of the collywobbles like I've never experienced before. As the giants came closer into view, I was reminded of an old sixties American television series I used to watch with my father called *Land of the Giants*.

'It also reminded me of *Gulliver's Travels*, *Sinbad and the Golden Fleece* and *King Kong*, the latter which I wish I hadn't brought to mind as it did not end well! After all, we are all descended from the apes, our DNA being little different from theirs. This little fact Darwin delighted in telling me while our feet were still firmly planted upon the Land of the Giant Seahorse. While upon these islands, several monkeys attempted to make a monkey out of us as we tried to capture them in a cage, and succeeded too I might add. Time after time they evaded all of the traps and nets we set down, leading Drake to joke that he wasn't sure who should be in the cage, the monkeys or some of his slow-witted able seamen, who were found wanting in this task. If the truth be told, he joked, they were less than able, the truth in truth at times is not a concept our captain, and I can't believe I am saying "our captain" about the great Sir Francis Drake, but nevertheless, our captain is familiar with, any more than our travelling companion and shipmate Hans Christian Andersen as both seem equally adept as spinning fairytales and fishy tales of the sea serpent that got away!

'But back to our run-in with the giants… while aboard the *Hind*, Alice looked as scared as I was as Neptune and Titan raised there ugly heads, and believe you me neither were what you might call as pretty as a picture, and we clung to one another like limpets to a rock. For a moment I hoped this was just a dream and asked Alice to pinch me several times over, which she did, and it hurt! And the clincher regarding whether this was or was not a dream\nightmare was when the Spanish shot a cannon across our broadside. Some ships in this world were nothing more than floating coffins, luckily the *Golden Hind* was made of sterner stuff, good old-fashioned English oak, or at least the stern was!

'As the Spanish came closer and we could see the whites of their eyes, we could see the fear in theirs matched ours. Some had a look of horror upon their faces when they saw Drake shouting "El Draque!", which I was later to find out meant "The Dragon". A dragon would certainly have made a most welcome ally in the perilous situation we now found ourselves, like Timaeus the defender of Atlantis, who could turn into a teal-coloured dragon at the drop of a pointy wizard's hat. Boy, would my history teacher at school be proud of me for digging up this Greek historical factoid\myth\legend\fairytale at such short notice. It's nice to see the steam search engine in my head is still shipshape and Bristol fashion, despite my little grey cells being shaken up as much as they have by this experience! Then out of nowhere another ship joined the fray, an English ship called the *Golden Lion*, Captained by Sir Walter Raleigh, who stood side by side with the *Hinde* against Philips' Spanish galleons.'

This was indeed a golden moment in more ways than one. Gulliver knew that this ship was normally captained by William Boroughs, who didn't get on with Francis Drake and who'd had a spat of their own. So when Drake first saw the *Golden Lion* he was hardly jumping for joy, although when he saw his friend with his brother John by his side, his face lit up like a lighthouse.

And then a rainbow appeared out of nowhere, although not in the sky, as the *Rainbow* was another ship in the fleet of the Royal Navy. Soon the *Rainbow* was joined by another English ship, the *Elizabeth Bonaventure*, a ship Drake was later to sail upon in the timeline in Gulliver's world, which had been on an adventure of its own off the coast of Santo Domingo. Gulliver was to wonder if Drake *was* aboard this ship; that really would be a turn up for the books, especially for his travel book! Two Drakes for the price of one, now that really would seem like black magic to the Spanish and the fairytale to end all fairytales. *Even Hans Christian would have trouble topping this one,* Gulliver thought, winking his inner eye like a cyclops! Then two more Spanish ships appeared out of the midsts of time and joined the fray, along with the Tudor warship the *Mary Rose*, which Gulliver had only seen in Portsmouth, or what was left of her.

And then the icing on the cake moment happened, and in truth when it did Gulliver found it hard to suspend his disbelief. *HMS Victory* appeared from its suspended animation in time to join the fray. Lord Admiral Horatio Nelson was standing upon the deck dressed up to the nines in his white breeches, blue and gold braded tunic with gold buttons to match and with what looked like a matador's hat on his head. Nelson took the hat off and waved it several times over his head to reveal a white wig with a pony tail tied at the back in a black bow. The men onboard the British ships went wild, throwing their hats into the air as if victory was secured and the battle already won, which perhaps it was.

And then the strangest most curious of things happened in this Goliath verses Goliath battle which wasn't to be expected, as Titan and Neptune stopped their personal squabble, over what I have no idea, and decided to intercede in the fight between English ships and the Spanish galleons. Wading in, Titan picked up the Spanish galleons and Neptune gathered up the English ships as if they were nothing more than toy ships sailing in a tin bathtub. The cannonballs bounced off of their massive frames as if they were marbles, and not the Elgin Marbles, I might add! The sea gods then held their respective catches within a hair's breath of their faces and we could all feel their hot breath, which nearly tore the sails asunder and swept us into the sea. 'The lateen sail was blown clean off like a moth's wing in a tailspin,' wrote Gulliver in his best English, as the gods held a small body of water in the palms of their massive calloused hands along with the ships. However, it was soon obvious to both us and the Spanish that these two giants of the sea meant us no ill will, both appearing as the most gentle of giants and as benign as the water upon a mill pond. Neptune had obviously been eating garlic, which left a bad taste in all of our mouths, as well as cheese, as some was still stuck in his beard along with hundreds of sea urchins and crustaceans.

Titan walked several hundred leagues in no time at all and placed the galleons down just off the Spanish port of Costa Dorada, while Neptune went in the opposite direction and set the *Golden Hind*, the *Rainbow*, the *Elizabeth Bonaventure*, the *Golden Lion*, the *Mary Rose* and *HMS Victory* down about a league from the English coast. Titan and Neptune then turned around, met each other in the middle of the Atlantic Ocean and kissed and made up, before taking a much-needed rest on their waterbeds at the bottom of the ocean.

Old Father Time said this really was too much excitement for a gentleman of his reclining years and when he got home he would be happy to just tend his beloved marigolds.

As a golden sun shone down from the sky, the *Golden Hind* and its crew were both literally and metaphorically sailing upon sunshine. The *Golden Hind*, all sails unfurled, apart from the lateen sail which unfortunately for the sailmaker aboard had sailed its last voyage, was flanked by the *Golden Lion* to its port side, while *HMS Victory* and the *Elizabeth Bonaventure* flanked it to its starboard side as they sailed into Portsmouth harbour all guns blazing (that was just metaphorically speaking!). Here they were met by an exultant Queen Elizabeth I. It appeared half of Albion was out to greet the *Golden Hind* and the cream of the Royal Navy. Somehow the population of England had heard upon the grapevine that Drake and his crew had embarked upon this impossible quest and had achieved their goal of finding The Last Bookshop in the World , oh, and in doing so had circumnavigated the world to boot. Apparently some people had heard the news by holding a shell up to their ears, which they'd picked up from the beach and which is where the expression 'having a word in your shell-like' came from, probably!

The queen invited all the crew of the *Golden Hind* to her place, which was a palace made of crystal in Old Londinium town. Later still she asked Drake exactly where The Last Bookshop in the World was, and that if he didn't tell her she would ex-communicate him, or worse, remove his head from his shoulders. Drake still wouldn't break the contract he'd signed in The Last Bookshop in the World, saying to the queen that no Englishman worth his salt would break his word, and if he did she wouldn't respect him. Drake desperately tried to steer the queen away from the subject hoping she wouldn't cast her subject, mainly Drake, out of her queendom. Far from being angry, Queen Elizabeth I was most impressed that Drake had stuck to his guns and said that anyway, she was only yanking his anchor as she knew exactly where The Last Bookshop in the World was. However, like Drake, she had signed the same contract and couldn't talk about its whereabouts either. Drake wasn't sure if the queen was telling fairytales or not!

Later Drake was knighted but not by a Frenchman aboard the *Golden Hind* like in Gulliver's world, but by Queen Elizabeth herself. A ballad was even written in Drake's honour entitled *The World Encompassed*. This ballad made Drake realize he had actually circumnavigated the world and some, well, even he, admitted his sense of direction at times left a lot to be desired. He also read accounts of his derring-do in a book called *The True and Perfecte* written by Thomas Greepe and printed in London by I. Charleswood, for Thomas Hackett. This book wrote of the 'Newes of the woorthy and valiuant ex-ploytes, performed and done by the valiant Knight Syre Francis Drake.' The book had no date upon it. Gulliver also read some of this book and noted how he wasn't the only one suffering from dyslexia.

Of course Gulliver realized that was just how they spelt things in Shakespeare's Ye Olde English Dictionary. The book also told of Drake's exploits in the West Indies, which included the Great West Indies Raid in his ships the *Dragon* and the *Swan*, which Drake said he couldn't remember anything about, which was a little strange. Gulliver thought this was either because he hadn't or the rum had gone to his head! There was even a poem written for him by a man called Robert Hayman who had met Drake on a steep Devon street in Totnes when he was but a small child of five. Drake had patted the boy on the head and gave him an orange and said to him, 'God bless, my boy.'

He did recall this event. Drake, who loved children,

never had children of his own. Perhaps that was why he took Gulliver and Alice under his wing, treating them as if they were his own children. The first verse of the poem went like this:

> The Dragon that over Seas did raise his Crest
> And brought back heapes of gold unto his nest;
> Unto his foes more terrible than Thunder.
> Glory of his age, After-ages Wonder,
> Excelling all those that excell'd before,
> It's fear'd we shall have none such any more;
> Effecting all he sole did undertake,
> Valiant, just, wise, milde, honest, godly Drake.

When Drake read the poem it bought a tear to his eye, although at the time he said the wind had blown a bit of grit into his eye which he was simply wiping away with his handkerchief.

Gulliver presented the queen with a map of their journey which he had sketched and then painted, as well as several pictures of mermaids and seahorses he had sketched while aboard the *Golden Hind*. However, Gulliver didn't give her his travelogue as he felt he may well have to edit it first in case he had said anything he ought not to have done. After all, like Drake, he had no desire to lose his head unless it was metaphorically speaking, and in truth, it is a lot easier to speak both metaphorically and literally if you have a head than if you do not!

While they were all in London, the queen decreed that they should all be given the key to the city, a golden key at that. Not only was Drake knighted aboard the *Golden Hind* but so was Gulliver, becoming Sir Gulliver. Alice became a dame, receiving her dameship from young

Queen Victoria, who at the time in truth was a little princess! Later still they got to ride on Stephenson's new-fangled contraption he called a rocket, although in truth it was closer to a train than a rocket. And after that experience they slowed things down a little by watching penny-farthing races taking place over London Bridge, which Old Father Time said was more his speed. That night they witnessed the most magnificent firework display imaginable, where Gulliver got talking to a man who said his name was Guy. These proceedings were both watched by Queen Elizabeth I and a young Queen Victoria, who as it turned out was most amusing.

Later there were some fireworks of a different kind when the man named Guy appeared to spontaneously combusted right in front of Gulliver's eyes. However, his eyes were probably playing tricks upon him, either that or the man was a conjuror, a master magician like Houdini. The icing on the cake was there was no marzipan on this cake, no sorry, only yanking your anchor, the icing on the icing on the cake was a full symphony orchestra that played Handel's *Water Music*, conducted by a little-known musician who could capture lightning in a jar, musically speaking that is. The man's name, which I'm sure is of little consequence to you being a wannabe named Wolfgang Amadeus Mozart, who probably wouldn't amount to anything, although that night he appeared to wave his conductor's wand like a wizard.

At the end of the piece, Gunner William Wigglesworth had the honour of firing the cannon, which was sitting aboard the *Golden Hind* at the time and which in turn was sat upon a becalmed River Thames. It was just unfortunate that the cannonball which was fired from the gun sank a ship in dry dock called the *Mary Rose*!

Only yanking your anchor, however, the cannonball did make a sizable hole in the Globe Theatre!

But as Shakespeare was later to say, 'Worse things happen at sea.' Anyway, in truth the building was old and desperately needed a makeover so no real harm was done. Some wag wearing a wig pointed out to the bard of Avon that unless he was very much mistaken, the Globe Theatre wasn't at sea. Shakespeare retorted that he was just being metaphorical and, if this wag wasn't careful, he would help him drown his sorrows and he wasn't being metaphorical either. Further adding that the Thames would be the perfect place for Shakespeare to help him drown these sorrows of his. Shakespeare, it appeared was fond of talking about himself in the third person. In this curious parallel world where time was mixed up, it was conceivable that there could have been three Shakespeares, one in the first flush of youth, one having a mid-life crisis and one in the autumn of his years! Mind you, what with the strange nature of this world, Gulliver wouldn't have been the least bit surprised if he found the Globe Theatre was underwater, which he thought would have pleased the mermaids and mermen no end.

The crew of the *Golden Hind* also saw the master magician Harry Houdini free himself from several chains, and a coffin that was encased inside a block of ice that was then placed in the River Thames. The Thames was partly frozen over at the time, hence the *Golden Hind* being becalmed as if in a tourist's snow dome, like the ones Gulliver had seen in the gift shop in the Globe Theatre in London in his time.

Quite how Houdini 'the Magic Man' achieved this miraculous conjuring fete even Gulliver was not sure, but it seemed in this age of the extraordinary, the implausible, the impossible, the fantastical, the miraculous, the phantasmagorical, such fetes were mere trifles and not in the least bit out of the ordinary in any way, shape or form.

The industrial revolution had started in earnest with the great exhibition at the Crystal Palace, which showed off the latest inventions of the time. 'This revolution will take a little bit of getting used to for the Elizabethans amongst us,' Queen Elizabeth said with a wry smile upon her royal countenance. However, in time the Elizabethans got used to it as the old ways mixed with the new, as it appeared it was meant to be in this weird and wonderful world of fantastical proportions that mirrored the earth of 2013, but only if you were looking in a crazy fairground mirror. Then Queen Victoria grew up and the realm was governed by two queens befitting of this golden age to end all golden ages. Now you would have thought this would have put Queen Elizabeth I's nose out of joint somewhat, but not a bit of it as she so wisely said, 'Two heads are better than one!' Now Queen Elizabeth had more time for kicking her heels up and having fun, which amused Queen Victoria greatly. This was no mean feat, as the older Victoria got, the less amused she became.

Gold is an attractive proposition which attracts both people and objects to it like a magnet. Two ages were said to be golden, the sixteenth century of the Elizabethan period of Drake's *Golden Hind*, where discovery of new lands was commonplace. And the nineteenth century where Caxton's printing press took over from the golden illuminated manuscripts, the age of the industrial revolution, with its golden age of steam and inventors who became not only heroes but national treasures too.

After the gods had shaken time up in this parallel

world which housed a parallel earth, the two ages were attracted to one another, like the dial of a compass is attracted to magnetic north, as they formed the new world. However, other time periods had also slipped into this world like grains of sand from the hourglass. But predominately the sixteenth and the nineteenth centuries reigned over this kingdom presided over by Queen Elizabeth I and more recently by Queen Victoria and Queen Elizabeth I. This is how Gulliver explained the world he was now living in in his travelogue, otherwise known as his book with words and pictures.

'Later, Queen Elizabeth thanked Drake for the books he'd given her, although she said one of them was a little too racy for her tastes. Later still, Drake laid his cape down in a puddle so Queen Elizabeth didn't get her pretty little feet wet, that actually weren't that little!'

Apparently Drake had heard Gulliver talking in his sleep saying. 'Don't let the queen get her feet wet. Throw down your cape, man, throw down your cape!' In this dream Raleigh appeared to be in somewhat of an agitated state, although this dream appeared to be more of a midsummer night's nightmare than a midsummer night's dream. Now Drake knew the ancients thought that through dreams you could predict the future. After all, Gulliver wasn't your average boy, Drake could see that, so thought he was preordained to save the queen from getting her pretty little feet wet, not realizing that was Sir Walter Raleigh's destiny. But surely such a small act couldn't change history, could it, a sort of butterfly effect in time?

The next time Drake sailed to Gulliver's Island he brought the chief the copies of Shakespeare's latest novels, although by that time, Shakespeare being as prolific as he was, he had written several more blockbusters.

Gulliver bought a house in the same street as Alice's

with the purse full of golden ducats the queen had given every member of the crew of the *Golden Hind* which, once again, seemed somewhat appropriate. The queen had a golden dog collar made for Beagle and he became the mascot of all shipfarers around the world. Books were even written about him, as were of *Gulliver's Travels*. The queen also had a giant golden anchor made from the gold Drake had plundered from the land known as the Land of Gold – Mexico. After which she presented it to Sir Francis Drake along with his knighthood, as by now Drake had become a national treasure. It seemed at this point in time that Sir Francis Drake definitely could have been said to have had 'the Midas touch'. Queen Victoria also knighted Isambard Kingdom Brunel for his engineering achievements and gave him some spare keys to the kingdom and the City of London just in case he ever got locked out.

Drake had procured a book at The Last Bookshop in the World which foretold of his downfall, a book called *La Dragontea*, an epic story poem by the Spaniard Lope de Vega of Drake's last voyage and miserable downfall. Drake, having read the future, wasn't sure what to do about it; should he alter the course of history or accept his fate, accepting what had already been written in print, for surely the future was written in stone and had been preordained before he had even been born? Drake decided to let things pan out the way they were meant to, after all, he wasn't a god, although at one time the Spanish sailors perceived him to be one. Drake thought wisely that if the bad parts of his life hadn't happened, the good parts wouldn't have happened either. It seemed some of Old Father Time's wisdom had rubbed off on Sir Francis Drake in this epic voyage of a lifetime, that and he thought the whole tale nothing more than what he called 'a Hans Christian'! in other words a fairytale!

The last recorded conversation Drake and Gulliver had was outside a large manor house in Devon called Buckland Abbey and it went exactly like this…

'Gulliver, my boy, it's been an honour to know you,' Sir Francis Drake said earnestly.

'You too, Sir Francis,' Gulliver said as a tear in his eye wasn't far off falling like ships fell off the flat earth.

'Sir Francis, that has a nice ring to it like a time bell. It seems, young Master Gulliver, that you were right all along. I would be happy to have you serve amongst my ship's company any time,' Drake said proudly, recalling when he had first met Gulliver upon the *Golden Hind* some time ago, a time no longer recorded. Nevertheless this was a meeting he would not forget for quite some time to come.

'It lightens my heart to hear you say so, Sir Francis,' Gulliver said, sounding older than his years, whatever they may be.

'How I wish I lived in such a fine place, Sir Gulliver, then my father, God rest his soul, would truly be proud of me,' Drake said standing in the garden of the estate looking at the great abbey that stood before him. This was the first time Gulliver had been called a sir and it made him fell proud, adding a good foot to his rather slumped frame as he stood erect like the mast of a tall ship. Now he felt like a man and not just a callow youth who was out of his depth.

'You do… or should I say you will… or should I say you have?' Gulliver said talking gibberish as for a moment he reverted to the stammer of his childhood.

'I see you've been looking into your crystal ball again, Gulliver. I won't ask you to tell me my future as I think a man dictates his own future. It is not for the gods to write the fate of a man, his destiny is in his own hands.

Don't you think so, my boy?' Drake said stroking his wispy beard as if he needed some reassuring on this point.

'Think? I think I think too much, sire,' Gulliver said as his thoughts turned to the Greek philosopher whose name had temporarily escaped him, the one who said, 'I think, therefore I am.'

'Yes, thinking is not all that it is cracked up to be, that's 110% sure, as you young people like to say nowadays!' Drake gave out a hearty laugh and the two parted on the best of terms imaginable.

Alice and Gulliver grew up together and became life-long friends. However, as time went by Alice could see by the look in Gulliver's eyes that he yearned to travel back to his own world and his own time. Alice couldn't bear to be parted from him, nor could Gulliver bear to be parted from Alice, who, he said, had a smile so infectious that the world would be a better place if everybody caught her infectious smile. Alice in all honesty was curious as to what Gulliver's world was like, a world where time still existed. Both Gulliver and Alice were in their late teens when this happened. There was one thing, however, that Gulliver had come to realize, that in this parallel earth, time did still flow like a river, it was just that it appeared not to as there were no clocks marking it. The speed of life wasn't as fast as in his modern world, more as if it were in slow motion like when they slowed down the beating of a hummingbird's wings in a wildlife documentary on the Discovery Channel. But time had definitely slowed down to a snail's pace and that wasn't just an illusion. When the gods had shaken this world up they had altered the structure of time and space. The waves that were now gently lapping on the shores of the cosmological oceans in this parallel world may have been invisible to the naked eye having been irrevocably altered, but they were still there. This meant that one day, God willing, a golden ship would be seen sailing across those waves in time and space in a voyage as fantastical as Drake's circumnavigation of the globe, a globe which due to its age could definitely be said to be the greatest antiquity of them all.

Gulliver was no Einstein, Newton or Hawking, but this was how he perceived time. Time was a deep blue ocean, a sea of tranquility where no mountainous waves were ever seen. This he wrote in his travelogue, which was definitely coloured by the synaesthete in him. And the tune he was hearing in his head when he wrote this? Well, it was more tunes than just one tune, a musical collage of *Surf's Up*, *Good Vibrations* and *Sail on Sailor* by the musical god-like genius of Brian Wilson of the Beach Boys, which seemed more than appropriate. 'Swimming in the deepest oceans on earth, sailing the seven seas, walking across the sands of time until I get to the cosmological oceans where I sailed away on the ship which I built with my own fair hand, a ship I named *Imagination*.' Although for Gulliver it wasn't to be a solo voyage as he had two other crewmembers aboard his ship.

Oh, and perhaps I should tell you that with the help of Alice 'the Mermaid Girl', Gulliver actually learnt to swim. He wasn't quite a merman, certainly not in the same 20,000 leagues under the sea as fish which swam in the oceans, but he could do a passable doggie paddle, or at least Beagle thought so.

Was Alice a real mermaid or not? That's a very good question. Unfortunately on that subject I'm sworn to secrecy.

And so Gulliver, Alice and Beagle returned to the cave with a diving bell designed by Leonardo Da Vinci himself. Da Vinci had heard of Gulliver's travels and had journeyed to Devon from Italy especially to talk to the boy the world was calling the 'Golden Boy' or 'the boy who held wonders in his hand'. As soon as the two met they recognized one another from their meeting upon the Black Sea. Gulliver told Da Vinci about his world and how he needed to get back there. So Da Vinci designed a diving bell which didn't look like a tin bathtub and one that two people and a dog could fit comfortably in to make such a perilous journey under the sea without be drowned in the process. Da Vinci's design was based on the pumping motion of a jellyfish as it pushes itself to the surface, an aqualung of sorts, a modern breathing apparatus not unlike the propulsion systems of a nautilus fish which lives in a spiral shell. Gulliver wondered if Da Vinci had ever met Jules Verne or H.G. Wells, which certainly would have been a meeting of minds that Gulliver would have liked to have been present at.

Leonardo had the diving bell put onto a cart drawn by a horse which transported it through the labyrinths of the cave to where the rock pool was situated. Gulliver, Alice and Da Vinci then offloaded the contraption into the water.

To Gulliver, the diving bell looked not unlike a miniature Unidentified Flying Object, although of course in this case it was an Identified Submersible Object.

What Leonardo Da Vinci didn't tell Gulliver was that he was working on a time machine which was very nearly complete and that he might well see him again some time soon.

'Well, Alice, are you ready?' Gulliver said looking at Alice as he climbed into the diving bell that was half submerged in the pool of the cave's lagoon with Beagle in his arms.

'Ready as I'll ever be,' said Alice as she stepped into the diving bell nervously.

'You know what happens in stories when you go from one world to the next, time hardly passes at all. And if you don't like my world you can always come back.' Gulliver said doing his level best to reassure Alice. Gulliver was pretty sure it would still be Sunday!

'Don't worry, my young friends, I have complete faith that my invention will get you to your destination safely,' Da Vinci said smiling warmly while stroking his beard, which normally meant he was nervous.

'If it's all the same to you, Leonardo, I feel much more comfortable when I'm worrying about something than when I'm not!' said Gulliver, who felt such a perilous journey required a certain amount of worrying for not to do so he felt would have been tempting fate. Gulliver had always felt, in his world the gods never liked it if you got too far ahead of yourself. The minute you said life was going swimmingly or things were plain sailing, the minute you were sunk, the gods made 110% sure of that!

Da Vinci showed Gulliver and Alice how his invention worked and what operated what, as in the diving bell there was a mass of shiny white china buttons, mahogany levers, brass toggles and weird-looking switches. He also told Gulliver, if he insisted in worrying, exactly what he should be worrying about the most, saying if any of the needles pointed to the furthest west or the furthest east it normally meant you were sunk, even if you were in the air at the time!

'Good luck and Godspeed. *Arvideci* to you and always remember these words, Gulliver, *sono il migliore, optimus sum, arvideci, arvideci*,' cried Da Vinci waving happily in their direction as he bid them a fond farewell.

Gulliver thought *arvideci* sounded like arrived and not goodbye, as if Da Vinci was welcoming him to this world, a *déjà vu* moment if you like. Gulliver had no idea what the words Da Vinci had said meant any more than he knew what half the words in the English language meant. But that was language for you, it was nothing more than a whole load of words cobbled together to fall where they may, as if in a snow dome that had been shaken up by God knows who, probably Shakespeare!

Later Gulliver was to find out these words in Italian and in Latin meant 'I am the best'. Now some could say Leonardo Da Vinci was being somewhat of a big head know-it-all geek that wasn't Greek, or more likely translated could mean, 'Believe in yourself, Gulliver. Be optimistic for you could do anything you put your imaginative mind to.'

And then the diving bell submerged under the water as a mass of rising bubbles rose to the surface in its wake and then it was gone, leaving the mirror image of Leonardo Da Vinci's face in the water of the rock pool. As a smile rippled across his craggy features you could say Da Vinci's face was quite a picture; if you had a highly attuned imagination you could almost say his face mirrored the smile on the painting of the Mona Lisa!

## EPILOGUE

# Time and Tide

The diving bell passed long strands of billowing seaweed and bemused sea life as it made its way through the dark murky water as it headed for the sunlight above.

'Look!' Alice cried as she pointed at a shoal of shimmering silver fish which darted past the window of the diving bell in the half light.

'It's a different world down here,' Gulliver said, unaware of exactly what he'd just said.

Gulliver would have loved to have seen more wondrous sights but these greenie dark black waters were not like the pristine crystal clear waters of the South Pacific or the blue waters of the Antiquarium.

The diving bell slowly rose to the surface in a motion best described as that of a jellyfish, in other words in slightly jerky stages. Da Vinci's design was simple, brilliant and effective and like a lot of his inventions, based on the designs of Mother Nature.

Nearing their journey's end and with both Gulliver and Alice metaphorically holding their breaths, disaster struck when the diving bell hit the bottom of a passing submarine.

'Water!' cried Alice, which being inside a diving bell wasn't the worse thing you could have heard unless the water was inside the diving bell. Unfortunately for Alice, Gulliver and Beagle, it was as water started pouring into the diving bell at an alarming rate. Gulliver was hoping the pump action of the jellyfish applied to the inside as well as the outside of Da Vinci's diving bell, but unfortunately it didn't!

This left no other option but for them to swim for their very lives. In this moment of madness Gulliver had the foresight to thrust his travelogue down his trousers in the hope it could be saved for posterity along with the travellers!

Gulliver watched the diving bell sink like the proverbial stone back down into the murky depths from whence they had come. Da Vinci's diving bell might not have seen them safely all the way home but at least they were almost there, and it wasn't Leonardo's fault the British Navy weren't looking where they were going!

A little while later Beagle and Gulliver emerged from beneath the waves but Alice was nowhere to be seen. Gulliver dived down several times but could not see her anywhere, he feared the worst and that she had drowned in the backwash of the submarine.

Disconsolately Gulliver swam to the dry land of St Mary's Bay in Brixham and with Beagle by his side walked back to his houseboat-cum-antiques emporium. As he did so he noticed that Beagle was no longer a puppy but was old and by the look of his hands and legs so was he. In fact he was thirty-five again; he hadn't aged a day in the time he was in the parallel world. In fact, to add insult to injury, it was a Sunday, the exact same Sunday that they had left this world on.

Gulliver later wrote in his travelogue that he felt like many moons had passed since he left his world when in fact no moons had passed at all, which was strange to say the very least. Mind you, in the parallel earth-cum-giant antique globe, the moon was a large moonstone, that and in that world there was no time to pass so was it any wonder it was still a Sunday?

Gulliver had always said Sundays went on for ever and it seemed he wasn't far wrong! Beagle still had his golden collar on, the one Queen Elizabeth I had given him on the parallel earth they had travelled back in time to, which at least proved this wasn't a dream. Having said that, as the parallel earth had no time perhaps that description is not all it should be. All Gulliver had on when he resurfaced in the Devon of 2013 was some very tight trousers and a shirt he'd split.

Gulliver continued on with his life as usual almost as if his travels hadn't happened but had all been just a vivid dream, although getting used to time again was a little strange. However, by this time Gulliver and strange were anything but strange bedfellows. He didn't tell anybody of his story, why would he, for whom in their right mind would believe a single word that came out of his mouth? However, Gulliver did write a travelogue entitled *Gulliver's Travels in Wonderland*, which he turned into a novel, although it only sold a few thousand copies around the world. No matter, he enjoyed writing it even if nobody enjoyed reading such nonsensical hogwash! Perhaps whoever read it would end up between the pages of the book travelling by his side on his fantastical voyage into the unknown. And at least it took his mind off feeling guilty that Alice had drowned in their attempts to get back to his world, unless she really was a mermaid and she had swum back to her own world, this at least gave Gulliver some comfort. Who knows, maybe his fantastical yarn would be turned into a film which would pick up several Golden Globes, perhaps even an Oscar or two. Well, one could dream, one could always dream.

Having written his first book and having read other people's books, Gulliver knew that all writers were as mad as a hatter and this to Gulliver's mind was not a fairytale. It was true, however, that some writers were madder than others, but they were all mad. This meant Gulliver felt write, sorry right at home in this noble profession which in part required you to use your imagination and wear a hat which said 'Not for sale!' upon the brim.

Gulliver still lived in the old world as he still worked in his antique shop which was still less than shipshape and Bristol fashion, although it was shipshape and Brixham fashion, well, after a fashion! Since his travels Gulliver felt reborn, like a kid in a candy store, even though his short return to childhood was over, well for the time being at least, and he didn't work in a candy store. Now every time somebody called him 'Sir' it made him stand tall both literally and metaphorically, whereas before it had just made him feel old. He may not have been a knight in his world but now in his soul he felt every bit as much a knight of the realm as Sir Galahad or King Arthur.

This uplift of spirit was helped by yet another strange event which began with the word however…

However, this wasn't end of story, not quite, for six months later Alice walked into Gulliver's antique's shop\boat as an adult. As soon as Gulliver saw Alice he knew it was her and she in turn knew it was Gulliver, simply by looking the other in the eye. They hugged as rivers of tears flowed from their eyes, which later Gulliver said might have flooded his shop if they hadn't stopped.

Apparently Alice had surfaced but had bumped her head on a rock, suffering from amnesia in the process. It was only a few days ago that her memory had returned and it transpired that she had been staying at a bed and breakfast house in the area. The lady who found her on the shoreline was the owner of the B &B who took pity on her as she appeared to be down on her luck, as she had no money and no means of identifying herself. Alice told the woman she couldn't even remember her own name and the police had no luck in finding out her identity either.

Once Alice regained her memory, she, like Gulliver, found getting used to a world where time existed quite strange. Now, for a girl who didn't known the meaning of the word 'strange' or 'time', this all took some time, how much I cannot say. However, Alice was familiar with the word 'curious', and it was curiosity (which in this case didn't kill the cat) which helped her adjust to this strange parallel earth which had an abundance of time in it which could be both valued and wasted in equal measures.

One particular fine day on the earth of 2013, the sky was full of balloons, or I should say hot air balloons of all shapes, sizes and colours, it was truly a glorious sight to behold. However, Alice was worried that the balloons would hit the roof of the world and burst or the roof of the ship's bottle, which of course in Gulliver's world did not exist. Alice also found the weather confusing and more severe than she was used to. Being in the confines of the ship's bottle meant the winds were lighter and it never snowed, although when it was very cold ice did form on the top of the ship's bottle and then fell in large sheets. This, if you were underneath at the time, wasn't much fun as Gulliver had found out to his cost, nearly ending up like an ice sculpture of Rodin's The Thinker. When the glass wall at the back of the ship's bottle iced up, climbers with crampons on their feet often scaled it, or at least attempted to!

When Gulliver looked back over his time in this strange world with the help of his travelogue he wondered how everything managed to work even though he had seen it work with his own eyes. Gulliver was fully aware that some time ago in his world there had been an experiment in a science laboratory where life had been conjured up in a beaker by a boffin, and that the earth, like the antique globe, was magnetic, and that life and water may well have been brought to the earth of the past via a comet or a meteorite. And although this still left his explanation of the parallel earth as woolly as a woolly mammoth, at least it made some sense out of the nonsense that was Alice's Wonderland. There were times Gulliver thought earth was nothing more than an experiment in a beaker, that beaker being the earth, as an alien lifeform looked on to see how their experiment was working out. If you thought about it, which Gulliver had, this made us an alien lifeform! Yes, Gulliver certainly had some imagination, which since he had come back to his own world was back to its old self, almost as if the child within him had been regenerated by his wondrous, fantastical 'out of this world' adventure of several lifetimes.

For the first time in her life, Alice saw and heard lightning first hand, which made her jump out of her skin and hide under the nearest table shaking like a leaf. Although Gulliver was used to lightning, he being the perfect gentleman crawled under the table with her and held her hand until the lightning passed. Yes, his world did take a bit of getting used to, Gulliver had said to Alice with a wry smile upon his face.

Time passed as it has a mind to do and in this world Old Father Time kept very much in the background, watching from a distance. But be in no doubt, the Guardian of

Time was there along with the gods sitting up high amongst the clouds in the heavens known as Mount Olympus. Gulliver eventually summed up the courage to propose to Alice, which he did in a rather romantic fashion while travelling on the Paignton and Dartmouth steam train line. Of course Alice said yes. Even more romantically, they had a maritime wedding, getting married on board the *Golden Hind*, the replica mind. The icing on the cake was that their wedding cake was of the *Golden Hind*, which was definitely a replica, with a married couple standing upon its deck. Just for the record, the cake had been baked by Heston Blumenthal, who like Gulliver was one of planet earth's true original thinkers. And they all lived happily ever after. Well, that's a nice ending but that's not quite the end of the story.

A year later in 2013 a terrible flood hit the coast of Devon and Brixham was flooded. At the time, Gulliver, Beagle and Alice were standing upon the deck of the *Golden Hind* as a wave swept them out to sea. (Once again this was a replica of the *Hind* and there wasn't an aardvark or zygote in sight as this wasn't Noah's or Gulliver's Ark!) At the time, to Gulliver's imaginative mind, it felt as if the *Golden Hind* was nothing more than a toy boat caught in a squall, or like a surfer riding upon a crest of a wave until the wave fell away.

Sometime later, the replica of the *Golden Hind* appeared out of the mists of time to see the *Golden Hind* surrounded by several Spanish galleons. As the *Golden Hind* sailed into view, the Spanish could not believe their eyes, it was true what everybody said about Drake, that he was a god and had magically conjured up another *Golden Hind* which was sailing full steam ahead in their exact direction. The Spanish thought this was a ghost ship and sailed off into the sunset with their collective sails between their legs.

Then the golden seas they were sailing upon became as becalmed as a mill pond. Were the seas actually golden? Well, there are such things as extremophiles which are microbes, and there is one such microbe called archaea which thrives in hot springs and black smokes upon the ocean floor. Some of these species consume the heavy metal dissolved in the water before excreting it as solid. This process produces gold from sea water, a form of alchemy some might say. Then, of course, there is another form of gold, in the oceans, black gold in other words oil which big oil companies wanted to plunder from the Artic and oceans of the world. This plundering of the black gold by the multi-national pirates had already had consequences which were not good for the life which lived in these places, something Gulliver strongly opposed. Gulliver had been very much a greenhorn in Alice's world, in this world he was very much into green issues realizing Mother Nature needed all the help she could get to stem the tide of global warming.

'You took your time!' said Drake as Gulliver, Beagle and Alice sailed into view. 'Only yanking your anchor, boy. Nice to see you again. I wondered where you'd disappeared to!'

'Just thought I'd take the old girl out for a spin across the waves of time to blow the cobwebs from her sails,' Gulliver shouted to Drake across the ship's starboard side as the two *Golden Hinds* sailed side by side as if it was the most natural thing in the world. One might have said these two ships were doppelgangers, mirror images of one another, if one had a mind to.

'That's taken the wind out of those Spanish sails,' Drake said grinning from ear to ear.

'Actually, technically it hasn't otherwise they wouldn't be sailing over the horizon,' Gulliver said taking the wind out of Drake's sails.

'So where does your fancy take you this time, Gulliver?' Drake said as he scratched his beard ignoring Gulliver's quip, although it may well have been that he was going deaf due to the noise of the cannons going off in battle.

'Well, I hear there is a place in the South American, Amazonian rainforest called El Dorado where a city of gold stands,' Gulliver said as he took out his spyglass and looked into the mists of time.

'Well, there's no time like the present, Gulliver my boy, after all, time waits for no man, not even Old Father Time! So hoist the mainsail, lads. Splice the what-cha-ma-call-it, oh, and nice to see you again, Alice, and you too, Beagle,' Drake said as Beagle leapt up onto the side of the replica of the *Golden Hind* and barked out his orders to Sir Francis Drake. It seemed to Gulliver there was plenty of adventure, out there if you were prepared to go to the ends of the earth and beyond to find it. Drake certainly felt there was plenty of the map that still needed filling in and he was intent on filling that map for both queen and country, or in this particular case, queens and country!

Gulliver wondered if there was such thing as a time map or a map of time itself. *That would take some time to fill in the blanks*, he thought as a smile appeared upon his dial as he continued to circumnavigate the globe of the imagination, a globe of unimaginable size which was never likely to be circumnavigated until the end of the world itself.

'Oh you might recognize this fellow,' Drake said nonchalantly, almost as an afterthought as Hans Christian Andersen appeared from below deck with a great big smile upon his face. And once again with no word of a lie, this unbelievable happening wasn't a fairytale! Gulliver could hardly believe his own eyes, he thought Hans Christian had got so thoroughly lost in a book in The Last

Bookshop in the World that he would never see the light of day again. Gulliver was later to write this in the epilogue of his travelogue: 'I know it makes little sense thus making it nonsense, but I think The Last Bookshop in the World should be added to the list of ancient wonders of the world, even if this wonder is in a parallel world!'

Having sailed into the mists of time upon the replica *Golden Hind*, Gulliver had returned to the age when he left the parallel world so now both he and Alice were eighteen years of age, and in dog years Beagle was a teenager too of sorts. With all this gallivanting through time, or a time without time, it made Gulliver wonder if he could send a message in a bottle through time. Perhaps he could even send a ship in a bottle through time. Perhaps a sculptor or an engineer could build a giant bottle and put a giant ship in it, a bit like the *Cutty Sark* in London. Mind you, in summer, due to the glass the heat would be stifling, although I suppose they could always fit air conditioning. I would say these were most curious thoughts indeed but in truth, for Gulliver, thinking-wise these leftfield thoughts were pretty much standard fare!

And that really is the end of *Gulliver's Travels*, or should I say *The Travels of Gulliver*? Hold your seahorses. What's that I spy through my magical telescopic time device, otherwise known as the Da Vinci\Galileo Optimum Timaeus Crystal Viewing Scope? Just give me a minute while I twiddle with this crystal eyepiece, just a few minor adjustments and as the mists of time clear… hey presto! I can quite clearly see a sequel of the swashbuckling variety sailing into view… End of the story, unless I'm looking through the wrong end of the scope and that's not a sequel I spy but a prequel!

If you enjoyed this book you may well enjoy some of my other fantastical books:

Professor Doppelganger
and the Fantastical Cloud Factory.

(The Nocturne Chronicles)
The Night Maze & the Looking Glass Girl

Thoroughly Modern Lilly

Letters to Queen Elizabeth Land

The Boy Who Lived in Rainbows

The Flat Earth Society & the Great Globe Conspiracy

www.markrolandlangdale.co.uk